THE ESFAH SAGAS:
ASHES OF AILUSHURAI

BY
CHRISTOPHER D. SCHMITZ

A DRAGON DICE NOVEL

© 2020 by Christopher D. Schmitz
All rights reserved. No part of this book may be reproduced, stored in a retrieval system, or transmitted in any form or by any means without the prior written permission of the publishers, except by a reviewer who may quote brief passages in a review to be printed in a newspaper, magazine, or journal.
The final approval for this literary material is granted by the author.
Dragon Dice and its terms including Esfah, Coral Elf (selumari), Dwarf (vagha), Lava Elf (morehl), Goblin (trogs), Amazon, Firewalker (Empyrea), Undead (bloodless), Feral (ghwereste), Swamp Stalker (sarslayan), Frostwing (Areosa), Scalder (Faeli), Treefolk (efflorah), Dragonkin, eldarim, Eldrymetallum, Magestorm! and Dragon Dice II: Gamer's Edition are trademarks owned by SFR, Inc.
Forgotten Realms and Dragonlance are trademarks owned by Wizards of the Coast.

PUBLISHED BY TREESHAKER BOOKS

THE ESFAH SAGAS

Rise and Fall of the Obsidian Grotto
Cast of Fate

The Relic Quests
Ashes of Ailushurai
Rise of the Champions (coming 2021)
Drakuwar (coming soon)

The Cyrean Songs
Chill Wind
Eye of the Storm
Secrets of the Shadowlands (coming 2021)

STAY UP TO DATE ON THE WORLD OF ESFAH!

Get a free copy of book 1 in the Esfah Sagas by visiting:

www.subscribepage.com/getfreedragondicenovels

Subscribers who sign up for this no-spam email list will get free books, exclusive content, and more! You'll get *Rise & Fall of the Obsidian Grotto* immediately… if you would like more details or want to follow the author, you can find his details at the end of this book.

BACKGROUND

Dragon Dice™ was originally created by Lester Smith and produced by TSR in 1995.It is an Origins Award winning strategy game where players create mythical armies using dice to represent each troop and is one of several collectible dice games that emerged in the 1990s. The game combines strategy and skill as well as a little luck.

After several years, TSR, now owned by Wizards of the Coast, had put Dragon Dice™ on hold to work on other projects. In October of 2000, SFR Inc. purchased the rights to Dragon Dice™.

Most of the races and monsters in original TSR Dragon Dice were created by Lester Smith and include some creatures unique to a fantasy setting and others that are familiar to the Dungeons & Dragons role-playing game. While the world of Esfah, where Dragon Dice™ takes place, has many similarities to that of Dungeons & Dragons, it is distinctly different in many respects. In some ways, there are greater unknowns and its history is both newer and older all at once.

Around the end of 1995 I was a teenager and avid board gamer who had a burger slinging job (which gave me a disposable income) and a car (that took most of my disposable income.) In addition to many other games I played as part of a regular quartet of gamers, Dragon Dice™ was one that we all enjoyed.

I fondly remember how the four of us would cut out of elective classes, study halls, and independent learning periods to meet up for gaming sessions. Dragon Dice™ came in a pocketable carrying bag which made it perfect for that.

We also had a mutual acquaintance. An older gentleman in town owned a new and used bookstore that also carried a limited supply of gaming products. Though he did not stock Dragon Dice™, he did have a copy of *Cast of Fate*, the first Dragon Dice™ novel which included a special promo die; I snapped it up right away as the most avid reader of the foursome (which lent itself to me become the dedicated DM for our role-playing game sessions and solidified my path as a story-teller.) The included promotional die was our bright and shiny object for months.

Cast of Fate by Allen Varney was not the only book set in the world of Esfah, though it remains one of the few. As I write and publish more and more fiction (both Fantasy and Science Fiction,) I tend to write the stories that I've always wanted to... and I've always wanted to have a voice in a shared universe. Creating a story within the Dragon Dice™ universe is something I've always wanted to do, so I give a special thanks to SFR, a company composed of true and like-minded fans who have kept alive a product that was one of the gems of the 1990s.

-- Chris

FOREWORD

In eons past, when time was young and creation malleable, the four powers of Nature -- earth, air, fire, and water -- the children of Nature, gods in their own rights, brought forth two races of beings to care for their fledgling world, created by the all-father, Tarvanehl. One race, the selumari or coral elves, was created to husband the fluid forces of air and water. The other race, the vagha, a dwarvish race, embodied the stability of earth and the tempering power of fire. Together, these two peoples worked to nurture their infant world into something glorious and beautiful.

But Nature had a nemesis in Death, the spirit of entropy. In imitation of Nature, Death brought into being its own races: the morehl, or lava elves, who worshiped fire and destruction, and the trogs, a race of goblins, who sprang from earth and corruption. From the moment of their creation, the morehl and trogs sowed conflict, defiling the very world that gave them life and corrupting the other races who tended it. War sparked over land and possessions. Soon, hordes of dispossessed selumari, vagha, morehl, and trogs swept back and forth across the lands of Esfah, locked in endless battle.

In their struggles for supremacy over the fledgling world, the First Races pressed other magical beings into their service. The morehl were the first to do so, bringing up fire-breathing Hellhounds and web-casting Driders from the deepest caverns below Esfah. The trogs followed suit, leading Trolls, Harpies, and other monsters into battle. In response, the selumari called forth Coral Giants from the ocean and swarms of Sprites from the skies. The vagha enlisted Gargoyles, Androsphinxes, and other creatures of the crags.

Conflict raged across the face of Esfah and Death delighted in the carnage.

Back and forth across the world, darkness battle against light. Each side pushed harder yet for victory and the battles grew ever savage and desperate. New races arose, each pressed into the fray of the bloody struggle that seemed to have no end in sight.

Saddened by the bloodshed, Nature, the goddess-mother Ghaeial, dealt death to preserve life. Death, the bastard child Malgrimm--son of Ghaeial and Selurehl, the god known as Void. Malgrimm reveled in the chaos, terror, and pain that war brought.

A time of champions arose to safeguard the realm. Wars continued and an entire age passed. Pockets of tenuous peace grew from apathy--a new trick engineered by Death to soften the resolve of Nature's troops, almost seeming to abandon his playground for the comforts of the Abyss--but his attention has never truly waned.

Esfah has never known true peace. It is not in the planet's makeup: this is where the children of gods war on their behalf. Both old and new races struggle ever onward--creatures inspired to greater ends, forever in search of either an end to the bloodshed, or carnage renewed, as each is bent towards his or her own ends.

Esfah cannot know peace. Malgrimm--the god known as Death--will not allow it. Only a few know his true name--and to speak it aloud is to court Death himself.

For a short video overview of Esfah's origins, visit
https://youtu.be/JhF8RPFkF9I

For up to date information on the world of Esfah, and all things
related to the Dragon Dice universe, including products and specials,
check out:

http://www.sfr-inc.com

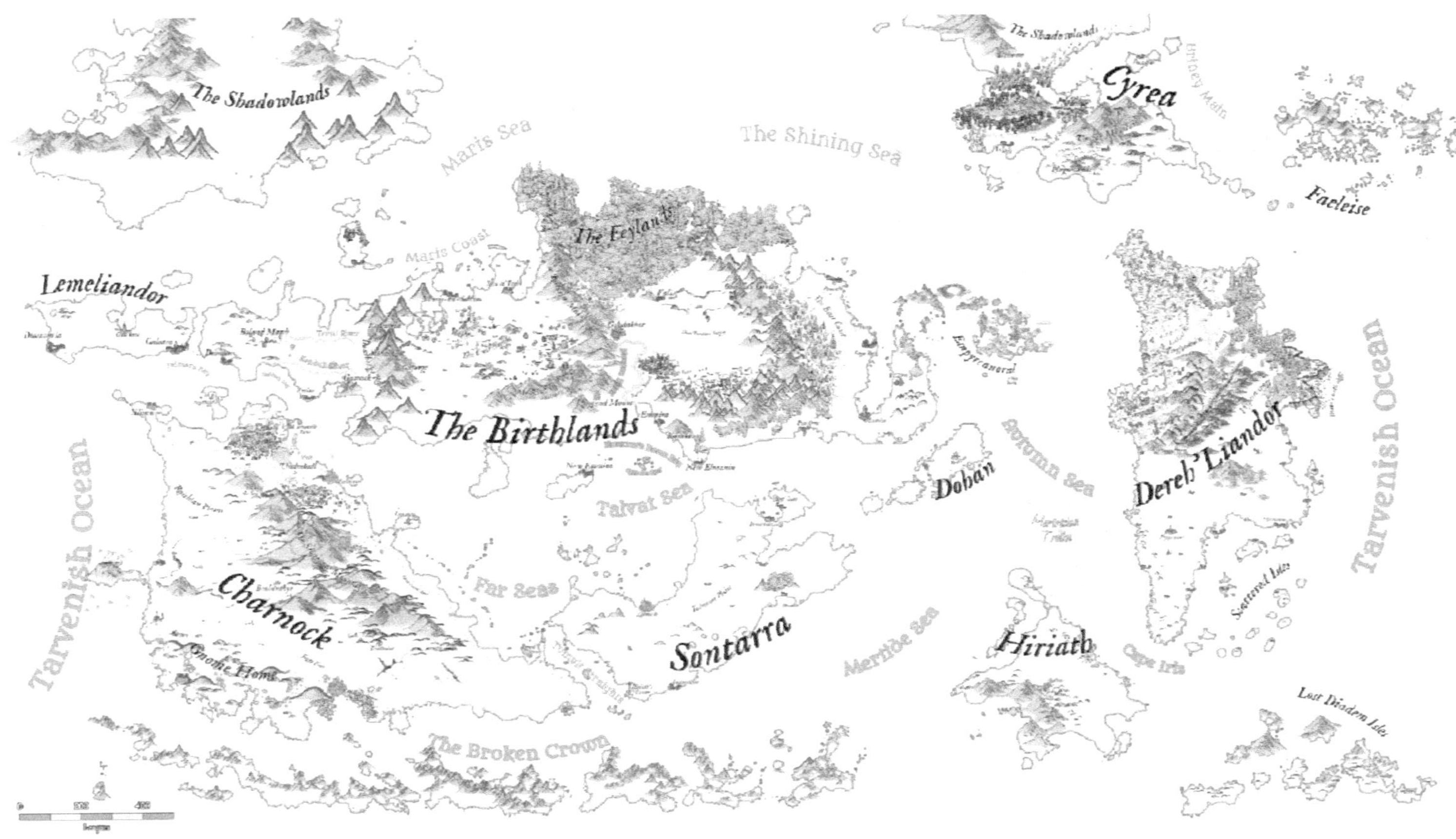
The Shadowlands
Maris Sea
The Shining Sea
The Shadowlands
Cyrea
Faeleise
The Feylands
Maris Coast
Lemeliandor
Tarvenish Ocean
The Birthlands
Dereb'Liandor
Autumn Sea
Doban
Talvat Sea
Tarvenish Ocean
Charnock
Far Seas
Sontarra
Meritte Sea
Hiriath
Cape Irla
Scattered Isles
Gnome Home
The Broken Crown
Lost Diadem Isles

PROLOGUE

Year 143 of the First Age

Melkior stumbled through a briar patch and cursed his way through the snags. Thick trees surrounded him, and hounds bayed furiously in the distance, dogging his every step as they had since he'd fled the smoldering wreckage of Lurneville on the edge of Ender's Gulf. The brambles tore his hands from his chest as he pushed through, exposing the gaping wound that had slicked his hand with blood.

His blood ran crimson, like the humans; though he resembled one in many ways, he was no mere man. Melkior was eldarim, both a mage and warrior champion… and by his efforts he'd just killed an entire tribe of men and women… and so many more—and after that came the fight against the elves, his friends—many of them *intimate*.

Ignoring the pain, Melkior snapped his hand back over the ragged tear in his flesh and tried to keep pressure on it. He glanced at his other fist; it was also slicked with blood, but not his own. Splatters of red and green painted him: red from the humans and green from the selumari, the coral elves who he'd been a sworn protector of.

A tracker howled not far behind him, ominous in the pale moonlight; it had his scent. The blue-skinned elves would be on him soon.

The wounded eldarim pushed ahead, though his lungs burned as intensely as the leaking hole in his torso. The captain of the elven guard, Leisterbane, would find him soon if he didn't quicken his pace. He was a formidable opponent—even for the eldarim champion—the demi-godlike acolyte. That Melkior could lose to Leisterbane in combat was not a possibility two days ago, before Melkior broke faith and attacked the selumari kingdom under his house's protection. But now, with so severe of a wound?

But even without his pet drake, Melkior was still formidable; dragon or not, he was still a Dragonlord. At his best, with his dragon at his side, none of the other champions from the other races stood a chance to beat him. He'd just proved as much in the secret room below his keep, battling and defeating the coral elf champion—though he'd paid a heavy price in the combat. He growled at the fresh memory. It had been her life Melkior tried to save… *their* lives… *together.*

Something made her betray him.

He grimaced at the hot wound he'd taken from her and bit back tears—more painful than the gash in his flesh were her words. Those had injured him worst of all. He refused to entertain them again.

"I'll be lucky if death does not find me first," Melkior panted, leaning momentarily against a tree and grinding his teeth against the pain. The hounds sounded their alarm again and the wounded fighter lurched forward, knowing he could not stay if he wanted to live another day. He took two steps and then tumbled to the ground.

Everything went silent. Blood still poured from his lacerated side, mixing with the silky loam to form a puddle of mud. Smells of lichen and stale water filled his nostrils. Pain wracked his body and told him that he still lived.

He touched his hand to the sticky wound and checked himself. Frankly, he was amazed that he had any blood left within him by now. *What happens when I run out?* The thought passed as quickly as it came.

Melkior rolled over and stared at the sky. *Let the hounds come… what good is living anyway, without her… my Princess Ailushurai.*

The moon was up, making her twice daily voyage across the upper atmosphere. Dead trees framed his view as they reached for the air like skeletal arms bursting up from their graves; they shimmered slightly from the glow of a nearby campfire. Such a light would surely draw the enemies quicker than expected, though he wondered that he hadn't noticed it earlier.

The fugitive rolled over and onto his knees; Melkior finally rose to his wobbly feet. A large pyre, built of charred skulls, towered in the middle of the glade. Flames licked out from empty sockets and gaps between teeth. Everything natural within the bubble seemed to have withered with decay. An ornate throne sat opposite him on the far side of the fire. A fair-skinned man with handsome features leaned forward from his bone chair; peering over steepled fingers, he watched Melkior intently, but said nothing.

With wide eyes, Melkior looked around the profane circle. The atmosphere dripped with corruption. Dread realization set in: Melkior had stumbled into a festration, an arcane bubble of evil where the presence of the Dark One lingered. Terror shot a jolt of adrenaline into his heart; it might keep him alive a few seconds longer, though the certainty that he would die in this corrupted, sacred ring gripped him.

Finally, the man stroked his goatee and waved him forward. He spoke from the throne as his eldarim guest arrived nearer the fire. "Greetings, Melkior. I have watched you from afar, like I watch so many of Esfah's citizens. The Teldrim you slaughtered were more children of Tarvanehl, the Creator… my enemy." The stranger regarded him coolly. "You once fought my forces as a major antagonist against me," his voice boomed, "but yesterday you murdered the Teldrim chief and wiped the stain of their presence from Esfah's face."

Melkior's gaze burned. He'd been the guardian of the coastal province surrounding Lurneville where his selumari friends had lived and watched the Teldrim with caution as the new breed of humans encroached—even encamped the capital. Melkior's voice remained flat. "Their chief wanted what was mine. He could not have her—did not *deserve her*."

The mysterious man grinned. "Ailushurai. The selumari princess… and Champion of her people. Another of my antagonists."

Melkior nodded measuredly and memorized the man's face and mannerisms. He looked demure, unassuming, even if he radiated evil. "Tell me your name."

He smiled and shook his head. "To say the name of one such as I means to invoke me and my power. Only those who are intimate with my ways may know my name and speak it freely."

"What do you want with me?" Melkior knew his time was fleeting, even if he hadn't heard a dog baying since before falling into the festration.

"Very direct." The mysterious man suddenly stood adjacent to him, startling his guest. "I offer you a deal. Pledge fealty to me and I will grant you the power you seek. You will become powerful and remain so with Ailushurai by your side… forever. In return, you will wage war as my general and raise high a banner in my name."

Melkior cocked his head. "A name that I do not know?"

"You know me by another name." He pointed a finger to the eldarim's torso.

Melkior looked down at his chest. It had stopped bleeding. His voice warbled. "Death?" Melkior's eyelids fluttered and his body tried everything in its power to shut down, veins completely drained—but still, Melkior remained standing by sheer force of will.

"I *am* the god they call Death… the Corrupter, the Harrower, and all those other names." He held up a small vial filled with churning, black ichor.

Melkior sank to his knees, unable to remain upright any longer.

"Swear it. Pledge yourself to me, body and soul, and you shall have this power! Say my name and remain on Esfah as a conqueror."

It took everything in Melkior to look up at the fiend who casually offered him limitless power. His head trembled with death throes, but he maintained eye contact even as his pupils began dilating.

"Say my name and be united forever with your beloved Ailushurai." A second unraveled with painstaking length. He yelled, *"Say it!"*

"Malgrimm!" the eldarim shouted, somehow knowing Death's secret name in the core of his being.

With the pretense of gentleness gone, Malgrimm grabbed Melkior by the face and squeezed his jaw open, pouring the contents of the vial down his throat. "Tarvanehl is dead to you; *I am your father now*, and this is my gift to you, my son," he hissed. "The Necralluvium."

With his last living breath, Melkior shrieked as the inky substance unstitched him body and soul and then wove him back together with black magic drawn from the void. His screams filled the festration grounds.

Malgrimm raked his fingers vertically across his new toy's chest. They cut like razors, shredding Melkior's tattered vestments, laying his naked flesh open to the sky, revealing a black tattoo where the god of Death had marked him with an arcane sigil.

A dozen elves burst through the foliage with blades unsheathed. They locked eyes on the enemy they had been tracking all evening.

Melkior stood and faced the threat. He looked over his shoulders, but the throne, mound of flaming skulls, and his new master had all disappeared. The selumari released their leashes, and the hounds raced upon him.

The eldarim smashed them apart with his fists, caving in the first one's skull, and the second one he dashed to pieces as they pressed for position. The final two ran away, yelping with their tails between their legs.

"Take him!" Leisterbane howled, commanding his troops.

Melkior drew his broken blade from its sheath. He suddenly remembered that it had shattered during the attack on the Teldrim when his glorious mount, a white dragon named Rahkawmn, crashed to the ground, a lance bolt piercing his chest. That moment had turned the tides of the battle.

The fallen eldarim threw away the useless handle as two selumari charged him.

Filled with rage and black magic, Melkior reached out his hand and channeled his new master's hatred. The elves staggered and tumbled to the ground, their bodies filled with rot and decay and their blue skin turned gray as ash. They writhed on the grass as Melkior, a converted lich, took their weapons. With a sword in each grip, he executed them.

Melkior snarled at the pursuit party and spat a challenge at Leisterbane.

The elite cadre of elves surged forward as a group.

Melkior whirled and spun like a razor-sharp cyclone, deflecting and parrying with uncanny ease... surging with power he'd never felt before. Elf upon elf fell like stacked cordwood, dripping thick rivulets of verdant blood across their blue tinted skin.

Malgrimm's chosen one plunged his blades deep into Leisterbane's chest, cleaving his heart, and defeating the elf warrior with ease. Finally, silence ruled the grounds of the dead zone. Melkior dropped the curved elven swords and put a hand to his chest. The wound had sealed up, gnarled and twisted, but Melkior could not find a heartbeat. Even without it, raw power coursed through his limbs, as if arcane energy had sheathed his very bones and he now wore flesh like one wears a cloak.

He whirled back to search for the festration a final time, but nothing remained of it save trampled grass now colored with the hues of spilled selumari blood. No physical sign remained of Lord Malgrimm, but his dark will still echoed in Melkior's mind. His and his master's desires aligned. Melkior now spoke for the god of Death as his chief acolyte.

Melkior's toe bumped something shiny. He bent low and retrieved the vial. The ampoule of inky black stuff had remained full and corked.

He returned to the killing field and poured a drop of Necralluvium onto each of the murdered selumari. They shambled and groaned and pulled to their feet, motivated by the lich's desires. The undead formed rank behind the ghastly Leisterbane who saluted.

"As I am to Malgrimm, you are to me, Leisterbane," Melkior commanded.

The corptic elf growled in response.

"Now," Melkior turned and looked to the distance where the coral elves had defended their home from his earlier invasion, "let us go and claim what Malgrimm has promised to me." He took strides towards the horizon with only one name on his lips. "Ailushurai."

CHAPTER ONE

Year 1127 of the Second Age

The red bearded dwarven King winked at his son Hy'Targ Sa'Mandr. Hy'Mandr, King of the Irontooth clan, grinned at the prince before plunging into the darkness nearest a stony embankment. High standing stones stood on the hills above the Jagra Flats and the town of Tenebrakth. The monolith obscured the deep crevasse which held the promise of adventure and riches in the hidden depths.

Hy'Targ barely recognized his father without his crown and royal vestments. Though his father often left on private excursions, this was Hy'Targ's first adventure. Even if the journey had not taken them much beyond their homelands, travel did not agree with Hy'Targ who preferred a library to even the foothills of the Stonejaw Mountains where his home was.

Despite the posh accoutrements of the castle, Hy'Mandr was vagha—and all dwarves remained swarthy and thick-bearded regardless of their environments or lofty positions. The king's royal responsibilities disagreed with his adventurer's wanderlust, and he intentionally left his beard as a wild growth of unkempt whiskers. Promises of travel and glory released a kind of inner glow from the old vagha. It had been too long for his comfort since he'd had the chance to escape the duties demanded by his throne.

King Irontooth clutched his prized, magic battle axe as he headed towards the tomb. He'd long ago named the weapon *Glorybringer,* which accurately identified Hy'Mandr's chief pursuit. The axe was a leftover relic from the Magestorm Wars, the ancient era of powerful artifacts whose existence nearly fractured the world of Esfah; the war's end split the dating system, instead. The first year following its cessation marked the beginning of the Second Age.

The prince followed his father and rubbed a wiry beard which clung to his face: a full beard by human standards, but barely more than stubble by comparison to his father. Ahead, the seasoned crew of dwarves located the hidden entrance to the catacombs they'd been questing after. Hy'Targ watched the King's old adventuring buddies as they plunged one by one beneath the inky veil of shadow. The ancient site had been rumored to hold a prize which Hy'Mandr, the Adventurer King sought.

Shielding his face against the late evening rays of Soll, Hy'Targ sighed as if he might experience discomfort away from the sunlight. He knew it was unbecoming of his race, and he blushed sheepishly, glanced up to take one last look at Rhaudian, the moon, before he hung his head and followed.

Like all vagha, his eyes adjusted quickly to the darkness. Hy'Targ found the others in a cluster, crouched around a patch of soil. He hurried over to them and let his father's crew explain what they'd found.

Mi'Darrio, a middle-aged dwarf by vaghan reckoning, and a qualified scout from his father's adventuring days— before he'd become king, traced a finger through the dirt while Tr'Gurn lit a torch to see best by. Dwarven sight was good in the dark, and with only a little light, they could see almost perfectly.

The king spat and nearby and grumbled, "trogs," while tightening a grip on the haft of Glorybringer. Hy'Targ noted his father's displeasure, but felt quite certain King Irontooth's voice carried a hint of glee at the prospect of encountering goblin resistance. Besides, diplomacy had never been the King's strong suit.

Mi'Darrio wrinkled his nose and shook his head, wagging his beard. "The footprints are certainly goblinoid," he said, "but they are quite old."

"How old?"

Shrugging, Mi'Darrio had to guess. "I don't know," he spat. "Older than you, ya mangy old coot. Bleeding ancient—I don't think anyone else has been this way in decades."

As if in response, the wind cut across the open mouth of the cave and moaned with a forlorn howl.

King Hy'Mandr lit his own torch and strolled deeper into the warrens. "Funny. The ancient crone who told us the tale of this place and it's monstrous guardian didn't say anything about trogs." He mumbled a judgment against the nearby settlement's powers of observation if the city watch let trogs sneak past unchallenged.

Hy'Targ grimaced. The crew of dwarves had managed to evade the prying eyes in the town of mixed races as well. Tenebrakth wasn't known for protecting its borders: they had a spiked palisade to keep out intruders. Outsiders weren't much of a concern for them beyond what goods they brought at market price.

With an unruly gray eyebrow, Mi'Darrio winked at the prince. "Don't worry, I'm sure we'll find the old spider if we push further into the cave."

Hy'Targ realized he'd been grinding his teeth. No wonder his father's friend thought they needed to comfort him. The prince did his best to set his jaw and keep his face neutral, like any seasoned warrior might, though he couldn't quite muster the look of excited anticipation that the others wore. He didn't have that much dishonesty in him.

Another dwarf in their party, Vy'Danis, put a fresh torch in the prince's hand and took up the rear.

Hy'Targ caught up with his father as the caverns widened into something shaped like a natural hall. The king clapped a thick paw upon his shoulder and rubbed it with a sparkle in his eye.

Pointing to the expansive ceilings of the grotto, they both spotted the silvery filaments which looped from point to point like bowing, laden stalks of grain. "Do you see the webs?"

Hy'Targ clenched his jaw and nodded. "This looks like the right place."

"Is it what you'd imagined?" Hy'Mandr asked enthusiastically. "I'm sure you've read about this sort of thing in all those books you keep busy with up in Ne'Vistar's tower?"

Hy'Targ bobbed his head reluctantly. He knew he needed to provide his father with some sort of answer. "Yes… and no. I've never heard the legend of Sshkkryyahr before you told me about this quest."

The king grinned. "It's not inna book cuz it's a *true* legend."

Hy'Targ cocked his head at the convoluted logic.

"If this giant spider's really as dangerous as they say it is, nobody with enough facts t'write a book ever survived its lair."

He didn't think that's how it worked, but Hy'Targ didn't want to press the point and argue with his father. After all, the King was the famous adventurer in their party… Hy'Targ had barely even left the castle before this. He much preferred the library or intellectual pursuits to sloughing through swamps or plundering crypts.

King Hy'Mandr's smile broadened as the swaths of silk draped lower and lower. "This is it boys. Let's spread out and find the beast, or its lair, at least."

"Kinda like the time we tracked those brigands down near Oxforge and then cornered an Umberhulk by mistake?" Mi'Lazlee brought up, grinning.

A chorus of chuckles rippled through the dwarves as they meandered deeper into the darkness.

"Aye. Those were the days. But today, we'll have our prize," Hy'Mandr promised to his six companions.

Hy'Targ rolled his eyes at all the tales of *the good old days*, but took his place in the search line. Alongside his father and the rest of the king's bearded entourage, he trudged through the dark chamber in search of the next clue that would hasten the end of this adventure and bear him back to his books in the royal library.

Hy'Targ reached over his shoulder and tried to massage the soreness from where the leather straps on his plate armor chaffed him. It took a bit of doing to get at the irritated patch of skin.

After a few blessed seconds of relief brought by his efforts, Hy'Targ cursed with the realization that he'd meandered off course. Spinning in a few circles, he finally spotted the glow of his companions' torches moving in the distance.

Hy'Targ quickened his pace and felt the flush of embarrassment redden his cheeks. He knew his father's insinuations had been right; Hy'Targ wasn't cut out to be an adventurer. For as long as he'd lived, his footsteps had always been smaller than his father's. King Hy'Mandr was right that Hy'Targ preferred time in the library above anything else.

Kicking a rock that skittered into the darkness, Hy'Targ felt resentment creeping into his core. He'd always been closer to the old wizard, his Father's chief adviser, than he was to the King—his father. Royal dwarven court was not an easy place to raise a child, and Ne'Vistar and his assistants had done most of the actual raising of the child after his mother, Queen Sh'Ttil, mysteriously disappeared when he was barely eight years old. Now forty, Hy'Targ was barely more than a child by vaghan reckoning—an unruly adolescent prince who rebelled by ironically preferring scholarly pursuits to the way of the axe in which he'd been trained.

He kicked the stone again as he caught up to the line and resumed course.

Hy'Targ gave the broken chunk of shale one final boot and it bounced off something nearby, impacting with a hollow *thud*. The prince traced its path through the darkness and found a mangled corpse of a long-dead trog.

The realness of danger closed in around him, and Hy'Targ's gut tightened. He looked up; more corpses lay strewn about a gaping hole he'd found which delved further into the depths ahead of him. The edges were sharp like jagged teeth and they guarded a deeper darkness below in the heart of the hillock.

He tried to whistle, but his lips had dried up. After a few attempts, he finally succeeded and called the rest of the party over to the bone littered section of the undercroft.

Hy'Mandr arrived first, skidding to a halt with his weapon in hand. He beamed with pride at his son's discovery and checked the area for any nearby threat to swing his axe at, but nothing remained alive to volunteer as a target.

Mi'Darrio poked a finger into the corpse. It's body, sunken and desiccated, looked more like a mummy than anything else. He turned the next adjacent carcass over; it appeared much the same. Something had tied the victim's limbs with fine silk and sucked its innards out, leaving the remaining refuse behind to litter the floor. "I think we're in the right place," Mi'Darrio agreed.

The king's grin broadened, and he bounced like an excited kid at birthfeast. He flashed his son a proud look.

Hy'Targ forced a smile. He would face a monster for his father; he knew it might someday be a talent required of him whenever he would have to assume the throne. Hy'Targ's faux smile nearly faltered at the thought of a title he did not covet. The wretched obligation of ruling a kingdom had brought his father little joy, and Hy'Targ had not hoped for it any time soon.

Tr'Gurn finally arrived with Jr'Dunn whose arm was slung over his shoulder. The fat, old vagha limped on a mangled leg that bled thick, red streams down the cuffs of his boot.

"What happened to you?"

Jr'Dunn shrugged. He bent low and pulled a broken piece of splintered ash from his leg meat. "I haven't seen one of these kinds of traps in over fifty years, now," he groused, half with pride for locating and defusing it in his misbegotten way. "Not since that time we raided the morehl Kingdoms and liberated all'o those kin from the Firehammer clan." He flashed King Hy'Mandr a stink eye. "Remember… that was afore you finally settled down… got all domesticated and married."

The king looked at the wound, thin lipped. "Yer gonna hafta head for the exit, old friend. No complaints… but I'd hate to lose you deeper in the tunnels and then have to carry yer gurk-lovin' hind end all the way back." He pointed to the scattered trog bodies.

Jr'Dunn looked like he might complain, but then nodded and turned for home. He limped away, chuckling, and slapped Hy'Targ on the shoulder as he passed. "I hope you're enjoying the chase, kid. Ain't nothing like an adventure—have 'em while you can, before you meet some pretty lass and leave all o' this glory behind ya."

Hy'Targ stared at the darker portal reaching for further depths. The prince swallowed the lump in his throat; he felt quite different about the matter.

Below the barrow cave, Mi'Darrio's kinsman, Mi'Lazlee, sidled up to the dwarf prince. He knew Prince Hy'Targ loved the tale more than the adventure and he reminded him of their purpose in plundering the cave.

"The old crone said that Sshkkryyahr stole magic from the gods. Using her webs, she intended to use them to spin indestructible materials for the early champions and tip the scales in favor of Death's forces." Mi'Lazlee told Hy'Targ.

Together they secured the rope to the base of a jagged stalagmite. Before leaving for their journey, the king and company had consulted the aged soothsayer who had lived in the catacombs prior to Hy'Mandr's kingdom being established. She'd kept the place clean and functional for a generation before Hy'Targ's birth. Despite her oddities, she seemed to know more stories than all the books in all the libraries of Gundakhor.

He continued, "The gods discovered her treachery and cursed her, magically binding her within this dungeon so that she could not aid Lord Death, the first-gods' bastard brother. They forced Sshkkryyahr to weave a set armor for a chosen champion—the one who would defeat Melkior."

Hy'Targ cinched the knot tight and raised an eyebrow. "Melkior?" Hy'Targ wasn't much of an adventurer, he knew that in his core, but old lore always lit a spark deep within him—even though he would rather experience the tale from the outside of a book's pages. He far preferred reading adventure stories to living them. "I've not heard of Melkior—and I'm widely read." The prince cocked a smile—it was the one area he could claim superiority over within this party, and he'd already surpassed most of Irontooth's scholars in sheer knowledge, but with nary a fraction of their years.

"That's not surprising," Mi'Lazlee admitted. "I only heard tales of Melkior as a child from my old Baba, up until my Gam told her they would frighten me and made her stop. Melkior was Lord Death's first general and his chosen champion, back when the gods still warred over their creation. Baba said he had been handpicked by Mal—"

Hy'Targ snapped off a wild-eyed look of warning. *To say the personal name of Death was to invoke him*, the old saying went.

Mi'Lazlee caught the gesture and chuckled. "I don't buy into any o' that religious nonsense," he said. "After all, if it were all as true as me own face, the armor would've been taken by the ones that rose up to stop Melkior so many generations ago—like the prophecy and punishment the gods cursed Sshkkryyahr with. In any event, Melkior's army was wiped out way back in the First Age."

The prince shrugged, following his logic. If all the old myths were to be believed, the armor would not be here because Melkior *was* defeated. Were it not so, he would still be terrorizing the continent of Charnock and even spread to the Birthlands and as far as Cyrea and the rest.

Mi'Lazlee continued and dropped Death's name without a second thought. "Anyways, *Malgrimm* used Melkior to launch the first raising of the dead, but he was ultimately defeated. Most of his legend is obscure, clouded by layers of teaching in the *old ways*... from back when people were still religious, that is."

Hy'Targ nodded, thin lipped, as they sauntered back towards the gaping maw. The hole led deeper into the dungeon. "So, are *you*?"

"Am I what?" the older dwarf asked.

"Religious?"

Mi'Lazlee chuckled. "The gods are certainly real—or real nuff, least-a-wise. Maybe the gods just represent good ideals or forces of nature. Magic underpins everything, lad, but *religion*? I'd rather put my faith in friends or the handle of a well-made axe than some invisible beings who pull the strings of fate."

Hy'Targ felt certain Ne'Vistar and the arcane class of dwarves in the Irontooth Keep would disagree. Much of the argument boiled down to familiarity. "But I thought you believed in magic—you can't deny the existence of what you haven't experienced?"

Mi'Lazlee shrugged. "I've seen it work, so I know it's real… *but the gods as actual beings?* I dunno bout all that… might not be so cut and dried as my Gam always said. Not ever'thing is literal, young dwarf."

Hy'Targ crooked the edge of his jaw. "But couldn't *they* seem as real to the *priests* as your *axe* is to *you*?"

The thought stood Mi'Lazlee up straight and the old dwarf furrowed his brow. He finally chuckled and shook his head. "It sounds like Ne'Vistar has got you all twisted up in philosophy." He gripped the haft of his weapon for emphasis; his heavy fingers clunked the handle like mallets on a war drum. "I believe in *this*." He grinned before they returned to within earshot of the others. "It's good that your father brought you on this trip… my old Baba… my Gam, too—they were both battier than a drunk mudblood." He tapped the axe-handle again. *"This*… this will always be there for you—it's our way… something you ought to know well before you gotta sit on your father's throne."

Hy'Targ didn't object; although he preferred a book to battle, *he was still vagha*, and knowing the way of the axe was a necessity. He followed in silence and shimmied down the rope, trailing after the rest of them as they descended into the sublevel.

Twenty feet down, the party regrouped in what they assumed was the lair of Sshkkryyahr. Darkness pressed in close enough that it robbed even their dwarf's keen sight and limited its range. A thin layer of sludge caked the floor.

The king and his company already had axes in hand. Webs draped around the perimeter. Cocooned bodies, long since drained of fluids, dangled above the roughhewn floor, twisting in the gossamer as slow as derelict selumari airships.

Rusted weapons and corroded armor lay discarded below where the ancient cadavers hung suspended nearby. The adventurers moved forwards with caution and toed through the sets of old, decaying mail. None of it fit the description of Sshkkryyahr's mythic armor.

They could sense the presence of something evil close by. Hairs pricked on the backs of their necks, and tension built in the humid, earthy air. King Hy'Mandr buzzed with excitement. "Are ye ready, boys?"

The king's remaining friends tightened fists around weapons and nodded resolutely. Hy'Targ grimaced to mask the nervous energy churning in his gut, but he nodded as well.

Hy'Mandr spotted a thin strand of silk crossing their path and held his arms wide, calling his crew to a halt as he bent to examine it. He reached out and tweaked a stray, silver filament. It shivered with micro-vibrations.

The vaghan explorers clutched their weapons tight enough that knuckles cracked. Several restive moments stretched out for what seemed to Hy'Targ like an eternity.

Just before they relaxed their postures, a massive beast lashed out through the curtain of webbing. It snarled and snapped, towering more than twice the height of even Mi'Darrio, the tallest of their number.

The arachnid creature roared and stomped its pointy legs down in an attempt to skewer the stout vagha intruders with its spear-like feet. Above the eight-legged carapace, the uppermost half of an elf's body sat perched in centaur-like fashion. Her fiery, red skin and pointed ears clearly identified her as one of the ancient monsters of old. Her uppermost half resembled the morehl species—the Lava Elves who came after; Sshkkryyahr hurled curses and shrieked with ravenous growls.

"That's no spider!" Hy'Mandr howled, swinging his axe in wild loops. "It's a durngam drider."

Tr'Gurn yelped and rolled under the beast to avoid being trampled. He bent askew two of the creature's legs and they buckled like a pair of green-broken ailanthus saplings. The drider wailed with pain and batted the dwarf across the subterranean hall.

Bolstered by the monster's wound, the rest of the dwarves raised their weapons and pushed forward, overwhelming the drider and knocking her to the ground. They brandished blades and pressed them threateningly against their enemy's soft spots after dragging her down to their height.

She shied back, stumbling anemically, and yielded to the intruders. The drider panted, gasping for breath. Her sunken features and sallow skin indicated starvation.

"You are not trogs," the pitiable thing wheezed.

The King puffed out his chest. "Are you Sshkkryyahr, the great spider?" Hy'Mandr demanded.

Sshkkryyahr bowed her face, "That is my name," her hissing voice sounded like talons raked across a scholar's slate board, "though I've not heard it spoken aloud for... many decades. What brings the vagha to my lair; who are you? What do you want?"

"I am Hy'Mandr, the Adventurer King, and I seek the prize of legend." He beckoned for his son to come closer and stand beside him as he claimed victory over the mythic beast.

Hy'Targ approached as directed, but he kept his knees bent and ready with weapon prepared in case Sshkkryyahr merely played with them. He did not trust a morehl monster to parley without duplicity. In every tale he'd read, magical beasts tended to act treacherously.

"You want the armor?"

The dwarven king nodded.

Sshkkryyahr attempted to rise. Stumbled once and then took a few hesitant steps on uncertain legs. "It is this way," she winced and moved slow as an injured ox.

The dwarves surrounded her as she led them deeper into her prison.

"The gods once walked among us, incarnate and full of themselves, capricious and toying with creations like playthings." She growled, "The goddesses Ailuril and Aguarehl bound me in this chamber and forced me to work for them until its fated owners would arrive to claim it… a champion of high destiny."

Mi'Lazlee chuffed under his breath and stifled a chuckle; he didn't mention that the gods had done so as punishment.

"What you seek is an armor so light that it weighs practically nothing, but remains nigh impenetrable," Sshkkryyahr promised. "The armor prophesied to be worn by the next champion of the gods. I will lead you to it."

Sshkkryyahr led them through the cavernous warrens and towards an area deeper within the heart of the crypt. The vaghas' primal senses informed them that the center of the dungeon lay ahead. A location ahead seemed to emit a natural kind of light, and the dwarves spotted it far off.

Underfoot, the floors took on a polished sheen and smooth, engraved pillars replaced stalactites and stalagmites. Mystic runes were embossed within tiles where they walked, and the dwarves' thick-soled boots clomped upon the surface as the huge antechamber yawned open before them.

The vertical columns formed a huge circle with magically lit torches. Each burned with flames the color of the four primary elements; scarlet, gold, cerulean, and emerald they cast illumination into the dark. Myriad colonnades surrounded a stone plinth erected at the center of the room and the object resting upon it that shimmered with a white light.

Hy'Targ bent a knee and ran a finger along the smooth floor as they approached. "This is excellent craftsmanship… dwarven?"

His father shook his head. "eldarim," he muttered.

The prince pursed his lips. *Then this place truly is old,* he thought. The eldarim, rare as they still were, had not been builders for eons, now… not for nearly eight-hundred years before the Magestorm Wars.

Sshkkryyahr entered the ancient circle. As the adventurers followed, the shape of the armor took form within the glowing bubble. It appeared to be nothing more than a simple, woven robe, resting upon a dressing mannequin.

Tiny zots of light flickered at the edge of the vaghas' vision like sunspots. Looking from the drider to the artifact, the dots seemed to shimmer ever so softly, trailing from one to the other like links in a featherlight chain.

"The binding spell which anchors me in this dungeon is connected to this foul armor," Sshkkryyahr spat. "I will be glad to be rid of it. You must break the enchantment in exchange for the armor."

Vy'Danis crossed his arms over his barrel chest. "I say we just take the prize and leave this foul creature here."

Sshkkryyahr recoiled indignantly. "You cannot! It is guarded by a powerful magic—the very same one that binds me to this place. To even try would anger the gods of Esfah." She skittered around the pedestal and motioned towards the high, arched ceiling of the casemate. Ancient runes encircled them, engraved upon stone tablets affixed far above. Each one had been fastened to the ring of rafters spanning from pillar to pillar.

With a rhyming cadence, the guardian pointed to the glyphs as she read:

"To the one without sight, sight will be given. To take the armor, a champion must fight, and a devil released. To dispel this ward, one must possess…"

Sshkkryyahr pointed to a silver plate affixed below the armor. Attached to the plinth, it completed the statement with a single rune for a word in old Eldari. *Compassion.*

Hy'Targ stepped forward and turned a circle. A sense of wonder overtook him as he examined the ancient letters carved shortly long after the dawn of the Elder races, the vagha second among them. He almost felt an affinity for adventuring grow within him, and then his eyes caught sight of more age-shriveled bodies beyond the ring of pillars. They appeared to be trogs, but he thought some of the armor appeared to morehl-like.

"It is a simple, but powerful ward," Sshkkryyahr said. "Read it aloud and complete the phrase by finishing it." She pointed to the last word written upon the shiny plaque below the armor.

The Adventurer King bobbed his head towards the discarded bodies that his son had spied. "What about *them*? Did they also try to release you?"

Sshkkryyahr feigned shock that the dwarf would not trust her complicitly. "None of these were adventurers of destiny. Besides, trogs can rarely read," she deflected, "and both they and lava elves are incapable of compassion."

Mi'Lazlee scoffed again. "Destiny is just something people invent as an excuse to write clever stories. Ain't no bards here; we each make our own destiny."

"Then take the take the armor," the drider challenged. She crossed her arms over her naked breasts and stepped back to let him pass.

Mi'Lazlee set his jaw and approached the plinth. He reached into the white light and tried to take it, but it would not move. He smashed the base of its mounting with his axe, but the impact only sent painful shivers up the vagha's girthy forearms. He grumbled, and then walked back to the others, cursing about magic under his breath.

"Can you not read?" Sshkkryyahr asked derisively.

"A'course I can! I read good." Mi'Lazlee defended.

"Then you know what is required to take the artifact. Speak the words. Release me and claim your prize." The ancient rhyme rumbled through each of their minds again and

Sshkkryyahr threw her hair over her shoulders, revealing her breasts as she teased seductively, "I assure you, boys… I can be quite a devil—when I'm not locked away from company."

Hy'Targ continued to study the inscription while his father stepped between the drider and the armor to inspect it.

"All magic has a cost," the king mumbled, thinking this exchange too simple. "Especially the kind of magic that might sunder the will of a god."

The prince narrowed his gaze at one of the runic plates as his father began reading aloud from them. Something about it didn't seem quite right.

"Per-throw-mah-nawz. Awnsooze awnsooze-yeebow. Oath-aw-law oo-ruze awnsooze…"

Hy'Targ squinted suspiciously. He'd learned quite a lot about Eldari rune-script and other languages with the help of Ne'Vistar's tutelage. The early plates that read *without sight, sight will be given,* looked kilter'd and slightly askew. An awful thought struck him: it could've been moved—rotated from the converse which would mean the *opposite meaning* was intended.

"…thoree-sawz rhy-tho hagawlahz. Per-throw lah-gooze."

Hy'Targ's gaze fell upon the plate and realization sunk in. *The eldarim did not believe in compassion*—they viewed it as weakness. In context, to them, the word would more accurately translate as foolishness, *not compassion!*

"No, wait," Hy'Targ yelled.

Too late—Hy'Mandr spoke the final word from the plate. *"Ingwaz."*

As if punctuating the broken enchantment, the binding spell holding Sshkkryyahr within the dungeon cracked with a boom like thunder and a sizzle like falling rain. The drider cackled manically as the aura surrounding the armor blasted apart, blowing back hard enough that it nearly extinguished the arcane light sources ensconced upon the pillars and knocking half the dwarves from their feet.

Hy'Targ rushed towards his father as the horrible price of the magic took its toll.

The king's eyes sank into his head and liquefied to bloody, milky leakage as he clutched his face and screamed. Opalescent effluence bubbled and ran down his beard in heavy rivulets as his sockets emptied of all but darkness.

With a terrible screech of laughter, the duplicitous beast, finally freed, readied her attack.

Chel walked along the Great Coastal Road and smelled the salty sea breeze roll off the Far Sea. It lay a few leagues to the east. She had walked a long way, trying to find work, but nobody in these parts would willingly hire a lava elf.

Her pointed, red ears picked up the faint sounds of travelers coming from the south. The stone-paved highway made it easy to pick out the distinct sounds of the wheels on the path.

"Probably heading for Niamarlee," the lava elf muttered. She hid herself in some nearby bushes and waited for the travelers to catch up and then pass her by. Her people, the morehl, were distrusted, often even hated, by the other races—especially the selumari. The blue-skinned elves had hated their red-skinned counterparts ever since the Dawn of War, thousands of years ago. The coral elves blamed the lava elves for most of Esfah's woes, and the selumari kingdom of Niamarlee was the next city on the road, which was marked by many smaller like villages, like the one she lived in.

Within Chel's town she had relative safety, provided she did not depart. Her mixed-race community demanded the races tolerate each other within the bounds of the law. Most towns were like that, though they each had individual ordinances, but Chel was a long way from town and the law didn't apply in the woods. A lone woman on the road could become easy prey. She did not want to end up some prisoner sold into slavery in a Shen la'Terl brothel… and Chel was known for her extreme beauty. She'd turned down several offers already.

Nobody would come to her rescue if slavers took her. Chel had no family—she'd been a drifter for as long as she could remember, like so many other displaced morehl children victimized by the aftermath of nameless battles.

Skulking further into the foliage, she waited behind cover. The small caravan traveled on foot; a locked carriage pulled by a pony accompanied the band of six dwarves. She relaxed. Dwarves could be cranky and stubborn—and they were relentless when provoked—but they did not bear any animosity towards the lava elves unless they had a personal history with them. Dwarves who were religious worshiped the same god as the morehl as often as not: Firiel—the god of fire.

Chel's stomach grumbled as the caravan drew nearer. She hadn't worked in quite some time—meaning it had been even longer since she last ate. Just because her village wasn't directly dangerous, the anti-morehl bias still made it difficult to find honest work.

Keen elven eyes let her see a great distance and she noted a lock bouncing against the carriage door's hasp. It was the kind she was most adept at picking, *and a lock meant something of value was within.* Chel hadn't always been such an upright community member. She'd moved in her search for peace but previously earned her keep sifting the pockets of others.

It had been a long while since she'd dipped into her dishonest skill set, but she'd grown desperate over the last several weeks. Chel needed someone to give her a break. The morehl didn't want to steal, but she had to make a score that so readily presented itself. She retrieved the lock-pick she always kept in her pocket.

Chel pretended to stumble out from the trees and feigned surprise when the traveling dwarves halted. She met their gaze and apologized. "Pardon me. I seem to have gotten lost. A filthy goblin stole my pack—all my food and belongings—ran right through those trees like a coward." She could see it in their eyes; her beauty fascinated them, and more so, their hackles were up at the prospect of a goblin thief accosting this damsel. The vagha felt the same racial hatred for them that the Seulmari had for the lava elves. Ancient grudges died hard.

The dwarven leader soothed her and checked her over for wounds. His whiskers twitched when his hands rubbed against her hot, red flesh during a brief examination. "You don't appear to be harmed, me lass," he said with a leading manner, searching for her name.

"Chel," she said.

"I am Brenton," he said.

Chel grinned. She could tell a lot about him by the naming convention. He wasn't a dwarf from the region—Brenton's name didn't begin with the ancient slave clan moniker. She guessed Brenton and his gang were from further south, probably from Lyandrica.

Feigning discomfort from the hot sun, she meandered closer into the shade of the wagon while the collection of five motley dwarves under Brenton's command watched from several paces away. Any seasoned vagha would know that lava elves didn't mind the heat.

Brenton's pupils expanded as he watched her and spoke like a braggart, trying to impress the pretty thing. "Me and the company are on our way to Niamarlee to meet a contact and bring him his cargo. It's going on up to Undrakull… probably intended for the markets." He confirmed that they'd come from the port city of Lyandrica.

The dwarf greedily licked his lips and his eyes drank in her form.

She could tell that he wanted her. Chel had all the power in that moment. After a few moments of meaningless small talk, she bit her lip and turned up her lusty charm. She stepped closer to Brenton, swinging her hips as she approached; he took a half step backwards and bumped against the side of the locked carriage.

"I've never been with someone so burly and strong," she said, wrapping a finger through his red and gray beard. She put her other arm over his shoulders and deftly picked the simple lock with the thieves' tool as she teased him.

An impassioned flame lit behind the vagha's eyes. "Well… I… morehl girls have always seemed to me to look… I mean…"

She let him flounder and set the hook deeper. Chel did not like playing the strumpet, at least, not unless she genuinely cared for her chosen mate, and Brenton was certainly not that. He was a mark. She'd not had a mate in over a year, and Chel wasn't even sure what she was looking for. She only knew that she'd know it once she found it.

They were out of sight of Brenton's companions, and the dwarf leaned forward to peek at them around the corner of the vehicle. He muttered to himself; there wasn't much he could do in this position.

Chel injected a sultry tone to her voice. "If only there was somewhere we could go for a few minutes of privacy? Maybe we could use this carriage?"

Brenton frowned. "It's locked, my pretty. I ain't even seen inside it—that was sealed up back in Lyandrica." His cheeks flushed. The dwarf's blood was coursing.

She pouted her lip. "It doesn't *look* sealed. That lock's not even closed; it's just hanging there."

Brenton glanced at it. "We'll I'll be…" He didn't give the lock a second thought. "I suppose we could steal away a few minutes." He began unbuckling his belt and loosening his trousers. "Take a few minutes for yerselves, boys," he shouted to his peers. "It's a good time to take a piss if ye need one! Maybe go search for that trog in the trees."

He stole another look around the corner to see his mates ambling off to do just that. Whether they need to relieve themselves or merely gave him a few moments and suspected their leader's intentions, Brenton couldn't be certain. He didn't care, either.

Chel opened the door and found a startled firewalker—an elemental race from the north-east, long thought to be a hybrid species of selumari. The guard's eyes seemed to burn with an internal, crimson fire. The empyreans were a warrior race and rare in these parts unless hired for a specific job, usually mercenary work—Charnock was about as far from Empyreanoral, their homelands, as one could get.

He glanced aside at the four bracelets resting on the seat opposite him. The warrior growled, and Chel snatched the quartet of precious bangles before the firewalker could draw his weapon. She sprinted away as fast as she could.

The morehl was fleet of foot, but the empyreans were revered for their quickness. Chel blasted past Brenton whose pants had wrapped around his ankles. He barely had time to mutter his surprise, and he yelped when the blue guardian shoved him aside to get past him.

Chel dashed down the highway as fast as she could. Seconds later she had sprinted well beyond the ability of the dwarves to find her. She looked over her shoulder and saw the empyrean was still in pursuit—and gaining on her.

Sliding the bracelets over her wrists, two on each hand, she turned a hard left and plunged through the trees. She could not face a firewalker and hope to live—they were bred for battle and their culture devoted itself to martial prowess. The only way to lose her relentless pursuit was to hide and hope he was a poor tracker. She slipped through tall trees and ducked below bough and branch, pushing her way through the bracken as she ran blind, hoping he could not find her. Perhaps plunging blindly through the woods would let her outdistance him as he slowed to trail her.

Chel looked up too late and collided with one very surprised elf, and they both tumbled to the ground. She stared at him wild-eyed and scrambled to her feet.

He was a tangle of arms and feet as he stood and floundered for words as he introduced himself, apologizing profusely. "My name is Jordyll," he said, oblivious to the fact that she was in hurry.

"I'm Chel," she said, catching her breath. "You are a Cursed One... a mudblood?" Chel asked, noting his dark gray skin. In every other way, he looked like one of the elves... but his color was wrong.

He ignored the slurs, so enamored with her beauty that he didn't seem to hear them. Chel looked into his eyes, noting some deep spark within him, a kind of kismet connection. She regretted her choice of words and hoped he hadn't interpreted them as an insult. *He was still an elf, and not a selumari,* she thought. Seeing his handsomeness, something kindled in her own heart as well.

Her pursuer crashed into the clearing where they stood, and Jordyll reacted on pure instinct when Chel screamed. He whirled around and hit the empyrean with his shovel, knocking him clean off his feet; the enemy landed flat on his back and did not move.

Jordyll knelt beside him as Chel fretted. "I didn't hit him that hard," he muttered, looking to Chel. Trickles of blood poured where his head had cracked against a jagged stone. "He was after you? Why?"

Chel stared long into her rescuer's deep eyes. She did not want to lie to him—even though it would have been so easy for her. "I... I stole something from him. He traveled with some dwarves down the road. I was just so hungry and morehl are so despised this far south. I... I..."

He looked at her, and his face softened. Jordyll pulled her into an embrace. Perhaps only the gray elves were more universally hated—and by *both* sides of their kin. selumari and morehl both considered them abominations.

As she looked into Jordyll's face, however, she saw something else. *Someone* else.

"Come," he said. "I know of an abandoned farm near the outskirts of the town up ahead."

"It's not near Niamarlee, is it?" She could not feel safe in the shadows of a coral elf castle.

"No." He took her by the hand. "We will be safe there. I will take care of you." He squeezed her and she leaned into his embrace, suddenly as enthralled with him as Brenton had been with her.

Chel knew in that moment, she'd found everything she had ever wanted.

In the low light of the crypts, flecks of white spittle flew from the drider as it reared back. Her legs nearly buckled on the damaged appendages where Tr'Gurn had hobbled it. Sshkkryyahr hammered down towards the blind king, trying to crush him with her weight.

Hy'Mandr spun and whirled. Unable to see her, the king was far from defenseless.

Even blinded, the Adventurer King could sense her presence well enough to pivot aside and make the monster's death stroke miss. She came close enough that she sprayed frothy saliva across his beard. In total absence of sight, Hy'Mandr shoved his son out of the path of destruction and swung his axe around, heaving it towards her head with a practiced, whirling motion. Glorybringer's keen edge sliced her face from lip to scalp, carving a jagged line of dripping crimson.

Her cheek and brow leaked steam as the morehl blood splattered in smokey splotches. Sshkkryyahr screamed and hissed curses, furiously swiping at the disabled king.

Hy'Targ tackled his father, rolling them both to the ground and barely evading decapitation. The remaining four the vagha had gotten back to their feet and charged against the salivating drider who seemed suddenly bolstered by her rage and hunger.

Sshkkryyahr sidestepped them, using the plinth as a guard, and maneuvered around her enemies. She reeled backwards to avoid an attack and then snagged a dwarf. Sshkkryyahr ripped Mi'Lazlee's arm from his body. Greedily tearing flesh from bone with her jagged teeth, she devoured half of it while in retreat. She cackled as she fled and clutched to her chest the first meal she'd earned in ages.

On the far side of the Eldari circle, Sshkkryyahr scaled one of the pillars with her massive spider legs. Moments later, she scrambled through a crack in the ceiling. Broken gravel and dust rained through as she collapsed whatever tunnel permitted her escape and blocked any pursuit from below by the same path.

Hy'Targ's father shook off the prince's embrace as he tried to make sense of what had happened to him. Finally, he relented and Hy'Targ led his father to his best friend, who sat nearby. Mi'Darrio cradled his brother who hyperventilated, babbling incessantly through the shock and pain of the severed limb.

Mi'Lazlee rocked slightly, trying and failing to get to his feet. He reassured everyone he was okay, but only flailed off balance after losing the arm. "I'm fine. I'm fine. I'm fine," he promised. "I'm…" the blood stopped spurting from his shoulder. He whispered, "I hear them… the signal horns of Tarvanehl… I see… I see the Eternal Lands…" Mi'Lazlee fell silent and even the blind king could see that the spark of life in his friend had extinguished.

With his father staggering behind him, Hy'Targ could only stand and watch under the magic glow of the elemental fires. His face darkened as he thought of how carelessly Mi'Lazlee had earlier invoked Malgrimm's name—Death's personal name—and he had come to collect his due.

Hy'Targ guided his father by the shoulders and helped turn him towards the exit, still uncertain how they would hoist him up from the hole where they'd hung the rope. Guilt pooled in Hy'Targ's gut. The one real skill he brought to the party had been his book smarts… and he'd realized the treachery of the drider's riddle too late.

The dwarves decided to leave Mi'Lazlee's body behind. They had to if there remained any hope of getting the king back to the Irontooth Keep with enough haste for the healers to attempt any healing for him. It was a tenday's journey home by mammoth, and that was only if no further incidents on the road slowed them down—and assumed Gunter's pass through the southern Stonejaw Mountains could be treacherous. King Hy'mandr's drakufreet mount, the only known one of its kind, could cut that time in less than half—but none except the blind king could ride the bronze colored dragonkin. Brentésion was notoriously temperamental towards any other handlers.

They had almost cleared the edge of the pillars when Hy'Mandr stiffened. "Well?"

"What is it?" Hy'Targ asked

"Well don't leave the bloody armor behind—if'n I've paid this heavy a toll, we better at least get something out of the quest."

Hy'Targ hurried back to the plinth and retrieved the armor. It was a fine knit, expertly woven from silks that hardly weighed a thing. He rushed back to his father and gave it to him.

The king felt the armor with his hands and tested it with stretches and vain attempts to tear it. Finally, he thrust it back to his son. His voice was warm and even-tempered. "Take it. I want you to have the armor."

Hy'Targ didn't really know what to say. His voice bordered on a whisper. "Was this prize worth it? When is the last time we needed such armor? We're not even at war…"

The king fumbled for his son's shoulders and then gripped him tight with hands like shackles. Hy'Mandr searched his son with the dark sockets where his eyes had once been; they somehow pierced to his soul, regardless of sight. "The prize was never a tangible *thing*, son… it was getting my ass off that durngam throne and having the chance to adventure with the only other dwarf I'd give my eyes for." He relaxed his grip and stumbled back towards his companions. "Someday, you will be king… and you needed to learn something from this quest—you need to know…"

Hy'Targ swallowed the lump in his throat and followed his father and their party as they continued through the subterranean dark.

Hy'Mandr, King Irontooth, continued speaking words that would haunt the prince for years to come. "You needed to know, son… there are some things you can't learn from books."

Two red-skinned elves skulked within the secret crypt on the Raithlan Plains. The older lava elf set his torch in the stand. Ripples of flame light danced over his deep, red skin and played across his wisdom lines and crow's feet near his black eyes. A younger morehl set down the bag of grave-robbing tools and wisps of dust curled up from around the duo's satchel, finally freed back into the air.

Marring the floor between the pair of raised graves, a patch of mold stretched across the stagnant puddle between them. Besides that, everything else remained fuzzy in a film of gray velvet giling.

"Nobody has been here in centuries," the young one said. He'd learned of this tomb from a greedy buyer in Giyrnach—the Dohanese was likely a fence for the artifacts he'd hoped to claim from the young elf's efforts. Dohan, despite the island's comparative size, was a hive of export—much of it illegal.

The younger elf had enlisted himself to Hartyuga and agreed to aid him in the plunder—he knew they had both searched for this treasure for some time now, and the younger morehl felt certain his secret buyer offered a higher price than Hartyuga's. Besides, the older thief refused to share the identity of his purchaser, which did not sit well with him.

Hartyuga had always thought himself something of a mentor to the boy, even if the junior elf had never accepted the fool's efforts to educate him. They'd pulled a couple jobs together over the last several years, but Hartyuga had only ever shown him one useful trick in all that time.

The older morehl grinned and said knowingly, "It's been longer than that, actually." He reverently approached the pair of stone sarcophagi and compared their inscriptions to the weathered parchment he'd kept on his body until now. The eldest kept his information close to the vest to prevent a double cross. He tucked it away after confirming his information.

Hartyuga dug a fingernail beneath the edge of a needle that he kept threaded just within the top layer of his skin and cast the minor spell he'd taught to his reluctant protege. It transformed into a full-sized pry bar in his hands. Hartyuga kept it hidden amongst the collection of secret tools stashed in his sub-dermal camouflage.

He rammed the lever under the heavy, stone lid, and the younger elf stayed him with a hand and a shake of his head.

"It's trapped," he said.

Hartyuga raised an eyebrow. "I thought I was the teacher, and you were the apprentice?"

The younger elf shrugged and rolled his eyes. "Well, you're apparently not doing very well, are you?" They'd both had different data sources pointing them to this crypt— apparently Hartyuga's was less well-informed than his Dohanese employer had been.

Frowning, Hartyuga dropped his tool. "And you have a plan, then… some way around the trap?"

The youth nodded. "Of course I do. Have I ever been ill prepared for any job these past couple years?"

Nodding diffidently, the older morehl stepped back and let his charge take over. He grinned and let the kid do all the difficult work. Both lava elves knew which possessed the more skilled hands of the pair.

Hartyuga retrieved his document and scanned it again. He grinned as he re-read the commission.

After rummaging through the tool sack, the younger of the red elves pulled out a set of stone cutting chisels and a hammer from his supply and tossed the sack aside to store their plunder within. "Tell me again who this buyer is and why he or she is interested in some collection of old bones?"

Hartyuga cocked his ear towards the door leading to the long stairs they had climbed. "Nice try. But I haven't known you long enough to trust you with that information. You can meet him when we get paid."

"Five years isn't long enough, Hartyuga?" His ears picked up on the distant noises, too.

The older one grimaced and stepped towards the door. "You're still a month shy of that first gig we pulled back in Maris-ta-Sehlim."

After chiseling a fracture line on the lid, the younger one frowned. "This will take a little while… find me some boards? I need to stabilize this corner, so I don't set off the pressure switch. Gotta keep the lid's weight on that trigger."

His partner didn't pay him any mind. He poked his head out the arched doorway. "I hear something. We're not alone."

"It's probably just that elderly human we snuck past when we entered the crypt. Maybe he's using this dungeon as his root cellar."

The elder elf scowled. "After all the traps we evaded, you really think one old man would casually come down here to pick through his sack of dried broomcorn or clusters of turnips?" He shook his head and hissed.

"Well, I don't know. Go and check it out, then. Unless you want to stay here and disable this trap, instead?"

Hartyuga scowled, but drew his flintlock in the first hand and a dagger in the other. "Not likely, kid. You get those remains secured—I'll deal with our intruder."

With his partner slipping back down the stairs, the young morehl grinned. He knew something that Hartyuga did not. If his partner had done his due diligence, he'd have learned the legends, and that a terrifying monster had inhabited the depths of this tomb. He didn't know a morehl he'd wager succeeding against a hungry Beholder, and Hartyuga didn't scratch the bottom of a list of lava elves he would ever bet on.

A flintlock's report split the musty air, followed shortly by Hartyuga's screams. They were cut short and followed by many long moments of silence. He knew his partner would not return, just as the young thief had hoped. Even though he found murder distasteful, he'd happily let natural events play out.

The remaining treasure hunter wedged a moldy board between the ceiling and the weighted trigger-plate. He smiled; knowing Hartyuga's buyer was irrelevant, he could find out who it was eventually, or find a new one in time if he hoped to cause a bidding war and emerge a very wealthy morehl. The lava elf picked up his stone cutting tools and got back to work. If his upbringing in the shadowy underworld of Maris-ta-Sehlim's thieving guild had taught him anything, it was the virtue of patience—and provided he could wait, these bones promised him a significant payday… and Nohdan planned to blow it all at once on a month of debauchery in the pleasure houses of Shen la'Terl… and then move on to the next job.

With one swift crack of the hammer, the lid broke free, and the trap remained intact. Nohdan grinned and looked up at the ceiling. Pinpoints of starlight shone through above the mossy growth on the floor; it would guide him towards the cracked, narrow exit, and back across the Far and Talvat Seas, ending back in Dohan… where his hefty payment waited.

CHAPTER TWO
(12 Years later)

Year 1139 of the Second Age

The collection of adult Amazons sat in the tent of meeting where a murmur of worry rippled through them. Each human spoke of recent events to their village chief and his companion, another of the elders.

Chief Geru traded glances with the aged singer of the records, Murthak the Skald. Together they made up part of the council of rulers from their community, the People of the Sun, who had built their home at the north side of Charnock where the Stonejaw Mountains turned to hills and met the plains. The eldest member of their committee, Trandlurthan, was not present, though the community had called a meeting he should have been at.

The chief bit his lip as a young man explained that his best sheep had been ripped apart in the middle of the night.

"We settled here four generations ago," the herdsman said. "We gave up the old, nomadic ways so we could stop fighting, so our flocks would increase in size, and so we'd have the security of the harvest... but now, we live in fear of the barrow's long shadow!"

A chorus of assents moved through the smoky tent. Chief Geru wiped away the sting of incense that bit his eyes and listened patiently. That was his job as the leader.

"We settled this land not knowing it was cursed," a woman spoke up. "Someone must do something." Voices agreed with her. "Three of us have died in as many nights... it's gone beyond just animals," she insisted to more applause.

The first man spoke up again. "We left much of our heritage behind when we traded sword and spear for shovel and plow, but we remember the old stories." A hush fell over the folk. "We remember tales and legends long forgotten. I believe this is the work of the mythical b'yandhar."

In the swelling silence, Murthak stood on uneasy, elderly knees. "You could be right," his gravelly voice echoed in the reverential quiet. "However, it could just as likely be a bugbear or a pack of wolves that has harassed and murdered our families and livestock. We also know there have been goblin movements to the east, and not far, at that."

The skald looked at each face in the room in turn as he surveyed the hall. "Has any man or woman here seen the b'yandhar? Would you know it if you saw it?"

Confused glances bounced back and forth among the tribe. None had ever seen it, and no one here could identify it, now.

"It is a monster," the woman insisted. "Its skin is covered with disease."

"I heard it was eyes!"

"Tentacles," someone yelled.

"...and it can cause disturbing visions and dreams and even kill a man with its mind."

"*Or* a woman," insisted a muscular female descended from the Amazon's warrior caste.

The skald quieted them. "The b'yandhar is a thing mostly lost to legend," he insisted. "Many conflicting stories exist—but we know that it lived in the crypt long ago and has slumbered since the first age... more than twelve hundred years, now. If it has indeed awoken, something must have caused it. Did someone here awaken the beast?"

Only silence responded. He nodded curtly and then returned to the Chief's side and took his seat.

Murthak leaned over to Chief Geru and whispered, "Trandlurthan is not present."

Geru bobbed his head measuredly. "He is nearly as old as you, was he not?"

"Older," the skald told him. "I do fear the worst for him. Every year since his son died, he's grown more eccentric than the last, obsessed with all sorts of alchemy and mysticism. I'm afraid it's madness that drove him to his hermitage up in the outskirts near the barrow."

Chief Geru frowned, but did not mention the old man's absence to the community. The last thing they needed was to add one more name to the recent death toll. There *were* deaths, and the issue would not likely go away until the culprit was discovered and dealt with.

"Will there be action?" a villager demanded.

Standing to address them all, Chief Geru held out his hands to ask for calm and attention. "Yes, yes. There will be action and soon. The elders and I will convene and decide the next steps to take, if this is truly the work of the b'yandhar, or whatever other evils might have crept out of the crypt." He searched the distance in the direction of the rugged hill where the old dungeon entrance laid.

The villagers were right. Something *did* haunt the warren tomb below the hillock. Something needed to be done… but the People of the Sun could never know what secrets their community guarded. Only the Elders should be cursed with that knowledge.

Nohdan stared at the exquisite blade in the moonlight. It perched on a gilded stand upon a dais in the middle of the chamber. "Some idiot called this thing the *Dragonstaff*?" He smirked and glanced at the works of art and other potential valuables hanging on the walls. "I guess Dragon*sword* must've already been taken."

He hung from the vertical cable of the castle he hoped to plunder and gazed at the valuable sword. Like most magic weapons, this priceless artifact was one of the relics crafted by master artisans prior to the Magestorm War, a legendary battle when nearly all the children of the gods went to battle with a glut of weapons that drew power from the heart of Esfah. Now, after so long had passed, the items grew rarer and more valuable, making them perfect marks for clever thieves.

Scanning the legendary blade, it looked like the real deal—and he'd seen several fakes. Nohdan had become something of an expert in Magestorm relics after identifying and stealing so many; he knew that Dragonstaffs came in many varieties and their cores were constructed of dragon bone. While many were, in fact, staffs, others had been integrated together with blades during their construction and had handles inlaid with dragon bone.

The fire-skinned morehl let go of his rope and left it to dangle from the chimney where he'd entered. There had been no fire—he'd paid one of the kitchen scullions to see to that, although natural fire, for short time periods, wouldn't harm a lava elf.

"Filthy selumari," Nohdan said under his breath as he silently cataloged all the valuables piled in the room. "Filthy *rich* selumari," he corrected.

The morehl slinked through the room to check for anything else he desired and then crawled up to the enchanted weapon and pulled it from its place of honor. Nohdan whirled its keen edge around with surprising ease; he'd thought it would have been heavier.

Finally satisfied, the thief pinched the grip of the sword and muttered the incantation. He'd learned only a few spells in his time, and each of them came in handy for thieving, but none more than this one.

Nohdan repeated the words like a mantra and with a steady cadence until the blade shrank and transmuted into a needle. He slid the needle into the calloused flesh of his forearm where he had hidden several other needles, keeping them just beneath the surface of the skin and above the nerve endings.

His employers across the Talvatic Sea would be thrilled—any of the Dragonstaffs would fetch a hefty sum, and Nohdan's exquisite tastes required regular cash to keep him happy. He looked around one last time for anything else he could easily steal before he absconded with the real prize.

The door suddenly burst in and the room filled with guards. Within mere seconds, it seemed like every elven blade north of Bralanthyr lay pressed to his throat.

Nodhan looked up and recognized the closest of the blue-skinned elves. "Hello, Prince Mantieth," Nodhan said with a smile. The guards shackled the red elf as he spoke.

Mantieth bowed. "My reputation precedes me," said the cocksure young elf.

Nodhan shrugged. "I saw a drawing of you once. You know, a catalog of royalty and the children of famous people." He left off the part about the roster's connection to an assassination request.

The prince shrugged and quipped without missing a beat. "I know you, too, Nodhan. Burglars who get caught often get sketched, and those prints are shared with others. You're not very good at this, it seems." He locked eyes with the thief; they could have been the same age, though vastly separated by culture, wealth, and skin color.

"Hazard of the job, it seems," sighed Nohdan.

Mantieth bowed, "It seems I'm not the first to catch you—but unlucky for you, I'll likely be the last."

"Wait," the morehl argued, "don't you even care that the Dragonstaff is gone?"

Mantieth shrugged; he had no interest in bartering with a thief. "Inconsequential. It was pretty, but far too dangerous to ever use in battle without the proper safety precautions. A weapon that summons dragons? History proves that is seldom a good idea. Besides, there hasn't been a significant war in decades."

Nohdan grinned as his guards pushed him down the hall. "That's something you selumari lack... an old-fashioned appreciation for an injection of chaos."

"I certainly do love things ordered. You'll see what I mean soon enough; every day is the same in the dungeons," Mantieth taunted. "Someday you'll lose track of the year." He grinned as the guards dragged the invader away, and then hurried off to tell his best friend, Elorall, exactly what had happened.

King Hy'Mandr Irontooth sat upon the throne in his mountainside castle and slumped with fatigue. In the most recent decade since the accident that claimed his sight, his ruddy hair and beard had turned to shades of ash and snow; his strong frame had bent and withered, and he no longer possessed the ability to pursue his life's true passions.

The last of his court's business concluded when Ne'Vistar approached from his side. The dwarven scholar laid hold of the king's arm. "King Irontooth," he had to rouse him from a near sleep. "Can you spare a moment of your time?"

Hy'Mandr turned to his adviser. "Eh, Ne'Vistar? What is it... is it Hy'Targ?"

"No, no. Nothing like that... but perhaps something far worse than you can imagine."

The king cocked an eyebrow and then reached for his cane. He used it to wobble up to his feet, and then guide his steps.

"Walk with me?" Ne'Vistar asked.

Hy'Mandr sighed. He'd just thought his day had finished, but he nodded. Ne'Vistar never wasted time at court with petty in-fighting between clans or other trivial matters.

The king could tell from way his cane clicked the ground, sharp and loud, that they were alone. "What is it, Ne'Vistar?"

"War," he whispered.

The king perked up. His eyes were gone, but he still possessed the hot blood and heart of a dwarf.

"But I've heard no rumors or tales of…"

"Of course you wouldn't," Ne'Vistar interrupted. "I've told no one. One of my young oracles, more talented than I've ever seen before, has had a vision. Blackness grows across all Esfah until it blots out every living and green thing. By its end, nothing is left but withered branch and broken bone."

Hy'Mandr hissed sharply. "Riddles? Speak plainly."

"Riddles are how the visions come, King Irontooth," Ne'Vistar insisted. "The oracle awakened from a trance, screaming and repeating a single name until he calmed enough to tell me his vision."

The king nodded measuredly and stroked his beard. Gravely he said, "Tell me the name."

"Melkior," he annunciated the name with cautious dread.

Hy'Mandr's face remained stony and unreadable.

"My King?"

The blind dwarf began moving again, heading towards the royal chambers. "Do you believe your oracle, Ne'Vistar? I've always been under the impression that Melkior is a myth… a legend we tell children to make them behave."

"He is a figure from our religion… his part of the story is a small, yet powerful one—purposefully left out of the annals, but surely the house of faith…"

"Bah! Faith. That's just a term for myths we tell *adults* to make *them* behave," he chuckled. And then his voice grew dark. "But I didn't ask about what people say or what books contain. I've known lots of people and I've read many books—

or at least I did before…" the crow's feet deepened at the edges of his empty sockets. "Tell me what *you* believe about this oracle, Ne'Vistar."

The old scholar wilted beneath Hy'Mandr's words. "I believe him." A few seconds of silence hung over the moment.

Ne'Vistar broke the quiet. "It has been over a thousand years since the last time the Mother or Father intervened in Esfah, but that does not mean they have abandoned us. It has been a test of faith. I believe a new time of champions is coming—I have long believed this. Melkior was Death's first champion. Something dangerous is coming—if not this mythical Melkior, then some new archetype… a new champion of death, perhaps."

Hy'Mandr nodded slowly. "I may not have your exact brand of faith, my friend, but I'm inclined to believe you… I can feel the gathering darkness."

"Sire?" Ne'Vistar squinted at him. He'd never assumed that the king possessed any of the kinds of the mystic sight or ability required of spell casters who worked magics with skill beyond the latent abilities inherent of all vagha.

"Not in a magical sense, ya durned fool." He shrugged. "Simple math. It's been far too long since anything drastic happened in Esfah. We've enjoyed too much equilibrium for our time—Esfahn history is soaked in struggle and war: pent up aggression is bound to break free sooner or later." Hy'Mandr paused at his door, his mood somber. "I'll make arrangements to bolster our forces and prepare our stockpiles and equipment, but quietly, in case yer omens come to pass," he said, and then he pushed through the door to his private quarters.

Ne'Vistar bowed and left the king to his rest. He did not tell Hy'Mandr the end part of the vision: that King Hy'Mandr led a host of warriors against the evil one, and there were also dragons.

Best not get his hopes up. Dreams and oracles often had symbolic meanings rather than literal ones... and what good was one blind dwarf, even if he were a king, against a dragon?

The *gruntch*ing sound of scooping dirt filled the hot air overlooking the People of the Sun's village, coming from behind the tiny, solitary house halfway up the knoll. It was the only sign of activity. All else was too quiet.

Bare-chested, Varanthl swung the pickaxe over and over as the sun crawled towards the horizon, casting the ominous shadows that crept closer to the old, stone building which he'd shared for the last year with his father.

Using all four arms, Varanthl crawled out of the deep hole he'd shoveled and knelt next to the body that he'd wrapped in a sheet and tied with a thin cord; covering his father seemed like the right thing to do, but also Varanthl couldn't bear to see him this way. He only wanted to remember Trandlurthan how he'd known him—constantly moving—and not how he was now: ashen skinned, silent, and wooden.

He did not know what he was supposed to do next. Varanthl stood, broad shouldered, well over six feet tall, and with two muscular arms on each side. It seemed appropriate to speak words of remembrance before placing Trandlurthan within the hole. Varanthl opened his mouth to speak, but did not know the proper words... there were so many things that he did not know. Varanthl was only one year old, after all.

His chest felt tight and his eyes burned with hotness, like when his father had told jokes or funny stories... but this was altogether different. It hurt. Sadness squeezed his lungs. He wiped his cheeks; until now, Varanthl had not been familiar with crying.

Finally, he lowered his father into the grave by the rope and filled the hole in with his shovel.

Varanthl went back inside and sat at the table in sullen silence. He always knew that his father had been old, but he'd never expected him to pass away so soon. As he'd always done, he set two bowls for the stew he'd prepared earlier and left his father's place set. The empty setting bothered him, reddening his neck.

He rubbed the old, raised scars at his joints. They itched whenever Varanthl grew anxious, and the seams crisscrossed all over his body, making him keenly aware that he'd not always been this way… been what he was now.

The loneliness of the surrounding silence crushed in around him. Still half-naked, Varanthl stood and held out the shirt his father had made for him; he'd sewn on two extra arms and extended the torso for him. Varanthl picked up one of his father's shirts and smelled it. Trandlurthan's tunic only had two arms—he knew he was different, but differences meant so little to families.

As he dressed himself, the edges of his frayed clothing caught on the crusty, metal emblem embedded in his chest. He pulled the shirt down, and the fabric muted the dull glow that it emitted. He massaged it absentmindedly. The metal thing always felt hot, but he didn't want to scare people away with his appearance. Trandlurthan had two arms, but he did not have metal intersecting his flesh. While most of Varanthl appeared human, those parts that were *different* were anything but human.

Varanthl thought of his father's words. "The metal thing keeps you alive, son. I cannot bear to lose you again, so leave it alone." He'd also said, "People will be scared when they first see you… until they know you as I do. None has ever existed like you before. For all the races created by the Mother and Father, there are still so many things that scare us. The world is full of both beauty and ugliness; what terrifies me is that we so rarely understand the difference between the two."

He sighed. Though he knew from his father that he had an uncle somewhere in the village, Varanthl had never met another person before. He used to sit outside at night and listen to the sounds of celebrations down the hill. He'd even crept down and watched the bronze-skinned men and women dance in the fire or caught glimpses of them working their fields.

Varanthl looked down. His lower right hand was that same bronze color, at least until his skin was crossed by a long scar where he'd once worn stitches—back in his earliest memories. He almost smiled at the memory; those stitches had itched like nothing he'd felt before or since.

He finished his meal and washed up. He put away the dishes and exited the hut.

Setting his face to the village, Varanthl began the trek down towards the community. The sun had almost set behind him, but the townspeople rarely quieted until it had been dark for a while.

Children looked up at his massive form, silhouetted by the colors of an evening sky, and then ran into their homes, calling for their parents.

"Please. Please," Varanthl called out. "My father, Trandlurthan is dead."

The few adult men and women who spotted him turned away and ran, fear in their eyes. Varanthl stepped after them, losing them in the shadows. "Why do you run?"

Someone yelled in the distance.

A whistling buzz trilled past his ear. Another one stopped with a thud; an arrow lodged in the turf near his feet. A mob of terrified people carrying swords, bows, and makeshift weapons gathered. One of them threw a torch at him; it bounced off his upper shoulder, scattering cinders that stung his cheeks.

"The b'yandhar," one woman screamed.

"It's a b'yandhar—it's hideous!"

"Four arms and covered in scars…"

"Murderer," another yelled, flailing another torch at Varanthl. "My wife is dead and gone."

He did not understand. "Not your wife… Trandlurthan is dead," Varanthl roared above the crowd, trying to make himself heard and force them to understand.

The mob howled and jabbed at him with weapons. Another arrow flew wild nearby. "It murdered Trandlurthan!" the next missile zipped past, nicking the patchwork man and drawing a stream of blood.

Scared, Varanthl turned and fled back up the hillside. The villagers pushed after him, but only to the edge of their homes and established a perimeter.

Varanthl paused halfway up the hill and turned to watch. They'd set up sentries to sound an alarm lest the creature return.

Dejected for having found no hope, their words stung his heart and he shambled back up the slope. He closed the door to his hut and leaned against it in silence. Rejection burned hotter than the thing affixed to his breast and it stung deeply, like an echo of the pain he'd felt when he'd found his father that morning, more still than he'd ever seen him.

Varanthl slid down to the floor and tucked his knees to his chest. For only the second time in his short, confusing life, he cried.

Br'Derluch sa'Terl stroked his long beard as he sat impatiently at the table, cursing below his breath. The dwarf groused with his vaghan aides seated nearby and behind him, equally frustrated. They'd been waiting a week already for the appointment with the selumari leader in his kingdom just up the coast of the Far Seas.

The coral elves seated across the table from Br'Derluch looked equally exasperated by the king's empty seat. selumari aides fidgeted and avoided direct eye contact with the irked diplomat from the Irontooth kingdom.

Finally, Br'Derluch slapped his hands on the table and stood with a huff. "I ain't gonna have any more of my time wasted. I don't care *who* it is that keeps me waiting."

The door to the chamber opened as he spoke, and the elven king's entry sucked the air out of the room.

Leidergelth, King of Niamarlee, took his seat and fixed the dwarf with his cool gaze. "I am told that you represent Hy'Mandr… King Irontooth?" He barely deigned to look at the vagha delegate. "You come to the selumari for what purpose? Perhaps your king couldn't find his way out of his own castle gates?" Leidergelth smirked.

Br'Derluch curled a lip, but didn't take the bait. "I'm here to discuss the Great Coastal Road," he puffed a hot blast through his nose, incensed by the gall of his insult. "Without a formal peace, trade has become tenuous… especially in the borderlands: on the road where enforcement of law is growing lax. We must decide who patrols where and who effects repairs?"

The King stared down his nose. "It has always been Niamarlee's position that we own *all* of the road. It was originally called the *Ahymoc-t'Ogan*: the Great *Coral* Road. We built it before the usurper…"

"*The vagha built it!*" Br'Derluch rose his voice.

Leidergelth grinned coyly. "*Slaves* legitimately owned by my kingdom built the road generations ago. We do not consent to any other agreement or interpretation of our mutual history."

"And a fine good job you've done, then," the dwarf spat. "Even on my way here my party was attacked by goblin bandits. The Irontooth Kingdom merely wants to arrive at some sort of arrangement that…"

"The Irontooth vagha have already taken enough from my people," Leidergelth interrupted.

"We *won* our independence from our *oppressors*," Br'Derluch fired back.

The king stood, ready to unload more regrettable words when Furtaevell, his primary adviser and chief enchanter, laid a hand on the king's shoulder. "What happened in the past is certainly regrettable. But it's already been done, and not by any of us in this room," Furtaevell insisted.

Leidergelth smoothed his rumpled vestments and sat, only a little calmer for it. "You have come into my home and brought me no tribute from your people."

Br'Derluch kept his voice even. "We stopped paying tribute under Hy'Loer the Chainbreaker. We come as a free and separate people offering terms for open trade."

The king gave him an evil eye and opened his mouth to speak, but Br'Derluch tossed a small sack onto the table, hoping to appease him.

Leidergelth reached for it and jingled its metallic contents. "It's not gold?" he raised a confused brow and spoke sourly as he undid the drawstrings. "Even if it were, it'd be awfully small."

"No gold," Br'Derluch said.

The king poured out its contents: small iron ingots.

"You can have your alchemists test it. It's from the latest vein we uncovered below our mountain—very fine stuff." Br'Derluch didn't understand the king's reaction. After a moment he asked, "Aren't you in need of local suppliers of quality metal? Don't tell me you're happy with the prices of that sub-par garbage they're sending you from Oxforge? With Vhandria's tariffs, plus transportation costs, there's no way you can get ore of the same quality fer a reasonable price."

Leidergelth slammed a fist on the table. He seethed with long-brewing rage. "That we're even having this conversation is ridiculous. Did that blind oaf of a king send you up the coast just to gloat how he owns mines that were once the selumari's?"

"I've had about enough of your insults!" Br'Derluch stood. "We brought a good faith offer and you wouldn't dare speak to Hy'Mandr like this. Even blind he'd…"

"He'd what? Chop at the air with that fancy axe of his?" Leidergelth leaned over the table. "We will not negotiate with the Irontooth Clan… from what I hear, his son can barely lift a weapon in his own defense. It won't be long before that sightless gurk's line comes to an end in his weakling son—but what would you expect from Gundakhorian trash?"

"How dare you insult the Queen…"

"Oh please, what do you even know about Sh'Ttil… besides that she is dead?"

Br'Derluch and Leidergelth were both on their feet, screaming at each other. The king waved his hands and walked towards the exit.

"Put as much hope as you like in your future, but without a strong Niamarlee, Irontooth is nothing. While your kingdom withers, I've put all my stock in the next generation— so if you'll excuse me, I'm going to watch my son's sparring match."

Furtaevell followed his king even as the dwarven delegate hurled well-deserved curses at them. The selumari adviser walked backwards, quietly promising Br'Derluch that he'd arrange for a future meeting, hopefully one with cooler heads.

The door opened to Prince Mantieth who stood in the hall as the royal party spilled into the corridor. He saw his father and stepped forward to greet him, then noticed the seething, red-bearded dwarf at the back of the room. Mantieth bowed to the delegate. "Good evening, fine sir…"

Leidergelth snapped at his son. "Never bow to a vagha—especially not one from Irontooth. They are beneath we selumari."

The coral elf prince stiffened, and his lips tightened. He offered an apologetic shrug to the diplomat and then turned to leave the dwarf behind as he followed his father's lead.

CHAPTER THREE

Hy'Targ Irontooth gently closed the door behind him. The Great Hall of the Irontooth castle's mezzanine yawned open before him and the pillars reached high overhead. It stretched a vast distance in each direction, connecting most of the vital parts of Hy'Mandr's kingdom under the mountain.

He walked the length of the Great Hall overcome by a dour mood as he pondered the news. Tr'Dyer, Hy'Mandr's physician, had not been optimistic regarding the king's most recent health update. The prince came from a second meeting and the head cleric had concurred with Tr'Dyer's diagnosis.

"His spirit is dying," they'd both said. *"He needs to feel his fingers grasp the handle of his axe again—feel the rush of battle and adventure... of course, without his eyes, the remedy would prove even deadlier than the affliction."*

Hy'Targ kicked a rock as he wandered away from the hospital. After more than ten years, he still cursed himself for not speaking up sooner in the den of the drider.

"Hey!" a young dwarf called and hurried after him. "Wait up, Hy'Targ."

Hy'Targ paused for him to catch up. He recognized him as Tr'Varris, a healer's apprentice who was about his age. Hy'Targ was familiar, though he didn't know him well, a natural consequence of his cloister in the library where the students of medicine often studied.

Tr'Varris breathed heavily once he'd closed the distance. "I couldn't help but overhear you back there with the healers. Restoring King Irontooth's sight would certainly be in the interest of everyone under the mountain. It sounds like you've exhausted most of the conventional wisdom from both doctors and clerics."

The prince cocked his head. "And you have some *unconventional* wisdom?"

Tr'Varris shrugged. "Perhaps. I heard an old tale about a magic item called the Kreethaln. It can supposedly heal any ailment. There were three Kreethaln that fell from the sky during the first age. Their magic was not of Esfah, but was something else entirely. They were Life-bringer, Wisdom-giver, and Spell-crafter. Do you know the legends?"

Hy'Targ nodded. "Aye. Everyone has heard it, at least a nursery rhyme accounting." A trio of mystic pieces, each with their own magics, had come from the skies, flung from some other source of Tarvanehl's creative endeavors and drawn to the face of Esfah by the madness in Karakto in 532FA when the early Magestorm relics entered play, dragging half the Daybringer Comets to the planet with deadly purpose. That had been nearly fifteen hundred years ago.

"All myths spawn from greater truths," Tr'Varris said, and Hy'Targ flashed him a knowing look.

The prince understood that Tr'Varris was a believer in the faith: he thought the old lore true, and Hy'Targ hoped he might be right... he remained undecided on the matter.

Tr'Varris said, "I don't know if it helps or not, but it was on my mind when I saw you searching for answers in the library." He clapped the prince on the shoulder and headed back towards the healer's house. "I hope you find the cure."

Hy'Targ puffed a blast of air through his nostrils and watched the medical student leave. "Unconventional wisdom," he muttered. *But maybe he's right. It makes sense that only an arcane remedy could fix a curse like the one that robbed his father. The Kreethaln, Life-bringer, might be exactly what he needed to end the curse... the houses of magic, medicine, and faith had each failed him.*

Lost in thought about the possibilities, he nearly bumped into Ne'Vistar, who seemed equally inattentive. Both looked at each other sheepishly and traded formalities.

"Walk with me," Ne'Vistar urged him. Hy'targ happily obliged.

"Might I be serious with you, Prince?"

Hy'targ nodded, not that his mentor had ever been anything but. "Please do."

"I do not believe your father is well," Ne'Vistar admitted. "Nobody says what they think, but I fear he may be dying."

"You're not wrong," Hy'targ said after a long pause. He set his jaw and recalling his latest meeting with the physicians.

Ne'Vistar locked eyes with him and asked gravely, "Do you feel adequately prepared to lead when the king passes?" He muttered a brief, superstitious ward to prevent his words from becoming an omen.

"I do not know," Hy'targ said. "I might be *ready*… but I do not know that I am *worthy.*"

Ne'Vistar's face softened at the answer.

Hy'targ blurted out, "I am thinking about going on an adventure."

The old scholar shot him a look like he'd shown up drunk for the formal summer rituals.

"To prepare myself," Hy'targ explained. "My father rebuilt his entire kingdom on principles he learned during his travels. Irontooth struggled under the kings before him—he must've learned *something* that made him a good ruler."

"Will undertaking a quest truly make you a better leader?"

Hy'targ shrugged. "I'm certain my father would think so."

Ne'Vistar searched his face. "And do you think your father is a good leader?"

The younger dwarf nearly shoved his elder. "Stop speaking in riddles, ya durned fool!"

Ne'Vistar smiled. "You may have more in common with him than you realize.

Hy'targ nodded grudgingly.

"If you feel strongly about it, I think that you should seize this chance while you still have it." Ne'Vistar's thoughts dwelled on the recent vision, and the image of the blind king trying to lead his army. "None can say for certain how much time any of us have; neither fate nor death discriminates between paupers and kings. Do you have a quest in mind?"

"Is there any truth to the tales of the Kreethaln? Surely there is at least *some* truth to the stories. I was on my way to the library when we bumped into each other."

"Information is old, and scarce, but there is some data written on the topic." Ne'Vistar turned to head there with him, trying to hide a placid grin. "I will show you the book you seek."

They walked to the tower mostly in silence and then meandered between the rows of dusty books and stacked scrolls. Ne'Vistar led him to the back corner where many of the most esoteric texts languished, awaiting scholars with obscure questions that each work had been written to specifically answer.

He pulled a musty tome out and handed it to the younger dwarf.

Hy'targ opened it and flipped through the pages; they turned as if they hadn't been handled in decades. He paused on one and examined the old print and plate stamp with ink graphics that depicted important events of the era, including the fall of the Daybringer comets in 532FA. One of the folios near the back had been torn out. He closed it and thanked Ne'Vistar.

Soll's morning light had brought out the confidence of the People of the Sun, and they'd climbed the hill in much larger numbers than what Varanthl saw the previous evening. They made a dull murmur as they came up the slope en mass.

Varanthl shrank back from the doorway after peeking through the window. An angry man pounded on the door. He demanded his father show himself. The crowd boiled behind him, clustering into knots of angry people who somehow made each other even angrier as they pointed and shouted.

"Trandlurthan! Trandlurthan, come out here," their representative yelled.

Varanthl desperately wanted to fling the door open and welcome them as family. He'd been taught nothing different—this one could have been his uncle for all he knew. Trandlurthan had shown Varanthl only kindness in all his days and had never demonstrated a need for suspicion. But last night, Varanthl learned to fear other humans. Not everyone was like his father… according to his recent experience, only few were.

Cracking the door only slightly ajar, the angry man's eyes bulged as he turned his gaze upwards to look at the massive Varanthl. He recoiled, pupils fixating on the visible scars and patchwork flesh.

"It's true!" he yelled, seeing no Trandlurthan within, and incited a riot. "The monster has killed him!"

The mob brandished their weapons, mostly pitchforks and axes, but a few carried swords and hunting bows. They began pelting him with stones. Varanthl slammed the opening shut and wedged a chair behind it as he tried to convince them he was no threat.

Windows busted inward as rocks smashed through. The door rattled as someone started pounding on it with a hammer. Villagers screamed and rallied more folk to their cause, "It's killed Trandlurthan!" and "We've trapped the b'yandhar!"

The door shook again and cracked. The hinges began to yield.

Varanthl looked around the small, one-room cabin—the only place he'd known as home—and panicked. He knew he had to leave and locked all his fond memories away in his mind, retrieved the empty bowl he'd set last night for his father, and chucked it through the rear window of the house causing it to break as the crowd surged against the front of the house.

Using all four of his powerful arms to avoid cutting himself on glass shards, Varanthl pulled himself through. He escaped out the back even as the mob busted through his door.

He had no plan—Varanthl only knew he had to get away if he wanted to stay alive.

His attackers shouted out his position and pursued him further up the hill. "Kill him! Kill the b'yandhar," they howled. "Don't let him escape!"

Varanthl crested the steep ridge on his powerful legs, using all his limbs to help scale the stony hillock. He turned back and then sank to his knees. Men and women had set fire to his home. Oily smoke rose high enough to sting his nose and mingled with the salty tears he tasted, giving a flavor profile to his grief.

The enemy scrambled towards him as best as they could, though some gave up and returned to stoke the pyre, content with that. More rocks flew his way, and he sat on his haunches, dejected.

An arrow whistled a shrill whine and lodged deep in his chest.

Varanthl sprang to his feet and roared with pain, tearing the missile from his flesh; bright pink blood bubbled out from the punctured lung. His attackers stepped back in shock, and then screamed their fury, reinvigorated. More arrows and stones flew his way and with more serious intentions.

He turned and fled the remaining distance up the hill to where the flat face of the crypt towered above even Varanthl. An ominous, black slit darkened deeper than the shadow that the barrow cast.

Varanthl paused. His father had warned him to never enter the tomb at the hill's peak. He swallowed the lump in his throat and massaged the wound from the arrow; it had mostly healed already—his wounds always did.

He did not know what this b'yandhar was that the villagers feared so much—but if Varanthl found and killed the monster, it might bring peace to the village. *Then, maybe they'll accept me? Surely this is all a mistake—surely, they will see I am one of them?*

Varanthl ignored the nervous fear welling in his gut. He ducked his head within the craggy entrance and plunged into the darkness.

Hy'Targ sat across from King Hy'Mandr at the feast-table in the royal supper hall. As usual, Hy'Mandr's closest friends joined them. They were more family than anyone else, and King Irontooth always had room at his table for any person who had previously quested with the Adventurer King.

Mi'Darrio had already drained most of a keg and slumped into a deep, drunken stupor at the end of the buffet while griping about how the ale-master's current brew seemed weaker than last years. Jr'Dunn and Vy'Danis, the only others to join them that night, briefly took their leave to retrieve a second barrel as the drunk Warchief had hogged most of the first.

The King sat awkwardly with his son. Blindness made it all that much more awkward; he couldn't pick up on nonverbal cues that allowed him to communicate on subtle levels.

"Father, I have important news," Hy'Targ finally said once they were alone.

"What is it? Something new you read?" He tried his best guess and find common ground to relate with.

"Yes… and no. I am planning to go on an adventure. I read about an artifact and I plan to search for it."

Hy'Mandr's brows raised above his empty sockets. The king nodded enthusiastically, not expecting this conversation at all, but keen to have it. "Tell me about this relic?"

Hy'Targ's book thumped on the table. Hy'Mandr could not see it, but could hear the pages rustle and almost taste the book-scent with his nose. It had to be an old tome.

"The Kreethaln. It is a magic artifact that they say can fix any person that is broken." He turned to a passage. "Here is a story of an eldarim who became paralyzed and with its help could walk again. There's another of a human child who grew back his entire leg after a week."

Hy'Mandr listened in silence, nodding along to show he tracked with him. "When do you go?"

"A few days. Maybe sooner." He paused as the other two dwarves entered with a fresh cask. "I assume you approve?"

"How could I not?" The King wore a smile. "The adventurer's road is where I found my truest self and I was not much younger than you."

"Where ye goin?" Jr'Dunn asked.

"I have a quest—an object I am planning to search for."

"Just as long as it's not true love yer after," Vy'Danis joked. "It's not a long walk, but I know where all the friendliest bar wenches reside. I can draw ye a map."

"No, no," Hy'Mandr waved them off, not wanting to end the conversation he and Hy'Targ had been having. "Pour us each a drink to wish my son well!"

The old dwarves happily obliged and passed the cups. They drained each mug and slammed them onto the table.

"Of course you have my full support," the King insisted. "Do you have a party?"

"A party?"

"O'course. Every crew should have at least six members. Lots of reasons…"

"I-I hadn't thought of that."

"Adventuring alone is a risky business. Let me send a few with you, just fer my peace of mind."

Hy'Targ bit his lip and nodded, he knew that as heir to the throne it might be a condition of his departure. "I suppose so. There are several things I could have overlooked." He pushed his cup away. "I am going to double check my lists, then, and think about what additional supplies I will need."

Hy'Mandr spread his arms and demanded an embrace. "Be careful on the road," He said. "Esfah has never been a safe world, and though it has been relatively quiet these last few years, I fear it may be getting worse and soon."

Hy'Targ thumped his father on the back. "I'll see you in the morning."

The king bobbed his head and waited until he heard the door click shut.

"Jr'Dunn and Vy'Danis, I'm sure I can count on you two to keep my son safe?"

"Of course," they agreed.

The King's brow furrowed, and he decided to bring them deeper into his confidence. "Ne'Vistar's house has had a vision of a rising evil. He said it concerned the rise of an ancient lich."

"Old wives' tales," Jr'Dunn scoffed and then quaffed from his mug. "Though I'd agree that enemies are everywhere and growing in strength. trogs have been sighted in the north again… but undead lords are difficult to believe in, and even the occasional bloodless wanderer has been rare in the last century, those rumors from Cyrea aside. Asides—that's halfway around the world." He took another chug. "I'd be more worried about how fast them goblins are breeding."

Vy'Danis chuckled, "And there's the selumari in the north to worry about as well."

The king slumped contentedly in his chair. "I'm not entirely certain that I believe in all this undead nonsense Ne'Vistar is concerned with, but I'm happy that my son has finally gotten the adventuring spirit. Try to keep out of his way as much as possible—let him undertake the quest. The world grows secretly more dangerous each year, and I fear it won't have me in it a lot longer."

His friends tried to disagree with Hy'Mandr on that point.

He held up a hand to silence them. "Don't try to honey-coat what I know is true. I ain't been well for years… and it ain't about me eyes. Really, I've been unwell since losing Sh'Ttil, and that boy is the last connection this world has to her." He sighed and let his queen's memory hang in the air for a few moments. "You two find four o' yer kin and travel with Hy'Targ. Make sure one of them is a bard. If my son accomplishes truly amazing deeds, I must hear a song about it 'fore I pass."

Jr'Dunn and Vy'Danis agreed while the king turned his thoughts inward.

"Hy'Targ should take *some* risks, though. Let him run the show," he sighed and began fumbling within his robes for something. "This is *his* adventure… not one of *ours*… maybe that's been the problem in how I been parenting all along."

He continued rummaging through his clothes until he found what he was looking for. He withdrew a tightly bound piece of parchment that had been sealed with a magic rune. The king held it to his nose and inhaled, finding the scent that had grown so faint over the decades. It had been a gift from his beloved Sh'Ttil before departing on his first adventure after their marriage, and he'd always kept it on his person in her memory.

Hy'Mandr found his long-time friend's arm and put a reliquary scroll into his hand. Both could feel its magic in their vaghan bones.

"An artifact?"

"Something for protection." The king slumped his shoulders. "It takes eyes to read it, I'm afraid. But you'll know when and if you need it—Sh'Ttil had always said as much." He grabbed his friend by the one final time. "Keep him safe..." his crows' feet smile showed he would've winked if he's still practiced that gesture, "just not *too* safe."

Wracking his brain over the final details of his trip, Hy'Targ paced in his bedroom. His decision to quest for the Kreethaln had been made several days ago, and thankfully, his father had left him to make his own arrangements for it.

Someone knocked on his door and Ne'Vistar entered. He carried a long, flat box and laid it on the prince's bed.

"What's this?"

"Isn't it the point of a gift be that the recipient opens it?"

Hy'Targ narrowed his gaze. "You and your riddles." He opened the large box and raised his eyebrows. "Glorybringer? My father's axe?" He hefted the famous weapon from its crate and examined it; it had been recently sharpened to a keen edge and polished, though finger marks on the haft had darkened where his father had often gripped the handle over his many years.

Ne'Vistar nodded. "He asked that I give it to you and pay close attention so I can describe your reaction."

He smiled warmly and lifted the double-sided battle axe with a mix of wonder and pride. Hy'Targ had barely ever touched the item before—he'd never had the reason or curiosity before now.

The old scholar handed him a second gift.

Hy'Targ unwrapped the cloth to find an empty journal.

"I trust you will record the details of your adventure?"

"Yes, although I have a bard as well."

Ne'Vistar grinned wryly. "Bards are notorious for embellishing where facts are concerned. I already have a spot in the library reserved for it."

"Thank you, my friend." He stood to leave. The party planned to depart later that morning.

Ne'Vistar cleared his throat and confessed, "I don't think your father likes me all that much... thinks I have influenced you over the years... made you into more of a scholar than the adventurer he'd been."

Hy'Targ cocked his head. "That's not true... at least, not that he dislikes you."

"Oh, but it is," he insisted. "And I can accept that. He *likes* his adventuring buddies... but he *trusts* me, and in a different way than the others. That is why he sent me to deliver the axe and to make sure you're adequately prepared."

"I don't understand."

Ne'Vistar nodded toward the dressing dummy that bore Sshkkryyahr's armor; it languished in the corner of the room. "I know you may feel guilty for wearing it, but do not make his sacrifice a vain one." The fact it hadn't been packed only confirmed the prince had intended to leave it behind.

Hy'Targ hung his head a moment and grimaced. Then he put on the woven silk armor, which draped more like a coat than anything else. He'd never actually worn it before. "It's kind of comfortable," he admitted as he adjusted the fabrics.

"Good. Now I can tell your father that you are truly ready."

Hy'Targ opened the cover of his journal before leaving and wrote the first header. *The quest for the Kreethaln: Lifebringer.* A loose leaf tucked behind the first page fell out and into his hand. One side had sketches of the three enchanted devices. The flip side contained a map and several notes leading north west of the Irontooth stronghold.

"This is your handwriting," Hy'Targ recognized scrawled upon the missing page from the old book taken from the library.

Ne'Vistar nodded. "I've been on an adventure or two in my younger days as well."

"Tell me about your quest… did you find it?"

Ne'Vistar grew quiet for several moments. "I once had a wife, many years ago—long before you were born. She was one of Queen Sh'Ttil's sisters, in fact. She fell ill, and I set it in my mind to locate it, for her sake…" he trailed off, choking on difficult words.

"What happened?"

"She died before I returned."

Hy'Targ remained silent, not daring to ask the question burning on his lips… *did you find it?*

Finally, Ne'Vistar continued, "I did not locate Life-bringer, but I found a man who knew its story. I suspected there was much more to his knowledge than he let on. You want to find a human named Murthak. Follow the map. You will find him."

Hy'Targ thanked him. "Do you really think I'll find it, or is my quest in vain?"

Ne'Vistar shrugged. "I do hope you claim the Kreethaln. The kingdom needs your father… or a man with his spirit."

Hy'Targ embraced him. Before he could leave, Ne'Vistar called out, "Do be careful. I fear that great evils awaken in Esfah. It would be best for all the races living under the face of the Mother and Father if any army that fights the blackness had Hy'Mandr's strength."

"What have you foreseen?"

He did not want to burden the prince with so much knowledge when he had his own task. "Nothing you should worry about… not yet. Find Murthak and complete your quest."

CHAPTER FOUR

Hy'Targ emerged from the subterranean corridors and walked into the open-air section of the castle grounds where the stables housed their mounts against the curtain wall. Hy'Mandr's kingdom was known for producing some of the finest mammoth steeds. His father's flag flew from the parapets upon the wall, and he spotted his adventuring crew mustering in the courtyard beyond the animal stalls.

While most vaghan tribes kept a small cluster of mammoths, the Irontooth kingdom kept dozens as a point of pride, and the sigil on their dwarven flag was the woolly beast. Hy'Loer the Chainbreaker, Hy'Mandr's grandfather and second king under the mountain, had been the stable master as a boy and a mammoth rider under King Gr'Nevuh who'd led them to freedom from Niamarlee by leading the revolt.

Gr'Nevuh had died unexpectedly, barely fifteen years into his rule and under mysterious circumstances. A simple vote of clan leaders put forward Hy'Loer. The vagha were drawn to leaders with moxy, and all the previous members of the Hy clan had more than their fair share—but most had failed to be qualified leaders, Hy'Mandr included. What Hy'Mandr lacked in administrative skills, however, he made up for in common sense. He'd appointed and empowered highly qualified leaders for domestic issues and regularly deferred to their wisdom.

Hy'Targ spotted his father standing next to the stable master in the courtyard. Hy'Mandr held the reins for Brentésion, his prized dragonkin mount. The draconic creature looked quite content to have been saddled; she hadn't worn her barding for many years.

"Father? I thought you'd be in court."

Hy'Mandr's empty sockets appeared to scan his son with futile purpose, but his face beamed regardless. "I would not miss this for anything," he said, and handed Hy'Targ the reins. "Here. You should take Brentésion. I cannot ride her and Eldurim knows how badly she needs the exercise." Ever since her discovery, the beast had refused to let anyone else ride her but the king.

She was not like the other dragonkin which could be clearly identified by the color of their scales, each attuned to the elemental nature of magic. Brentésion was metallic bronze in color and something else altogether. She stood a head larger than even the mammoths and could have been mistaken for a young dragon she was so large.

Hy'Targ looked at her nervously, unsure that Brentésion would let him ride. He'd never attempted it before, but the previous stable master had tried once. They'd had to find a new stable master after a brief funeral.

Hy'Mandr wrapped an arm around his son and called to Brentésion; he cooed, and spoke to her like she was a puppy. The beast lowered her head and nuzzled against the blind king. "I want you to go with my son," he said. "Bring him safely to glory and help him as you have helped me."

Brentésion sucked in a big lungful of air, taking in Hy'Targ's scent. The dwarf prince was afraid for a moment that the drakufreet might belch a hot blast of flame on him, but the creature merely snorted and lowered his head to allow the son to ride. Hy'Targ climbed aboard Brentésion's back and all the onlookers, mostly vagha but also a few conscripts from other races, watched with wonder.

The king's grin spread a mile wide. He could somehow sense that his mount had bonded with his son—even if his eyes could not see it. He heard the subtle gasps of the others.

Brentésion, with Hy'Targ upon his back, took a few tentative steps and then seemed to relax as if finding his comfort level. Hy'Targ had held his breath the entire time. Finally, he rubbed the dragonkin's neck, and she leaned into his stroking hands and accepted the bond.

The prince looked back to see his father, and his eyes caught sight of a familiar old dwarf upon the castle wall: Hy'Drunyr, brother of the king. Their eyes locked only momentarily and then he disappeared into a hallway. Hy'Targ wondered at the look his uncle had given him. Hy'Mandr and his brother had not always gotten along, though Hy'Targ did not know what old rift had driven them apart; he only knew that they were not on speaking terms and that he'd traded barely more than a dozen words with his uncle in all of his short life.

Hy'Targ wondered briefly after his father's safety, and then put it out of mind. The king's guard was formidable enough to quell any internal mischief—and Taryl was never far away from the king's side. The prince scanned the courtyard looking for Taryl, but the eldarim soldier was notoriously difficult to find when he wanted to hide, and the bodyguard was usually perfectly blended into any scene where he could provide help at a moment's notice.

Even knowing his father could not see him, Hy'Targ waved to the king. Finally, he spotted Taryl and nodded to the dutiful warrior who would safeguard the throne. Taryl returned the gesture with a curt farewell and then Hy'Targ guided Brentésion towards his company of fellow travelers and their mammoths, and together they headed down the slopes of the Irontooth Mountain.

Hy'Targ and his company rode for several days on their beasts, heading west, deeper into Amazon territory. Vast swaths of flatlands and plains spread between pockets of hill, valley, and forest giving their mounts relatively easy travel. Brentésion loped happily alongside the six mammals, each one bearing a single rider.

The ancient vagha had domesticated the great creatures early in the first age, breeding some for speed and others for strength, though none of their breeds quite matched the massive bulk of the wild mammoths that once roamed the countryside. They were no longer found in the wild, except for an occasional spotting from sailors who claimed they still roamed in the frosty Shadowlands near the north pole. Hy'Targ had only seen the undomesticated variety depicted in books, but legend held that they'd been transformed into the largest of the feral folk when the Mother returned to walk again upon Esfah at the beginning of the Second Age. Hy'Targ didn't often leave the Irontooth Mountain and had never seen a ghwereste before. He hoped this journey would enable him to cross paths with one, though he did not expect it.

Brentésion carried him at a steady pace which the mount easily managed, even if she'd gotten a little pudgy in her last decade of disuse. The ground underfoot had been tilled; farms and rocky outcroppings dotted the landscape and small hamlets could be marked by distant spirals of smoke from hearths and homes. A larger hill rose in the distance, crested by a stony berm. Bronze skinned humans came out to greet them as the train of mastodons and one drakufreet approached their village. A clutch of youths hung behind the man who greeted them; children hovered close behind the greeter, curious of the woolly beasts and especially of Brentésion.

"What village is this?" Hy'Targ asked in the common tongue.

"My friend, my friend… we are the People of the Sun."

The dwarf nodded; Ne'Vistar's book had noted the name of their people. "I am looking for Murthak. Is Murthak still the skald? A mutual friend said I should speak with him," Hy'Targ said.

"Murthak? Yes… he serves the chief," the man pointed ahead to the village.

Vy'Hrothgyr, the party's bard, edged his mount closer to the conversation. He jotted notes in a journal of his own while the prince continued conversing.

Hy'Targ looked at the man, excited for their first local contact made since leaving the castle a week ago. "Are you familiar with the legend of the Kreethaln?"

The man squinted, searching his memory. "No," he said, and Hy'Targ believed him. "We haven't kept much to the old stories, although we've been very interested in the tale of the b'yandhar, lately." The man grew excited. "One emerged from the crypt recently, four arms and covered in scars… hideous as the day is long. It killed several of our kin before we drove it back into the tombs."

"Thank you," Hy'Targ said, unsure of what a b'yandhar was. He assumed it was some local legend or a corruption version of an old term. He waved to the cadre of children and then led the caravan towards the village in search of Murthak.

Hy'Targ sat in Murthak's tent, curiously observing the old Amazon with weathered skin. The skald's skin tone seemed curiously darker than the rest of the villagers. Jr'Dunn and Vy'Danis stood outside with the rest of Hy'Targ's escorts while the prince shared his quest with the human.

"Yes," the wizened, old man confirmed the legend. "I have both seen and held the Kreethaln, though that was very many years ago."

"Can you give it to me?

"No."

Hy'Targ stared down his nose at him.

Murthak grimaced beneath the dwarf's glare. "I can see you will not be deterred… you already know much about the device and I believe you when you tell me your intentions are pure," he explained. "The vagha have long memories, longer than that of the humans. Our clan has forgotten its old legends. We fight no wars, and we pay no tributes. Generations ago we settled in this area for one purpose: to guard the Life-bringer and keep it safe. Our people think we came here to cultivate land and prosper—and we are happy to let them think as much, but our purpose is higher: a vow made long ago. If we could have destroyed the Kreethaln, we would have. Destruction of powerful artifacts is the best way to prevent evil forces from capturing them. We've forgotten the lessons taught by the Magestorm Wars."

"Then it is here?" Hy'Targ asked. "You have the Kreethaln."

The skald opened his mouth to say something, but held his tongue.

"Please, you have to tell me where it is. Ne'Vistar, the chief vagha scholar of the Irontooth Kingdom sent me to find you so I could claim it. His last words to me were a portent of great evils awakening in Esfah—we need the Kreethaln to fight against it."

Murthak grimaced, and then his stern facade cracked. "I'm sure you do; I have had similar omens. But I cannot give it to you."

"Is it because of this b'yandhar creature?"

He shook his head with a stiff neck. "You must have heard the prattling of our common folk. A man who is recently dead was the device's holder. His family had been its guardian for nearly a thousand years. We settled here so that it could be best safeguarded—partly by letting its legend fade into obscurity." He sighed and repeated, "Our people have forgotten its own legends... but you dwarves have not."

Hy'Targ tilted an eyebrow.

"My brother, Trandlurthan, died recently. It was natural; he was old. Trandlurthan's only son died two years prior. A couple nights ago some overzealous villagers, thinking they'd cornered the b'yandhar, burned Trandlurthan's home to the ground. I could not help you even if I was willing. Only *he* knew its location."

Hy'Targ's heart sank, and he frowned at the bad news. "I'm sorry for your family's losses."

Murthak tilted his head to accept the kind words.

"Would it be inappropriate to look through the remains?"

"I sifted the ashes myself only this morning. I found nothing, but you may also look if it gives the necessary closure to your quest."

Hy'Targ got up to leave. "If your people no longer have the device to guard, there is no reason to stay settled here. Will the Amazons return to the old ways and take up swords again if there is indeed a great evil?"

"We have more than one purpose here," Murthak insisted. "We watch over the grave of Ailushurai, the first selumari champion. Our people were tied to hers in the ancient days. We are content to remain here in her honor."

Hy'Targ thanked him again, and he took his leave. Outside, he spotted a thin wisp of smoke still crawling skyward atop the nearby hillock. His mind kept mulling over the name as he led his entourage up the hill. *Ailushurai, where have I heard that name before?*

Hy'Targ and the others found the blackened husk of the building laying in a heap upon the barren ground. Little else remained and only a few live cinders at the central pile eked out enough smoke to sting their vagha eyes, and that but barely.

"I found a grave," Vy'Danis called. He hunched over the unmarked plot of soil and raked his fingers through it. "Not more than a week old."

Hy'Targ gave up searching through the ashes and joined him. "This must be where Murthak's brother was buried." He checked the sky and frowned at what he was about to suggest. "I think we ought to exhume the body."

Jr'Dunn looked at him sidelong and then shrugged. "It is certainly what your father would have done. It's likely a dead end, but is the only possible place to find a clue, given the fire."

The rest of the dwarves nodded, agreeing to the grisly task. "But we should wait for the cover of night to do it, for decency's sake," Hy'Targ said, examining the surrounding soil. He spotted a set of large, human footprints in the soft dirt. He checked the area and found another set of them near a trampled patch of turf where the crowd had chased this monster he had heard about. The traffic headed up the hill.

Hy'Targ turned his gaze up and spotted the fletching of an arrow sticking up like some forsaken monument. He walked towards it and scaled the steep berm where he plucked it from the ground. Nearby, another arrow laid in the grass; the tip was bloody and appeared relatively fresh. Red had dripped onto the blades of grass and dried, marking the direction the wounded thing had fled: straight towards the stone wall of a barrow. The blood couldn't have been more than a few days old or the morning dew would have dispelled it.

Jr'Dunn and Vy'Danis joined him as Hy'Targ pulled Glorybringer from its baldric sheath and gripped it tight. He stood before a tall crack that led deeper into a steep descent; it delved into the heart of the hillock. Long ago, someone had engraved runes vertically alongside the fissure. They read *Crypt of Ailushurai.*

Hy'Targ called down the slope to the remaining four dwarves. "Circle the mammoths and Brentésion around the grave for privacy. Start digging when darkness falls… discreetly." Hy'Targ nodded to Jr'Dunn and Vy'Danis who flanked him on either side, and then the three vagha plunged headlong into the darkness.

Days ago, Varanthl had made a wrong turn. The winding passages looped back and around, confusing him and forcing the lost soul to meander through the dark for hours and hours before he had a chance to catch his bearings and finally begin mapping his location.

Varanthl crawled below a low overhang in the dungeon and then stood to his full height. His eyes had attuned to the dark long ago, after the villagers chased him into the crypt. Tiny pinholes of light pierced the darkness at different junctures, giving limited light that split the black at irregular intervals. Varied smells of mold and pooled water from old rains' seepage filled his nostrils.

His stomach rumbled in the unnerving quiet. It sounded like a menacing growl in the darkness. It unnerved Varanthl until he realized it had come from his gut.

Nearby, he spotted a rat pausing to drink at a fetid puddle. For generations, the rodent lived in absence of predators; the rat did not spook when Varanthl approached and he snatched it up and broke its neck. Also finding a creeping, bitter root that he knew was edible, Varanthl devoured them both as quickly as possible, choking to keep the vile tastes from lingering too long on his tongue.

He turned a circle in the chamber and found a collection of armor and weapons stocked in the hidden room. Varanthl did not know what a b'yandhar was, and he assumed that the Amazons did not either since they had attacked him, but he assumed it must be dangerous, whatever it was.

Varanthl rummaged through the equipment and found the largest coat of scale mail he could find and grabbed a nearby rusted dagger. He split the sides to cut it into a vest capable of freeing all four of his arms. Putting the dagger in his boot, he pulled a huge sword off a weapons rack.

Trandlurthan had talked him through some basic combat maneuvers, but he'd only ever used a stick before. He'd never held an actual sword. That fact had never bothered him until now. Varanthl had always assumed the maneuvers his father taught him were simply good exercise… and a good skill worth learning, like proper table manners. He never thought he would need to take a life in defense of his own.

He walked close to the walls and found another crevasse where the earth had eroded away. Varanthl dropped to a knee and peered through. It opened into a natural warren. By contrast to the carved, geometrical halls he'd been trapped within, the other side curved with organic arches and slopes. This part had been burrowed, not built by skilled craftspersons.

The dungeon where he'd been wandering, carved out by the ancients, showed no sign of the monster that Varanthl was accused of being. He assumed that these natural caves might hold more promise.

Varanthl's heart pounded in his ears; he assumed he would soon encounter the b'yandhar. Clad in the stolen armor, he clutched the blade and rolled through the crack. If he was to be accepted by the villagers, he knew that he must first kill the b'yandhar.

Hy'Targ walked ahead of Jr'Dunn and Vy'Danis. The two older vagha traded knowing glances and let the prince walk ahead, honoring the king's desire to let his son find his salt and craft his own glory.

They'd ventured down and into a lower level, navigating the twisting halls in the darkness. Luckily, they could still see because of their keen, dwarven sight. The walls seemed covered in ancient iconography that depicted skeletons rising up to overthrow a selumari kingdom; they dragged a coral elf princess to her grave; a pale eldarim with empty eyes led the forces of Death.

The dwarf company came to a room that split off into three pathways. Hy'Targ licked his hand and held it up to each passage. He detected a slight airflow on the two side tunnels. The one in the middle had dead air.

"This one," he nodded to the center hall. "This one terminates," he peered through the dark. "Likely ends in the heart of the barrow." His words hung heavy—what awaited them at the bottom? Crypts and caves were fundamentally different, each dangerous in their own ways. Not that the prince had much actual experience with them—but he had read many books on the subject.

Hy'Targ took two paces through the passageway when he heard a distinct *click* underfoot. He whirled, wide-eyed as a massive block slammed down behind him, cutting him off from his peers.

Beating futilely on the hunk of granite, he could barely hear Jr'Dunn and Vy'Danis on the other side; the blockage muffled their voices. Hy'Targ felt the vibrations of dwarven hammers trying to break through from the other side.

Eventually it stopped, and those faint voices faded altogether. Hy'Targ was left alone in the dark.

He turned to face the long hallway and descended further into the belly of the crypt. Still, tiny fissures allowed air to flow and light to leak into the depths of the craggy barrow. It eventually emptied into a deep room with tall sides that yawned open on top. Hy'Targ came to a spot where hallways split, and the two paths in opposite directions. He immediately recognized that he'd stumbled into a giant maze.

Hy'Targ marked the sides of the turns with a stick of chalk he kept in his pouch. It indicated which way he'd come, but the maze quickly proved too advanced for that to be a method that would get him through it quickly.

He retreated the way he'd come and walked back up the slope to gain some elevation over the maze. Hy'Targ prodded the crumbling pumice near one of the cracks that shed light into the maze. He rammed the butt of Glorybringer against the soft stone over and over. Eventually, he broke through and widened the hole enough that he could see the entirety of the maze. On the far side, a large opening seemed to indicate the maze's end point.

Hy'Targ took out his journal and drew a sketch of the map, standing on his toes to make sure he recorded every visible twist and turn he would encounter. He studied it for a few moments and then picked his way through and to the other side.

Knowing the way through, the maze took only an hour to traverse. He kept a sharp eye out for traps, but didn't detect any, though he suspected that the wrong paths he'd been clever enough to avoided might have hidden many nasty surprises.

He emerged on the far side of the maze and discovered a crumbled section of wall where a natural grotto opened through the wreckage. Hy'Targ figured the cave looked as if some huge creature might have used it as a den. He opted to continue through the halls in hopes of finding any kind of answers, clues, or persons who could help him find the Kreethaln.

The dwarf smirked as he came to a spiral staircase near the crumbling warrens. He realized he hadn't given any thought yet about how to escape the dungeon. *Surely my father would be proud.*

Hy'Targ began the slow ascent on stairs, ascending one flight at a time. The steps should have been rounded by use over the ages, but the corners of the lonely stair treads were almost sharp, still as new as the day they'd been hewn from rock.

Many minutes later, he paused for breath. The staircase continued to climb.

CHAPTER FIVE

Sweat dripped into Varanthl's eyes as he walked through the underground grotto. He stepped cautiously, vaguely aware that something else hovered in the dark with him. The four-armed man moved as silent as a cat; his heart pounded in his ears.

The combined humidity and stillness of the air made the cave swelter like hot breath. He hoped that moisture wasn't due to the size of the lungs from whatever creature shadowed him in the blackness.

Varanthl felt its eyes on him, unnerving him to his core. He gripped the extended hilt of his sword with all four hands and searched the darkness for the predator, certain that it must be the b'yandhar.

Finally, Varanthl came to the end of the tunnel. Leaning against the curving dead-end, he spotted countless bodies littering the floor. They sat against the wall in defeat, weapons laid at their feet, abandoned to the eons. Most of them wore an armor the same or similar to what Varanthl had donned. At least one was different, more recent.

He whirled around, sensing the evil presence in the darkness. Clutching the sword, he demanded, "Show yourself!"

Varanthl's voice reverberated off the dank walls and a spheroid creature materialized with a roar. Leathery flesh sagged and hung from the beast's bulges which might have once boasted thick plates of chitinous, natural armor. The thing had shed them over a vast length of time spent languishing in this pit. A central eye burned brightly above its toothy maw, and withered tentacles ended with shriveled polyps that Varanthl suspected had once been additional eyeballs. It did not look healthy.

The thing slobbered glops of foamy saliva and Varanthl felt waves of energy slam into his body. They did little else, but they made him feel strange. With each pulse, the device on his chest seemed to vibrate defiantly as if it counteracted the magic.

With each blast it sent, the b'yandhar's main eye reddened with further rage at its impotence and from a growing hunger borne of desperation.

Varanthl suspected the creature used magic on him. His father had told him about the art of spell craft, but luckily the spells did not seem to affect Varanthl as intended.

The b'yandhar roared again and startled Varanthl from his thoughts. Finally, it charged at him, shrieking, and tried to gore him with its crooked, spiny teeth.

Varanthl swung his blade, but even in a feeble state, the weapon glanced aside as if it were a mere flyswatter used against an angry warthog; the blade fell away and into the darkness. He ducked underneath the creature and snatched the nearest weapon he found, a surprisingly heavy mallet. Still on his knees, he twisted his massive torso and swung the hammer by its long pole. The heavy end smashed the b'yandhar in the rear before it could turn back to him and the impact of the mallet sounded like an eggshell breaking, sickly wet and crunchy.

The monster shrieked, grievously wounded, and Varanthl scrambled to his feet, still clutching the weapon with one of his hands. His heart leapt in his chest and he rushed at a full tilt back towards the entrance with the wounded beast glaring daggers at his back.

Varanthl dashed beyond the edge of the b'yandhar's cave and skidded to a stop with the beast roaring behind him. Surely the creature would chase him down in the maze where he'd wandered for the last couple days! Then Varanthl noticed a small door leading to a staircase. He was certain the beast was too large to follow him up it. He ducked his head and began climbing.

Hy'Targ crept through the room as he tried to meter his breathing. The long climb had taken a toll on him and his thighs burned. It wouldn't have surprised him if the stair that began in the depths of the earth would have emptied out on the top of the hillock's capstone. Instead, it spilled into a landing with a door that hung slightly ajar and revealed an old storeroom.

The chamber's light sources bled through the cracks and gaps with increasing frequency, making the room appear bright by contrast even though the color had turned a deeper shade of yellow to indicate the sun had nearly gone down, though its amber hues still spilled through microfractures like ribbons of illumination.

Rows and rows of shelves lined the walls. Ancient artifacts leaned upon them. Anything with leather or fabrics had long ago moldered and turned to rot, but some of the items were gilded with precious metals and still offered gleaming hints of their value beneath a layer of dust.

Two stone sarcophagi rested in the center of the room; both had heavy lids stamped with wax seals. The closest one had a long board wedged between the ceiling and the corner of the ossuary. The lid around the wedged post had been cracked.

Curiosity got the better of him.

Hy'Targ might not have been a mason, but he was a dwarf after all. He examined the rock; the fracture had telltale signs that tools had been used to create it. The dwarf looked closer at the sarcophagus. The seals had been cut, and the lid had been engraved with a name in old elven script, the same as he'd seen on the dungeon's entrance. *Ailushurai.*

Someone else had inscribed words upon her tomb. They were ancient, but obviously came later. *May she never depart from her lover's side.* He recognized an arcane marking, but also noted that the seals had been broken. Whatever spell had been bound to the contents must have already been activated.

What can be the harm in peeking? the dwarf asked himself. *Maybe there's a link to the Kreethaln.* He pushed the lid half off and tipped it up on its end. He hung onto it while he examined the boxes' contents. Nothing remained within but dust and scraps of ancient cloth that disintegrated at his touch.

Hy'Targ lost his grip on the lid and he tried to get a fresh grip on it. Accidentally bumping into the vertical beam, it slipped free and crashed to the floor along with the lid that broke to pieces. The busted corner where the post had been pressing against a trigger-plate popped free with a noticeable click. A mechanism engaged without the weight of lid or beam to secure it.

The adjacent sarcophagus clicked with additional sounds of mechanical release. Sounds of sucking air like a rushing wind nearly deafened the vagha, and then everything grew far too quiet.

He pulled his axe to his side and held it at the ready.

The remaining lid flew from its place and smashed a collection of shelves on the far side of the room. Lit by a fell, green light the bones stitched themselves together and dust rushed into a swirl and clothed the ghastly skeleton with material that knit itself into emaciated skin that draped over the bones as the figure stepped free from his cage. An intricate tattoo in the shape of a binding sigil marked the skin of his chest.

His empty, black sockets locked on Hy'Targ and it hacked with a raspy cough. They burned with intense darkness until the dust formed sunken eyeballs within them. "Where is she?" he demanded.

"I-I don't know what you mean," he stammered.

"Where is Ailushurai? Where is my beloved?"

The pieces suddenly fell into place in Hy'Targ's mind. All at once he remembered reading the *Tragedy of Ailushurai* after Mi'Lazlee had piqued his interest in the tale shortly before the older dwarf's demise in Sshkkryyahr's dungeon.

The lich glanced down into the empty ossuary Hy'Targ had opened. His eyes burned. "Where are her bones? What did you do with them?" his voice dripped with hostility.

"Nothing! I only just arrived."

The fiend's gaze burned with an evil light and he roared, "Who dares steal Ailushurai from Melkior?"

Hy'Targ tried to take a step away from the undead eldarim who moved on hesitant feet as they still took form by the power of whatever magics had triggered Melkior's revival.

"Tell me where she is? So help me, I will burn the world of Esfah to a blackened husk and rain plagues upon her soil until only dust of the grave remains. Until she is returned to me, every tree will wither and women shall wail for unborn children! Their bastard flesh shall return in the dead of night to devour their grieving mothers. Darkness will fall upon this land… and when we are reunited, I will release an even greater winnowing as I prepare the way for my lord Malgrimm." He locked eyes upon a terrified young vagha and clarified. "The god of Death."

Hy'Targ whirled around and fled as Melkior tried to seize him. The fiend lunged forward; Hy'Targ ducked under his bony arms.

The dwarf instinctively turned to run. He took two steps towards the door with Melkior bearing down on him. A massive, four-armed humanoid burst through the opening at a dead sprint and crashed into Hy'Targ. Both toppled onto the emaciated lich and bowled him over.

Melkior sprang to his feet and yanked a rusty sword from the ground. The new intruder brandished his hammer;

Hy'Targ held his axe. All three traded glances with each other, wondering who would make the first move.

Hy'Targ tried to keep the nervous warble out of his voice and guessed at the human-like creature's body language. "You're not with the evil lich?"

"Is that guy in league with the b'yandhar?" four-arms asked, nodding to the lich.

"What's a b'yandhar?"

"The evil creature that lives in this dungeon."

"Then yeah. I would guess so. I'm Hy'Targ," he said from the side of his mouth as he repositioned to firmly face only the undead.

"I'm Varanthl." He copied the dwarf's gesture and faced the lich.

"Enough!" Melkior shouted.

Hy'Targ and Varanthl each took a half step towards each other.

Melkior tensed and hefted his weapon. He grimaced as if the act caused pain; he was still weak from his reconstitution. The lich stepped towards a shelf and grabbed a Wayfare Orb where it rested. He twisted the two halves of the device and then disappeared in a flash like lightning leaving Hy'Targ and Varanthl behind in the darkness of the crypt.

Varanthl stared curiously at Hy'Targ. Finally, he asked, "What are you?"

Hy'Targ stopped pounding on the ceiling with a steel pike he'd found. He raised an eyebrow. "What do you mean?"

"The Amazon people don't always have beards like yours," Varanthl said. "And they're generally taller."

"I'm a vagha... a dwarf. Who *are your* people? You don't *look* human."

Varanthl clamped his mouth shut.

Hy'Targ started jamming the pole into the ceiling again and knocked free a significant chunk of crumbling stone. "Do you know who your people are?"

After a silent moment, he flatly said, "No."

"You are a homunculus," Hy'Targ recognized, looking over his scars with cold detachment. "An artificially created life form… similar to a golem, but made through science instead of magic… so also *not* like a golem."

"My father never told me…"

"Your creator," Hy'Targ started to say, and then stopped himself when he saw the look on Varanthl's face. He diplomatically corrected himself, "would be the same as your father." He poked the stone overhead a few more times and freed another hunk of stone. A hole opened above them and exposed the sky.

The strange allies pulled whatever rubble they could find into a pile that they scaled and used to escape the crypt.

Hy'Targ stretched in the waning scraps of sunlight. More than most other dwarves, he preferred the sunlight over the shadows—even of his own home. Varanthl stood tall and stared into the distance, not turning back to even glance at the Amazon tribe below them. The plains stretched away into the distance.

The dwarf prince crept to the edge of the hillock's peak and spotted his party getting to work within the circle of mammoths. They'd circled the mounts around the grave and begun digging behind them. Jr'Dunn and Vy'Danis were with them. Brentésion had curled up near the woolly beasts and taken a nap.

He returned to Varanthl. The homunculus's dark mood spilled over to Hy'Targ. The dwarf waved his hand towards the horizon and said, "Melkior is out there, somewhere. He is an ancient evil and must be stopped before he regains his full power."

Varanthl did not turn to look at him.

"You should come with me. We need to find and stop him."

"No," Varanthl said. He explained, "I need to find my people… but I have no people." He sighed. "I need to find out *who I am*." The homunculus looked at all four of his hands. Two of them were different from the others. Patches of his flesh had come from different skin tones… different people. "You understand?"

Hy'Targ nodded and compassion brightened his eyes. "I do. Good luck."

Varanthl fixed his eyes on the distance and began walking.

Niamarlee's ivory buildings hung gray beyond a veil of haze in the background. A salty tang hung in the air that rolled off the coast as Sh'Zzar meandered through the long rows of wilting crops.

"You were right to call me," she said with her husky voice. The silver-haired dwarf glanced down at several plants with different markers; Sh'Zzar hadn't assumed she would have been the only help that the farmer would bring in… especially given the anti-vaghan sentiments of their local culture… and especially towards the member of her clan. For him to call on *her*, things must have been dire.

Walking the rows, Sh'Zzar spotted at least a dozen marked plants. None of the other sorcerers or alchemists had proved capable of helping.

"Can you help? I can't afford to lose my entire crop." The coral elf bit his lip and offered her a less than a fair wage for her assistance: the *vagha price* the locals called it. "I can give you a five-piece of silver."

Sh'Zzar grabbed a handful of soil and let half of it run through her fingers. "Have you ever been cursed before?"

The farmer gulped and slowly shook his head. "Not to my knowledge."

"Well this is definitely magic," she said. "Perhaps you've offended someone, and they decided to blight your fields." Sh'Zzar held his gaze while the farmer did mental calisthenics necessary to decode her threat: *his offer was offensive, and if he didn't come up with something better, he'd be* doubly *cursed.*

After he'd sweated long enough, the vagha sorceress gave him a new price—a fair one. "I charge a gold ten-piece. That is my standard rate. I can help you, and if I can't you won't be compelled to pay."

The farmer refused to look her in the face and only stared into the distance and grumbled, not wanting to pay a dwarf anything but the vagha price. He'd already paid a selumari enchanter and had no success.

She continued anyways. "If I was selumari, you would say my age was a sign of wisdom and valuable experience," Sh'Zzar said, though not unkindly. "I can fix it... the problem is in the soil and not the plants." She waved to the marked crops to indicate her point. "Whomever else you've consulted didn't have the skills to fix your issue. You need someone who specializes in earth magic."

The farmer grimaced and nodded, agreeing to her price. He sighed, "How soon can you start?"

"Soon," she said. "I simply need to get some items from my home. You'll make your harvest, yet."

She turned and then hunched over, nearly collapsing from the sudden pain. Her chest burned with black fire, as if some deep seed of dread had suddenly sprouted and coiled itself around her internal organs.

"What is it? What's wrong?" The farmer rushed to her aid—suddenly concerned for a dwarf's safety… she was suddenly valuable to him.

"I-I don't know. A terrible feeling… something magic. An overwhelming sense that an ancient evil has revisited this world." She fixed him with dull, ashen eyes. They were normally brightly green and full of sun.

Sh'Zzar didn't tell him the second part of her dark premonition: that her family was somehow tied up in the event.

CHAPTER SIX

Still clutching the magic orb that had transported him, Melkior re-materialized a hundred leagues away. He stood in the middle of a field, naked in the failing sun and glad for the crisp night air that crept across the pasture. A billow of fog rolled through a distant tree line, Melkior suspected it hid a bog and all sort of creatures his enemies would consider Death's minions.

He took a deep breath to steady himself. Melkior was precariously low on energy, but that would improve with every passing moment that the dark magics wove him back together. He moved on stiff legs as joints rotated, grinding bone against bone. His cartilage had not yet fully formed. The lich ignored the pain and focused on the rage he felt over the abduction of his beloved.

Melkior would retrieve her remains—even if he had to dismantle Esfah stone by stone to get them. They were *his*, as much a part of him as his own skeleton and bound to him by the promise of the dark lord. Melkior brushed his fingers over the tattoo emblazoned upon his chest—the sigil bound him to his beloved, and them both to Death, as if three strands of a braided chord; without her he would never be fully complete.

He looked past Rhaudian to assess his position. Leguin hung bright and ruddy just above the horizon as Esfah's sister planet in orbit reflected Soll's light through the dark. Based on the stars, he was able to assume a heading and then angled himself towards his home. The wrecked tower at the edge of Ender's Gulf had become a deadlands when the citadel fell to the Seulmari army in their mad pursuit of Ailushurai's corpse— during the lich's descent into the Abyss when Melkior wrested

Ailushurai's soul from the clutches of the void-god himself, Selurehl, and bound it to his flesh with ink.

They sacked the tower while the Champions of the gods, and their allied Amazons, whisked Ailushurai's body away, presumably to hide her at Xlinea—or perhaps the humans would send her over the Tarvenish Ocean and hide her half way around Esfah in Dereh'Liandor or Hiriath.

The lich grimaced. Two sensations were inescapable for him. He felt the magic of his tattoo—it was the mark the void god branded him with, and it bonded her to him. He would always be drawn to Ailushurai and he *would* find her. Secondly, Melkior could sense the works of Malgrimm's hands and was eternally driven to complete his dark lord's will.

He sensed the distant deadlands even now: little grew there, and the scarred face of the planet rejected life itself. His home had once been a thriving region... and he'd personally killed it, creating a kind of permanent festration to honor his dark lord.

Melkior put one foot in front of the other and began the long trek forward, feeling the machinations of Malgrimm's wicked drive. He might not yet possess Ailushurai's remains, but he would find her in time. Recovering her bones was the end goal, not the first step—he had to honor his Lord Death in the meanwhile.

A figure standing in the field caught his eye. Melkior stared at it for a few moments, assessing its threat level, and finally approached what he recognized as a scarecrow.

The effigy hung on a pike, meant to ward the crops from the birds. He snatched a ratty cloak from off it. Wrapping the shawl over his undead form, he tested the pocket and then put the wayfare orb into it for safekeeping. It would take a significant amount of time to recharge and would be more useful if needed again once he had his bearings and a location. Blind jumps, such as the one he'd just taken, were inherently risky.

He began his walk, feeling less pain. He assumed his joints had grown back ligaments and synovial fluid.

Plodding onward, he grinned. Melkior would first raise his army—and then he could put serious attention to the search for his beloved.

Soll's rays crested the barrow above Trandlurthan's demolished home where the dwarves had made their camp. With the sun still creeping above the horizon, Vy'Danis spotted a mammoth in the distance. It approached at a steady lope, bearing a single dwarven rider.

"Prince?" he called out to the groggy vagha who'd stayed awake well into the night recording the most recent leg of his quest in the pages of his journal. He'd felt compelled to document the release of an ancient evil, even if his part in it carried a dose of shame.

Hy'Targ sat near the fire with his journal in his lap. Next to him sat Vy'Hrothgyr who jotted notes inside his own as he hummed a well-known pub tune. Hy'Targ set his record down and then flipped it closed as the bard tried to copy off it.

The prince retrieved a collapsible spyglass from his gear and put it to his eye. The rider was still a long way off. He handed it to Vy'Danis who peered through.

"It's Mi'Darrio," Vy'Danis confirmed.

"Trouble?" Hy'Targ speculated, suddenly afraid for his father. Wild speculation towards his uncle tried to find root in his imaginings.

"Not likely. The pace isn't urgent enough for that."

Hy'Targ nodded and returned to the campfire. His gut twisted with worry for his father, even if the Warchief's posture did not seem anything to fret over. A black thought struck him, *perhaps my father has died and Mi'Darrio means to seat me on the throne? I'm not ready for that...*

He put on an extra pot to brew tea in advance of his arrival and tossed a bundle of colored sticks into the embers. The twig cluster, arranged by vaghan alchemists, spat out a thick plume of colored smoke to signal their location to the traveler. He would recognize the dwarven smokestick.

Mi'Darrio finally arrived and dismounted after the sun had fully risen and begun to warm the morning air. While making repeated assurances that King Hy'Mandr was fine, he joined his fellow vagha around the fire and offered greetings. Mi'Darrio glanced sidelong at the freshly turned soil of the nearby grave. "A little grave robbing, eh? Looks like a true adventure you're having. A quest is rarely a quest without exhuming a body or raiding a tomb."

"That's a check for both options," Hy'Targ said and took a sip from his mug.

Mi'Darrio raised his brows and Hy'Targ shared the complete account of what had transpired in the Crypt of Ailushurai. The corpse that the others had retrieved from the fresh soil yielded no clues.

"A dead end," Mi'Darrio noted. "Your quest has not ended, but has certainly complicated with this Melkior figure."

Hy'Targ looked over the rim of his cup and then drained it. Mi'Darrio's indifference to the mention of such a villainous figure unnerved him. "There must be something else going on. Why did my father send you?"

Mi'Darrio bobbed his head. "Hy'Mandr's oracles have had inklings that a great evil would rise. None of us took it seriously; we assumed it was some kind of symbolism for the political turmoil up in Niamarlee. Who could have known Melkior was real?" He put a hand on the prince's shoulder and explained his seeming indifference to such a dark turn. "It was prophesied—there was nothing you could have done to prevent the evil one's escape. Fate played its fiddle and you danced—as we all must."

Hy'Targ swallowed the lump in his throat, he hadn't fully realized the seriousness of his involvement in Melkior's resurrection until that moment.

Mi'Darrio continued. "Your father sent me to give you this letter and to bring back a report."

The prince rubbed his face and accepted the letter. He opened it and read.

Hy'Targ, you are an adventurer now, a model dwarven warrior—if you succeed or not. Whether you bear such a title is irrelevant; I may not have been an ideal parent, but I am proud of you in every way... I was proud before you undertook this quest and will ever be regardless of its outcome. I may not have my eyes, but I see you perfectly.

Father.

The king's sloppy, blind scrawl signed the bottom haphazardly by his own hand.

Hy'Targ folded the parchment and slipped it into his pack. A burning ache lit in his gut. With no other leads on the Kreethaln, he'd considered returning to Irontooth just that morning. He clenched his fists and turned to his fellow vagha.

"Melkior is a real threat... one that rose from myth and childhood tale, but he did so because of my actions. This problem is my responsibility to correct, prophecy or not. I need each of you to tell me whatever stories you know about this bogeyman. We have to go after him while there is still a chance to stop him... before he can regain his full strength."

"What shall I tell King Irontooth?" Mi'Darrio asked.

Hy'Targ handed him his journal. "Read this to him; I wrote down everything that happened in the crypt. Tell him my adventure continues." The Prince felt certain his father had to know—if Hy'Targ didn't stop that Lich, someone would need to come after him, and someone else after that. If someone did not stop Melkior, it would only be a short time before he wiped out all life on Esfah.

Melkior's bare feet stomped unfeeling over the broken gravel of the barren land on the northern peninsula which jutted into the Far Sea on the north side of the Ender's Gulf and where Hadden Bay terminated across the far side of the waters.

The land had blackened and slumped as if Nature herself had tried to slide the region off her face and drown it in the sea. Only scrubby growth and copses of weeds struggled beyond the wasted soil. Swamps ringed the western edge and wild tangles of nutrition-less fruited callery, thick with long, spiny thorns, promised false respite to any local wildlife.

He moved with singular purpose and plodded onward until he climbed a gentle rise to sloped up to the ruined foundation of his keep. An ash-blasted stone foundation, much of which had crumbled into heaps of broken shale, was all that remained of his once ivory citadel.

A fell wind blew through his ancient home and a raven screeched overhead. The very shadows felt alive to Melkior. He could sense the pulse of his master in this place.

The lich climbed the wreckage of a staircase. It led to what was once the third level of his tower. Barely a perch remained, and he stood upon it and looked over his domain. Heaps of wreckage stood as monuments to the wars of the first age. Some of the remains he did not recognize; he could only assume that others had waged battle here in the millennium that followed his exile from Esfah.

Melkior descended the stairs. Fond memories crept into his heart, memories of sneaking Ailushurai up these stairs and to his chamber. His reminiscence turned to ash, rotting in his heart when he saw the old blade. A broken Teldrim sword laid on a step and Melkior hissed when he recognized the tribal emblem upon the hilt. He'd paid his mortal life to blot out the race of horse-lords.

He left the fractured weapon where it lay and meandered back into the main chamber. Only a small part of the lower structure had been laid bare before the open sky and much of it remained intact. Melkior picked up a time-stained bust that lay broken on the floor and set it back on the pedestal it had been thrown from. He aligned the sigil on its base with the engravings on the plinth and turned the bust to trigger a switch.

Beneath a moldering scrap of rug on the floor, a hidden door slid open. His secret room remained unmolested, and he descended the steps into the darkness.

His lich eyes saw perfectly in all conditions. The couch, where he'd laid Ailushurai as she had died by his hand, had succumbed to time and collapsed upon itself. It was the same place where, after a night of intimate coupling, she'd first told him her father had arranged her marriage to the Teldrim king—and of her intention to honor it.

Some wounds could never heal. The rage in the undead eldarim's heart burned so hot that it lit fire to the ancient sconces still attached to the walls. Leaving his tattered cloak in place, he donned a pair of breeches and boots that were left here since the first age. They'd barely retained their integrity, but they sufficed for his needs: he'd transcended the need for fashion. He slung a baldric across his shoulders and retrieved a now ancient bastard sword from his collection.

Melkior licked the blade and tasted the rust upon its edge. He smacked its flat side against a stone corner, and the oxidation splintered and broke free as the sword's metal shivered with keen ringing—the song of battle. Eldari craftsmanship endured the test of time.

Why the Creator-Father, Tarvanehl, had chosen to create the Teldrim, a race of nomadic horse-lords, forever eluded him, but Melkior had made it his mission to eradicate them before they could spread across the face of Esfah and cause further harm. The cost had been high: severing the bond between the eldarim and selumari champions, sundering lovers. Exterminating the Teldrim had done worse: it forever set the eldarim champion against even his gods.

In the torchlight at the edge of the room, a secret doorway was built into the cliff face below his keep. Melkior walked towards it, wanting to look out and see the ruins of the ancient selumari city that his forces had destroyed. The great Lurneville was a jewel to behold and rested upon a massive cliff plate that jutted out over the water, shored up by pillars that supported its base.

In the attack on the Teldrim, his dragon, Rahkawmn, had burned the Teldrim's encampment to the ground on Ailushurai's wedding day. Now, he wanted nothing more than to dash whatever remained of the city into the sea.

His toe caught something, and it skittered across the ground. A glass vial rolled to a stop just before the door. He bent to retrieve it and grinned.

Leisterbane, his undead general, had left an ampoule of Necralluvium behind in the old keep. Melkior's last commands to him had been to fulfill Malgrimm's wishes by infusing every dead warrior he found with a drop of the Necralluvium and then subjugate the living races and overtake all the seven continents and the scattered islands.

Melkior burned with the need to reclaim Ailushurai and reanimate her as his own. In his mad pursuit, he had charged Leisterbane with directing his armies until he reunited with Ailushurai. Melkior had not returned from his quest; the former Dragonlord had suffered too traumatic of damage after the remaining champions allied against him with their life-based magics. He'd fallen on the Raithlan Plains.

Leisterbane had been a necessary part of the campaign against the living—one that could survive Melkior. Whatever became of him, Melkior did not know, but he could sense that the undead selumari still remained active in Esfah. Like Ailushurai, Leisterbane was bonded to him.

Melkior assumed that his loyal servant had seen to whatever magics in the crypt had revived him. His former peers, the Champions, might have laid he and Ailushurai to rest in a proper tomb, but only Leisterbane would have engineered his return.

He slid the glassy container of churning, inky fluid into his belt pouch and flung the door open. The old battlefield sprawled below him: the lands once under his protection remained desolate. Few stones still stood from the forgotten elven kingdom of Lurneville. Only foundation walls remained, standing at busted heights like some kind of maze.

The sight pleased the lich as he surveyed his domain, planning his next move. Only one goal burned in his corrupted heart, reuniting with his beloved Ailushurai, and to do that, he needed bodies and information. This time, he would temper his passion to reclaim her, and he would send his minions to locate her first.

Melkior left his home and spotted a yellowed patch of ground in the distance. He smiled wickedly as he walked for it. Bones. Huge bones the size of rafter beams lay beneath a sheen of fine silica that had blown away in patches to expose ribs.

He approached with a kind of reverence and took the vial of Necralluvium he'd discovered and poured several drops onto the chitinous material. The festering ichor seemed to bore its way inside the porous surface. Vibrating within the soil, the ground trembled. Moments later it heaved and bucked as the great dragon buried below shook itself free from the bonds of time and decay. Rahkawmn roared with a barely rage held in check by eons; leaves upon a nearby copse of bushes quaked with fear and fell to the ground.

Melkior laid a hand on the necrotic dragon. It shook the dirt from what remained of old scales that still stubbornly clung to the beast's shredded hide. Rahkawmn laid his head low for its master to place a reassuring hand upon its brow.

"Our time has come again, my friend." Melkior clutched the vial of Necralluvium. "But his time I will not waste further time by exhuming an army and invigorating them with a million drops of black." He held the ampoule high as he toasted himself. "I alone will control the dead. They will come to my beck and call and shall live again by my pleasure; I alone will sustain them!"

Melkior tipped his head back and drained the murky fluid, swallowing every vile drop. His knees buckled, and he clutched his gut, cackling maniacally. "So much power," he whispered, climbing to his feet. "And it will only increase as I claim what Malgrimm has promised me!"

He closed his eyes. New sensations rushed into him.

"I can feel it—every festration on the planet. The scent of death calls out to me from every tomb. Every pocket of wild Necralluvium Leisterbane released into the seas, below the soil, and over the land is open to me."

A few skeletons laid exposed to the elements, and they rose at the lich's command, but teetered on shaky, brittle limbs. He planted his earlier urges into them and filled one with his knowledge of alchemy.

"Create the morehl's flintlock powder... lots of it. I want you to smash Lurneville's support pylons and push it into the sea. This land is *mine*, now, and I want nothing to remind me of the selumari taint."

The corps of long-dead minions scurried off to begin their task with singular purpose.

Melkior meandered further and sensed where other bones had been buried and better preserved. He pointed to a patch of dirt and clutched the air as if he held the crossbars of a marionette. He lifted his tagged talons and a crew of six skeletons dug themselves free from their repose. Broken armor hung off them in a slouching cant, displaying long-forgotten Teldrim sigils.

The lich's eyes opened, burning with fury. "You are my chosen scouts." Melkior reached down inside and drew on the death magic welling up within him; he blasted them with a wave of hot, acrid energy that devoured any vestiges of organic material. It burned their whitewashed bones and darkened their ossein scaffolding; the edges of joints and cracked bone glowed where the flames' heat concentrated like charcoal. Their old armor sizzled and fell to the ground around the blackened skeletons' feet.

Melkior breathed onto each of them, imbuing them with the memory of his beloved, sharing her scent. He instilled within each his same devotion to her. Like bloodhounds, they would be drawn to the bones, or those with connections to them.

"Go. Find my bride."

With a chattering and clacking of their bones, the burnt ones retrieved ancient sword and shield and departed for the hunt. As Malgrimm's vision for the subjugation of Esfah motivated Melkior, so did the Lich's passion drive his minions towards the lost bones.

"Malgrimm's vision shall come to pass. Once Ailushurai is at my side, all the dead shall rise. Then... all Esfah will fall."

The dwarves sat with their feet to the fire. They had all heard some version of the Melkior story as children. Most were similar and revolved around the champions of the first age, of which Melkior was the chief, before his terrible fall under evil's thrall.

The four natural gods had appointed a chosen one from each of the elder races to act as their guardians against the Misbegotten One; even the morehl and trogs had a champion—

they were tainted by the power of Death, but they also shared in devotion to Firiel and Eldurim. Death had intervened and corrupted the eldarim champion, manipulating world affairs so that he could twist Melkior into his tool.

Hy'Targ listened intently as each vagha shared. All eyes turned to the bard at the end of their telling.

Vy'Hrothgyr bobbed his head. "There is a song I know about it. It is not a popular tale—leastwise, it ain't never won me a drink in any pub. The Tragedy of Melkior is not a happy tale, too difficult to drink ale by," he sighed. "But I can tell it to ye."

The bard's voice rumbled as he sang the low song with a pleasant, but somber baritone.

Protector of peninsulas north and pride of the Far Sea,
looked long o'er the lands of Lurneville.
Mighty stood the massive tower of Melkior; champion of
eldarim and chained of heart to the maiden faire,
Beloved lark of Lurneville, the elven 'eroine Ailushurai.
Loved the dragon lord of the ivory castle. Forbidden
love, elf champion faire and Melkior.

Then the Teldrim came from father Tarvanehl; they
shook the shores with shoe and hoof.
They carved and cut a home for cairn and on horse and
beast-built treasure for their brood.
Fleet of foot and fine of aim the kingdoms quaked at
camps of Teldrim.
Wise ones woe to wage a war, lord Lurneville parleyed
for alliance bonds.

The Teldrim king To'ur pledged true to Wed they lovely
lady Lurneville.
The deed dark'd eldarim heart and drove Melkior to
mad'ning ends and pacts with Death-god foe.

Draw dragonkin and Eld'rim knights, drake Rahkawmn is hie; grabbing groom Melkior turn't while tents of Teldrim burn.

Strike selumari safeguards, sword and shield; break oaths with others, sever all that binds.

Ailushurai approached ivory keep avowed, too take To'urn and twain once strong troth of love.

Ailushurai's eart assunder, she bled betrayed by her belov'd.

Cataclysmic conflict the champions fought and quarreled, Teldrim To'urn bled last below the tow'r of ash

And barbarian blade bled Ailushurai's breast. Misfortune murdered his would-be mate, miserable Melkior.

Extinction end, every Teldrim ere does while Coral-folk cried as Lurneville collapses, burns.

Leisterbane led legions low and ruined Rahkawmn and routed kin. And chased the cur from keep and castle.

Selumari saber struck true and sound pierced flesh from said sad eldarim, re-moved, disgorged with mortal wounds Melkior met cursed [Vy'Hrothgyr coughed to cover the word and avoided saying the forbidden name of Malgrimm].

And struck dark bargain, though dead he stood cut coral hearts twith cult's deathseed corrupted Leisterbane's corpse.

Carried hither the champions came allied to cause, making Melkior face their allied might.

They faced the foe with fury bravely fought, and side by side they slew their scourge by Tarvanehl's spirit.

A champion's life eschewed by spell transact, and gave Melkior to the grave again, entombed forever.

And lich Leisterbane scourge of the living left the underground and unleashed the first plague of undead.

"What does it mean, Vy'Hrothgyr?" Hy'Targ asked.

He shrugged. "There's a certain amount of interpretation to everything," he said. "It's an old song and filled with symbolism. Who really knows what's what when you peel back the layers of religious iconography and shades of nuanced history?"

Hy'Targ started down his nose at him. "You really are a terrible bard, you know that? You can remember stuff, but don't even know what it means?"

Vy'Hrothgyr laughed. He agreed with a wink, "Aye. I might be the worst… but I'm *your* bard."

Hy'Targ raked four fingers through his hair and beard. "Gods… I'd better not die on this quest—not if *you* survive. Who knows what ye'd say bout me when I'm gone?"

With a wink, Vy'Hrothgyr laughed. "In my defense, I may be a crummy bard, but my limericks are pretty amazing."

Hy'Targ rolled his eyes.

"There once was a prince from Irontooth. He met on a quest, a pretty young lass…"

"Enough of that," Hy'Targ stood. He looked north. "We do learn from the song that Melkior's base is the desolate lands on the peninsula up the coast of the Far Sea. I think that's where we will find him; he must have returned home while he re-gathers his strength. I've seen a few old maps that even indicated the wreckage of the old Ivory Citadel remains; that corroborates our direction. What do you think, Mi'Darrio?"

The older dwarf grinned. "I think I want to hear the rest of that limerick so I can share it with the king when I return."

Hy'Targ glared at his father's friend and Vy'Hrothgyr winked at Mi'Darrio.

"All right, all right," Mi'Darrio grew more serious. "I think it's the right move. But don't go rushing in directly." He drew a map in the dirt. "This way is filled with obstacles that will take you days to get around: bogs and foothills plus lakes and rivers. That terrain changes seasonally." Mi'Darrio drew a line that meandered around and up. "Take the Great Coastal Road up through the kingdom of Niamarlee. It's a further distance, but you'll arrive quicker and fresher from the travel with a packed road underfoot."

"Thank you," Hy'Targ said. He sprang to his feet and began immediately breaking camp for the journey.

Mi'Darrio clapped him on the shoulder and said his goodbyes; his spirit remained jovial, but a deep worry burned beneath the veneer of mirth—the threat of this lich had seriously worried Mi'Darrio. He would need to ride back and inform the king immediately. Mi'Darrio realized the prince spotted his fear and the dwarf doubled down on his regular jovial nonchalance. He called to the bard, "Vy'Hrothgyr… you owe me the rest of that rhyme 'fore I depart."

CHAPTER SEVEN

Varanthl walked through the trees in silence. He had traveled several days since leaving Hy'Targ at the crypt and the homunculus had regretted most every step since. The dwarf had been the only person he'd met so far who had not tried to kill him on sight. Then again, he'd taken care to stay out of view whenever possible, not that there had been many opportunities to meet folk in the wilds or plains.

Gradually, the sparse copses of tree and bracken grew less intermittent and hills and valleys broke up the flatlands with occasional patches of variation. Trees took over as the norm and plains became the rarer sight.

From one rise, Varanthl could taste the subtle difference in the air, they grew closer to the sea. His creator—father had told him about the Talvat and Far Seas.

Varanthl decided in that moment that Trandlurthan was his *Father, not merely his creator*. He did not know if he was created by him or some other, and he never would, but that did not change who Trandlurthan was to him.

He paused in the middle of wondering what experiences he'd like to have. He decided he would very much like to see the ocean.

Varanthl stopped on the elevation where a clearing had opened and stared at the sprawling landscape below, assuming that the thick, dark line on the horizon was a great body of water. Another line snaked between the trees and swaths of land that had been cut and plowed.

From his vantage Varanthl traced the great row's path from village to town as it moved across the countryside. He committed as much of its general layout as he could to memory and began his trek further towards the sea.

Varanthl could sense he drew nearer the road as the sun crept towards the horizon and his nose caught a wisp of wood smoke. He lingered near the edge of the trees and observed for a few moments.

Two figures moved across a field, pushing a wagon filled with produce. Varanthl stood still and watched them: a tall one and a shorter one. *A father and a son?*

He observed them from a distance, keeping as hidden as possible. Varanthl grew keenly interested in the two. Were all fathers and sons like he and Trandlurthan? He did not know.

The homunculus followed them towards a bend in the road and quickened his pace to avoid losing them. He hurried around the curve and the father stood there waiting for Varanthl.

"Welcome, friend," the older one said. "My name is Jordyll. This is Gherbin, my son."

Varanthl nearly stumbled as he came to a stop. Aside from Hy'Targ, his other recent interactions had made him suspicious. "How is it you call me friend?"

"You're a big guy, dressed for battle… I figure, if you wanted to kill us just for being frehlasuhl, you'd have done it by now. I spotted you some distance back."

Varanthl realized that he still wore the armor and carried the warhammer he'd taken from the crypt. "Frehlasuhl?"

"All the better that you don't know the term," Jordyll said with a hint of relief.

Varanthl scanned the duo. They appeared to have mottled gray skin; when he looked closer, he saw it was covered with colorful spalts of red and blue that were so dark they looked almost black. Red eyes, and hair as white as snow stood a stark contrast. He glanced at his own skin, stitched together to make a mixed pattern of tan and ivory like their spalting. "The frehlasuhl are elves?" Varanthl stared at Jordyll's pointed ears, not intending any rudeness. "I've never met an elf before."

He nodded measuredly, wondering how such a fact could be, given Esfah's glorious diversity. "Of a sort... yes." Jordyll scanned the homunculus. "You look famished—practically dead on your feet," he said. "Come with us. I can feed ye at least."

"Daa," Gherbin objected.

Jordyll waved his complaint off. "There will be plenty to eat, and there's always more water for the broth."

Varanthl didn't quite know what to say, though his stomach did rumble at the thought. He'd managed to catch a rabbit a day ago, but occasional berries and roots had not been enough to sate him. "Th-thank you," he stammered, simply glad that his odd form had not scared them away. "I would like that very much."

Br'Derluch paced in the main chamber of Niamarlee's makeshift consulate. The fact that the elves hadn't forced them to lodge in a hostel at their own expense had proven the first and only promising sign that their diplomatic mission could end favorably.

Wo'Dunnia and Fi'Krayg, Br'Derluch's companions, sat on the chairs at the edge of the room where they played a kind of elven strategy board game made of two-colored coral pieces. The burly Fi'Krayg cleaned his fingernails with an axe and shook his head as the scrawny Wo'Dunnia made his move.

Fi'Krayg, the delegate's bodyguard, had slaughtered the much younger Wo'Dunnia's stack of pieces. "Have you even played this game before?" Fi'Krayg asked. "I thought you diplomatic types were supposed to be good at strategy?"

Wo'Dunnia shrugged. He was short for a dwarf, and as scrawny as a selumari, besides. "You're about to fall into my trap, you know." He steepled his fingers as he sat back after making a bold move.

The bodyguard gave him an askew look, made a simple move, and won the game. "Yer awful at this. How's about something new? Arm wrestling?"

Wo'Dunnia frowned. "I might need them to remain unbroken—but I'm quite certain I'd win in a footrace, if you want an actual challenge." Before pursuing diplomatic pursuits, Wo'Dunnia had been well known as a sprinter and even been a part of an athletic team that competed in a tournament hosted by the Vhandrian kingdom.

The duo turned their attention back to Br'Derluch. The diplomat brooded nearby, traveling the length of the floor, turning, and repeating his trip like a pendulum clock.

"We've been sitting on our asses for days," he hissed. "I don't think that daft elven king has any intention of giving us another audience."

Fi'Krayg curled a lip. "There are other ways to get his attention... perhaps a more aggressive approach?"

Their leader shook his head. "I don't think we want to risk rekindling the old war," Br'Derluch cautioned, "and I'm sure that's what would happen... but if we don't see some kind of movement in a few days, we might consider abandoning our mission for a later date. Timing may not be in our favor this year."

Wo'Dunnia leaned forward. "The time is right. Hy'Mandr was right to send us; his contact in Stonehome indicated a coming price hike on all Vhandria's iron exports. They are *selumari*, sure, but that don't make em stupid by default."

Br'Derluch groused some more underneath his breath.

"Give him a few days," Wo'Dunnia said. "I heard some talk about a big celebration: some important event in honor of his son. I'm sure he must be quite busy given the circumstances."

"Fine, fine," Br'Derluch rumbled, pulling Wo'Dunnia out of the chair. "Then gimmee yer seat. Fi'Krayg needs some decent competition, and you're rubbish at this game."

The dwarven diplomat reset the game pieces. "I will give Leidergelth a few days past this celebration, but that's it. If he continues wearing my patience afterwards, I'm gonna stick him for an extra ten percent beyond what Hy'Mandr was willing to give him on those export rates."

In Leidergelth's supper hall, the other selumari politely applauded for Prince Mantieth. The younger coral elf bowed as his father, king of Niamarlee, toasted his son.

Mantieth blushed as the king sang his praises: how he'd bested contender after contender in combat, led diplomatic missions to sensitive kingdoms, and fulfilled other duties demanded by his royal status. Deep inside, it burned Mantieth up to know that he'd never been in any real peril—each of the accolades were just empty praises about battles with wooden swords and dignitary visits to castles owing Niamarlee's support via old allegiances.

"Of course, apologies came on behalf of Queen Naemyar who wishes she could be here, but you know how your mother's travels take priority," his father told him.

Mantieth thanked him diplomatically. Like all the rest, he knew she was never coming home. Some rift had come between Leidergelth and Naemyar ten years ago, and she remained abroad by her own will and remained for most of the last decade to her family home in Cyrea. The prince remained stone faced, but silently resented his father's unyielding will; he knew more than most what personal havoc it could wreak.

Leidergelth didn't notice his son's tepid response. The king's most recent praise was for the closest thing the prince had had to an actual victory. Mantieth had captured the morehl thief, Nohdan. "Even though that rapscallion somehow taken the Dragonstaff—likely his partner got away with it—he'll still pay a stiff penalty. My Mantieth cornered the red skinned beast at sword point."

The coral elf's ears perked up. He locked his gaze on his father. Leidergelth's eyes glistened with fear—fear that his son could've been injured—even as he embellished the tale. Mantieth understood why his father had paid experts to train and prepare him for the rigors of war, though that scenario looked like it would never come. The king's fear also explained why he'd never let Mantieth experience any actual threats outside a controlled environment.

Mantieth smiled with thin lips. As the only son and heir to the throne, he sympathized—and he assumed the back alley gossip about his mother was right, she was never returning, but his heart yearned for so much more than a life trapped within the royal walls. He was bred and trained for battle; cooping him up burned him to the core. Mantieth scanned the room and looked for his best friend, Elorall, hoping she might have returned early from her trip. They'd grown up together, and Elorall had already been on several exciting adventures on behalf of her father, the king's High Enchanter.

He hid his disappointment for her absence and raised his wineglass in salute, responding to the King's toast. Mantieth drained his glass.

His coming of age celebration was planned to take place in a few days. Then, the party would escalate parades, feasts, dancing. He grinned. His father might play it safe in diplomatic situations, but he knew how to throw a party in true selumari fashion. Mantieth both assumed and hoped that Elorall would be back by then; life seemed more interesting whenever she was around. Her father's reins were not quite so tight as Leidergelth's.

The majordomo rang a bell and the final course came out. Servants bore great platters laden with fine deserts and more wine.

Mantieth stepped backwards from the revelry, fading into the crowd, and swiped a flagon of wine, two glasses, and a pair of desserts. He bowed out as the guests happily scarfed down the sweets oblivious to the fact that their guest of honor had absconded with the wine and now wandered the vacant halls.

Anyone of importance was invited to the pre-feast festival, and he did not see any of the vaghan diplomats at the event—not surprising given his father's prejudices. Tonight, the royal staff was reduced to a skeleton crew and the corridors remained mostly empty. Mantieth sighed at the excess of it all and slipped into the bowels of the castle where he rapped on a thick, wooden door.

Fiery eyes greeted him through the Judas hole. "You again? I already told you I don't want to share my stories; my tales are my own. Hire a bard or visit a library, for Firiel's sake," Nodhan spat.

Mantieth held the wine and cake up for viewing. "How about a trade, then?"

The prisoner's dark eyes lingered on the cake. Elegantly frosted, berries perched upon it's whipped peaks like acrobats about to launch into performance. "All right then," the lava elf acquiesced, tilting the goblet so that it fit through the bars.

Mantieth poured the fine red blend at an odd angle to fill the cup and slid the cake through the food slot.

"I'll keep talking as long as the wine keeps pouring." Nodhan admitted that he had traveled most of the settled regions of Esfah though he'd grown up as an orphan on the streets of a free-city east of Emmira. He learned the ways of all the folk who made up the kaleidoscope of races in a free-city of Port Orric. There, members of the thieves' guild recruited and trained him, eventually taking him to the metropolis of Marista-Sehlim as an official member when he turned thirteen.

Mantieth kept pouring the flagon, jealously listening to tales of intrigue, adventure, and hardship.

Even tipsy from the wine, Nodhan realized how Mantieth hung on every word of how he'd stolen the priceless art collection from a pompous lord near the Maris Coast and tapped in to his vast connection of criminal operatives in order to fence it and locate details on the next mark from an information broker. He raised the full glass and toasted the prince, even though he knew his tongue had become looser than normal from the wine. "I've stolen just about anything there is to steal—even the reliquary bones belonging to some old, elven princess..." The morehl chuckled. "Big deal she was among Nekarthans—elven secret society stuff. Apparently, they cast some kind of magic so they'd revive their champion." He took a huge swig and drained the last of the drink, trying not to think about the secret society who still followed Nekarthis, the necromancer responsible for the Magestorm Wars. "There's always a way out of any trap."

Mantieth smirked. "Typical lava elves and their Death worship..."

"Who said anything about it being only the *red-skinned* elves? Just because our heritage was initiated in Death doesn't mean we're all evil—and it doesn't mean all selumari are good."

Mantieth curiously regarded him. "What do you think, Nodhan, are *you* evil?"

Nodhan trailed off in thought for a long moment. The tips of his ears felt warm; that meant the wine was working. Finally, he shrugged and came back the subject at hand, but dodged the last question. "There's a market for everything, you know. May you someday find the little piece of the adventure you seek… and finally be worthy of all those fancy titles they use for you."

Mantieth stiffened. The barb, truthful as it was, dug deep.

"The wine is gone," Nodhan said flatly and returned to the bunk in his tiny cell. Their deal had ended.

Mantieth shut the slider on the Judas hole, wrung his hands, and returned to his quarters.

Mantieth walked the streets of the city. This late, only few were still out and about in Niarmarlee. He shook his head as he stretched his legs and inhaled the fresh air. None of those who *were* awake recognized him—in truth, they didn't even make eye contact.

For a moment at least, the elven prince was free from the obligations and duties of his father's house. In that moment he felt free—perhaps not as free as the morehl thief whose freedom led him to a selumari dungeon, but free enough.

He let his thoughts consume him as he wandered, assuming that his absence from his own party hadn't even been noted. Mantieth did not notice when a charred skeleton, clothed in the black of night, cocked his head in the shadows and took note of him.

The skeletal hunter sniffed deeply and stared at the blue-skinned prince, but remained hidden in the darkness.

Varanthl followed Jordyll and his son through the trails that led from his modest fields and towards his home. The trail came in from the rear and snaked a winding path between the trees; the homunculus peered through the foliage and could see that a much easier, straight and packed tributary of the Great

Coastal Road should have been easily accessible from the last field. It would have made transit easier, especially with a loaded cart.

Jordyll winked as he caught his guest's eye line. "No sense risking danger, friend."

Varanthl rubbed his chin. He realized, "You… don't want to encounter others?"

Jordyll half-shrugged. "Community is not a high priority for the frehlasuhl." The farmer realized he needed to explain. "We are a forbidden people. The grey elves are products of morehl and selumari parents—not a thing looked upon kindly by either side. It is a forbidden union."

"Maybe you could live among the dwarves? I met a decent vagha recently. They seem like they…"

"The funny thing about hate is that it's contagious," Jordyll cut him off. "The frehlasuhl are barely an afterthought for even the most benevolent. Even the vagha call us Mudbloods and, like all races, are quick to shun us." He looked far and away and whispered, "Or worse."

They walked a few silent steps and Gherbin told him softly. "They killed Maa… just for loving Daa and having grey children." His face clouded. "It's a cosmic comedy that being the child of more than two gods could be such a curse. Ghaeial and Tarvanehl would be so disappointed in their children's creations."

Quiet fell again, except for the creaks of the laden wagon's axle as they traveled. Varanthl felt an instant kinship with these unjustly hated people and his jawline softened.

"She was a beauty," Jordyll said, mostly to himself. "Raven-black hair and crimson skin. Those mischievous morehl eyes… those sparkling black eyes… and hips that curved like…" he made a gesture with his hands as if caressing them.

"Daa!" Gherbin hissed with embarrassment.

Jordyll's cheeks burned a deeper gray. His bright smile faded. "A group of drunk selumari from the city ahead caught her on the road and burned her alive." He swallowed hard. "Do you know how hot something must be to burn a lava elf?" He sighed as they approached the trail's end.

A small yard opened around his meager home with a grass lot that had been pecked down to a reasonable length by the farmer's poultry. "I'll go tell Ferth that we've got one more for supper," Gherbin said, hustling ahead. He glanced sidelong at the visitor and then hurried into the house.

The cart halted in front of a lean-to and Jordyll began unloading the contents: a few buckets of edible crops and a mound of hay for the goats. Varanthl noticed a bracelet dangling around his wrist. Gherbin had worn one just like it.

"It ain't worth much," Jordyll explained to Varanthl. "Can't even melt it down—the rings are fireproof—I don't suspect that even dragon's fire would do the trick."

The farmer continued, "Not much in my home worth stealing, either," he explained. "Not that I'd ever accuse… just being up front with ye. I don't know your purpose on the road, after all."

Before the mudblood could spear a load with his pitchfork, Varanthl wrapped his four massive arms around the hay load and hefted the entire mound over his shoulder. "Where do you need this?"

Wide-eyed, the farmer showed him to his depleted stack and Varanthl deposited it while kid goats pranced happily around his feet, bleating joyous approval.

Jordyll grinned; in a few moments, his guest had done the work of four and in half as much time. "Where are you going after-wards, friend?"

All four of his arms shrugged. "Nowhere in particular. I had to leave my home. My father…" he trailed off leaving no question of what had happened.

"If you like, I have a few jobs you could help with, if you needed a bed and want to earn your keep."

Varanthl nodded. "I'd like that very much." He laid aside his hammer against the shed and shrugged off the archaic armor he'd worn. Only a thin tunic covered him.

Two hours later, he followed Jordyll inside the house. Smells of the cooked meal tantalized Varanthl's senses.

Jordyll buzzed with excitement. He rubbed Gherbin's head and tousled his hair. "You wouldn't hardly believe it, son. We accomplished nearly a full day's worth of work already."

Even the child, cold to the idea of a guest, seemed to warm with his father's enthusiasm… and the fact that he wouldn't have to help unload hay after supper.

A grey skinned female, close in age to Gherbin, set the food at the rough-hewn table.

"This is Ferthalin," the farmer introduced.

"You can call me Ferth," she said with a smile and sparkling eyes which must've belonged to her mother. Her mottled skin glowed slightly redder than her brother's.

The lilt in her voice made Varanthl think her younger than her brother, and on the cusp of her teenage years. Warmness spread across the homunculus's chest, and he finally felt that peace he'd lost with his father's passing.

Like her brother and father, she too wore a bracelet, except she wore one on each wrist.

"This is Varanthl," Jordyll introduced. "He is going to stay with us for a period. Maybe now we can finally repair the barn and mend the fences," he suggested. "That might allow our flock to finally start growing again—if we can just keep out the swamp crawlers.

"Swamp crawlers?" Varanthl asked.

"Local trog's pets. They look like dog-sized insects and aren't particularly dangerous, but they've gotten a taste for goat flesh."

"And chicken," Ferth added.

They gathered around the table and sat. Before Varanthl could reach for the food, his new family bowed their heads briefly and Jordyll offered a word to the gods. "Father Tarvanehl and Mother Ghaeial, we thank you for continued protection, and for our food, and our new friend Varanthl. Gods watch over us."

The gray elves hummed a matching note in agreement, and they all opened their eyes and reached for the food.

CHAPTER EIGHT

Elorall sat next to the driver of the horse team that pulled her wagon. As part of the caravan that traveled the Great Coastal Road, her carriage's strongbox held the object they'd been sent on behalf of King Leidergelth to retrieve. The other carts and riders, all selumari, sandwiched hers in the center. The youthful selumari stood on the toe board to let the wind hit her face. They'd just gotten close enough to Niamarlee so that she could get a faint, familiar whiff of salt that rolled off the Far Seas.

She spotted several brown forms in the distance as they merged ahead onto the Great Coastal Road bearing on an intercept course. Light glinted off one of the figures—some kind of brassy hued dragonkin. Drakufreet were not common; but she'd seen them on occasion, but never any this size or color. Elorall couldn't be certain if their presence was coincidental or not.

The wary selumari called out a caution signal to her escorts. Four coral elves traveled ahead and another four behind her. Her troops converged to assess the road before them.

Elorall shaded her eyes against the sun and looked into the distance. "Seven vagha on riding mammoths, and a drakufreet… traveling beasts, not the heavier war animals," she reported. The pachyderms each still dwarfed the elves' horses, but were distinctly smaller than the heavies she understood that the dwarves often bred.

"So no threat then?" her driver asked. "I'd always assumed *all* beasts could be used in battle, you know—you just got to try hard enough."

"We're on the king's business," Elorall said. "We must always assume ill intent by outsiders." She knew that

Leidergelth entertained a crew of vaghan diplomats… she assumed things would not go well. The King's temper and stubbornness could rival that of any dwarf. "We'd better announce ourselves and call them to stand down as we pass," she said, noting a marker stone along the highway—they were in Niamarlee's land and could exercise such a demand to give them the road.

Their horses rode up on the vagha with a burst of speed and then hers pulled back as the driver yanked on the reins. The dwarves had crossbows out in a flash, and the elven aggressors had arrows knocked and ready equally fast. Both sides yelled indiscernible demands at each other as they gestured with their weapons.

Elorall's voice pierced the cacophony. "I am Elorall, the official envoy of King Leidergelth of Niamarlee. Yield the road until we have passed!"

One of the mammoth riders stiffened tall and held up a dwarven war-axe. He shouted back, "I am Prince Hy'Targ, son of King Hy'Mandr and heir to the Irontooth throne." His booming voice made her sit up and take notice, though his tone belied the look in the prince's eyes, and she suspected a false bravado.

A tense silence burgeoned within both groups. Neither wanted to back down as a matter of principle.

"State your business on the road," Elorall said, more politely than previous. Her troops had begun to relax their postures, but only slightly. The dwarves did likewise.

"Just traveling," Hy'Targ said.

Elorall bid her escorts to lower their weapons, and they complied. She looked the vagha over: as well as she could tell, the prince seemed a similar age to Elorall and her friend back at the castle, Prince Mantieth. "You're here for Mantieth's coming of age party?" she guessed.

He shook his head. "We're quest-bound north of Niamarlee."

She nodded measuredly and then all heads snapped west at the sound of a goblin battle horn. "trogs!" the selumari shouted.

From atop his woolly mount, Hy'Targ stood in his barding and extended his spyglass. He spotted movement down the road. A throng of green-skinned fiends dragged several timbers across the path.

"They've blocked the highway with a logjam," he said, checking the other direction and spotted goblinoids fleeing back into the woods. "Behind you, too."

The mammoths closed in to form a defensive position around the elves.

"It looks like you could use some assistance," Hy'Targ offered from his seat upon Brentésion.

"We appreciate it," Elorall nodded. "There have been increased raids in these parts lately." She stood tall on the carriage and glanced inside to verify that her cargo was still secure.

All the combined forces readied bow and bolt and stared at the tree line which crashed and buzzed with approaching troops. Leaves rustled and branches shook violently. They'd be through in a matter of moments.

"Any second now," Elorall muttered through grit teeth.

Varanthal sat at the supper table. He'd spent the last couple of days laboring on Jordyll's small farm. He enjoyed the work; it made him feel a part of something noble, helping the group eke out a living amongst the wild elements that conspired against them. The homunculus took quickly to the frehlasuhl family and proved adept at farming under Jordyll's tutelage.

After another day's work, he joined them in the customary prayer and breaking of bread. Ferthalin broke out in song. Varanthal sat and listened, entranced by both song and the girl's voice. She sang of a fair elven woman named Chel who was the most sought-after female of her village, but Chel left it all behind for a secret lover who had captured her heart and given her four beautiful rings.

"I think you might be part songbird," Varanthal said once she had finished.

Ferth giggled and reached for a plate of biscuits. "Now you must sing for us," she insisted.

Varanthal looked from face to face. "Oh no, I…"

She stared at him with a cross look. "But you *must*," Ferth insisted. "One person shares and the other gives back. It's what family looks like. Sharing of songs is a tradition."

Varanthal's spine tingled and his cheeks warmed. "Very well," he said. "But I am not terribly talented at songcraft. I only really know a couple."

All members of the family watched him with interest. Ferth leaned forward and rested her chin on her hands, waiting intently.

The homunculus cleared his throat and began his song, a tale his father had taught him about the creation of Esfah.

M'oer Ghaeial and Father Tarvanehl
Sang o'er the world creating all
Lonely to'ger, she and him
They brought forth son: Eldurim.

With him of earth their hearts did fill
They kissed like wind creating Ailuril.
The house of gods began to swell
And fiery passion birthed Firiel.

Yet Esfah dry lacked wat'r and well
So come forth they bid did Aguarehl.

Varanthl paused for a second, furrowed his brow, and then continued singing,

And Ghaeial taught them how to craft
And they created folk from great to last.
Eldarim and dragon kin and kind
And songs to stand the tests of time.

"I know this song," Ferth piped up. "But you forgot a verse."

Varanthl looked down sheepishly. "I left it out on purpose," he said. "I don't like the part about the family's breaking or the part of Death's conception." He tightened his lips and thought of his father. "I don't like death."

Ferth smiled back at him and then began the rest of the song. She sang along with Varanthl about the creation of the primary races. His voice carried the tune and her melodic additions flitted around his like a happy sparrow. They finished the piece and Gherbin and Jordyll leaned forward and clapped for them. Their bracelets bounced on their wrists.

Varanthl watched and took a bite of chicken and grains from his plate. Something niggled at the back of his mind as the clues knit together. He looked at Ferth and asked, "Your mother must have been Chel? Was your father the secret lover with the four rings?"

She nodded, giving a knowing smile. "My mother taught the song to me, but she says that Daa helped her write it."

Ferth stood and walked around the table. She removed one of Chel's bracelets and slipped it around Varanthl's wrist. "This means family."

The homunculus's cheeks burned as he bit back tears. "It is the most precious thing I've ever been given." He turned it on his wrist, admiring it.

She turned to her father. "And now it's Daa's turn to sing."

Jordyll winked. "I think we ought to hear from Gherbin, first."

The youth looked up, his face stuffed with food and surprise as he peered around the table. With his cheeks bulging and caught by the sudden demand, he was neither able to deny it or fulfill it. The rest of them laughed as the boy scrambled to swallow and protest his turn to sing.

Arrows and bolts streaked towards their marks as Hy'Targ and Elorall commanded their troops. trogs fell as soon as they popped their heads up from the tall grass and gave their enemies targets. They howled as they fell within the marshy heather along the road. What the trogs lacked in terms of protection they made up for in numbers—a horrible tactic, but one made practical when each goblin sow birthed eight new imps each spring.

The goblin army launched missiles from slings and crude short bows, targeting the coral elves' horses first. Elorall's beasts shrieked and fell in a panicked, bloody tangle before the swampy foes began creeping further out from the foliage.

Hy'Targ ordered that the mammoths move behind the wagons to give them better protection from the enemy projectiles, and he crouched behind Brentésion's massive head as the trogs' pellets zinged around him or bounced off the bronze dragonkin's armored hide. The impromptu alliance of vagha and selumari rallied for cover and continued showering the goblins with their dwindling supply of missiles.

A second horn blew from their battle line, and the trogs stopped returning fire. A short pause developed organically, and the goblins shouted a war cry from their hidden positions as they bolstered for martial combat. Behind the thickets, trees split with deafening peals as a massive pair of trolls charged from the ruined greenery, shrieking loudly and with an insane rancor. The closest one emerged fully and cracked a cask of rancid goblin gutchurn. He cast the empty keg at the enemy as he ran and it smashed against Elorall's carriage, rocking it violently enough to break an axle. The second one had crouched within the tall reeds and disappeared.

On instinct, the elves poured arrow after arrow into the towering brute nearest them. It moved with uncanny speed. A wave of snarling, cackling goblins rushed forward on their monstrous ally's heels; many even passed it in their battle fervor.

Hy'Targ's troops drew axes and Elorall's pulled swords as the trogs closed the gap. They hacked apart the first wave as it breeched their defensive line; the quickest and cockiest goblins became the deadest ones the fastest. The second wave crashed into them harder and as a more unified front after learning from the first scouts' attempts.

A cadre of shriekers surged through the devilgrass. Both the dense foliage and the goblins it hid suddenly burned with blue energy. It withered and lit on fire as Elorall blasted them with a jolt of lightning from her fingertips.

Hy'Targ raised an eyebrow and the coral elf spell caster winked at him in response, revealing her nature as a spell caster. The dwarf whirled his axe and lopped the head clean from a trog's shoulders. Both were grateful their first encounter had not come to blows.

One massive troll, easily taller than the mammoths, cackled as it arrived and kicked the closest wagon, splintering it to pieces and obliterating it. The wreckage smashed two selumari to the dirt several cubits back. The troll turned and roared, reaching out to snatch Elorall and her friends. They scattered, dashing through enemy formations, cutting them down as they went.

Hy'Targ's two experienced guardians, Vy'Danis and Jr'Dunn, each clambered behind the reins of the largest of their two mammoths and charged through the grass nearest the Great Coastal Road. They trampled the snarling fiends as they swung the creatures' tusks from side to side, razing great swaths of the stumpy, angry goblins. Many of them near the rear turned and fled back for the safety of the trees, rushing past and under the watchful eye of a slightly larger goblin who wore red and white paint. The trog commander, too, slinked further into the trees to avoid any missiles from the travelers and escape beyond range of the mammoths.

Leaping from his cover, the other troll blindsided both Brentésion and Hy'Targ. The vagha rider fell to the ground as the dragonkin groaned in surprise. The peaty monstrosity wrapped his strong arms around the beast and tackled it. Goblins in the rushes netted him in thick cords to prevent Brentésion from unfurling his wings and escaping—the entire encounter took mere moments. The troll and his minions dashed deeper into the towering devilgrass leaving only Brentésion's neck and face exposed; woven rope bound his mouth shut. The drakufreet's eyes locked on Hy'Targ as he rolled to his feet; they pleaded for his support. And then the troll heaved and yanked the copper beast into the grass and disappeared.

Hy'Targ howled and ran for his mount's aid only to be met with a hail of trog bullets. One glanced off his shoulder and the prince whirled back to safety behind the demolished wagons. He gritted his teeth and vowed to reclaim his father's prized steed, though he didn't know how or when it could be done.

Another coral elf fell below a crushing throng of swamp-footed trogs as they emerged from the reeds. The elf's voice seemed to drown in the swarm as they overwhelmed him.

They pulled him to the ground and shivved him repeatedly with their crude weapons.

A similar crowd amassed around Vy'Hrothgyr who fought them off bravely despite the wound on his side where an enemy had stuck him with one of their jagged weapons. The prince watched the shifting devil grass—if he didn't pursue Brentésion now, he might lose him forever!

Vy'Hrothgyr had just begun to falter when Hy'Targ rushed at the piled up trogs near the side of an elven cart. The dwarf cursed, hot blood boiling at the loss of so prized a mount, and swung Glorybringer wildly, cleaving goblins three and four at a time with each zealous swing.

Trogs yelped and scattered as Hy'Targ rescued the bard from certain doom.

Hy'Targ slapped his bard on the shoulder. The anger in his voice made his voice crack, "Sing about *that*—and no bawdy limericks," he yelled through blood splattered lips, stained with the ochre yellow of goblin ichor.

Vy'Hrothgyr grinned manically and he and Hy'Targ both went opposite directions, killing trogs with reckless abandon.

The remaining troll fixated on Elorall and tried to snatch the spellcaster. He chased her around the central wagon, which laid busted open from the battle. Screeching, it leapt over top of the broken vehicle; using both fists it tried smashing her to paste with meaty fists balled up like hammers.

Elorall dove beneath the wrecked carriage. The cart's driver looked up from where he'd been hiding, wild eyed, as those huge mallets smashed him into the ground.

The troll lost sight of Elorall and shrieked. Denied the sport it wanted, it kicked one of its own goblin comrades, punting him across the field like a rag doll. Turning back, the beast spotted Hy'Targ and pounced.

Hy'Targ lunged forward just in time and scrambled for safety to avoid the driver's fate.

Elorall dashed from beneath the nearby broken boards and wheels and plunged her sword deep into the troll's leg. Aiming for the lower tendon, she hoped to cripple it. The blade lodged in thick troll flesh and the monster shrieked and whirled on her, batting her away. She fell back to the dirt near the wrecked wagon.

The troll turned back on Hy'Targ as it dislodged the elven blade from its corded muscle and snapped it like a twig. Hy'Targ's eyes widened, and he hoped the bard wasn't about to write about his demise.

Reaching over a broken beam, the female elf snatched a blade from the bed of the destroyed carriage and unsheathed the fine weapon: the cargo they'd carried. She sprinted up the boards and used the seat to springboard off as the troll reached for Hy'Targ. The added height gave her just enough reach to slash clean through the beast's malodorous hide and sever the troll's head.

Its enormous body collapsed at Hy'Targ's feet and the bulbous head rolled into the grass with a stupefied look frozen upon it. A retreat horn blew, and the goblins routed back for the forest.

Elorall used a rag to wipe the remaining blood from the weapon, though the metal seemed to drink it in. "A vorpal blade," she explained to Hy'Targ as they took stock of who and what remained of their crews. "One of the mystic weapons leftover from the Magestorm Wars."

She had lost a few of her coral elf escorts and all their horses. The dwarves were scuffed up, but, aside from the abduction of Brentésion, were in relatively good shape considering the size of the army they'd fought back.

"What were they after?" Hy'Targ asked, wondering if they had specifically attacked to steal his mount, or if stealing the rare drakufreet had merely been their leader's afterthought.

He grimaced as he stared towards the trees where they'd dragged his father's steed. All his vaghan pride demanded he pursue them and take back the dragonkin—and then he remembered his timeline.

Hy'Targ spat into the dirt, still clearing out the taste of goblin blood from his teeth. There would be a reckoning, someday. Brentésion would be reclaimed—but now was not the time.

"Senseless violence," Elorall muttered a response. "What else do goblins ever want? They've been stepping up their attacks lately. Maybe they're starving in their swamps… needing to branch out and push their borders further? These were mostly younger, unblooded forces."

Hy'Targ rubbed his chin and looked at both the north and south blockages. "I'm not convinced it was so simple," he said. "Something's driving them. Someone with a rudimentary skill in tactics." He pointed to the blockades. "Their attacks aren't normally this well thought-through, are they? Have you known goblins to block roads and drive monstrous champions like a spearhead?"

She shrugged and slid the sword, Mantieth's sword, into the frog of her leather belt for safe keeping.

Suddenly, the headless troll's body got up and lunged for Elorall. Quick as lightning, Hy'Targ swung his axe, howling in surprise when Glorybringer sparked into flame. The weapon tore a chunk of the troll open and the entire monster lit up like a strawman. It took three steps towards the trees and then finally collapsed, lying dead in an immolated heap.

"I didn't know it could do that," Hy'Targ muttered awestruck, implying surprise from both axe and enemy.

Vy'Danis, nursing a slight limp, slapped his ward on the back. "Yer father always tried to get 'er to light, but was never quite able to get it to spark up in battle." The old dwarf shrugged. "He won that thing in a duel long before you were born, but none of us ever really believed it was a Magestorm artifact like that fancy sword," he bobbed his head to the blade at Elorall's side.

The vagha climbed their mounts and offered hands to their new friends and pulled them up to ferry them home. "We'll get you to Niamarlee," Hy'Targ promised, taking Vy'Hrothgyr's mount and making him ride behind Vy'Danis. "It's on our way, though our errand is one of utmost urgency." He explained their situation as briefly as possible as they traveled, hoping he could request help against Melkior from Leidergelth's forces. "This fight belongs to more folk than just us. If we're right, all of Esfah is at stake…"

CHAPTER NINE

Selumari flags waved in the breeze above Leidergelth's castle at the heart of Niamarlee. The train of vagha-driven mammoths entered the city to much fanfare of the locals as their parade drove the coral elf survivors towards the inner curtain wall that protected the royalty. High overhead the castle, a set of towers supported an eyrie to house the large birds that selumari cavalry sometimes kept. Even further yet, a coral airship glimmered slightly, awash with cloud.

The collection of coral elves seated behind the dwarves waved off the guards near the fortified barbican and the sentries allowed them to pass within. The woolly caravan came to a halt within the castle's main court.

Furtaevell stood behind the king's majordomo. The High Enchanter stood on his toes to try to spot his daughter in the crowd of visitors. Relief washed over his blue face when he found her.

The elven king and his entourage flowed out from the castle's main gate and diplomatically greeted the caravan. Behind King Leidergelth, Prince Mantieth hurried down the steps as Elorall dropped from the back of the furry beast. Behind her came a battle-axe-toting dwarf, seemingly young for his company. He plopped to his feet adjacent her.

"King Leidergelth," he bowed with the trained motions of nobility. "I am Prince Hy'Targ, son of Hy'Mandr, King Irontooth."

Leidergelth smiled and returned the bow, although he seemed somewhat disinterested and indifferent of his presence, despite the significance of a prince's arrival. Irontooth royalty had not entered the castle walls of Niamarlee in two generations, and the last time had resulted in bloodshed.

Elorall bowed before her king. "Prince Hy'Targ and his party rescued me and your cargo from marauding trogs. They grow bolder and attack travelers even on the Great Coastal—Coral Road," she corrected and used the term her leader preferred.

Leidergelth gave her a cursory nod. "Yes, yes. My cargo… it is secure?"

"Yes." Elorall unfastened her belt and turned over ownership of the vorpal blade.

The king drew the beautiful sword and examined it in the light. He could feel its hunger, greedy for blood, as the weapon pulsed in his hand. Leidergelth slid it back into the sheath and made a grand show of handing it to Mantieth.

He announced so that his entourage could hear the proclamation, "My son, champion of the selumari. I give you this gift on your coming of age… a sword worthy of such a lofty call."

Mantieth smiled and thanked his father. He cringed only slightly from the undeserved accolades and fastened the blade at his waist, handing his previous sword to Virakh, his father's majordomo. Leidergelth's assemblage applauded him as he straightened his tunic, making the sensations of unworthiness worsen in his gut.

Hy'Targ noted the selumari prince's tepid reaction and raised an eyebrow, but said nothing. Instead, the dwarf approached the king again.

An expert in diplomacy, the king introduced his son, turning a shoulder to the heir of his neighbor's throne. "Mantieth, do you know Prince Hy'Targ of the Irontooth Mountain? They dwell in the mountain to our southeast."

"I don't believe we've had the pleasure," Mantieth bowed.

The dwarf gave a curt one in response. "A mark of peaceful times, I suppose," Hy'Targ said. "Actually, King

Leidergelth, I hoped to speak with you in private on an important matter…"

"Are you part of the diplomatic mission from your father?"

"Well… no," Hy'Targ stammered. "I was on a quest on King Irontooth's behalf when…"

"A quest? You certainly *should* speak with my son. Mantieth is our most capable adventurer. If you are looking to share stories of action and derring-do, speak with him." The King turned to his entourage and returned to the castle, leaving Mantieth and Elorall behind with the vagha.

Before following the crowd of self-consumed elves, Furtaevell grabbed his daughter and looked her over while Hy'Targ stared incredulously after Leidergelth. He checked over his daughter for injuries and frowned at her bruises and scrapes.

"I'm fine," she insisted quietly, and then pointed out that the entourage was leaving without him.

Furtaevell frowned, but kissed her on the head, and then hurried away. "We'll catch up later, daughter."

"Sorry," Mantieth said once they had gone. "He's been very focused on Niamarlee as of late and hasn't had much time for exterior concerns."

"Like protecting the Great Coastal Road?" Hy'Targ groused. It was no secret that the road had grown increasingly dangerous these last few years, but the dwarf hadn't experienced anything like it until now.

Mantieth started to object at the grumble some tone in Hy'Targ's voice, but then shrugged. It had been a fair observation. "The trogs should certainly be upgraded from an *occasional nuisance* to a regular, albeit minor, threat."

Hy'Targ turned to Elorall. He noticed her posture shift and saw her eyes twinkle as she stepped closer to Mantieth. He had to burst her bubble, "I thought you said we could get help in Niamarlee?"

She nodded. "Mantieth, you really need to convince your father to lend aid to these dwarves."

Hy'Targ nodded and explained. "The demon lich Melkior has risen anew and on the border of your lands. I would turn back and seek help from the vagha, but time is a premium; I surrendered my own mount—Hy'Mandr's prized dragonkin—to get here as fast as possible. Every day Melkior roams free he regains strength. He will soon be able to raise a new army of the dead like we have not seen since the First Age."

Mantieth looked skeptical. "Isn't Melkior just a legend?"

"Believe me, I'd rather be doing anything else," Hy'Targ said, shaking his head. "We believe that he's gone up the coast of the Far Sea and is headed to the old Ivory Tower— used magic to take a massive head start."

"It's a deadlands there, now," Mantieth said.

"Isn't that where you'd expect the bloodless to retreat to?" Elorall asked.

The blue-skinned elf shrugged reluctantly. "I confess I don't know much on the topic of the undead."

"Well, you better get some learning," Hy'Targ said bluntly. "You are Esfah's best hope at convincing your father to help us."

Mantieth nervously ran his fingers through his greenish hair. "Well, according to him, I'm some kind of hero already, so it ought to be a piece of cake, right?"

"Let's hope so. For all our sakes."

The selumari prince rolled his eyes. "Any advice on how we can convince him?"

Hy'Targ signaled for his companions to service their woolly mounts. "Yeah. By knowing a thing or two about history and how the bloodless ravaged our peoples in the past. Do you have a library?"

Hy'Targ walked through the rows of book racks and scroll cases, scanning titles embossed on spines and covers. He led his two elven companions through the stacks as if he'd been there before. All libraries of any quality had a kind of natural flow that made them easier to navigate.

"I thought you were an adventurer?" Mantieth asked skeptically, eying the bookish vagha.

The dwarf spat a cough of laughter. "Me? No. My father is the adventurer. I've always seen myself as more of a scholar."

Elorall grinned. "A scholar with an axe? That's something new—and I've seen you use it."

Hy'Targ shrugged. "Not all learning comes from books." He dragged his fingers through his beard, remembering where he'd gotten those words. He mumbled, "I'm starting to sound like my father."

One title caught his eye, and he pulled the book off its shelf while he continued browsing. Finally, he found a volume of *Histories of Wealhtheow the Scop* which boasted the correct century noted below the title of the encyclopedia. They'd named the series after the prolific researcher who originally compiled and penned *The Book of the Land* in the first age.

Hy'Targ sat at a desk in the silent hall and cracked the massive book open. It was an exhaustive type of tome, filled with more details than most cared to ever know; it was the kind the prince liked best. He flipped forward in the histories until he located the information on the uprising led by Melkior.

The tale recounted, over pages and pages, the same general details as Vy'Hrothgyr's song, *The Tragedy of Melkior*. He flipped further and found detailed accountings of lost troops and lineages that ended in the conflict. A block print gave a graphic depiction of Lurneville where it jutted out upon a cliff over the sea; the eldarim Champion's tower towered on the hill nearest it like a sentinel.

Another chapter wrote detail after detail about the Teldrim race which Melkior had annihilated. The race seemed similar in many respects to the humans and their Amazon warrior caste, although they had darker skin and lived nomadic lives; they bred horses and lived in tune with nature. Only a handful of the race remained alive post-Melkior... too few to remain a viable line.

Hy'Targ flipped forward several pages to a chapter on Leisterbane, Melkior's acolyte. A drawing of a black jar labeled its contents as Necralluvium. The verso page filled with a giant inkblot and a description of how the dark, viscous fluid had been unleashed upon Esfah by Leisterbane who used it to awaken the dead in the post-Melkior era.

He returned to the Teldrim section. Some past scholar had written additions into the margins, likely done within the last hundred years; he or she had listed the remaining lineages. They broke out into family trees with lines crossed out to indicate those who had died or received wavy underlines to indicate where the line had become so diluted that Teldrim blood was no longer worth recording.

Written around the sketch of the Teldrim crest, genealogy trees crossed to show where they'd tried to isolate the purer line. Only two names remained, brothers: Murthak and Trandlurthan. Hy'Targ grimaced when he read it and flipped the pages back to the main text on Melkior's uprising. He slid the book over to Mantieth.

"Important stuff in there. Better learn it, and fast." He tapped the page with the most important part of the account and picked up the other text he'd pulled from the archives.

While the elves scanned the pages, Hy'Targ flipped through a tome detailing the obscure legend of the Kreethaln devices which were evidentially created from eldrymetallum: the metal of the gods. He scanned the pages quickly, learning little new, except that it seemed the tale was more widely known, and was therefore a hopefully true account—something more than just a local myth. A line jumped out at him from the text. *The Gremmlobahnd came the same time as the Teldrim, the infants of Tarvanehl's races, and they became keepers and protectors for them. Their nomadic mobility made them a race of secret holders and the keepers of many mysteries.*

Elorall looked over his shoulder. "Who were the Gremmlobahnd?"

"You haven't heard of the gnomes?" he tried to hide a scoffing tone. "Esfah's been home to lots more kith and kin than just the elder races—born of Ghaeial or not." He did not want to dwell on the long-forgotten gnomes. If they did not secure Leidergelth's help, they might all meet them too soon in either the Bright Shining Lands or in the Abyss.

Hy'Targ stared at the reference, noted the page, and then continued. The book said nothing more about the Teldrim. The only new information he found verified the other devices besides Life-bringer: the other two Kreethaln.

Mantieth finally spoke up, "It says here that Melkior was obsessed with Ailushurai, the selumari princess. Even in death, he pursued her. He planned to reanimate her body so that he could have her in death, despite her ultimate rejection of him in life. If he reclaims Ailushurai, he could wield the power of Death incarnate."

Hy'Targ turned and looked at it. It went on to indicate that the collective champions of the races had stolen her body and used it to lure the lich out of safety in order to meet him on the field of battle.

Elorall leaned over their shoulders and flipped the page back to a two-sheet spread with a woodblock print. The graphic depicted a horde of skeletons rising from graves and devouring all Esfah at Melkior's command.

Mantieth stared at the illustrated horrors and whispered, "We've got to stop him from getting those bones."

"Believe the word of some *dwarf*?" King Leidergelth's booming voice bled through the thick chamber doors. "Do you even know about his father, the *Adventurer King*? He carved his entire kingdom out from lands that once belonged *to us*. His father fought my father in the last revolt—and we gave them land so that our generations could have peace. *How do we know that this is not some vagha ploy meant to take even more from us?*"

With his crew remaining in the courtyard, Hy'Targ sat on a step outside the king's door. Elorall leaned against a pillar next to him.

Some more mumbled words blurred unintelligible between the postern and their ears, spoken at a more moderate volume. Several minutes passed until the door finally opened just enough for Mantieth to escape.

His posture indicated a new coldness towards Hy'Targ. "He forbade any of his selumari from helping any dwarves beyond whatever assistance they would give to regular travelers passing through Niamarlee. He stressed the *passing through* part."

An awkward moment of tense silence passed. Elorall broke it. "So how do we help them?"

"We cannot." He crossed his arms.

Hy'Targ frowned and turned away from the other prince. "I knew it was a mistake to stop so long here. I've wasted precious time."

Elorall stood between them. "What is it with you two all of the sudden." She turned to Mantieth. "You were eager to help the vagha only minutes ago… before talking with the King."

Mantieth sighed. "Apparently our fathers are not the best of friends. It sounded like they have reasons to distrust each other."

"*So?*" Elorall spat. "Since when have you given a damn about what your father thinks? It's pretty shoddy timing to start right now." She looked at both of them. "Neither of you are your fathers. It is time to be your own person and actually *do* something worthy."

Both of them nodded and relaxed.

Hy'Targ bowed. "I do thank you for trying. It would be easier to vanquish Melkior with an army at my back. But I must go... I cannot wait around while the lich gains strength. I'm sure you understand, if we fail, he will come for *your* people first before his growing army of undead sweeps further south into vagha territory."

Mantieth bit his lip and whispered to his friend, "You trust him?"

Elorall nodded. "He saved my life when he had nothing to gain for it."

The elven prince turned to Hy'Targ. "You are correct. With an army of coral elves, you might stand a chance, but they will not rally behind you. You cannot take a full company of our troops, but what about the two of us?"

Hy'Targ nodded measuredly. "Aye. I would gladly have your assistance. After all," he winked, "I hear one of ye is some kind of elf champion or something?"

Mantieth grinned, and they clasped forearms. "I will pack quickly. Give this writ to one of your dwarves and have them pass it off to the stable master. They will provision your companions immediately so we can depart as soon as possible—we must depart before sunup, but first we have a visit to make."

Hy'Targ looked at him quizzically.

"I think I know an elf who has visited more places than I could ever imagine; he might have some inside information for us." He waggled the book he'd taken from the library. "Sometimes a guy can learn a thing or two from a book," he grinned and then tapped his head, "but not all knowledge is written on pages."

CHAPTER TEN

"Psst. Hey! Nohdan." The insistent, familiar voice woke him from his slumber.

The lava elf yawned and draped his thin blanket over his shoulders as he crawled out of his prison cot. Every vertebra in his back cracked.

He recognized the voice. "Mantieth… I swear by Firiel that I'll murder you if this isn't an official reprieve with orders for my release… it's the middle of the night and I don't want to…"

The Judas hole slid open to reveal the prince's eyes. Nohdan felt certain he was not alone, but the urgency in Mantieth's voice sobered him quickly.

"I must know something… you struck me as widely traveled and you've crossed paths with information brokers, heretics, mages, and the like."

Nohdan inclined his head. "All that is true. But what is this about?"

"What do you know about the Teldrim and Melkior?"

"I don't know anything about… wait—Melkior? Aren't the Teldrim the guys that Melkior wiped out? I don't read much history… but that's all from some child's tale, right?"

"You mentioned something previously that made me think you knew something about him. Melkior was madly in love with a selumari princess named…"

"Ailushurai."

Mantieth's eyes wilded. "I knew it." The prince moved back as some minor scuffle ensued outside the door. A new set of eyes peeked through, barely able to reach tall enough to peer through the port and into the cell.

"What do you know about her?" Nohdan grinned, holding all the cards. "I know that her body once lied in repose alongside the evil lich's, and that there is a group of morehl who believe in some crazy prophecy about his resurrection. As soon as he is reunited with Ailushurai, Melkior will reign terror across all Esfah."

The selumari's eyes widened at the casual telling of such zealous faith. "How do you know such things?"

Nohdan stood tall, "Because I am the one who stole her bones on behalf of an insane morehl warlock. He happens to belong to that cult. It was easy, too—they were left lying in some ancient eldarim convent. The cult of Nekarthis thinks the bones can control Death's chief general if they could animate them first," he scoffed and rolled his eyes. "They still believe in the power of the Netherwold."

Mantieth leaned in again. "Can you bring us to them— the bones?"

Nohdan laughed. "Could I? of course I could. But everything has a price."

"What is freedom worth to you?"

Nohdan shrugged. "Given enough time, I'll escape from your prison. I think we both know that."

Mantieth stared into his onyx eyes. "It is my Name Day tomorrow. If I ask my father for anything, he will give it to me without hesitation. I am leaving right now, and you will bring me to the bones. Otherwise, I will stay and ask my father for your head at sunset."

The lava elf stared back into his captor's unflinching eyes, unable to tell if the prince was truthful or not. "Fine," he said. "I'll bring you there. It's not far, but it is dangerous."

A pair of manacles slid through the food tray.

"What's this?" Nohdan complained.

"I think you know. I'm not taking chances."

Grumbling, the morehl reluctantly put them on. The door swung open to reveal Mantieth, a female selumari, and a dwarf. He followed them out and into the hall.

"This is Hy'Targ and Elorall."

Elorall leaned towards Nohdan and squeezed shut his manacles, which he'd left open enough that he might wriggle free. They clicked tight once fully closed.

The crafty Nohdan grinned with a shrug. "It was worth a shot."

The sun had not yet risen, and Rhaudian had nearly completed the second pass of its regular circuit across the sky. A portcullis raised on the curtain wall which separated Leidergelth's castle sanctum from the rest of Niamarlee.

Mantieth skulked ahead of the party, leading them through the gate, and then closed it behind them. Little moved in the dark except for the shuffling of the tethered vaghan mammoths that waited for them.

Vy'Danis and Jr'Dunn stood over a small fire nearby with the other four dwarves. They'd kept a vigil as appointed. Another four vaghan figures appeared in the shadows and they looked down their noses at the cuffed morehl who their companions dragged behind them.

Only Vy'Hrothgyr appeared amused. No doubt it gave him ideas for new verses to record within the bard's journal as he chronicled their adventure.

"Springing a prisoner from the clink might make this mission difficult," Vy'Danis objected, keeping his voice as muted as possible in the dead of night. "If he doesn't want to keep silent, he could bring the…"

"He'll keep quiet," Hy'Targ promised. "Nohdan can ride behind you. If he acts up, you have full permission to cold cock him."

Vy'Danis nodded solemnly.

"Now where do we go from here?" Mantieth asked the lava elf.

"North, along the coast," he said. "There is a volcanic plateau… do you know the one?"

The coral elves nodded. "The city of Undrakull?"

Nohdan nodded. "I will take you to the bones and the one who purchased them; he lives in the morehl city."

"I know the fastest route," Mantieth said, scrambling up a mastodon to sit behind his vagha escort. "Head north on the road. We'll abandon it for the lesser used trails tomorrow morning, before anyone can scramble an eagle rider to scout our position. My father won't realize we are gone until this evening when I fail to arrive for the feast being held in my honor." He rolled his eyes, glad to escape yet another of the stodgy events.

The others nodded, agreeing with the plan, and then began a lazy trot through the streets of Niamarlee. Dwarven drivers kept their beasts moving at a steady lope, balancing maximum speed against the quietest lope they could run the animals at.

Hy'Targ glanced backward as his pachyderm followed the others. Bright and full, Rhaudian had begun to set upon the high curtain wall of the king's keep. His heart startled when a figure turned to stare at him, slow and predator-like it perched upon a bastion rib with shimmers of lunar light peeking through the gaps in its body.

The black skeleton stood silhouetted against the moon. It tensed and then leapt with a lung-less, ravenous shriek that could only come from a fiend with arcane origins.

"Problem!" Hy'Targ yelled to his party, no longer caring about selumari ears. "A spy; a spy from Melkior!"

The other dwarves glanced back to see the black monstrosity chasing them through the cobbled street. It pursued with unnerving speed. Even in the deep night, its burned bones seemed darker still and absorbed whatever light Rhaudian or the occasional oil street lantern could give. It sprinted with violent effort and gained on the crew, pumping its arms, clutching a buckler in one fist and a sword in the other.

"Hie!" shouted Jr'Dunn as he urged his mammoth to full speed. The others matched him, and they galloped wildly through the otherwise quiet avenue.

Mantieth and Elorall turned their bodies and drew their bows. They loosed arrow after arrow, but the missiles glanced off the bloodless charger who paid the bolts no mind. Their projectiles had no effect on them.

"The emblem!" Mantieth shouted, noting the decoration on the fiend's equipment. "It's a Teldrim sigil."

Hy'Targ risked a look back and saw it clearly: the same symbol they'd seen in the library sketches was engraved on the demon's shield.

Before the creature could catch them on the paved streets, the riders broke through the edge of town and galloped across the packed dirt and flat stone of the northbound Great Coastal Road.

Elorall stared at it in terrified wonder. The thing had locked eyes on Nohdan, as if it somehow knew the morehl had once come in contact with the sacred bones.

The lava elf risked a look back, recognizing the same thing. He gulped anxiously. Not understanding the connection, he asked, "What have you guys gotten me involved in? I think I'd like to go back to prison, now."

Elorall ignored him and muttered a few words of an incantation. She raised her hands to the sky, balancing precariously behind Vy'Hrothgyr on the rump of his mount. The air crackled overhead, and she shouted the final word of her spell. A flurry of snow and ice formed and spun above her; she wielded it like a weapon and blasted the skeletal stalker with a burst of snow and bitter cold that slowed its steps.

Still, it pushed forward, snarling at the cold which stymied its progress. It pressed harder, fuming with toxic rage.

The selumari caster, still growling arcane syllables at the bloodless and keeping her spell active, uttered a few more words and her frigid fury shifted from snowy cold to chunks of hard ice. First small, the balls of hail grew in size and intensity until they increased into boulders and smashed the beast apart.

Black bones scattered across the road, crushed beneath the shower of icy rocks that piled atop the chitinous debris. The mammoths finally pulled away and gained ground.

Hours later, as the ice melted under the growing morning light, none were around to see the lifeless pieces slowly shamble across the dusty road. Imbued with evil power, the fiend began to reassemble.

Given the extra boost of speed at the beginning of their day, the adventurers made excellent headway up the northern road, though they frequently looked over their shoulders for either undead or selumari interference. None ever came.

By evening they took over a small glen off the road and rested their animals. The dwarves built a fire and pitched lean-to tents within minutes.

Vy'Hrothgyr prepared food from their fresh, elven provisions and they laid down to sleep as if it was serious business. The trip had begun in earnest, and they knew that every leg of it would only grow more dangerous.

Hy'Targ awoke with a start as his dwarven companion nudged him. His shift for the night-watch had begun. He sat up, bleary-eyed, and tended the fire. It had not been stoked large, for the sake of stealth, but it dwindled too low for his comfort.

The edges of the glade boasted rough stumpage that he could investigate for burnable lumber. Hy'Targ wandered just beyond reach of the light provided by the dying embers as he searched for firewood. His toe kicked something hard beneath the matted grass, and he bent to examine it.

Still groggy, he grinned at his good fortune and scooped up a bundle of split logs left over by the last group to use the clearing as a campsite. He turned back and dropped the armload at the sight he found.

Nohdan crouched near the fire with a set of lock picks in hand. Hy'Targ had no idea where he'd gotten them.

"Hey!" the dwarf shouted, startling the crafty lava elf.

He looked up as the manacles fell from his wrists.

Hy'Targ charged forward, drawing Glorybringer as he ran.

Nohdan dropped his lockpicks snatched and drew Mantieth's vorpal blade from its place next to the sleeping elf. It sang a wicked song as the sheath released its hungry blade.

The vagha prince slowed his gait at the sight of the deadly weapon.

Nohdan whirled around and motioned as if to fling the magnificent blade at Hy'Targ, and then the weapon disappeared in the dim light.

Hy'Targ did a double take, looking over his shoulder. The weapon had simply disappeared! He had no idea why the criminal would even attempt something so foolish. He turned back to Nohdan and saw the morehl used the distraction as an opportunity to flee.

"Wake up! All of you! Nohdan is escaping!" Hy'Targ shouted as he chased the lava elf into the woods.

Vy'Danis reached for his axe, cranky from having his sleep interrupted. "I shouldda expected as much. Tried to warn em," he muttered. "Kids these days never listen…"

CHAPTER ELEVEN

Hy'Targ stared over his shoulder dumbfounded, just as Nohdan had intended. The morehl was used to using misdirection to create opportunities, and the red-skinned elf used an old trick to his advantage and then seized on its window. He turned and dashed into the forest, hoping to lose his pursuit in the trees with his cover made ever darker by the late hour and still pinching the needle between his thumb and forefinger.

Safely hidden within the foliage, he held the needle that had been Mantieth's vorpal sword only moments ago. He slid it into the callous skin of his forearm where he'd kept his lock picks up until now. Nohdan grinned at his own cleverness and then dashed further still into the dark.

He had no idea what the skeletal creature was that pursued him. The vagha and the two meddlesome coral elves he could easily elude, but he trusted only his own instincts to keep him safe from a bloodless. Nohdan was more vulnerable than ever with the motley collection of travelers keeping him confined in chains. Terrifying as the black skeleton was, he'd much prefer taking his chances in freedom while hunted than in captivity—especially with that untested twit, Mantieth, guarding him.

Branches cracked behind Nohdan as the clumsy dwarves crashed through the trees. They practically broadcast their positions to him.

Nohdan sprinted only a little further down a wild animal trail and then leapt onto a tree that looked easy enough to shimmy up. He grabbed handfuls of moss and hauled himself higher before perching inside a hollow at its top where he held his breath.

The lava elf nestled himself into the berth and watched his pursuers chase down the animal break and over pursue. He raised his eyebrows; it turned out the dwarves were decent trackers after all—had he not hid, they might have caught him, eventually. Two vagha milled about below the tree where he crouched and then finally split, running in opposite directions.

Nohdan finally relaxed and exhaled the tense lungful of air when something snaked around his ankles. He tried to scream, but another strong, vine-like hand wrapped around his mouth. The entire tree he sat in cracked and shifted as it rustled and moved. A booming voice called out.

"Good sirs. Are you searching for a red-skinned imp? If you have misplaced one, I might be of assistance."

Nohdan flailed impotently as the nine-cubit tall treefolk plucked him off its head and hoisted him high, dangling the thief a healthy distance in the air.

Hy'Targ and Elorall were the first to return.

"There you are," Elorall accused, looking up at the trapped prisoner.

"Thank you, kind efflorah," Hy'Targ greeted the treefolk. "It seems you have found our wayward prisoner."

The treefolk inclined his stumpy head towards the dwarf in greeting. "It seems I have. Is it vermin? Would you like me to dispose of it?" His strong grasp tightened and Nohdan's panicked protests muffled under its bark-skinned grip.

"No, please. We need him," Hy'Targ insisted. "He is supposed to guide us to an item we must protect if we are to stop a great evil from returning to our world."

The treefolk shook his leaves as if the notion gave him a chill. "Adventurers, eh? Perhaps I can offer you a trade?"

"What do you have in mind?" Hy'Targ asked. By now, the rest of his crew had arrived.

"My name is Rhyll'ee-vrng-nrnnnvv," he introduced himself in his native tongue, which sounded more like the creaking of windy branches than words. "You may call me Rhyll. I am searching for a cure for my people. Something is making the efflorah of my region sick. We call it," he paused, searching his mind for words that would translate to the common tongue, "Gray Blight. It has seized most of my grove. Many of them have wasted away. I… I was told not to leave the wood, but I was the only one not taken by the blight. Something in the water, methinks. The water had a black, churning slime. It even got Lavrildr…" he leaned forward with almost youthful enthusiasm as he described her, "She's a piney young efflorah… very prickly boughs," he said lasciviously, making the dwarves laugh and cringe at the same time.

"We will do our best to find some kind of cure if we can," Hy'Targ said, thinking back to the black slime he'd read about in the selumari library. "You are welcome to accompany us. Your Gray Blight sounds very much like a sickness caused by the Necralluvium."

Rhyll stiffened, not understanding.

"It's part of the same evil we are trying to stop," Hy'Targ informed him.

Rhyll set Nohdan down in front of his new friends. "Very well. I will help you confront this evil if it might save my Lavrildr. My people have quarantined themselves in a stony area alongside the Far Sea where a dryad tends them. I do not know how much time they have."

Hy'Targ scowled, "You and me both."

Mantieth jabbed a finger into Nohdan's shoulder. "My sword?"

The morehl scowled. "Fine, but an illusionist never reveals his tricks." He turned his back to the crowd while pulling the dragonstaff needle and returning it to its normal size; making one fluid motion, he made sure they could not see how he did it. Nohdan gripped the pommel and mumbled a simple illusion spell, changing the handle's grip to look more like the stolen vorpal sword so long as it did not come under intense scrutiny. He grinned at his trick and hoped the cocky selumari wouldn't notice the difference.

Nohdan finished his spin and offered it back to Mantieth, who snatched the blade and sheathed it without a second thought. Hy'Targ pocketed the lava elf's lockpicks as Elorall retrieved the manacles. The morehl hid his smile as they clamped the shackles back around his wrists. If they were going to keep him close by and bound by chains, he figured he might as well have some fun with them.

Br'Derluch stormed down the hall with his two companions in tow. His flush cheeks and squared jaw where his beard bounced barely contained his anger. Wo'Dunnia and Fi'Krayg kept in lockstep with him as they searched the castle for someone who could answer their questions.

Coral elf soldiers watched them carefully from the corner of their eyes as the delegate stomped through the corridor. The dwarves grumbled about how the selumari were already stirring rumors and accusing the delegates of kidnapping the much-loved Prince Mantieth… and they'd only now learned that Prince Hy'Targ had been in the city because of local gossip.

The vaghan emissary refused to let a lie get the upper hand in their negotiations. Br'Derluch would not be anybody's scapegoat.

He saw Furtaevell exiting a room up ahead and bellowed at him. "Oy! You—I need to have words with you and your king!" Br'Derluch hustled to catch him.

Furtaevell stiffened and tried to close the door before Br'Derluch could see that King Leidergelth was inside.

"Is he in there? That's him." Br'Derluch wedged a foot in the door before it closed.

"The king is…"

"Too busy to talk to diplomatic guests? He'll talk to me—and he'll do it now, Furtaevell. Why was I never informed that my Prince had arrived in Niamarlee? I demand to know his whereabouts."

Amid all the dwarf's bluster, a hand reached out from through the door and stayed Furtaevell who spat and sputtered, caught off guard. The door opened, revealing King Leidergelth and his cold demeanor.

"You were not informed because I withheld the information," he retorted with a voice like cold steel. Guards drew close in order to protect the king. He narrowed his eyes at the hotheaded diplomat. "I think your bluster might be all for show. How about *you* tell *me* where Hy'Targ is… I'm sure that is where I will find my missing prisoner… and *my son?*"

Br'Derluch looked at him cross eyed. "I have no idea what you're talking about!"

"Which is exactly what I would assume you'd say if you were a collaborator in Mantieth's abduction. Was it you who hired the morehl thief to steal one of our greatest weapons?" Leidergelth nodded his head to his guards, and they put hands on their hilts. "How long have you wanted to see Niamarlee burn from dragon fire?"

"That's preposterous!"

"Take them!" the king growled.

Fi'Krayg's hands flashed, and the dwarf bodyguard snatched a small axe and a dagger from beneath his cloak. He leapt in front of Br'Derluch. "It's a trap—run!"

Br'Derluch stumbled as he whirled around. The selumari soldiers closed in and Br'Derluch shoved Wo'Dunnia past their line. "Get out of here—tell King Hy'Mandr we are betrayed!" The elves were on the diplomat a moment later, wrestling Br'Derluch to the ground.

Next to the king, Fi'Krayg howled with rage and the Leidergelth's personal guard fell on him with their blades. The stubborn dwarf refused to surrender even in the face of overwhelming odds. He forced their hands as Furtaevell tried desperately to restrain the elven soldiers in order to retain any possibility of diplomatic negotiations—Fi'Krayg's bright red blood splattered across the High Enchanter's robes.

Wo'Dunnia dashed down the hall like a jackrabbit. Elves tried to tackle him as he neared, but the lanky vagha juked and slipped beyond their reach.

Another band of sentries roared around a corner, hemming him in.

The dwarf dashed to the second-floor window and leapt through with barely a second glance.

His pursuit skidded to a stop and looked out across the courtyard, seeking him with their keen, elven eyes.

"He's gone," one yelled, unable to find him.

Someone screamed out the window above them and they turned their eyes up, just in time to catch sight of his boots slipping behind the buttress where he'd climbed.

"He's gone up top-the bleedin gurk scaled the coral brick…"

"Sound the alarm!"

Wo'Dunnia sprinted through the corridors which narrowed the higher up the keep went. He took a hard left and ducked through a door that led to a steep, spiral staircase; the dwarf heard footsteps behind him, stomping nearly as loud as the chiming signal bells.

He slammed the door shut and rammed his dagger into the frame in order to pin the barrier closed. Wo'Dunnia knew it wouldn't last long; he leapt the remaining stairs two at a time until the vertical passage emptied into a long, open plank of stone.

The dwarf dashed across the landing path atop the castle's roof and into the covered eyrie. He snatched a nearby shovel and rushed upon the caretaker before the old selumari even knew he was there. Wo'Dunnia clubbed him unconscious with a swift crack to the head. He rushed deeper into the enclosure before the elf had fully collapsed in an unconscious heap. Ankle ropes tethered half a dozen massive eagles within their berths.

Wo'Dunnia smashed the first five of them on one shoulder as he rushed by. The gruesome cracking sound made the damaged birds shriek all that much louder. He leapt onto the barding of the last one and released its lead rope.

Behind him, the door from the stairwell finally burst open and the royal guards reached the eyrie.

Suddenly glad for his comparatively slight size and weight, Wo'Dunnia urged the raptor over the edge of the building, hoping that steering the creature was as easy as the selumari riders made it look to be. The bird flapped his wings and cleared the edge of the castle, mainly for self-preservation. Wo'Dunnia tried to manipulate the creature with different tactics that he'd learned riding ponies, lizard mounts, and whatever else he could think of. He struggled to do it, but found enough sense of control that he thought he might actually survive. The eagle tried to glide back home twice, but then began obeying the witless pilot's commands.

He looked over his shoulder once he got the eagle pointed towards the Irontooth Mountain and glanced nervously at the Coral Airship overhead—he'd be out of range in a few moments and the bloated skyboats were notoriously slow until they'd gained enough momentum. The airship wouldn't be a problem if there were no more eagles and riders upon it.

Behind him, three guards forced the wounded birds into the air to give chase, urged onward by impatient riders who refused to heed the birds' pained screeches. Eagles and riders both shrieked loudly as they plummeted to their deaths on broken wings.

Wo'Dunnia gripped the reins, gritted his teeth, and flew towards the horizon.

Melkior sat on the third floor of his ruined citadel, beneath the gray, burnt sky that hung above. Tireless, bloodless workers shambled past him, carrying new hunks of obsidian; undead masons slowly reconstructed the once ivory stronghold in shades of black harvested from the defiled and broken earth. A trio of them rolled a cask filled with black powder out from the tower and pushed it through the wreckage of the old town on their way to the beach with an altogether different assignment.

He'd closed his eyes in meditation and communed with the deepest, foulest magics of Esfah. With powerful talons, the undead dragon Rahkawmn stood watch over his master, protecting the lich with diligent loyalty. The sentinel loomed above the busted citadel like a watchful gargoyle.

From his trance, Melkior felt every seed of corruption that fouled the environment. Every spring of roiling Necralluvium, deposited long ago by Leisterbane, availed itself to him. Every festration opened to his sight as if a blooming flower. They connected to him through the spirit of Malgrimm... somewhere at the furthest reaches of Esfah he sensed his minion's spirit. He would call upon Leisterbane when the time was right.

He felt the potential in the soil, dead bodies scattered below him. Bones turn in mass graves, steeped in the Necralluvium's oily filth; animated corpses waited for his beck and call. He communed with undead, carrion, and other spies, but he still could not find the object of his desire: his beloved Ailushurai who had been laid to rest in a tomb alongside him. He'd slept for so long that he did not know when or who had taken her from him—his beloved was snatched away from him for the third time.

Rage boiled up within him at the thought of her being stolen again. His mind flung back to that fateful day and he let his mind stray into memory: the *second* time she'd been taken from him.

Melkior remembered descending into the heart of the Abyss and risked all to reclaim Ailushurai's soul from the maddening jaws of the hell-scape where Selurehl reigned—he was called Void, Tarvanehl's brother and the father of Malgrimm himself. With Ailushurai's spark of life extinguished, she could only be reclaimed from the afterlife by permission of the third member of the elder gods. Passage through the Abyss was Voids purview. While the ancient sages and sorcerers had sometimes come and gone undetected, taking a soul from the nether was a different matter entirely.

He'd only barely wrested away ownership of Ailushurai's soul by convincing the god Selurehl of his commitment to prospering his son, Malgrimm, and pledging to annihilate the remaining champions of the gods: his onetime allies.

Melkior's plans for Ailushurai were loftier than mere animation. He did not want some mindless automaton—he wanted *her* restored to him, mind, body, and soul and had claimed the very deed to her spirit. Selurehl had written that deed with ink upon his chest.

Death's general had come out of the trance to discovered that his previous allies, the other Champions of the gods who he and Ailushurai had once fought alongside, had taken her body. He learned that his former friends hoped to hide her remains in Xlinea or send them further over the sea so that Melkior could never restore her to life.

Leisterbane, his general, had been tasked with remaining in Melkior's deadlands and spreading Malgrimm's darkness across the land while the converted lich went off on his mad venture.

The resulting battle had been deliciously horrific. His former compatriots fought and paid with their lives in their efforts to keep him from his lover. They clashed upon the Raithlan Plains with legendary fury.

Melkior relived every moment in his mind, re-visited every kill as he slew his former friends. One by one they fell; as they laid dying, Arfetsus, the Amazon hero clung to the body of Ailushurai, unwilling to give her up. Bleeding on the ground lay the vagha, Klagend and the morehl, Aeschere.

As Melkior advanced on her with singular and deadly purpose, Aeschere and Klagend lent Arfetsus their very spirits and the Amazonion spell caster channeled a dreadful, powerful spell and touched the lich with the very thing that could undo him: a spark of life. The heroes traded their lives for a powerful burst of life-instilling energies, forcing them into his corptic body; the lich could no longer function as an undead. Life sapped the spirit of death from him.

In order to keep him from reuniting with Ailushurai, his best friends willingly laid down their lives to confine his soul within the prison of his flesh as he crumbled. Thus ended the first age of champions. Arfetsus's followers and the eldarim among them built Ailushurai's tomb in secret and honored the dead by their burial.

The lich snarled and returned to better memories of him and his beloved. He remembered the warm days when he and Ailushurai sunned themselves in their secret beach-side hideaway. They would occasionally sneak away to the grassy coastal land and make love amongst the heather and watch the twice daily moonrises above the horizon and guess what secrets the bright planet Leguin could hold. That was before *the interloper* To'ur entered the scene with his army of horse-lords and encamped around Lurneville, stealing Ailushurai for the *first* time.

Melkior's reverie ended when his senses caught a faint odor. He opened his eyes… he was not in his body, but within the body of his scout—one of the Burned Ones he'd sent into the world to locate her… it was faint, but a morehl to the south carried it. *He had handled her bones.*

The skeletal creature pursued the lava elf until it could go no more, temporarily smashed beneath a glacial blast conjured by a selumari. Trapped beneath the ice, his sight faded into a frosty, white mist.

Melkior scowled and concentrated his energies elsewhere. Using the magic pent up within his black heart, he urged the undead up from the surface, calling to them, demanding that they answer his call to muster.

The lich shared his sight with Rahkawmn, and the dragon flapped his mighty wings, tattered as they were, and took to the sky. The wighted creature had slowed considerably in death, but he remained as powerful as he ever was in life. Rahkawmn angled for the southern horizon; if its prey was there—if the bones were near the elf, the dragon needed to be closer for his master's purpose. As soon as the scouts located a clue again, Rahkawmn would be prepared for action.

Watching his oldest friend go, Melkior smiled at the dragon. Melkior would find the lava elf and he would have his answers—and armed with that knowledge his growing army would march across the face of Esfah and take back what was stolen.

CHAPTER TWELVE

Nohdan sat grumpily behind his vagha babysitter as their mounts rushed forward. Mid-morning was in full blossom and the party had made considerably better time than the elves had guessed given the creatures' size.

Rhyll walked alongside the mastodons, standing only slightly taller, and taking long strides to keep up.

"Our trail turns off from the Great Coastal Road about a league ahead, past the next farm, just ahead," Mantieth promised. "At this rate, my father's scouts will never find us… not so far out."

Hy'Targ glanced backwards and remembered his own father's words before departing. *Esfah has never been a safe world, and I fear it may be getting worse.* Hy'Targ decided he'd been right all along: it was safer to explore his world from the chair of a library than by adventuring.

The small farm, mostly surrounded by thick copses of trees, slowly came into view as they plodded on. Hy'Targ's mammoth seemed jittery. The dwarf smelled the air; he tasted it heavy on the breeze: iron. Blood.

Slaughtered animals lay strewn all over the field, laid haphazardly within their own bloody pools. Whatever had killed them had done it for sport rather than for food.

Hy'Targ called them to a halt in front of the farmstead's main road. He stared at the house, uncertain if he'd seen movement or not. "What could have done this? trogs?"

Mantieth grimaced and scanned the scene. Blood splattered across the door frame; its plank construction hung shifted upon busted hinges. "I don't know. Maybe monsters? There are no tracks." The hard-packed earth had not received rain enough to loosen any soil near the Great Coastal Road.

They turned their mounts into the approach and walked them cautiously towards the house. Nohdan, thinking about the black skeleton and fearful of another encounter, hissed, "We don't have time for this. We should be on the trail by now."

He may have been right, but the party ignored his protests.

Hy'Targ nodded to four of his fellow dwarves, who climbed down to explore the farmhouse. The vagha tentatively approached and crept into the house with axes in hand. Moments after the door closed, shouting erupted inside.

Vy'Hrothgyr's distinct voice howled, "A monster!" And then sounds of a scuffle.

One dwarf went flying through a window, one of Jr'Dunn's kinsmen, Jr'Orhr, busted through the glass and rolled across the lawn, slightly dazed. "So much blood inside," he mumbled.

A massive creature busted through the front door with Vy'Hrothgyr chasing him out, bleeding from the scalp. "The monster! He did this—I saw him holding the bodies of the children..."

Elorall and Mantieth had arrows nocked and ready in a flash.

"Stop!" yelled Hy'Targ, looking at the four-armed creature. "I know him." The dwarf prince slid to the ground and rushed to the homunculus who had helped him days earlier. "By the gods, Varanthl... what happened here?"

Varanthl looked up, bleary eyed and with all four forearms stained red with blood; his torn shirt hung wide open to expose the stitch-scarred flesh beneath. "Hy'Targ... Hy'Targ, I should have gone with you when you invited me. D-dead. The family of mud-bloods. They're all dead," he wept.

But Hy'Targ only half heard him. He was staring at his friend's chest. There, through the rip in his shirt, he saw it plainly. Hy'Targ recognized it from the sketch: Life-bringer.

The Kreethaln he sought was attached to the homunculus's breast.

"But he's covered in blood," Jr'Orhr protested. The scuffed dwarf picked himself up from the ground carefully in order to avoid the busted glass.

For a moment, Hy'Targ felt tempted to simply agree and execute the creature so he could take the Kreethaln from Varanthl's chest. He tightened his lips and brushed the tickling whiskers away from the edges. His conscience would never let him rest if he did.

Varanthl sat on his knees, hands covered up to all four elbows with the blood of friend and foe, a red and yellow painting only broken up by the bracelet he wore on each of his four wrists.

The dwarven prince recognized the look on his face. It was the same one he wore when he'd learned of the loss of his mother, Queen Sh'Ttil.

"Of course he's covered in it," Hy'Targ bit back. "*Everything* is covered in blood. Wouldn't *you* be a mess if you'd tried to protect someone from this kind of onslaught?"

Jr'Orhr grumbled, but conceded the point.

"Tell us what happened," Elorall said softly while Rhyll walked a nervous loop around the perimeter.

"Horns… battle horns, and then they came, snarling and pounding blade against shield. They swarmed over the land, coming from the trees. Some small, some bigger than me. Green and oily," Varanthl shuddered.

"trogs," Mantieth spat.

Hy'Targ scanned the destruction all around them. "I don't know about your northern goblins, but the small pockets nearest us don't kill like this. They take only what they can claim for their meals—and they're not particularly skilled for war." He bit his lower lip, "Unless..."

Vy'Danis put a heavy hand on the prince's shoulder and nodded. "It's not some hunting or raiding party. It's like the other ones we encountered before Niamarlee: young and inexperienced ones... a new brood. A large one—but someone is blooding them."

The elves traded worried glances. "This... this was *practice*?"

Hy'Targ nodded. "Whoever is in charge wants to make sure his soldiers have seen battle and tasted blood."

Every member of the party whirled to face the woods on the west. A horn trumpeted within the trees.

A swamp crawler trotted out from the foliage. It resembled a twisted horn-beetle the size of a wolf. The animal opened its split jaws and scooped up one of the few remaining chickens that meandered around the property. The filthy beast swallowed it whole. Startled when it saw the rescuers; it turned and shrieked at the non-trogs.

Mantieth put an arrow through its head. Bloodthirsty cries reverberated in the western woods.

"I think it's time to go," Nohdan barked, shaking his chains for emphasis.

"I think he's right," Elorall said.

Varanthl stood to his full height and stepped back towards the house to grab the hammer he'd brought with him from the crypt. His armor laid strewn in pieces nearer the building, useless and hacked apart after the initial trog attack.

The dwarves turned the mammoths away, and another horn pealed in response. East. Through the trees the adventurers spotted a dark line of invaders crossing the Great Coastal Road, hemming them in with a wave of green hide and yellow eyes.

"There," Hy'Targ pointed. A tall goblinoid wearing red and white paint dropped the war-horn so that it hung around his neck on a leather cord.

He snarled at them, amber eyes recognizing the party from the earlier attack with the troll. Mantieth loosed an arrow, but the fiend stepped back behind a kite shield which caught the missile. It bore a sign of the Niamarlee army; he'd obviously taken it from some fallen selumari.

The dwarves brandished their axes and roared with defiance. "To the mammoths," Vy'Danis urged. "We can trample the lot of em if they get close and make a break for it."

Three vagha and Mantieth took one step for the mounts and then fell to their knees, too nauseous to move. Even one of the mammoths bowed, panting and shivering as if it might not survive the sudden wave of sickness.

"Magic," Elorall hissed, spotting the trog mage who stood near the painted goblin, decked out with a headdress and breastplate made of yellowed bones.

It flung a ball of black death magic at them.

Elorall splayed her fingers to the air and erected her shield just in time. The cloud of diseased filth splattered around them and dissipated like a swarm of flies.

The mage sneered and threw another spell, which split apart into javelin-like missiles. They rained down on them like jagged missiles of ballistic death magic.

Their coral elf caster groaned. Her protective shield held, but barely.

Cries of the enemy encircled the party from every side. They couldn't flee without leaving some behind, and they could not all fit inside the house.

"The barn!" Varanthl pointed, he scooped up Mantieth with one set of arms, and the vomiting Jr'Orhr in his others as he led the sprint. The mastodons trotted after him, recognizing it as the last place of safety. The sickened mammoth tried to run, but faltered. Rhyll turned to drag it behind him and managed to coax it into the shelter.

Trogs charged out from the woods behind them and swarmed across the farmstead, pinning them down inside the barn. Their victorious cries echoed so loud they vibrated the wooden shakes protecting the outbuilding from the weather.

Mantieth groaned, trembling on the floor alongside the others afflicted by the palsy. Elorall's blue skin had also turned a lighter shade. She paled as she struggled to rebuff the constant enervations of the skilled trog mage. All eyes looked to Hy'Targ.

Through the slits in the wood panels, they watched the farmhouse ignite as marauding goblins lit it ablaze.

Worry bled into Rhyll's voice. He might have survived on his own against arrow and bullet... but fire was a threat in a class apart for the treefolk. He asked, "What do we do now?"

Varanthl's grip tightened on the haft of his hammer as he watched from the cracked doorway of the barn. He stood side by side with the dwarf and assessed the dire situation.

"Last time we saw each other we faced overwhelming odds... looks like one of us is bad luck," Hy'Targ said. He suddenly hoped King Leidergelth's eagle riders might have been shadowing them this whole time. Maybe the selumari forces would ride to their rescue at any second.

The goblin death mage strolled cockily between his rioting troops and the bunker where they'd cowed the adventurers. Behind him, the swarm of trogs bounced up and down enthusiastically, like greenish yellow waves breaking upon a shore. He cast spell after spell, wearing down Elorall's ability to resist the death magic.

Varanthl watched the female caster wilt beneath the pressure. His jaw set and righteous indignation welled up within him. He caught sight of the bracelets he'd put on each wrist as a reminder of the family that took in the homunculus: Jordyll,

Gherbin, Ferthalin. Varanthl's normally soft-spoken demeanor broke and his eyes burned with anguished passion; he kicked the door open with a furious roar and charged towards the goblin mage.

The trog army froze, surprised by the four-armed maniac. Their death mage blasted him with bolt after bolt of black magic that would have given even a dragon pause. With each spell, the thing on Varanthl's chest pulsed with a jolt of invigorating energy; the arcane power sloughed off his barbarian body, splashing harmlessly aside like water off duck feathers.

He crossed the path in mere seconds and hoisted the hammer high above his head. Hurled it down upon the trog spell-caster, the impact smashed him to gooey bits as if he were an egg. Varanthl looked up and roared at the army, which pressed in on every side.

Goblins everywhere froze with fear. Most of them were still young, and so many recoiled.

In the stillness that followed, the vagha rushed from the barn. Three of them rode mounts and tore through the flanks, trampling green skinned thugs while their mammoths trumpeted. Rhyll plowed through another flank, crushing the little green soldiers as if they'd been mere fungal polyps on a log. The terrifying howls of an enraged tree-beast routed the unblooded warriors, and they scattered before him. Rhyll stomped them out like little fires, splattering ochre blood as they fled before him.

Elorall followed them out, blasting the goblins' rear line with an icy wind; she flung a bolt of lightning into the only crowd brave enough to stand their ground and the smoldering trogs collapsed in a singed heap of dead flesh.

Alleviated somewhat, Mantieth staggered to his feet as the worst of the palsy lifted after the sorcerer's demise. Nohdan watched him anxiously from his spot in the barn, eagerly waiting for the elven prince to drive his disguised blade into an enemy.

Hy'Targ's axe cut through trog after trog. He cleared a path before Varanthl and locked eyes, staring down the red and white smeared commander.

The trog leader glared at the dwarf and the homunculus who stood side by side, threatening him with murderous stares. Finally, the commander blew the horn for retreat.

Goblins fled back to the cover of the woods and swamps. Catching the last line of trogs in route, the painted commander screamed back, "We will be back—and next time, with our warlord. He will tear your flesh from bone."

Varanthl snarled at him in defiant response. Mantieth and the others finally caught up to him.

They caught their breath as they watched the trogs disappear beyond the horizon. Finally, they allowed their fatigued shoulders to slump. A long, wordless silence passed over them and the heat of the burning house warmed their faces as they recovered.

"What now?" Varanthl finally asked.

Hy'Targ rested a hand on Varanthl's lower shoulders. "This time you come with us." He scanned his companion, careful not to let his eyes linger too long on Varanthl's chest. "Truly, I'm not letting you out of my sight again."

Varanthl nodded solemnly. He twisted the bracelets on his wrists as he watched the flames of what had become an unanticipated funeral pyre.

"We'll give you a few moments," Hy'Targ said, letting the homunculus mourn while he and the others prepared their mounts to resume the trek. They needed to reach Undrakull soon… and to hopefully do so without adding yet another powerful enemy to the line of them arrayed against the party.

Hy'Targ thoughtfully bit the interior of his cheek. The entire journey had been one disaster after another. He'd found the object of his quest—and even that, too, had become another complicated situation.

Furtaevell awoke in a cold sweat. He flopped over to the side of his bed where he kept a journal in his nightstand.

With his daughter's disappearance, along with Mantieth's, he already worried constantly for her safety, but he refused to jump to unfounded conclusions. Before falling asleep, Furtaevell had convinced himself of the most obvious outcome: that Elorall had finally succeeded in wooing the clueless prince and they'd absconded for a few nights to indulge themselves in the impetuous nature of young love.

The arcane vision he'd received dismantled that notion. A future that he'd just seen shredded his heart and turned his stomach.

Scribbling feverishly, the mage made sure he recorded everything he'd seen in the spectral dream. His hand seemed to move of its own accord, detailing the entire sequence of events and drawing horrific, detailed depictions of it. As the omen's grip released, his hands slowed, and he dropped the charcoal stylus he'd used to draw the portent scenes. He'd created pages and pages of text and illustrations by magical impulse.

Furtaevell gasped as he read the notes back: he'd seen his daughter, laid dead and split open upon a wasteland; rotting corpses with hollow eyes ate her soft parts. She had vagha companions who were already dead and pulled to pieces. Mantieth fought blindly as he bled out from his empty sockets; a terrible lich finished devouring his eyes which he'd scooped out with clawed fingers.

Prince Hy'Targ was there. His arm, as well as Elorall's and Mantieth's, wore matching bracelets. A fourth laid at the bottom of an uprooted tree that burned with fire. Flames covered everything and eventually they consumed even Mantieth, who collapsed in a blazing heap.

Furtaevell pitched back over the side of the bed and vomited all over his floor. He wiped his mouth and trembled, recognizing the signs. Despite his rank and power as an enchanter, premonition had never been the gift most inclined to him, and whenever it struck, nausea and vertigo always accompanied it. Though it was rare for him… when it *did* strike, the oracular visions were powerful and accurate.

He rolled to his feet and took two steps, stumbled, and fell to his knees, sending the book sprawling. Furtaevell puked again. The king had to know that he'd had the dream.

The results of his fevered artwork laid open, splayed for him to see when he bent to pick up the journal. A detailed sketch stared back at him: the visage of Melkior, the dread lich general of the First Age, he'd drawn at the center of the two-page spread. Melkior held Mantieth's severed head in one hand and stared forward as if the drawing could see whoever looked upon it.

Furtaevell's heart leapt, and he snapped it shut.

After getting to his feet and steadying himself, the arcanist headed for King Leidergelth's chamber. He cursed Leidergelth's legendary stubbornness—*that vagha prince told us what his quest was, and the king dismissed him!* Despite the hour, the selumari king had to know what was at stake with the dwarves' mission… Elorall and Mantieth were certainly among them, and their mission was a doomed one.

CHAPTER THIRTEEN

Wo'Dunnia felt himself growing faint atop his winged mount. He'd been flying for a long time, and he hadn't eaten or drank anything since his escape from Niamarlee. His thirst was only aggravated by the rushing wind that parched his mouth and dried his eyes; the dwarf was too afraid that he wouldn't be able to get the bird into the sky again if they stopped for food or water... and that's provided he could even figure out how to land the durned thing.

The eagle also suffered the same ways. Wo'Dunnia had spent much unnecessary time fighting with the bird who kept trying to veer towards rivers or ponds. Finally, with the Irontooth mountain finally looming large where it protruded up from the Stonejaw Mountain Range south of Niamarlee, the eagle realized their destination.

After circling around the main portion of the exterior fortress at a high altitude, the bird began a spiraling descent with large, lazy loops.

Far below, Wo'Dunnia heard the blow of a signal horn, and his heart leapt. "They've spotted us," he told the bird.

The eagle cocked one amber eye back to its rider, but only momentarily, as if to insist that it be fed and watered in exchange for its services... and soon.

Wo'Dunnia leaned forward and patted the mount, and then nearly fell out of the seat when the bird bucked and rolled. The dwarf yelped and grabbed a hold of the barding.

Crossbow bolts zipped through the air near them.

"Hey, you blind dolts!" Wo'Dunnia screamed as his mount tried to flee.

He managed to wrangle the bird back around and angle it back to the fortress amid the lookouts on the defense tower firing at them. His eagle interpreted Wo'Dunnia's maneuvers as an attack and curled its wings, coming back at a steep trajectory that picked up speed. The diplomatic aide remembered too late that their airspace was protected by old accords, and they'd always insisted enemies with flight ability not violate their boundaries.

Too late now! He'd never arrive alive at the proper landing place after entering the no-fly zone. His only hope was that one of his kin would realize it was a vaghan rider and not a coral elf.

Wo'Dunnia howled and slapped the reins, trying to slow the bird. More pointed death flew at them like deadly hail.

Finally, afraid that he was going to crash, he yanked up on his reins and jerked the eagle's head high. His ride flared its wings wide and slowed so sharply that it nearly stopped entirely. It hovered for a long moment, and then the vagha sentries riddled it with missiles.

The majestic creature tumbled the last thirty cubits to the ground and Wo'Dunnia clutched it all the way down like a flume rider, screaming dwarven curses the whole way. It crashed to the dirt inside the walls and scattered gravel and feathers, skidding to a stop more quickly than the diplomatic aide who rolled another dozen cubits.

Wo'Dunnia finally tumbled to a stop in front of the dwarven security outpost. He barely managed to open his eyelids through his abrasion covered face and looked up to find the deadly end of a dozen crossbows pointed at his face.

"It-it's a dwarf," one of them said with surprise.

"Take me to General Mi'Darrio," Wo'Dunnia barely croaked.

"The Warchief is not here. At least, I don't think he has returned. He's away on King's business…"

"I don't care *who*," Wo'Dunnia blurted. "Take me to *someone*… or the king himself. I have grave news."

The travelers looked over the shoulders for the remainder of the trek to Undrakull. Constant paranoia kept their chatter to a minimum, aside from Rhyll's occasional comparison of nearby trees to his beloved Lavrildr. Not much else said, and a wave of relief washed over them as the rise of the plateau finally etched itself upon the horizon.

Finally, they broke through a foggy bank between the trees and the vertical cliff face. "Is it always so foggy here?" Elorall asked.

Vy'Danis nodded. "It has been every time I've been near," said the old vagha. He and Jr'Dunn had traveled more than the rest combined, except for the morehl. "I bet that one knows why," he waved towards Hy'Targ.

The prince smirked. "You know, reading is not a character flaw, Vy'Danis."

He shrugged, but Hy'Targ continued. "There's a lava flow beneath the city, it's why the morehl tunneled up and into the plateau instead of down and into the surface. The magma burns off a lot of the swampland's excess moisture creating the fog."

"Good," Elorall said as they settled the mammoths down and prepped themselves. Typically, such thick banks of mist were the result of conjuration, and none were in a fighting mood so soon again after the most recent goblin attack.

Rhyll rumbled around in the wispy fog bank behind them; he shook his branches and basked in the cool moisture. Jr'Dunn followed his nose and led the first of their mammoths towards a pool of water. Right before the beast plunged its trunk into the still water, the treefolk grabbed the animal and yanked it back. The mammoth snorted in surprise.

He pointed to the water, "Do not drink here," he insisted, and took Jr'Dunn closer after he settled the thirsty animal down.

Finally, Jr'Dunn spotted it. A dead lava elf lay face up at the bottom of the shallow, fetid pool. Most of its skin had eroded away or been devoured by tiny, aquatic carrion. It's empty eye sockets and most of its skull wore a patch of black, inky ooze that floated like a slime.

"That's it. That's the same stuff that gave my grove the Gray Blight."

Jr'Dunn nodded. "I'll find somewhere else to water 'em."

The older dwarf passed by Hy'Targ and his elf companions, who still were not ready to release the thief, Nohdan, even though the morehl argued for it.

"Nohdan *is* right about one thing. We can't all go in," Hy'Targ stated the obvious. "We'd be spotted right away."

"I have a plan for that," Elorall said. "The four of us will go in. I'll cast a disguise spell to conceal our identities."

Hy'Targ and the two selumari looked to Nohdan, who nodded skeptically. "It could work," he said. "But you will need to follow my lead once inside. Her magic can make you *look* like me, but you will *never* truly be morehl. There is more to an elf than just his or her skin color." He held up his bound hands and shook them. "I cannot do this in chains. This mission will require your trust."

Mantieth frowned and threatened, "Very well, but if you double cross us in there, you are the first one who dies."

Nohdan nodded. "I expected no less."

Elorall cast her spell, and their figures shifted slightly. No changes appeared more dramatic than the hue of their skin and hair, which deepened to match the dark crimson worn by Nohdan.

The true lava elf grinned at the disguised dwarf. "You're still a little short for a morehl."

Elorall turned to cast another spell, summoning an even denser wall of fog. The bank of mist settled over the crew they left behind and concealed them as they rested while the others searched out the bones. Securing them was only the first step—they would still need to face Melkior… but they had to remove them from the field of play first if they were to stand a fighting chance.

Varanthl wished them luck. "Please don't die. If you do, I'd have to kill all these lava elves inside, and I'm certain some of them are very pleasant folk."

Hy'Targ clapped the homunculus on the arm. "Keep an eye out for us; watch our back. I have no idea what's really inside that city, but if the bones of Ailushurai are actually there, then there's a good chance we are courting even more trouble by trying to steal them."

Nohdan quipped, "Well, it's a good thing you're bringing me along. I'm sort of an expert at stealing these bones."

The morehl turned on his heel and walked towards the plateau. The vagha traded silent, well-wishing nods, and the rest of the party followed their guide.

A large opening tunneled through the side of the plateau's vertical face. Gravel and loose scree formed a sloping road that led up to the entrance. Several morehl soldiers stood watch at the gate and a short line of merchants sat in the queue outside as they bartered with the troops for entrance; none of those folk were lava elves; morehl were free to come and go from the city.

The motley mix of races in the line pulled rickshaws or drove ponies with wagons laden for trade. A bedraggled dwarf with an eyepatch and a wooden leg successfully bartered his way past the entrance and pulled his cart inside.

"Don't pass deeper than the main hall," the guards warned him. "Your life depends on it—only morehl are allowed beyond it... lava elves *and her*... the matron."

A nearby guard threw a pebble at his companion. "Why'd you go warning him... he's just a crusty old vagha? Nobody cares if he wanders off and gets himself gutted for not knowing the rules." They paid the disguised adventurers no mind and didn't even give the fake lava elves a second look, letting them freely pass into Undrakull unmolested.

Hy'Targ's lip curled as they mocked the vagha tradesman, but he said nothing as he and his companions passed the crippled vendor. An expansive hall yawned open before them that bustled with traffic and a vibrant community of mixed races.

Fine, stone craft pillars extended floor to ceiling, nearly three hundred cubits! Hy'Targ marveled at it briefly, wondering how the morehl had achieved such marvelous workmanship... then he spotted their makers marks—grooves and stamps that functioned like a signature for its creators. Dwarves had built this: most likely slaves early in the second age. Undrakull had been a possible source for the anti-vagha sentiments that led to Niamarlee's earlier enslavement of his people—a curse that lasted for several generations.

Buildings and freestanding structures stood within the great hall where non-segregated commerce boomed. Undrakull's streets buzzed with activity and movement. Long cords stretched across the walls high above where flags hung and flapped overhead in the hot winds. In true morehl fashion, rings around the walls of the city displayed the corpses of long dead lava elf soldiers; they'd been stationed high above in corptic repose so they could watch over their city for all time. That was the highest honor for those fallen in battle.

The heat in the place made the adventurers' garb chafe uncomfortably at best. The magmic flow created a kind of convection system that moved the air through the interior of

Undrakull Commontown until it exited the porthole vents dug into the sides of the plateau.

Nohdan walked at a brisk pace, nearly slipping away from his charges, but they'd determined not to lose him in the crowds of Undrakull's Commontown market.

They'd neared the far edge of the dwarf-made chamber and skulked around a portal to a carved stair that left the area. Hy'Targ caught up and grabbed him by the arm. "Where are you taking us?"

Nohdan eyed him quizzically. "You did not think this was the *real* Undrakull?" His mouth twisted with distaste. "This is merely Commontown. Anyone can enter here; where I am taking you is into the heart of the true morehl city... where only lava elves may go."

He shook his arm free as the others arrived and ducked through the portal; this one seemed built with far less aesthetic in mind. Gone were the fine grooves and flat surfaces. A dark warren with twisted tunnels wound through the stone like bowels of the great plateau. Walls of the grottos plumed with lichen, mushrooms, and other foliage that glowed with dull illumination; most of these plants were toxic to other races, but consumed by the morehl as delicacies. Some passages looked like old lava tubes, crusted and sharp with igneous traits, others were pitted and jagged as if hewn by a race with little appreciation for stonework.

The tunnels mostly increased the elevation and eventually looped back around before yawning wide and into another cavernous opening. Railings on the far edge guarded against the steep fall off a balcony edge which overlooked Commontown. The updraft fed a hot wind into Undrakull, which kept the climate stiflingly hot and threatened to dry the eyes of Nohdan's companions.

More huts, built of lava stone and mortar, populated the actual morehl city. The exterior foundations of the fancier homes boasted more corpses. Skeletons of family members were built into the foundations, noble and positioned with heads up; enemies likewise, but with heads buried and bodies inverted to mark them shamed for eternity. Despite the uniformity and morbidity of their materials, the structures somehow seemed more opulent than those buildings below in Commontown. Red lights of fire and alchemy dotted the streets between the structures, along with the dull sheen provided by more lichens and fungi.

In the center of the community towered a large building that had obviously once been a temple. In the dim light, they could barely make it out, but noted that all religious iconography had been stripped from the facility.

Nohdan splayed his arms wide and introduced the town to his fellow traveling companions. "Welcome to Undrakull."

King Hy'Mandr Irontooth sat on his throne in the empty chamber, contemplating the news. Mi'Darrio had only just recently returned with a report of his son's quest. It sounded as if Esfah had grown more dangerous than expected these last twelve years.

He ground his teeth, wishing he could do something other than send emissaries to talk on his behalf. Hy'Mandr cursed the darkness and leaned over his seat to lay a hand on the armrest of the vacant queen's chair, wishing his bygone wife could advise him.

Hy'Mandr sighed, and then the door burst open as Taryl entered.

"My lord," the eldarim called out as he approached with a quickened pace. "Taryl here. I need a word."

The King bobbed his head, identifying him by his voice. He'd employed the eldarim champion for many years. Aside from his adventuring buddies and maybe Ne'Vistar, there was nobody he trusted more.

"News from Niamarlee."

Hy'Mandr's face twisted into a frown. "I'm guessing by your speed that it is not a positive report?"

Taryl shook his head, but only for his own benefit. "No. Wo'Dunnia has arrived on a stolen eagle."

"Wo'Dunnia... *the runner*?"

"Yes. He was the aide to Br'Derluch..."

"Was?" Hy'Mandr stood to his feet, heat rising off his chest.

"Ne'Vistar approaches." Taryl greeted the scholar as a second pair of footsteps entered. The eldarim.

"I came as soon as I heard," the old spell caster said, slightly winded.

"Report," Hy'Mandr bid Taryl to continue.

"There must have been some a mix up in Leidergelth's castle. The selumari king accused Br'Derluch of helping your son free prisoners, steal a powerful weapon to use against Niamarlee, and possibly kidnap Prince Mantieth."

"That's preposterous," Hy'Mandr spat. "He's on a quest near the amazon plains, one that only recently turned him towards the wastelands on the upper peninsula. And besides— have you *met my son*? He wouldn't hurt a soul, except to maybe drop a book on his foot."

"Regardless, they killed Br'Derluch's bodyguard and captured your emissary."

The king growled and shifted on his feet. He reached back to where Queen Sh'Ttil's axe leaned against the empty seat and grabbed the handle. He'd given it to her as a wedding gift and knew she'd always preferred to carry a weapon fit for a male. She had been a slave before becoming a queen—and a good axe meant it would never happen again.

Hy'Mandr squeezed it firm in his vagha grip, feeling his salt.

"Orders, sir?" Taryl asked.

He paused for a moment, letting the anger course through his system and reinvigorate him. "We march on Niamarlee and show them the strength of the vagha who they've insulted for far too long."

"W-we?" Ne'Vistar clarified.

"I'm not sending my army to Niamarlee without their king. Blind or not, I'm going with, even if only to inspire my troops."

Tension in the room hung thick and palpable as the blind ruler navigated the stairs leading up the dais to his throne.

"Well, what're you waiting for? Assemble the forward army," he ordered. "Ne'Vistar, I'm leaving you in charge in my stead, just like the old days. Mi'Darrio, too. He just got back and has Hy'Targ's journal. I think you'll find it interesting… but plenty of time for reading later."

King Hy'Mandr stood straight and walked confidently from his throne room with perhaps more vigor than he'd shown in years.

CHAPTER FOURTEEN

The four morehl, who were mostly not morehl, walked through the Undrakull streets.

"I retrieved the bones for a warlock who lives in that building," Nohdan indicated the former temple of Firiel. "He had only recently risen to status, but he functioned something like a city administrator."

Elorall cocked an eyebrow. "Undrakull does not have an Emperor? An alternate form of government?"

Nohdan shrugged. "More or less, but who needs politics when you have magic?"

The former temple loomed into view as they drew closer. "The same goes for religion, eh—who needs it?" muttered Hy'Targ without expecting an answer. The symbols of devotion to Firiel, the goddess both the morehl and vagha worshipped, lay busted in a heap where they leaned against the building.

Nohdan continued, "His consort is the morehl matron of this city, a broker of information—and a formidable enemy—so be aware of word games. I believe she helped him rise to position, so if Krierfar the warlock defers to her, then follow her lead; she wields much power."

The selumari glanced at him hesitantly. "You sound like you won't be there?"

"I will make introductions," Nohdan said, "but I must take Hy'Targ around back to collect your prize from the vault." He tightened his lips, hoping he didn't conceal his true intentions: if someone else carried the bones he hoped the bloodless hunter would chase *that person* instead.

"Vault?"

Nohdan chortled, "Of course. With what they paid me to collect these relics? Of course, they will need to keep them safe. Krierfar was something of a fanatic, he and the matron both. They were both high up in that Nekarthan Cult I mentioned once to Mantieth. I had to pretend I was as fanatical about Melkior worship as they were just to get paid and get out safely."

They shot the lava elf worried looks.

"The cult believed that they could control an awakened Melkior if they had Ailushurai's bones… they paid, and so I delivered the bones.

His party mates stared at Nohdan with bulging eyes. Elorall hissed, "You gave a warlock bent on releasing Death's chief general a tool to wipe out all life on Esfah? *And for a payday*?"

The lava elf shrugged. "It was just a story, it's not like I believed there was any truth to it."

"But you left Melkior in the other tomb. I was there, I saw it," Hy'Targ said.

"Well, I'm not *stupid*," Nohdan defended. "It may just be a story, but why take the risk. I heard the old tales, all fifty different versions of them. I knew better than to risk awakening a monster like Melkior… I don't believe most of the religious nonsense, but it doesn't mean I'm going to tempt fate by speaking Death's name or setting off traps that awaken undead lords."

"You read the inscription," Hy'Targ realized.

The others all looked at the dwarf in disguise.

"It read, 'May she never depart from her lover's side,'" Hy'Targ pointed out. "You jimmied the trap to get away… you knew someone put a curse on it, or that the trap would somehow activate this whole thing."

Nodhan shrugged sheepishly. "I'm guessing they were surprised when I turned up alive with the bones… I told them it didn't work and that the cult's counterparts possess the matching set... Melkior's."

Elloral cocked a judgmental eyebrow. "Why?"

"We don't need anyone else chasing down those bones and accidentally awakening the lich."

"Except that it's exactly what happened: he was still released," Hy'targ said. Deep down, though, relief washed over him. This whole debacle was a product of Nodhan's greed and not a result of his carelessness.

The morehl defended against their judgmental gazes. "I'm a thief, not a murderer, I rather like the world just the way it is. But they didn't need to know *that*—or that Melkior's body still laid where the eldarim dumped him centuries ago. Now let's go get those bones and get out of here."

The group stood outside the gate leading to the warlock's estate.

"You wait here, Hy'Targ," Nohdan instructed. "You might look like one of us because of the spell, but your dumpy vagha posture would give you away instantly. Just try to act like an elf... think graceful thoughts. Your life might depend on it."

Hy'Targ glared at him, but watched the mixed company of elves enter the warlock's doors. He did have to admit they had a certain graceful elegance. Remaining outside, he leaned against a wall... as gracefully as he could.

Varanthl sat glumly in the mist outside the perimeter of Undrakull. He didn't like the sitting and waiting; silence crushed him, put him inside of his head, back inside the loneliness where he felt the sting of loss. He had liked Jordyll's farm—there had always been something to do, a reason to keep busy, some next task.

He turned a bracelet around on his wrist and tightened his lips as he examined them. Each one was inscribed with a symbol and the name of Ghaeial's children. It was the children of the gods, except for the misbegotten one.

"I think it will be okay," Rhyll's voice rumbled in the nearby mist.

Varanthl looked up at him.

"The others, I mean." The treefolk said, curling his toes into a pool to drink. "They seem quite adept, though I can't say I like that lava elf fellow." Rhyll looked down at the homunculus. "And you, too. I think you'll be fine as well. You're with family now."

Varanthl grimaced and rolled the handle of his weapon in his grip, turning its heavy head. He said flatly, "I have no family."

Rhyll frowned, trying to understand what he meant. "My apologies. Treespeak doesn't always translate perfectly. We have a saying, *whenever we are together in heart and mind, we are family*." He looked away wistfully. "I wonder how my family is doing… my other family."

The homunculus frowned. "No. You got the saying right," he mumbled. "I'm sure they are fine."

They sat in relative silence for a moment. Varanthl sighed, exhaling his internal pain. Rhyll did likewise, though his treespeak sounded more like yawning, cracking branches in the wind.

Vy'Hrothgyr sat nearby, humming a tune and pausing to restart and then jot down notes in his journal where he recorded the party's progress, as well as other songs and rhymes he'd come up with.

A wet noise, terrible and guttural, broke their reverie. A mammoth drinking from the pool hacked and gargled; it's terrified chortle attracted the dwarves who rushed through the mist.

The beast collapsed with its airways blocked. Its eyes grayed, riddled through with bloodshot streaks and burst capillaries.

"She's choking on something," Jr'Dunn yelled, holding back the others in case the animal panicked and trampled them. "We can only hope it will pass before she does."

Varanthl scowled and ignored him. He laid one hand on the beast's face to comfort it and used two other arms to hold its mouth open wide. Plunging his remaining hand into the pachyderm's throat, he leaned in as far as he could.

"I—I've got a hand on it. Some kind of blockage." He pulled and stepped away, clutching an inky mass. It roiled in Varanthl's grip.

Rhyll recoiled. "You've touched the Gray Blight!" He looked at the pool he'd been drinking from, the same one the mammoth had drank from, and pulled his toes back out. "You must chop off your arm before it seeps into your flesh!"

Jr'Dunn pulled his axe, but Varanthl stared him down with a glower. The dark slime jerked and pulled, trying to escape from the homunculus rather than burrow its way into a new host. He dropped it to the dew slicked grass; it didn't leave behind so much as a stain on him.

Jerking and rolling like a ball pushed by a dung beetle, the wet mass crept back and towards the mammoth whose final groans signaled a losing fight against the Necralluvium lodged in its throat. Black spiderwebs creeped up and into the whites of her eyes.

Varanthl kicked the black slime wad into the stagnant pond and away from his party.

Jr'Dunn leaned an ear against the creature's throat and shook his head. "I fear it's in her lungs."

The homunculus gripped his hammer and looked from mammoth to dwarf. Jr'Dunn nodded solemnly.

Varanthl lifted his weapon and caved in the doomed beast's skull, ending its misery.

"We can't let anyone find it here before our mission is complete," Jr'Dunn whispered.

Rhyll picked up the dead mount and spun a wide arc, flinging it as far as he could into the center of the cursed pool. It gurgled pitiably and then slipped slowly beneath the surface, taking a chunk of the party's morale with it.

"Where is Krierfar?" Nohdan asked as he entered. His two companions followed a little behind him. "I've come to see the warlock."

The matron leaned forward and rested her bony elbows on the armrests to her over-sized lounger. "I'm afraid the warlock met an unfortunate fate several months ago… Nohdan." She squinted as she searched her memory for his name. "I have taken over his duties in his stead."

He gulped and averted her eyes, trying not to look at the jagged pink scar that marred her face. A moment of panic ripped through him—he hadn't told Mantieth and Elorall not to look at it. Nohdan hoped they had the mind and manners enough not to stare. She was quite fair aside from that blemish, so it was sure to be a soft spot for her.

"What business brings you back to Undrakull?"

"Information. I know you are always purchasing it—and I knew you'd be especially interested in this."

She grinned wickedly. "News is always an interesting topic. I heard you were caught months ago and are now rotting in the prisons below Niamarlee."

Nohdan winked. "Reports of my capture were greatly over-exaggerated."

"You escaped?"

He shrugged. "It was not difficult. The prince is a soft-headed fool… thinks too much of himself, and likewise, his father the king is even worse. I tricked him into setting me free." Nohdan could feel Mantieth's icy stare on his backside.

"I have heard as much about him," the matron finally said, relaxing. "So, what is this news?"

"*Melkior*," he said.

She leaned forward on the edge of her seat.

"You told me to bring you any others I found who were dedicated to Ailushurai and Melkior. These ones I brought alive. They are very eager—very dedicated believers."

"Yessss," she hissed. "I could use help from loyal adherents—and have developed a plan… after verifying your bones through mystic means, I think a pilgrimage to the World Wound is required. Perhaps on the next Turambar's Day when magic is the strongest."

Nohdan did his best not to grimace at the thought. Who knew what manner of black magic she could conjure within the Netherwold, the black pit in the crags of Dereh'Liandor? But the next Turambar's Day celebrations would not begin for three more years. The morehl stepped aside to turn over his companions, but held out a hand to receive payment for his services.

She raised her eyebrows. "I thought you were a true believer? You would extort me over this?"

"Of course I'm a believer," he lied. "But information is *never* free. You'd suspect my allegiances if I left empty-handed… *I know I would.*"

The matron grinned mischievously. "You are quite right." She tossed him a small bag that clinked of gold coins.

Nohdan bowed and exited.

Turning to her new guests, the matron offered them each a seat and poured drinks from a flagon. A gentle steam rose from each cup. "morehlian bloodwine to celebrate our lord," she said and passed them each an ornate goblet, not leaving them an option to decline.

Elorall choked down a gulp of the blood and wine mixture. Mantieth tried likewise, but almost wretched in his cup. He pretended to drink instead and allowed a little dribble to leak down his chin.

The matron stared at them long and hard, addressing them with steely, black eyes. "So, who are you, really?"

Nohdan left the building and whistled to Hy'Targ. The disguised dwarf snuck around the fence and joined him at the rear of the building.

"Good news," Nohdan reported, "I don't think there are any other guards inside. No opposition at all… just the matron. I-I think she ate everyone else."

"*Ate them?*" Hy'Targ's eyebrows rose in surprise.

The elf shrugged, continuing around back and motioned for his companion to return his property. Hy'Targ gave the elf back his lock pick set, and Nohdan got to work. Moments later, the latch popped, and the door swung freely.

Slinking down the halls, barely audible voices echoed through the corridor, muffled by doors and distance. A familiar quality in the timbre of the voices resonated between Hy'Targ's ears. He assumed it was something in Elorall and Mantieth's tone, or perhaps it was that barely discernible sensation of muffled words on the cusp of understanding. He shook his head and followed Nohdan.

Finally, the duo arrived in a large chamber; massive doors stretched floor to ceiling barring their path, and the vault rose even taller than that. Hy'Targ guessed that the vault must've been the interior of the steepled tower that rose high above the structure.

"That's a big vault," Hy'Targ whispered, looking at the puzzle box with spinning dials and runes that controlled the lock.

Nohdan nodded. "The matron is something of a collector. She keeps countless artifacts inside it." He moved to the lock and tried a combination as Hy'Targ asked him a question.

"Why are you helping us, anyway? You could've lost us in Commontown or in the tunnels," Hy'Targ commented, glad the morehl hadn't tried it.

The code Nohdan entered failed. He shrugged but didn't make eye contact. "I figure that black skeleton is still after me… and probably because of my connection to these bones. If I can give them to someone else, I'm hoping it'll have a new victim to chase. I can wash my hands of the lot of you once and for all and get back to Maris ta-Sehlim." He glared back at Hy'Targ and explained simply, "Self-preservation." He hadn't been this truthful in years; it made him feel gross.

Nohdan turned back to the lock and cursed as his combination failed again. "I memorized the code last time I was here… just in case I ever needed to return. I'm sure it's got to be the same." He rubbed his chin in deep thought as Hy'Targ hovered at the room's entrance, still trying to make out those words down the hall. "It must take more than one set of hands," Nohdan muttered. He located and marked the dials, which kept resetting on him as he completed the code.

"Hy'Targ. Come here," the lava elf hissed, explaining that some of the tumblers would automatically reset as the next dials in sequence were moved. "Hold these two runes in place while I complete the sequence so they don't default on me."

The dwarf held the two knobs and watched Nohdan turn the next four rune dials on the eight-letter sequence. The fifth he held, and then he turned the sixth. A click vibrated through the door as it unlocked.

They slowly pushed the door open to reveal a treasure trove of arcane artifacts. Hy'Targ took a step back and gulped at the sight of a towering blade golem. He reached for his weapon, but a second glance proved it was deactivated and harmless until awoken. The over-sized humanoid construct gleamed with jagged edges sprouting from its armor; he'd never seen one before and understood they were one of many terrifying creations made during decades leading up to the Magestorm Wars.

Nohdan rushed past the dwarf and to the center of the vault where Ailushurai's bones rested in a place of honor upon a velvet cushion. He brushed the bones aside and cut the cushion open with a jagged forearm of the blade golem. After shaking out the stuffing onto the floor, he dumped the sacred bones into the makeshift sack.

The prince hung back. Something in his gut bothered him… niggled at his consciousness.

Hy'Targ asked, "Nohdan, if she's alone, then how does she open the vault?"

Nohdan didn't even look back, but concentrated on tying the sack with a silk cord he'd swiped from a nearby tapestry roll.

"How does she do it, Nohdan? What kind of morehl eats her own people?"

Nohdan turned and gave the dwarf his sack. His eyes turned to the mountains of treasure… it was more than he could fence in a year. The original *Book of the Land* was too big to carry, nearly four cubits across, but next to it rested a tome that was far more valuable. An ancient book he knew he could easily steal.

"Hurry up. We've gotta get out of here—right after I snag a few pieces for all my trouble."

Hy'Targ took the bag from the thief and turned back to the hall where they'd left their companions with the matron. He realized the morehl was dodging his question. As he tied the velvet bag to his belt, Hy'Targ demanded an answer in an angry tone. "Who is this matron?"

CHAPTER FIFTEEN

Mantieth gripped the arms of his chair with enough force that changed the color of his knuckles. Elorall noticed his stress and put her hand over top of his.

The matron pressed her point. "I ask, 'who are you, really?' because I fear our dear Nohdan is not a true believer. He is useful for certain purposes, but is primarily interested in how many coins fill his purse. So, I ask you again, *who are you*? Are you dedicated believers willing to sacrifice everything for Melkior? Because I know how to revive him."

She rose to her full height, lifting her body higher and revealing that only her top half was lava elf. The rest of her was a giant spider. "My name is Sshkkryyahr," said the drider, "and I have served the lord Death since before he walked the face of Esfah as Malgrimm—since before Malgrimm chose Melkior as his general and poured a destiny of malice into him."

"W-what do we need to do?" Mantieth asked as Sshkkryyahr walked a circle around the room.

"How may we help bring about the return of our lord's chosen one?" Elorall said more eloquently.

"Ah," Sshkkryyahr wheezed enthusiastically. "You've heard the old prophecies about Melkior's resurrection? Perhaps the other cults around the world are not as forgetful as I'd believed."

Elorall tried interjecting a word, but the drider prattled on with excitement.

"Melkior is forever tied in life and in death to Ailushurai. His bargain with Selurehl, Lord of the Abyss, was a contract: binding even for the power of the gods. The closer Ailushurai is to Melkior, the more powerful he becomes—such that he could even return from the grave under some conditions."

"Could he be awakened without her?" Elorall asked.

"Were it so, I believe that he already would have," the drider continued. "I have owned her bones in secret for a decade now. But prophecy is a funny thing, it takes shades of meaning and symbols can change through the ages. But I feel that I may be able to return Ailushurai to some semblance of life—such an event would surely trigger Melkior's return to this plane."

Elorall looked nervously to the door. She knew they had to stall so Hy'Targ and Nodhan could acquire those bones. "How? I am interested in what magic could make that happen— once the spark of life has faded from this plane, I thought recalling it was impossible?"

The drider smiled wickedly. "The World Wound of Dereh'Liandor. It was ripped open during the Magestorm Wars and exposed an entrance to the Netherwold. From that realm, even the extinguished spark of life could be heard by Ailushurai. With her return, so would come Melkior's."

"Couldn't you do the same with Melkior?" Mantieth asked.

Sshkkryyahr eyed her with a glimmer of paranoia. "Why do you ask? Do you know where the body of Melkior is?" she loomed higher, taking a threatening posture.

Elorall recoiled involuntarily.

"O-of course not," Mantieth defended. "Of course, if we knew, we'd tell you immediately! We want the same things."

Sshkkryyahr hissed, but skulked back to the other side of the room. "Once Melkior has her back at his side, he will fulfill his oath to Death and raise an army so large that not even a total alliance of the races can stop it!" She looked aside, "To raise her we must open the veil and raid the Abyss, and the journey to Dereh'Liandor will not be easy. We shall need things I cannot easily acquire from Undrakull; I need outside agents."

The drider looked down on them. "The ritual will require sacrifice... the blood and souls of an eldarim and a selumari. I have secured a certain book; wrapped in dragon hide and written upon pages made of vagha skin, it is said that Malgrimm himself penned the Book of the Void. One chapter details Melkior's grief and hints at how to resurrect them both... among other things."

She stared intently at Mantieth's neck. After a few seconds she furrowed her brow. Her stare became overt enough that he wilted beneath her gaze.

He tried to distract her, keep her talking. "But... why would Death care enough for one servant to lay out a path for his return?" his voice warbled as Sshkkryyahr took slow, methodical steps towards him, each one loaded with lethal potential.

"Don't you understand, child? *Malgrimm is his father*, just as much as yours... who sits on the coral throne, *child of Leidergelth!*" As quick as lightning, she snatched Mantieth by the throat and hoisted him in her choking grasp.

Sshkkryyahr batted Elorall aside as if she were made of straw. The elf cracked her head against the wall, and her disguising enchantment fully dispelled.

"morehl do not sweat in the heat," Sshkkryyahr hissed into the prince's face, leaking further perspiration under the heat of her breath. "It appears that I have already secured one half of my necessary sacrifice."

The drider dangled Mantieth in the air. He kicked his feet as she raked a talon menacingly against his face and licked her lips. "Foolish, little imposters. I sensed the magic all over you the moment you entered. Your caster is weak, like a morehl infant."

Sshkkryyahr whirled at the quick and heavy vagha footsteps behind her, too late. Hy'Targ rammed into her massive thorax with a heavy shoulder and a full head of steam.

She dropped Mantieth into a heap as she sprawled backwards. Hissing like a snake, she collected herself and sneered at the familiar dwarf.

"It's you!" Hy'Targ shouted, staring at the scar his father had left on her face. His grip tightened on Glorybringer's handle.

"My bones!" Sshkkryyahr snarled, recognizing the pillow sack hanging at Hy'Targ's waist. "The bones of Ailushurai!"

Without a moment's hesitation, Hy'Targ dashed through the room and swung his axe. "You cursed my father!" he chopped through the table she tried to use as a shield. Splinters of jagged wood exploded, damaging her hands.

Sshkkryyahr lunged for a tall apothecary rack—for anything nearby that could be used as a weapon against the raging dwarf. He'd quickly hacked his way through whatever she scrambled to defend herself with.

"You took his sight!" he smashed through the alembic distiller set she flung at him.

"Wait—hold your axe! Without me, King Irontooth will never see again." Sshkkryyahr gambled. "I-I can reverse the spell, I can…"

Hy'Targ shouted over her. "There is only one way to be certain that you'll do no further harm to Esfah." He hefted his axe.

Sshkkryyahr snatched Mantieth by the leg and lifted him in place as a shield. She curled her lip, daring the dwarf to strike as she hedged towards the exit.

Hy'Targ's nose wrinkled as he weighed the odds.

A sizzle of frigid energy cackled over his shoulder, and the odor of ozone tickled his nose hairs. "Whose magic is weak, now?" Elorall growled behind him with eyes blazing azure.

Sshkkryyahr's arms frosted over, locking her shoulders and elbows in a sheaf of ice. Her black eyes widened with terror as Hy'Targ took a final step.

"Wait—I can…"

"For my father!" Glorybringer lit with volcanic fury to match its wielder and he split the drider open, lodging the fiery axe-head in her morehlian torso, a mere hands-breadth away from a stunned Mantieth.

Sshkkryyahr dropped dead in a shrieking heap of convulsing legs.

Mantieth scrambled to his feet, joining his companions who rushed for the door.

Elorall paused, "Wait! What about Nohdan?"

Mantieth frowned and nodded, "He hadn't agreed to come any further than Undrakull."

Hy'Targ looked back at the hallway leading to the vault. He hesitated, and then decided, "Leave him. If he didn't follow me, then this is where we part ways… perhaps he's right where he's always intended to be."

Hy'Targ, Mantieth, and Elorall had only barely gotten beyond direct sight of Sshkkryyahr's compound when they heard the bells ringing. Armor plates clacked against each other as lava elf troops rushed down the streets and someone cried out, "The matron is dead! Someone has killed Sshkkryyahr!"

The intruders hurried to put more distance between them and the old temple. They turned a corner and a morehl sentry spotted them. "Intruders! Intruders," he screamed, putting an alarm horn to his lips, he blasted a signal.

Mantieth snapped his bow to the ready and loosed an arrow. The scout's signal trailed off with a choking warble as the lava elf fell stone dead at the end of the alley. "Come on!"

Mantieth sprinted the opposite direction, and the others followed.

Hy'Targ huffed and puffed on his shorter legs, slipping slightly behind the two selumari. A group of soldiers dashed towards them from the shadows and drew firearms. The invaders rounded a corner, trying to lose them; flintlocks fired behind them and ball shot ricocheted off the stone building just at their rear.

"Can't you disguise us again?" Mantieth asked.

"It doesn't work like that," Elorall wheezed, pumping her arms. "It won't work with them actively looking for us, but I have another idea."

They sprinted around another building and headed towards the warrens.

Behind them, Undrakull's soldiers dashed around another turn, catching only fleeting glimpses of the murderers who killed their leader. Voices howled and horn toots communicated to other catch-and-kill teams.

"They're headed for the warrens—trying to escape!" one lava elf shouted as they pursued.

"They'll never escape. Sound the general alarm!"

A morehl guard split off from the pack and sounded a signal. A massive gjallarhorn, crafted from the wreckage of a dragon killed in the First Age, rumbled with a bass vibrato. It shook the Undrakull plateau and alerted every soul in the city and in Commontown.

High pitched sirens went up all across Undrakull. The cacophony rang through the stone of the plateau as every station picked up the alarm and the lower sentries closed the entrance gates, eliminating all roads in or out. Every morehl troop was put on high alert.

Nohdan dashed through the Undrakull streets, expertly avoiding suspicious eyes. He moved quick when he could and walked nonchalantly whenever he might be seen. The thief clutched the item he'd stolen from the drider's lair and held it tightly beneath his cloak.

All around him, doors slammed shut and shutters closed as the city went on lock-down, making it easier for the troops to find the intruders. Nohdan bit his lip—the longer he remained in the open, the more suspicion he would garner.

A squad of sentries dashed around the corner just as Hy'Targ and the elves sprinted past. Nohdan raised an eyebrow. Something was not right. The dwarf ran in the lead—Hy'Targ had never seemed the speediest of the crew. He did a double-take as the soldiers raised their weapons and fired at them with a cloud of blue smoke.

Bullets whizzed past Nohdan's ears and zipped right through the intruder's forms. *An illusion!*

He looked beyond the firing line and saw Hy'Targ, Mantieth, and Elorall—the real ones—sprinting away and in the opposite direction. They turned out of sight, not foolish enough to try escaping through the warrens where they'd entered.

The morehl forces spat profanities in their native tongue, realizing they'd been tricked. One of them leveled a finger at the thief. "You—I don't recognize you. And I know *everyone*," the red skinned elf accused.

Nohdan put a hand on his chest, feigning bewilderment at the accusation.

"Wait," said another soldier. "I recognize him."

Nohdan relaxed slightly and began telling an easy lie he'd used so often before. "Thank you, sir. I've just recently relocated to…"

The guard continued with his interjection, "I saw him with the intruders in Commontown only an hour ago."

"Get him!" they screamed, and they launched themselves after him.

Nohdan wheeled around and sprinted back the way he'd came. "You're going the wrong way!" he shouted—trying to wave them off and send them after intruders he'd cut ties with. "They went *the other way!*"

The thief spun on his heels and dashed down an alley, doubling back the other direction and skirting around his pursuers. He flung himself through the opening and into the next street, skidding to a halt in front of a creature whose hideous visage froze his hot morehl blood like ice. Sudden fear nearly liquefied his guts.

A black skeleton stood in the middle of the road, sniffing and staring down the path Nohdan had come by, anticipating his presence. The bloodless scout gritted its dusky teeth as the lava elf blanched under its empty-socketed gaze, and then it lifted its head as if it caught the scent of something stronger.

The Burned One whirled on its feet and sprinted away into the darkness. Nohdan knew in his gut what it found. If it had locked onto Hy'Targ and the bones, he wanted no involvement with the adventurers—regardless of any kind of corporate guilt he shared by awakening the dreaded Melkior.

Nohdan turned and fled in the opposite direction, shifting the bulky item he had taken from the vault beneath his cloak in order to run faster. The elf wished the book had been something he could turn into a needle to hide—but that trick only worked on mostly metal items.

He leveled his head and hurried away in search of a back door—surely some delinquent lava elf had left a secret back door out of Undrakull somewhere and Nohdan would find it. The morehl had no intention of being captured this day.

A cool wind blew off the coast of the Far Sea, laden with the scents of coral and seawater. The dwarf spell caster saw a customer approaching through the courtyard of her home.

Sh'Zzar greeted the selumari at her door and welcomed them in. The coral elf did his best to avoid cringing at the earthy appearance of the vagha's small bungalow erected on the edge of Niamarlee. He took the seat she offered and sat with rigid posture and on the very edge of the wooden, high-backed stool—a sign that he'd likely come to her from the sections of the city that housed the members of the higher-casted elves.

Her magic was powerful and in high demand. Visits from nobility or their servants were not uncommon, despite the second-rate status Sh'Zzar had as a vaghan alien. She couldn't help but grin as the elven fop sat with his knees pulled up too high on the furniture sized for dwarves instead of elves.

Rather than get to the point and alleviate his discomfort, Sh'Zzar turned to her stove and grabbed a kettle. "You must let me make you some tea," she said, stretching this humbling moment out as long as possible.

"Oh. No thank you…"

"Nonsense." She interrupted him. "I insist."

Finally, she poured a dose of the oolong and floral scented brew into a glaze-fired clay mug. The elf declined her offering again, hiding his mild disgust at the notion of utensils and cups made of anything but shaped coral.

While Sh'Zzar sipped her tea, the elf explained his case. He was a merchant with many items traveling along the trade routes, and he hoped to put her services on retainer.

"You are a world traveler, are you not?"

She narrowed her eyes at him over her mug. "Not the last time I checked."

"My apologies, I thought the prefix in your name indicated the Shree surname. I am acquainted with the Shree family up past New Elrannin, across the Talvat Sea."

Her lips tightened, and she shook her head.

His brows raised, "Surely you wouldn't be local? That *would be* a rare lineage."

Sh'Zzar scowled at him. "Where my clan hails from means very little compared to what skills I offer. You came here to commission me for a task, not draw my family tree. Tell me about your job or leave me be."

The merchant blinked, taken aback. "Yes. Well. I'm sure we've all got secrets. I'll leave you to yours and expect you'll leave me to mine when the time comes for you to render services, should you accept the job. Now, on to business."

Sh'Zzar nodded measuredly. She drained her cup and refilled it again. "I'm listening."

CHAPTER SIXTEEN

Varanthl stood next to the tethered mammoth and stared through the mist at the dim silhouette of the plateau. Plumes of volcanic smoke rose off its edges, creeping towards the sky.

"Something doesn't feel right," Rhyll said, standing next to the homunculus. "I thought they would have returned by now."

Vy'Hrothgyr's shape appeared through the fog, kiltering back and forth as he ran, almost making a waddling motion. He'd been posted as a scout nearest the edge of the arcane, misty shroud.

Panting and out of breath, he managed, "Horns… sirens… something's gone wrong inside. They're closing all the gates leading in or out of Undrakull!"

Jr'Dunn and Vy'Danis met up with them and got up to speed. "I knew this would happen," said one. "Probably betrayed by that bloody lava elf," growled the other.

Vy'Drisick, Jr'Orhr, and Jr'Tarl joined them in the fog, completing the assembly.

"What do we do?" Rhyll asked worriedly.

Varanthl set his jaw and stared at the looming, distant shadow. He said nothing, but knew they must still be alive: Elorall's misty shroud remained.

"Only two options," Jr'Dunn said. "We either continue his quest without him—try to face Melkior without the others…" he trailed off at the implication of their friends' fate.

"And the other?" asked Rhyll.

Jr'Dunn frowned. "We fight."

His kinsman, Jr'Orhr, scoffed. He still bore the cuts on his face from being thrown through the window at Varanthl's first meeting. "Fight a mountain?" He shook his head and grimaced. "There is another option. We ride for Irontooth and raise an army."

The bard grinded his teeth. "The whole point of this mad mission was to prevent the lich from getting those bones! Once he gets them, Melkior will be nigh unstoppable," Vy'Hrothgyr argued.

Bickering broke out among them. As the dwarves argued amongst themselves, Varanthl hefted his weapon and started walking towards Undrakull. Rhyll blinked twice and followed him.

The vagha finally realized they were short their largest two members.

Jr'Orhr hissed, "That's insanity."

Vy'Danis grinned through his gray whiskers. "Yeah, but it's my kind of insanity," he retorted. "Always choose action over the alternative," he spat. "It's the vagha way."

He caught up to the homunculus. "You have a plan?" Vy'Danis asked.

"Kill them all. Don't die," he stated simply.

"Not much of a plan."

"Better than arguing."

Vy'Danis nodded. "I'll give you that. I'm with you."

The closed gates of Undrakull barely came into view as they strode beyond the edge of the fog. The dwarf stayed him with a hand. "Do you think a mammoth could fit through there?"

Varanthl shot him an appreciative look and tried to guess what he was planning. He nodded. "We fight… but not to win?"

"Right," Vy'Danis said. "Rack up casualties, cause attrition. We just need to do enough damage to make them give us back our friends and send us on our way."

"Good," Varanthl exhaled the tension built up in his lungs. "I didn't really want to die, and I don't think I can fight them all—even with all of us combined."

"Well, yer not as dumb as ye look." Vy'Danis turned and signaled to the others. "Ready the mammoths," he yelled. "We got a plan! A big, crazy, plan."

"Are we gonna survive this plan?" Jr'Dunn fired back.

Vy'Danis shrugged and flashed him a goofy grin.

Hy'Targ and his companions sprinted through the side streets of Undrakull with the long legged Mantieth in the lead.

"But the exit's *that way!*" Hy'Targ wheezed with the sack of bones slapping rhythmically against his hip.

"Which is where all the guards are running to," Mantieth fired over his shoulder.

"Then, where are we going?" asked Elorall.

They broke out from an alley and neared the edge of the morehl city. The invaders ran in the opposite direction as the troops who headed downward through the winding grottos that descended through the plateau and into Commontown.

Mantieth said, "Just trust me. I have a plan." They rounded the last building and stared out over the distance between the row of poorer morehl homes on Undrakull's outskirts and the overlook where one misstep would send them hurtling to their deaths nearly three hundred cubits below on the streets of Commontown.

His lungs were so tight he thought they might seize up. Hy'Targ looked back as they finally paused for a moment to catch their collective breath.

The dwarf's heart plunged into his gut when he spotted it. A dark skeleton leapt down from a terrace. "Run!" he yelled, not waiting for them to ask for an explanation.

The dwarf sprinted as fast as he'd ever gone before. Still, his elf companions easily passed him. A short distance ahead of him, the elves slid to a stop before they could fall careening over the edge.

Running with reckless fury, the burned skeleton shrieked and closed the distance, gaining on Hy'Targ.

Mantieth scooped Elorall up and into his arms. She clung to his body with a mix of fear and arousal. The selumari prince placed his sheathed, enchanted blade over top of the long cable where flags were hung and told her to hold on tight.

He launched himself over the edge, riding his secured weapon across the sky and speeding across the breadth of Undrakull Commontown. The hot winds from the volcanic updrafts buffeted them, but Mantieth gripped his purchase all the harder despite the sweat glistening all over his body.

They tore through the massive banners, and the large spans of fabric fell lazily ground-ward. Curling, they danced gracefully to the floor in the updrafts.

With the enemy on his tail, Hy'Targ leapt through the sky and reached over the cable with the haft of Glorybringer, following Mantieth's lead. Momentum rocketed him across the zip line only a short length behind his companions. The coveted bones hung precariously from his belt.

Screeching, the skeletal scout leapt after him and snatched the cord as well, tirelessly tailing its prey, even gaining on them.

Elorall concentrated in order to cast the spell and iced the line behind Hy'Targ, raising up jagged frost crystals. The relentless fiend lost its grip on the zip line as the lumpy bulbs of ice threw its grip askew. With a demon wail, it plummeted the full distance until it hit bottom with a horrendous clatter. The force of the impact smashed the bloodless scout to pieces, scattering it across the streets of Commontown even as the guards quarantined the city and began searching for the invaders among the detained traders below.

Someone spotted the falling plumes of fabric and looked up in time to see the vagha and selumari as they skidded to a halt at the end of an air vent a great distance above the surface. The exit valve allowed the air to escape and kept Commontown from becoming so inhospitable that other races couldn't come to trade their wares.

Signal horns blasted again as the travelers ducked through the large aperture. Hot winds threatened to push them from their perch near the hole. They shared the ledge with the long-dead heroes of Undrakull's past. Mummified bodies of deceased morehl warriors ringed the walls high above Commontown like grimdark wainscoting.

They were trapped.

"Now what?" Elorall howled above the noise of rushing air.

Booming reports overpowered the winds behind them as the ball-shot of morehl flintlocks sizzled through the air and skipped off the nearby stone escarpments. One shot lodged in the chest of a morehl corpse and the thing crumbled and broke free. The mummified remains lurched forward like a bloodless, and then tumbled over the ledge.

Hy'Targ pushed between them and into one of the air valves. "Now we jump!" He stepped through the vent and emerged outside. Outside the plateau, he sagged to his butt and slid down the nearly vertical face of the monolith at speeds like the zip line. The elves took the plunge behind him and all three skimmed down the edge of the natural structure like rocks skipping across a lake; behind them, lava elves screamed for their heads and demanded the guards reopen the gates so they could pursue. If anything remained of them after flinging themselves off the edge of the stony mesa, they would invert their bodies and bury them in the foundations of their homes.

The remaining five mammoths emerged from the mist, accompanied by Varanthl and Rhyll. Somewhere inside the Undrakull gate, lava elves blew horns.

Trading nervous glances with the others, Varanthl asked, "Did they see us coming?"

Jr'Dunn shrugged, and the company picked up the pace, rushing towards the plateau. "We ought to be able to slam through the gate and breach the tunnel."

Their mastodons picked up speed, and the horns blasted again.

With a loud, cranking sound, the gates began to creak open.

"Go! Run!" they heard shouted from off to the side. Hy'Targ, Mantieth, and Elorall headed towards them in a dead sprint, shouting and waving their arms to indicate the urgency of the situation.

Varanthl and the party whirled on their heels and matched course with their friends.

Hy'Targ fumbled with the rope that tied the sack to his waist. He finally pulled his dagger and cut it free. "Vy'Hrothgyr!" he yelled.

The bard looked down to his prince running alongside him.

Vy'Hrothgyr threw him the bag. "Your mammoth is the fastest! You must take Ailushurai's remains to my father—stop for nothing!"

The bard tried to protest.

Hy'Targ cut him off. "Black skeletons."

Vy'Hrothgyr set his jaw and turned his eyes forward, taking his new duty seriously.

Hy'Targ waved on some nearby kinsmen. Jr'Dunn and Vy'Drisick went with Vy'Hrothgyr; they crashed furiously into the distance as the other mammoths peeled away, turning towards the swamplands surrounding Undrakull. "We've got to draw them away," the prince insisted.

"The lava elves or black skeletons?" Vy'Danis asked as the group paused before the edge of the marshy forest where tangled vines and hanging moss draped like ghastly figures before them.

"Both," Hy'Targ said, "but let's hope there's just the one skeleton… and pray that he chases *us* instead of the others. It must not get those bones."

"What's the play, then?" Mantieth asked. "Are we just a diversion?"

The dwarf shook his head. "It's the same as it ever was. We head off Melkior and destroy him before he consolidates power."

Whumpf! Something echoed sickly in their midst and Vy'Danis's mammoth groaned and slumped, spilling him to the ground as the beast fell head-first to the peaty floor. The creature's eyes bulged out and half its face burst open. They heard the report only after seeing the damage.

"Sharpshooters!"

Before they could turn the remaining beast into the woods, a squad of riflemen opened fire causing an eruption of acrid, blue smoke. The mammoth reared back, dumping its two riders, but also shielding them as the lava elf missiles peppered its body with wounds that ripped them apart with catastrophic damage.

"Everyone down," Vy'Danis urged as they huddled behind the bodies of their dead mounts for protection. Spherical bullets zipped past their heads as they bunkered for cover. The safety of the trees lay only thirty cubits to their north-west.

Elorall hissed as she tried to summon another bank of fog—but the stress of the drider's encounter, the sprints, and improvised escape had proved too much for her to keep up with. "I'm sorry. I'm sorry…" she muttered like a mantra, verging on tears.

Mantieth squeezed her hand. "It's okay. You need to rest."

Morehl ball shot smacked around them, violently upturning divots in the ground between them and the tree line. Undrakull's soldiers understood it was the traveler's only option for a safe escape.

"We've got to get to the trees," Hy'Targ insisted. The heavy fire dwindled as the morehl flintlock team waited for better shots to present themselves. "We gotta take out their sharpshooter, first."

Mantieth nodded soberly and nocked an arrow as the dwarf Jr'Tarl readied his crossbow. The selumari stood at the same time as Jr'Tarl and on opposite end of the mammoth they used for cover. Jr'Tarl fell stone dead with a sniper's bullet between his eyes before he could even raise his weapon.

The selumari's arrow streaked to its target, lodging in the eye of the morehl commander who had killed Jr'Tarl. The lava elf reeled and collapsed to the dirt. Mantieth sunk to safety, too—but too slowly to avoid all enemy missiles.

A bullet tagged him as he spun back, splitting his neck with a bloody streak. He collapsed against the fleshy belly of their mammoth-shield and slapped a hand against the wound. Viridescent blood streamed through his clutched fingers where he staunched the wound.

Elorall shrieked with panic. Suddenly invigorated, her eyes blazed white like lightning. Seeing her friend wounded got her hackles up.

"Let me see it," Vy'Danis insisted, peeling the elf prince's hand away nervously. He sighed with relief. "It only grazed ye. Gonna burn like crazy, but you'll survive it."

Elorall bit her lip and groaned as she summoned another bank of heavy mist thicker than any she'd ever made before.

"Let's go!" Hy'Targ yelled. His company rushed from their place of relative safety and dashed blindly through the fog. Bullets sung around them as they charged, but fired randomly into the wild. None of them found a mark.

Moments later they found themselves hidden well inside the trees and still pressing forward. The bank of fog had turned from a cool, summoned mist to a humid and boggy murk.

They plodded north towards the busted ivory keep of Melkior. Hy'Targ prayed to Firiel and all the other gods that Vy'Danis got those bones safely to his father—and if they could spare any grace, that they'd live long enough for the dwarven army to somehow arrive and help stop this creature of pure evil.

CHAPTER SEVENTEEN

They'd paused barely long enough to catch their breath. Vy'Danis leaned against a gnarled tree, huffing and puffing more than the rest. What he lacked in youth, the old dwarf made up for with experience. Right now, however, he was cursing his decision to come along instead of sending one of his younger kin—he'd often adventured with Hy'Mandr, but the Adventurer King never sprinted.

Vy'Danis stared back the way they'd come, watching for any kind of pursuit from the lava elves—*or a black skeleton.* Next to him, Elorall doted on Mantieth, tending his wound.

Hy'Targ approached and cocked his ear to the path they'd blazed.

"I think we finally lost them," Vy'Danis said.

Rhyll turned, and Vy'Danis spilled to the ground in surprise; he hadn't even realized he was resting against the treefolk in the dense, swampy wood. Vy'Danis did a double take between the Rhyll and a bent cypress and shrugged when he realized his mistake.

Somewhere along the way, their wooded path had turned decidedly marshier. Murky pools of sludge dotted with duckweed stretched between the copses of trees to form sticky sloughs. Cypress knees grew in knots and clumps of panic grass clotted the vile-smelling strata. Travel became a laborious task.

Rhyll looked around. He hummed deep in thought and then realized his companions did not sense what he did. "You do not feel that?"

They all looked at the treefolk.

"What do you mean?" Hy'Targ asked.

"The shaking… vibrations in the soil." Rhyll dug his root-like toes deeper into the dirt. "Something is coming…

something big… or something lots." He shrugged as only a tree can. "Maybe both."

Tired as the dwarves were, they urged everyone to a quickened pace. Only Varanthl seemed unaffected by fatigue. His keen eyes scanned the distance for any sign of enemies.

"We must continue heading north," Hy'Targ said, though his voice hinted at the desire to make camp and get some much-needed rest. "We're maybe a few days from the ruins of Lurneville… and Melkior."

They trudged through the bog for a few more hours. On the verge of exhaustion and collapse, the difficult terrain finally opened and provided patches of raised ground hard enough to travel by. A network of trails spread out on various paths, worming varicose through the hammock-forest canopy like spiderweb veins.

The crew checked with Rhyll regularly about whatever he was sensing. He merely scowled, still unsure of what new thing trailed them. He only knew that it continued to its pursuit.

"Given our luck," said Hy'Targ, "it's not likely to be anything good."

Far in the distance, a horn blew—not the brassy signal pipes of lava elves, but the guttural, organic cry of a hollowed tusk. They'd heard that tone in recent days before.

"trogs," Varanthl growled.

Propelled forward by the threat of the goblin horns, the company slogged through the twisting paths heading ever north through the vast expanse of peat and mire. Fatigue set in their bones as they moved with only short breaks to sleep and nibble at whatever foodstuffs had been in their packs when they'd fled Undrakull.

Two nights had passed, since Undrakull and the regular cries of goblin signal horns grew slightly closer on their heels each day. Without question, the enemy had certainly picked up their scent, and their dogged pursuit eroded any confidence that the mixed party possessed. They lost all hope they could somehow escape the swamp without having to face them.

After pushing themselves harder through the latest part of the morning, before the sun burned off the cool mist, the party paused to rest. For the remainder of the day, until the sun began its downward descent, the fetid air would turn sour and cling in their nostrils, making their haste that much more unpleasant.

Hy'Targ and Varanthl rested in the shade of some hanging moss, nibbling on a wafer of bread and cracked-pepper jerky from their stores. Hy'Targ tossed him a water skin, and the homunculus took a gulp.

The dwarf grinned and began to chuckle like a lunatic.

Varanthl was keenly aware of his limited knowledge of cultural norms. He stared at the dwarf, certain he'd committed some faux pas he did not understand. "What? What is it?"

Hy'Targ waved the comments away. "Nothing… I'm just starting to think that you might have made the better choice when we first met."

Crossing all four arms, Varanthl cocked an eyebrow.

"You left—got away from this foolish mission."

Varanthl fidgeted with his bracelets, thoughts turned towards his frehlasuhl family. "I'm not so sure my choice was best. But now that I know what's at stake, I'm certain this is the right place for me. If we can defeat Death, even if it's only a chance to do so, then it's one we must take." He tossed the bladder back.

Hy'Targ lifted it in salute and took a swig. "Well said."

"What would you be doing right now if not for this quest?" Varanthl asked.

"Probably have my nose in a book," he chuckled. "Probably hiding away from the world up in the tower where I can have a little bit of peace. O'course my father would grouse about it—tell me I need to be out living a life rather than reading about those *others* who did… and now, here I am."

"You do not get along with your father?"

The dwarf shrugged.

"My father was a great man," Varanthl said. "I wish he was here, now."

Hy'Targ sighed. "Mine is okay, I guess… I know he means well."

"Well mine can be a real bastard," Mantieth muttered from across the path under a willow's shade. He sat back to back with Elorall who scowled disapprovingly at the prince's comment.

Hy'Targ and Varanthl both laughed.

"Nah. He's all right," Hy'Targ said about his own father. "We're just different in many respects—but my father is a lot like yours. A great man—er, vagha, in his own right." He stole a glance at the thing on Varanthl's chest and then looked into the distance. "I really would do anything for him. He's more suited to this sort of adventure than I am."

Varanthl smiled warmly. "I hope I can meet him… when this is all over, of course. He sounds like quite the hero."

Hy'Targ glanced again at the homunculus's chest where the kreethaln peeked out from the tears in Varanthl's tattered shirt. "He really is. I hope that you get to meet him."

Elorall threw a twig at Hy'Targ. "Hey. Don't sell yourself short. From where I sit, you look like you've handled this mission as well as anyone could."

Vy'Danis walked over, leaving Jr'Orhr to stand guard and watch their rear. Something in the way he walked… like a cat stalking prey… grabbed Hy'Targ's attention.

"Something the matter?"

"They haven't blown their horns in hours."

Everyone perked up and stiffened. "Could that be good news?" Hy'Targ asked. "Maybe they lost our trail… maybe they gave up and went home?"

Vy'Danis's gray whiskers turned sideways as his lips thinned. He opened his mouth to speak when the foliage crashed. Goblins mounted on wardogs and wolves burst through the leaves. They screamed and darted down the trail with stone axes and jagged knives at the ready. Their animals slobbered and snarled.

Mantieth drew his bow and plugged two wardogs; their riders tumbled to the dirt. Jr'Orhr ran to quickly fall on them with his axe before they could right themselves.

Another three riders on wolves circled around the small camp and then made their move, running for Elorall. They charged straight down the path and suddenly disappeared with a loud clapping sound as Rhyll stepped onto the road and punted the three into the distance. Their bodies broke through the canopy with a *swish* as they sailed out of sight with pained sounds, having never noticed the efflorah from amongst the trees.

Six more riders came at their flanks, three on each side. Mantieth's bow took down one on his side before they closed the gap and Rhyll smashed one of the others. The final one ducked under him and rode on for Elorall-determined to put down the spell caster. Mantieth abandoned his bow and drew his blade as it came close; the disguised blade's keen edge rang with a menacing sound. The treefolk stomped the rider to goo at the last second.

On the other side, two wardogs snapped and snarled as they tried to outflank Varanthl, who swung his hammer in wide arcs to keep them at bay.

Vy'Danis lunged at the third rider, who mistook the eldest of the party as easy prey. He overextended his swing and let the trog rider grab it by the handle. The goblin sneered victoriously. His cackle quickly turned to gurgling shrieks as

Vy'Danis pulled his dagger and repeatedly stabbed the goblin and his mount, dragging them both to the ground.

Hy'Targ finally caught up to the long-striding homunculus and brought Glorybringer to bear. Varanthl spotted him coming and shifted his grip to his higher set of hands and swung a roundhouse blow towards the wardog rider. It whizzed inches away from the enemy's face. The trog sneered at him while Varanthl turned his back and brought the hammer to bear, smashing the head of the mount on the opposite side.

Before the remaining trog rider could pounce on the exposed homunculus, the enemy noticed Hy'Targ too late, charging beneath Varanthl's wild, high blow. The dwarf swung his battle axe as if he were chopping wood. The blow ripped the goblin rider in two halves and Glorybringer lodged in the wardog's spine, breaking it with gruesome sound.

The homunculus pulled his hammer from the scraps of the wardog's skull and gray matter, searching for the goblin rider who had already scrambled and routed.

"I got him," Jr'Orhr called, snapping his crossbow to attention. He whistled between his tight lips and sighted down his rail.

Foolishly, the trog turned ever so slightly to look back at the sound. Jr'Orhr's quarrel caught the goblin in the neck and tore out his throat, spilling mud-yellow blood across the path.

The creature flailed and clutched the wound. He stumbled near a slough and then pitched headlong into the brackish water, floating face down.

Further down the road from where the wolves had attacked sat the fastest of the mounted goblins. Sitting atop a dusky leopard, the lead scout watched his cavalry units fall. He put a horn to his lips and blasted a menacing note that echoed through the trees. The sound scattered a murder of crows that had greedily gathered to feast upon the battle's losers.

All eyes turned to the leopard scout who sneered and turned his animal back towards the shadows where he could continue to pace them and inform the others of the party's position. They'd never catch him with such a speedy creature at his service.

Elorall screamed defiantly and drew on the arcane power in her core. An azure bolt of lightning shot from her fingertips and caught the leopard and rider. They collapsed in a heap of burned fur and convulsing limbs. Her companions rushed over to the trog and grabbed him by the throat. He wheezed with a death rattle as they dragged him from the mount.

Its leopard lay dead, covered in heat blisters that bubbled upon its smoldering hide.

"Where are they? How close is your army?" Hy'Targ demanded. "How many are there?"

The scout's broken voice merely laughed with a deep, unsettling kind of death groan. "He's coming for you…"

"Who? Who's coming?"

With his final gasp, the goblin wheezed the name, "Ratargul the Smotherer." The trog fell limp and its eyes glazed over.

The adventurers traded glances with each other, and then the quiet pall that hung above the mossy canopy broke as a horn answered the leopard scout's signal. Three other horns picked up the call, and none of them were more than a quarter league away. The enemy was arrayed across the woods behind them— and they were close.

Rhyll led the charge, smashing through the trail; he cracked branches and tromped down snarls of tangle-fern. Boughs shook, and vines caught frequently around his head. The time for stealth had passed. Every few minutes they spotted a new trog ambusher lurking in the trees or errant sling bullets tore through the foliage nearby.

Their pursuit converged, crushing around them. trogs shrieked and hissed from the trees and scampered after them through witchgrass and thorny bracken.

A roar shook the trees, and heavy footprints thundered on the trail. The monster they belonged to demolished the low-hanging branches with a cracking thud. It charged forward, undeterred and ripping through the leaning branches.

A head taller than Varanthl and wider around than Rhyll, it locked glowing yellow eyes on its prey.

"A shambler," cried Mantieth. "Ratargul is a shambling mound!"

The creature roared in defiance. Jogging just behind him was the goblin commander, sporting his crusty paints of red and white.

Hy'Targ set his jaw as his blood heated. These were the same goblins who had stolen Brentésion. But he could spot neither the troll who had taken her, nor the mythic dragonkin herself. trogs were not that stupid, it seemed. *The troll must be with her somewhere else… I will get her back—I swear it.*

Ratargul tromped forward on large strides. His hulking arms ended in fists with viny tendril whips. Every piece of him looked bred from the sludge at the bottom of the bogs and laid over thick, corded muscles.

Without warning, Rhyll stopped short on the path. His companions piled up against him, and the enemies began to close the gap, charging on them.

Elorall threw up a protective wall of magic just in time to catch the projectiles flung by the goblins. "Why are we stopping?" she strained against the sheer volume of missiles incoming, but demanded an answer for their stoppage.

Rhyll turned worriedly. "The path! It's riddled with Gray Blight." The road they were on was the only way forward. Deep pools of murk and filth surrounded the trail on either side.

Hy'Targ looked past the treefolk. Ichorous black ooze pooled near the trail. It hung in sheaves off trees and clung to moss. The contagion danger was everywhere.

Behind them, Ratargul howled. Two tons of raging, carnivorous plant life threatened to break them apart in mere seconds. All hope seemed to shatter in that moment.

Vy'Danis reached into his pocket and pulled out the ancient scroll King Hy'Mandr had given him at the trip's start. "No durned better time than now." He broke the seal on the scroll and read the words on the old, magic-imbued paper.

It flashed with a bang of arcane power. The scroll incinerated with a flash of light and fire, releasing the pent-up spell.

The ground rumbled and heaved; it bucked and raised up to form a protective wall as Vy'Danis summoned the heart of a mountain. "Huh," he muttered. "So *that's* what it does."

Towering more than a hundred cubits high, the spontaneous hill cut them off from the enemy. The jagged outcrop spread far enough to create a wide wall that ended in the pools of filthy murk. Even if the trogs trudged through it, it would take them hours—and nobody guessed that those bogs were safe—even for goblins.

Elorall slumped against Mantieth, fatigued and strained beyond her normal limits.

Hy'Targ scowled, sucked in his breath, and strode into the plagued trail, picking his steps one at a time and thankful for Vy'Danis's quick thinking.

"I've got a bad feeling about this," Rhyll complained, watching his companions enter. "Our chances might be better with the trogs."

They heard scratching sounds as Ratargul and his minions scrambled up the pile of earth on taloned claws and paws. Some of them had found a path they could climb *over* the thing. Finally, even Rhyll ducked his head and pushed forward into the path.

Ratargul and a clutch of his more talented minions had made it over the barrier. They stopped at the edge, refusing to press into the spoiled foliage.

Hy'Targ and his company stopped only momentarily to look back and watch the monstrous shambler who refuse to go any further. A keen intelligence burned in the monster's eyes; he understood the threat of the blight.

One of his goblins stepped into the trail, testing the way forward, and the shambler crushed it with a roar that bordered on fear. He looked up and met gazes with Hy'Targ, as if promising they would meet again… if the dwarf survived the perils of the deep swamp.

The dwarf turned his head and returned to the road with a new appreciation for the dangers of the bog. There were things here far more dangerous than goblins. Hy'Targ looked around, thinking of one danger in particular: burned skeleton trackers… they hadn't seen one since their flight from Undrakull. He frowned. That most likely meant bad news for Vy'Hrothgyr the bard.

CHAPTER EIGHTEEN

Slick with perspiration, the mammoth steeds below Vy'Hrothgyr, Jr'Dunn, and Jr'Tarl frothed at the mouth. Their pelts had foamed with oil and sweat as the dwarves drove their beasts to such reckless speeds that it would surely lame their mounts, if not kill them.

As much as vagha loved their mounts, the creatures didn't matter—only the bones did. The dwarves could always breed new mammoths, but they might not have another chance to stop Melkior. They'd spotted a black skeleton for the first time one day ago and then lost it when they crossed through a river. Now, there were two of them, barely blips on the horizon behind them, running in dogged pursuit, but the vagha knew that they could close that distance in short order. The dwarves could not stop. They could not slow.

On the horizon, the bastion walls of the Irontooth Kingdom jutted out from the Irontooth Mountain, their clan's home. The sight brought such joy that even their despairing steeds had quickened their steps as they raced across the open field on the mountain's approach. Relief finally overrode their fatigue.

"We're going to make it," Vy'Hrothgyr cried, "We're really going to make it!" He glanced down at the cursed bag that bounced upon his hip, their weight pulled at the bard's belt like a millstone. His mastodon, faster than the rest, galloped ahead of the other two, breaking away and charging for the main gate.

Jr'Dunn spotted friends standing upon the walls, watching their hasty return with puzzled faces. Mi'Darrio waited above the main gate with Tr'Gurn and Ne'Vistar, members of the King's inner circle. They suddenly turned their noses skyward.

A terrible, guttural screech rent the sky and a shadowy pall fell over the riders like an eclipse. The two in the rear didn't hear or see the monstrosity, but they felt the white-hot pain that seared through them, blasting their skin to ash and cinder. Dragon's breath struck the beasts directly and obliterated the mammoths. Their corpses tumbled and spun with the momentum of their speed, scattering bone and flesh across the heather. Rib cages of two once-mighty steeds rolled across the plains like tumbleweed.

The fearsome Rahkawmn howled one more time in victory and then plunged down from the sky and snatched up Vy'Hrothgyr, mammoth and all, barely two hundred cubits in front of the dwarven gate. vagha stood on the parapets, wild-eyed. A few of them managed to fire ballista shots from their defensive towers, but the bolts bounced harmlessly off the hide of the corptic, rotting drake. Rahkawmn bent his head and ripped the mammoth in two halves. It dropped one half, holding the other as it leaked entrails across the countryside. Rahkawmn clutched Vy'Hrothgyr in its other massive paw and lumbered into the distance on slow but powerful wings, climbing high into the sky.

Mi'Darrio had already burst through the main gate and skidded to his knees. The general was the first to arrive at Jr'Dunn's side. He rolled his friend over, exposing the charred and blackened flesh that had gnarled with the heat and crushed against the gravel of the fall. Tr'Gurn arrived only moments later with Ne'Vistar still coming far behind.

Jr'Dunn could only stammer through his lips, frozen by shock and damage from the fall. "Melkior… Melkior… Melkior…"

"What? What is it? Where is the prince?" Mi'Darrio shook his friend—demanding information before the stout dwarf lost consciousness, perhaps forever. "What happened; where is Hy'Targ?" he shook his friend.

King Hy'Mandr had left Mi'Darrio in charge during his absence. Blind though he was, the Adventurer King had taken the bulk of the army and gone out to war.

Jr'Dunn's eyes snapped back open, wide and awake. The shock had set in so deep Jr'Dunn no longer felt pain. "Melkior has the bones... black skeletons... chasing us for days!"

"But what does that mean?"

Ne'Vistar pulled near with another dwarf on the wagon they had commandeered. A painted pony pulled it faster than recommended.

Jr'Dunn tried to sit up; his eyes screamed with pain and he growled through it as the adrenaline and shock begun to wear off, "Bring me to the king, right away!" Unable to move properly with his damaged limbs, he finally collapsed from the pain. His eyes spotted something ahead, and he pointed to the singed item in the dirt.

"The King is not here, old friend. I'll have to do," Mi'Darrio said.

The wounded traveler didn't seem to hear him. He barely managed to croak, "The book... Vy'Hrothgyr's journal. The bard wrote down everything. Grab it... The King will want it if I don't... if I don't..." Jr'Dunn stuttered and then trailed off, finally passing out from the pain.

With the road ahead more dangerous than ever, Vy'Danis insisted on leading the party through the swamp. The older dwarf muttered something about duty to King Hy'Mandr and how he'd lived long enough so far—if any should fall to the black poison, it ought to be him.

Hy'Targ and the others let him take that role and followed the eldest adventurer. The crew carefully picked their way through the treacherous, black leakage that dripped from trees and puddled on the ground in murky deposits.

The speed of caution halved the distance they could cover in a day, especially given Rhyll's size. He found it difficult to navigate some of the tighter spaces and had to frequently suck in or even tie back some of his boughs.

Supplies ran low as they traveled, and so they cut their rations even shorter, knowing that only more hunger and thirst awaited them in the future. Days had stretched out into a gray lump of time, and the canopy overhead blocked out the sun with multiple shades of drab. More leaves had turned ashen than remained green at the darkest part of the forest, and the travelers could not remember how much time had passed since they entered.

They pushed through the dead zone with tense muscles and quiet resolve. In the dark of night, other-worldly groans kept them awake, but its source never approached the light of their dim campfires which belched blue, peaty smoke.

Finally, they spotted one of the undead groaners during the day. It seemed more like an apparition: a creature walking down the forest trail. The figure had once been a trog. One foot had been gnawed away and so it limped, but moved with sentient mannerisms.

Vy'Danis cocked an eyebrow. They'd all learned from his cautious skepticism. The bloodless didn't mind its steps and walked through a puddle, clumsily splashing Necralluvium around its crooked goblin legs.

Mantieth loosed an arrow, but the thing continued its approach. He nocked another, and the others added missiles to his. Feathered shafts protruded from the zombie's rotting flesh, but the thing kept coming, picking up speed with every step that it took.

Finally, the trog rushed towards them. Behind them, they saw others like it emerging from the swamp. Gray blight clung to them like a fungus, and weeds hung like swamp curtains.

Hy'Targ readied his axe as the undead goblin closed to striking distance.

Rhyll slammed the creature with his mighty fists. He pounded the next one, and another, and another as they rushed mindlessly from the black heart of the swamp. Finally, silence reigned again. A pile of smashed goblin corpses blocked their path.

The treefolk pushed the mound of cadavers aside, and they toppled into the bog. Their gas-filled body-cavities emptied and the dead things gurgled and hissed, sinking slowly into the depths of the muck-bottomed fen with a curious stench.

"What does it mean?" Varanthl asked, watching the blighted bodies disappear, "aside from that this is why the trogs knew better than to come here?"

"It means we're on the right course," Elorall said. "We must be getting close to Melkior. This is a result of his influence."

They took a moment to rest in the heavy, sweltering air. Rhyll tapped Varanthl on the shoulder. "A word in private, my friend?"

The homunculus nodded, and they took a few steps away from the party. Varanthl looked at him curiously.

"I do so hope that my beloved Lavrildr is okay." He paused mournfully. "She is… family."

Varanthl did not speak, he merely listened.

"She took the blight… before I left, it had gotten deeper into her rings than we'd realized." Rhyll looked Varanthl in the eyes. "I remember what you did… with the mammoth outside of Undrakull."

"I don't understand," Varanthl finally stated.

"I believe you are uniquely immune to this plague." Rhyll turned his hands over to show his friend the patch of festering, black bark on them.

Varanthl's face darkened. His friend had caught a splatter of Necralluvium during the attack, and his tawny bark-skin turned a pallid hue of dappled gray where it had touched the stuff. As the homunculus watched, the infected spots expanded incrementally.

"Please," Rhyll said. "I cannot let the infection take me… I've seen it, seen what it does."

Varanthl looked up at him. "What are you asking of me?"

Rhyll's voice was low and serious. "Remove it."

The four-armed creature nodded measuredly. He used two strong hands to hold Rhyll's arms still and drew his dagger with the others. One at a time, Varanthl cut away great sections of Rhyll's hands.

Trembling like a branch in the wind, Rhyll shuddered as the homunculus cut on him. He groaned slightly, trying to remain as stoic as possible, but Varanthl had to slice away much of his friend's xylem, carving deep down past the woody cambium layer to make sure the Necralluvium had not advanced, and to make sure he could finish excising the infection before it spread.

Finally, he finished. Varanthl stared at his friend's wounded hands for several long minutes. Satisfied he didn't see any of the creeping Gray Blight grow upon the wounded efflorah, he grabbed his friend's hands and clutched them. "You should be okay," he reassured him.

Rhyll let out a pained sigh. "Thank you," he said as the others readied themselves on the trail to continue their journey. "I certainly hope that this Gray Blight can be cured, or its secrets laid bare after we capture or kill Melkior."

Varanthl bobbed his head and agreed. "From here forward, we must take care to pick our way through here as quietly as possible." He kicked the contaminated carvings he'd trimmed from Rhyll's hands and scattered them into the slough so he wouldn't have to cut on his friend's toes off next.

He wiped his hands on the grass sprouting nearest the patch, and then he opted to simply chuck the dagger into the duckweed. There was no sense in taking any risks with such dark alchemy.

Niamarlee stood a good way off. Towers and spires of elven design rose above the distant haze that obscured the reaches of the Great Coastal Road.

The air in front of the vaghan army twisted and warped momentarily as a spell disturbed the natural order. Rippling like a tidal pool, the air shimmered and belched out two figures and then untwisted, returning to normal and completing the incantation.

Taryl held up a hand and stayed the army that had taken a defensive position against whatever might pop out of the spell's opening. The eldarim champion charged towards it, reaching for his sword, but pulled back as he recognized the figures who emerged. Mi'Darrio and Ne'Vistar approached the eldarim general.

"What are you two doing here? You're supposed to be minding the king's business."

"Urgent news," Mi'Darrio shot back.

"So urgent that it required both of you?"

Ne'Vistar nodded gravely. He pocketed the wayfare orb and allowed it to recharge.

Taryl hurried the two dwarves into the king's presence. The king traveled in a secured wagon large enough to fit several advisers. Taryl crawled in after Mi'Darrio and Ne'Vistar.

King Hy'Mandr tilted his ear towards his trusted advisers, but scanned them as if he could actually see, at least in part. "What is so important that you…"

"We can't go to Niamarlee," Ne'Vistar insisted.

"I can bloody well do what I want," Hy'Mandr snapped, cranky and cooped up from the road. "I'm the king."

"If we stop to siege the selumari, Prince Hy'Targ will die," Mi'Darrio insisted.

Hy'Mandr's brow furrowed.

Ne'Vistar explained, "There was an attack on the mountain…"

"Leidergelth?"

"No. Everything from Hy'Targ's journal was accurate. Before the prince left, our seers had a vision, and it is coming to pass. The bloodless are returning to our land. An undead dragon just wiped out half of Hy'Targ's companions, who originally rode north with him. The dragon burned them alive on our very doorstep and took the bones of Ailushurai." He briefly ran down what had happened since Mi'Darrio met with the adventurers after they'd exhumed the body near the human settlement a couple weeks ago. "Hy'Targ and the others still press on for the Ivory Citadel of Lurneville."

The king's face darkened, and he tilted his head towards the old magi. "But they're just bones, right?"

Ne'Vistar shook his head. "If Melkior gets them, the lich will have enough power to raise an army the likes that Esfah has never seen—power promised to him by Malg… Death. It was promised to him long ago, before the first Champions of the Gods ended his reign of terror."

Hy'Mandr grimaced and bit his lip as he contemplated the possible courses of action. "Ne'Vistar," he asked, "who did you leave in charge of the throne?"

The old scholar shrank away from his words. "I, um… I had to make a difficult decision… the heads of the families started bickering over who would act as steward; I think they believed you wouldn't return from this battle with your, uh, condition."

"Out with it!"

"They were at each other's throats, as if the acting ruler might have a stronger claim to the throne if you didn't…"

"I said to tell me," Hy'Mandr insisted.

"Your brother… but we left Tr'Gurn with him," Ne'Vistar answered, as if that was some small consolation, but everyone knew Tr'Gurn was easily plied whenever alcohol was introduced to a situation. "And also Wo'Dunnia, the sprinter who served the delegate at Niamarlee."

The king sighed and set his jaw with a curled lip. Finally, he said, "What's done is done. We'll just have to hope by Firiel and Eldurim that my screw-up brother doesn't do too much damage in the interim."

Nods circled through the king's company.

Hy'Mandr gave the order. "Taryl, tell the army that Br'Derluch will have to wait. Take the caravan further north… as fast as we can possibly manage, but we've got to skirt the elven city. We can't risk them wanting to stop and scuffle, and we all better pray Leidergelth doesn't decide to make a play for our mountain while we're gone. That durned brother of mine might just give it to him," he muttered.

The king bit his lip and smoothed his unruly, red and white beard. "What I wouldn't give for some new champions," he said.

Ne'Vistar cocked his head and leaned closer to his leader. He looked him over curiously, staring into his face. He whispered. "Hy'Mandr… can you *see me?*"

The king smiled. But shook his head. "I remember yer ugly face. I'm glad to be blind… but I started sensing light and dark the other day." He waived away any hope the dwarves might've leapt to and pounded on the wall of his carriage. "Hop to it, Taryl," he ordered. "We're in a hurry and can't stop to quarrel with the elves!"

CHAPTER NINETEEN

Vy'Danis motioned for all the party to duck down and remain quiet as they approached. His companions slowly crawled towards the dwarf's forward position to see what he'd found.

A gloomy fen spread off from the trail ahead and a mound of muck rose from its center where a cluster of men with flesh like snakes had gathered. Few of the scaly folk meandered around the tiny village; mud and stick huts were arrayed so that they circled a central pyre. Only one of the structures looked considerably different from the others.

Poles of the peculiar hut stretched the flayed hide of some monster wide, or perhaps it was an enormous molting. Upon the door flap hung bone decorations and baubles from a myriad of cultures which were formed into a curtain that veiled whatever remained inside. The slimy citizenry seemed to give the hut a reverential step as they moved by it.

The remainder of their tribe waded through the marsh, dragging their victims through the quagmire as they struggled against their bonds.

"sarslayans," Hy'Targ identified them. "Swamp stalkers," he clarified with their common name. The well-read dwarf pointed to the captives who looked like animal-human hybrids. "They're all ghwereste, the feral folk."

Vy'Danis placed his hand on the prince's arm. "I don't care who they are… I only care about navigating us around this gods-forsaken place undetected."

The snakemen trudged out from the sloshing, filthy swamp and threw their prisoners to the ground before the deathly tabernacle. Black muck matted their fur and clung to the ghwereste.

Furling wide the entry to the odd tent, a terrifying sarslayan slithered from within. Below the monstrosity's bone, feather, and onyx headdress, his piercing, amber eyes searched the prisoners. He hissed and uttered a string of commands in a foreign tongue.

"Where is it?" he hissed in the common language and caressed the face of half-man, half-badger with his talons.

"Come on," Vy'Danis insisted in hushed tones. "We've got to get out of here. Keep on mission."

"Where is the seed?" the sarslayan chieftain roared. "Our spies know you have it."

"Wait," Rhyll said, suddenly very interested. "What seed…"

Vy'Danis bit his tongue as the party revolted against the common sense he urged them to.

The ghwereste refused to answer, and so the chief threw his writhing arms wide and made a guttural proclamation.

One of the swamp stalker guards bellowed in the common tongue for the feral folk's benefit, "The ceremony of the Watery Death! Bring out the waters of Lethial."

Hy'Targ and his companions watched in horror as two scullions dragged a heavy stone pot from the tent of skin and bone. A dark, stygian slop splashed up as they dropped it before the leader, who threw a fistful of powder into the fire. It flashed with a dazzling light, pulsing and flickering in a rhythmic fashion.

"Don't look at the light," Hy'Targ whispered as the sarslayans forced a lynx-folk to his knees and grabbed him by the fur at the back of his head. They peeled his eyelids and forced him to stare into the flames until his pupils contracted to black orbs.

Somewhere behind them came the sound of tribal drums. sarslayans swayed and chanted as they gathered around the ceremony.

The mage directing the ceremony plunged a dagger into their captive and drained his blood into a bowl; so entranced by the lights, the wounded creature didn't even flinch. Dumping the blood into the cauldron, the scaly one slashed his hand and added several drops of his own to the mix.

Swamp stalkers grabbed the entranced one and dragged him to the stone pot while the badger-folk screamed, pleading with them to stop. Pleading with his friend to snap out of his fugue.

Hissing at the badger-folk, the sarslayan chief obviously believed him to be their leader.

The snakemen forced their enchanted victims head into the oily water. He awoke and thrashed, trying to pull free, but the enemies held him fast while they dragged another two of the feral folk towards the flames.

Enemies kicked the back of their knees and forced them into the mud and watch the enchanted fire as they struggled.

With a final lurch, the drowned one surrendered. Moments later, they pulled him free. His eyes shone the same sickly yellow as the sarslayans. The newly transformed clutched his face when they released him, scratching at it as though he were molting. Patches of hide and skin scraped free and hung from him in fleshy chunks.

The convert pointed with a reptilian talon; his ghwereste flesh had torn free from his digits. "Grarrha has it," he shrieked, both body and mind enslaved to the swamp stalkers. "He has the Seed of Hope!"

As Grarrha, the badger-folk, struggled and protested, the revelation momentarily shook their last two companions free of the effects of the enchanted flame.

Rhyll groaned something in treespeak.

"What is the Seed of Hope? You know it?" whispered Mantieth.

He bent his head slightly.

Hy'Targ nodded as well. "It's from an ancient, epic poem, *The Soldier's Journey*, by Elius Lawfollow, a selumari. Don't you guys read your own classics?"

Mantieth looked to Elorall. Both shrugged.

"It's an allegory. A metaphor for the journey towards goodness. The Seed of Hope is like a golden seed that produces an inner light: hope."

"No," Rhyll rumbled his quiet disagreement. "It is real and not figurative. And there are few such seeds remaining in existence."

Hy'Targ raised an argumentative eyebrow. "I've actually studied the epics quite a bit. Many scholars have written on the subject. So, unless you've seen it..."

Behind them, Grarrha howled, insisting, "I lied—I lied to you all. The seed is not real, I just needed traveling companions..."

Grarrha fought against his captors. The secret company of travelers were unable to help. They could not intervene and remain hidden.

The treefolk motioned the vagha over to a nearby stump and pointed to the gray wood which long ago succumbed to breakage. "I've not seen it before, but the memories of trees are longer than the words of scholars." He pointed to the stump's age-faded rings. "Can you read these? They are the memories of this one."

Hy'Targ shook his head.

"I can. Any efflorah could look into this one's past." Rhyll tapped a dark ring near the pith. "This tree was named Nrrng'uhl-yeee-vnrvv. It did not see the seed. It could not. It was merely a tree, not an efflorah like me. But Nrrng'uhl-yeee-vnrvv believed in the Tree of Hope with every fiber of his xylem. You've not seen Firiel or Ailuril, and yet you believe... so it is with faith. Sometimes we see the effects of the gods but not the substance of them."

Hy'Targ nodded measuredly. He could accept that, at least in part.

Screams erupted from the village as the two ghwereste fought back, head-butting their captors. A mob of sarslayan tackled one to the ground.

The other feral folk threw himself into the pyre, refusing to be turned by the poisoned waters. He writhed within the flames as he screamed, "Grarrha, run!"

Rhyll tensed to intervene, but Vy'Danis held his hands up. "No! *We cannot get involved.* We must move on to the keep—we can't fight Melkior if we're all dead! Ye just got to trust fate—the gods know what they're doin." Logic had proved useless to motivate them, and so the dwarf tried a different tactic: invoking the sovereignty of the gods. "If it were their will for us to intervene, we'd be in the thick of it with that ghwereste already, and nothin we do could stop it."

The treefolk stood down even if he did not like the command. He dared not argue if the dwarf appealed to the gods.

Across the fen, Grarrha shook himself free and dashed further into the camp, not away from the crackling fire. He body-checked the mage-chief and shoved him into their makeshift shrine. A post snapped and collapsed it.

Before any enemy could catch him, Grarrha dunked his head into the vessel of fetid water where his friend had drowned. Grarrha took a deep gulp and then spilled the container of sacred drink.

Filthy swamp dwellers leapt for the hallowed basin and for their leader, trying to save whatever they could of the liquid. Grarrha used the distraction as an opportunity to escape. He dashed around a mud hovel and then splashed through the murk, circumventing the rest of the sarslayan village.

Vy'Danis urged his party, "Come on, now! It's our time to get away." He tromped down the trail on high alert. The others followed, trying to move as stealthily as possible, but also at top speed. With the swamp stalkers distracted, they'd certainly be able to maximize their cover.

They'd gotten nearly half a league away when a ghwereste with ratty, mired fur burst through the foliage and onto their path. His lungs heaved as he paused for breath.

Grarrha took two steps towards the party and then bent over and puked up the vile waters of Lethial that he'd drunk. The unctuous mix of crimson and gray spilled across the rugged road and a brilliant, shimmering seed fell from his mouth.

Drums sounded in the fen behind them, and the ghwereste snatched the golden nut and pocketed it. He looked at them all, only identifying them as something other than sarslayan. Grarrha hacked and spat one more time. "Please, you've got to save me!"

Vy'Danis bit his lip and frowned, cursing both irony and all three sisters of Fate for suddenly imposing the gods' mission upon him.

"One of my closest advisers has had a disturbing dream," King Leidergelth said. The selumari king sat outside the locked door where the recently escaped morehl had stayed.

From his prison cell, Br'Derluch rolled his eyes, but finally decided to engage the elf. "Maybe give him a glass of warm milk and send him back to bed," he scoffed.

The king ignored the snarky comment. "I wouldn't say he is my friend... kings can never *truly* have friends; kings do not have equals... but if friendships were possible, I would almost say that Furtaevell is mine."

"So, what do you want, then... to talk about your feelings? I'm starting to wish I would have joined Fi'Krayg and pulled my knife on ye. I could be dead right now... if only I wouldda played my cards right," Br'Derluch lamented with as much sarcasm as he had whiskers.

Leidergelth clearly paid him little mind. "Furtaevell is a talented arcanist… very powerful… perhaps the most powerful mage in Niamarlee." He paused and added below his breath, "At least, he's the most powerful selumari."

"Is there a point to this?"

He looked at the prisoner through the slot on the door. "Furtaevell only rarely has visions of the future, but when he does, they *always* come to pass."

Br'Derluch met his gaze through the hole, finally convinced they'd begun to engage. His posturing ended, and he recognized the king was genuinely fearful. "What did he see?"

Leidergelth's throat tightened. "My son… dead. His daughter… dead. *Your prince… dead.*"

The dwarven delegate pulled his stool closer to the door and sat. "And this fate is certain?"

With a grimace, Leidergelth shrugged. "Uncertain. It is theoretically possible that we could change this outcome… if we act appropriately."

"So, you come looking to me of all folk for answers—a vagha?"

"Visions are funny things. Sometimes they are symbolic. This deathly figure in the dream, for instance, it could be anything… it might not even be literal. It could even be a stand-in for Hy'Mandr who thinks to wage war on us." Leidergelth opened Furtaevell's journal to the terrifying image of Melkior that the enchanter had drawn in his fever state.

Br'Derluch studied it and scowled. "If you're asking me if my king could commit such an atrocity, my answer is no."

"He was en route to lay siege to Niamarlee, only recently. Something turned him aside."

Br'Derluch hid a relieved smile. He realized Wo'Dunnia must've made it home to rally his leader for aide.

Leidergelth asked, "What would make a king do that?"

"Yer a king. Ask yerself."

"I'm asking *you*. What would make the proud Hy'Mandr turn his army aside when he'd set his mind to siege Niamarlee?"

Br'Derluch reached slowly through the hole and put a finger on a spot in the detailed sketch: the dwarf. "His son. Hy'Targ means everything to the Adventurer King. Even dwarven pride pales in comparison.

Leidergelth turned the book and examined it. He hadn't noticed anything in the background before, he'd been fixated on the grisly depiction of Mantieth. Br'Derluch had pointed to the body of a fallen vagha in the background, and he was not alone. There were others there, too. "How do you know that is Hy'Targ?"

"It looks like him, and that axe... see the runes on it? It's Glorybringer. It belonged to Hy'Mandr. The King always said he wanted to pass it on if'n his son ever took up adventuring. I can't say for certain who the others are."

Leidergelth stared a moment longer at the image. If forced to admit it, he thought all dwarves looked alike.

"And where is Hy'Targ now?"

"Adventuring," Leidergelth mumbled, convinced by the evidence. He swallowed the lump in his throat, plagued by the implications of Furtaevell's vision.

"Tell me, Br'Derluch, do you share Furtaevell's belief that the vagha prince's mission is cursed?"

"It don't matter two scratches what I think. But you'n yer kind keep thinking and acting like you're better than the vagha. Are you gonna keep thinking that if Hy'Mandr gives up his grudge to save his son, and you don't even try to rescue yers? What truly matters is what *you think*... and what you decide to do with that."

King Leidergelth scowled. He closed the enchanter's morbid journal, stood, and walked away.

Distance drowned the sounds of the pursuit drums and the swamp-stuck party slackened its pace, but only slightly. Vy'Danis wouldn't allow anything slower than a brisk walk. Finally, wore out by a full day of travel at the fastest speeds possible, they broke camp many leagues away from the sarslayan site.

The group built no fire and kept as quiet as possible. They all needed rest and so they kept no watch, but Vy'Danis set a few wires on the path and rigged them to bells. They slept only lightly, and only for a few hours at a time before rising groggily to their feet in the early light to do it all again.

Their feral-folk companion eventually shared his mission after they'd put enough distance between them and the enemy. "I was sent by the sylvans of the Feylands," Grarrha said, piquing the interests of the others. Even Vy'Danis bent his ear; the Feylands were clear on the opposite side of the next continent across the sea and their forests sprawled for more than two hundred thousand square leagues until they ended at the coasts of the Shining Sea. "Only myself and one other knew the true nature of our mission, my mentor, Negnathae. We collected the seed in secret, traveling all the way to Reeves Island, a place under human control. It lies south of Hadden Bay between Dehnlee and Xlinea.

"I became separated from him when the swamp stalkers attacked. Now, I must get the seed back to where it can be planted and protected."

Ever the doubter, Jr'Orhr piped up, "Yer goin the wrong way if yer tryin to get back home."

Grarrha nodded slowly. "You know the tale of the Gray Wanderer?"

Only Hy'Targ nodded. He understood it as another name for *The Soldier's Journey*.

"The seed needed to be fertilized, first," Grarrha said. "It won't sprout if it's not first activated… we needed the waters of the River Lethial… a cursed stream that dried up more than a thousand years ago. The sarslayan keep traces of the original waters for their ritual of the Watery Death."

Grarrha recited a passage from the epic, quoting two relevant pieces.

The Abyss
is wrought with rage;
passions of hate churn there.
Its walls are of cloven fears
pegged by spikes of despair.
In its depths lies the River of No Return;
the stench of sluggish waters
couples with terror
and bears bitter fruit…

Beside him was a broken bough,
Its end tipped with wilted silver petals
And a golden nut.
He kept the Seed,
Its beauty his only talisman against the Dark.

Hy'Targ asked, "Are you saying the Dark is a reference to the shadow creature defeated by the Amazon hero at the dawn of the Second Age?" He bumbled through his memory for a few moments. "Lyander, was it? I can never remember it… human names never make sense to me. The same story from where Lyander's Pass was named—just south of Gundakhor."

Grarrha nodded and shrugged. "That may be so. We encountered no resistance on the island, though none would have known where to look if not for the instructions we received before leaving the Feylands." Grarrha continued quoting the passage.

The Dead Zone

Has no heart, no soul.
To wander there long
is sure and certain death.
But it became the soldier's home,
and he is its gray wanderer,
its keeper of the last Seed of Hope.

"Until the seed could be activated by the lifeblood—the same sluggish waters of the cursed river that spawned it—possessing the Seed is a mere vanity… but if the seed becomes alive…" he trailed off.

Hy'Targ raised an eyebrow. "Encountering the swamp stalkers was always part of the plan?" he realized.

Grarrha nodded and then picked up the pace. The party had slowed during Grarrha's telling.

"What? What do you plan to use the seed for?" Rhyll asked.

"For centuries, there has been a dark blight spreading across the face of Esfah," Grarrha insisted. "Perhaps you have seen it. An oily black. It has taken the seas, corrupted the soil, and I fear that in time it could twist the other gods, too… perhaps it will become a cloud and overtake Ailuril's domain. I do not know, but it must be stopped."

Hy'Targ glanced aside at the nearby hanging moss fronds. They dripped with Necralluvium.

"Evil marshals its forces. Large-scale wars may have grown cold these last two hundred years, but only because Death has changed his tactics. Death subverts good, weakens it and corrupts it from within."

Vy'Danis listened intently, but coaxed the team back along the trail as they slowed again.

"How so?" Hy'Targ asked, looking for clarity. Not an argument.

"Nodhan said that it isn't only morehl who join these psycho death cults," Mantieth mumbled. "Could selumari or even vagha be working for the dark one?"

Grarrha offered his take on it. "Look at the results. selumari fight the vagha over something as trivial as land. The amazons—human warriors—have become either fearful or apathetic. The eldarim's line is diluted and scattered in diaspora. The Arcana Veil dividing the realms has stiffened… in days of old, any dwarf or elf could harness the elemental magics. Now only those who have the innate talents can harness them—and how often do you see the drakufreet? Dragonkin have nearly vanished from this world except as an occasional novelty. This blight is a part of that. The Tree of Hope can dismantle that curse."

Hy'Targ frowned. His gut still burned with the loss of Brentésion.

They resumed a speedier pace as Rhyll spoke, "I believe him."

Elloral slowed and cocked her ear. She'd always been more perceptive than most—it was partly what had opened her mind and giftings to magic. She stared far off, sensing something the others did not.

"What is it?" Mantieth asked, walking near her. He turned his head as well, hearing it clearly in the pause.

"sarslayan drums."

CHAPTER TWENTY

The drums boomed loudly on their heels as the party dashed through the winding paths. Their trail twisted and turned through the sloughs, forcing them to run maddeningly long distances while the sarslayans cut directly through the muck of the fens and snaked their way towards them on an intercept course. The scaly creatures splashed on all sides of them, threatening to overtake the fugitives.

Finally, the first of the reptilian creatures burst through the foliage. Jr'Orhr quickly cut him down, and Mantieth and Elorall snap-fired a few arrows into the reptilian stalkers who harried their rear.

Sarslayans leapt from the trees, thinking their superior numbers would make reclaiming the ghwereste easy. Varanthl and Hy'Targ hacked their way through the surge of voracious monsters.

"We could really use your help, Rhyll!" Vy'Danis shouted as he mowed down two serpentine warriors wishing for another attack from mighty efflorah like the one he'd displayed against the goblins.

Rhyll stood protectively next to the badger-folk. He shouted, "I must save Grarrha!" He pushed the feral one towards a nearby tree that seemed to still have some life left in its roots.

The treefolk ignored the pleas for assistance, instead searching deep down within himself as he tried to muster whatever magics he could. He growled, feeling a strain in his core. "Elorall, I need assistance. Feel the soul of this tree, summon whatever energy you can from Aguarehl and channel it into this one!"

She hurried over and summoned her innate arcane powers. Elorall bit her lower lip and gave Rhyll a tenuous look. "Something is hampering my power—something nearby."

They turned as one and looked at the swamp. A scaly beast rose from the water, parts of its old flesh had been torn away to reveal the new, puckered scales. Fetid mire clung to the once fine feathers of the converted owl-folk.

Grarrha stiffened and stepped back aghast. "Negnathae!"

The mutated ghwereste hissed as it shook the mud from its body. Hunks of owl flesh fell off it as the hybrid approached. It grinned as it continued negating Elorall's energy and its beak slid off its face, splashing into the water.

"Negnathae knows what I possess," Grarrha yelled. "We must not let them acquire the Seed!"

The massive owl-folk approached, squishing through the mud with hideous resolve. Smaller hybrid sarslayans flanked him, ready to sacrifice themselves in order to obtain the prize for their tribal chief.

Mantieth plugged several of them with arrows, but more kept coming. Elorall and Rhyll stared at the tree and redoubled their arcane efforts. "We must open the heart of the tree—all trees are connected by the heart of Esfah. I know the spell; we can send him straight away to the Feylands if you can muster the energy!"

Swamp stalkers pushed Hy'Targ and Varanthl back towards the others. They backpedaled dangerously close to Rhyll and Elorall. Grarrha turned and looked to the path; he considered fleeing and taking his chances on foot. He looked back at the corrupted owl-folk, knowing that he'd never make it on foot.

Negnathae continued dispelling Elorall's mystic energies, and he and the others strode forward, confident in their overwhelming numbers. As Varanthl ducked beneath the raking claws of a serpentine sarslayan, he smashed his hand into a wad of inky Necralluvium.

Swinging his hammer, he smashed through the stalker's lower body and then shot back up to his feet. He hurled the wad of viscous gunk and hit Negnathae in the face.

The converted ghwereste shrieked and flailed as the Necralluvium crawled across Negnathae's head. His flesh sizzled, and he clutched at it, only spreading the oily mass further.

All eyes turned to the beast, including the sarslayan minions. They stopped in their tracks, fear and panic turning their golden eyes a deeper shade of yellow.

Mantieth seized the opportunity and put an arrow through Negnathae's heart.

Negnathae screamed one last time, pitched headlong, and fell dead into the murky water. He bubbled and tipped like a breeching ship and then sank beneath the surface.

"Got it!" exclaimed Elorall. She squeezed her hands together and pulled them apart as if she'd squeezed an invisible accordion. Focusing on the energies she summoned, that special spark that connected her to Esfah's heart roared to life. She channeled that energy into Rhyll, combining her magic with his as if braiding the energies together so that either could shape a spell.

At Rhyll's direction, the tree unstitched itself and opened like an organic door, releasing an inner light. Minor globes of magic hovered like sprites, inviting a passenger within.

Grarrha felt for his pocket to be sure that the seed remained out of sight and where he had put it. He panicked only momentarily when he could not locate the rigid bulge and then calmed as much as possible, given the circumstances, when his fingers laid against the round shape of the sacred seed buttoned within his pocket. He quickly nodded his thanks to Rhyll and Elorall and then hurled himself through the magic aperture within the tree. It quickly enveloped him, and he disappeared, knowing he would emerge fifteen hundred leagues away.

The other sarslayans screeched and recoiled as the ghwereste disappeared with his prize, but they did not attack further. Instead, they slinked back down and into the water where they watched from afar but refused to engage them. With Grarrha and the Seed gone, the interlopers served no further purpose except as mutates, and they'd proven themselves to be too difficult of prey to risk taking them.

Warily, Grarrha's rescuers disengaged and left the realm of the swamp stalkers behind.

By the end of the evening, there was not even a hint of sarslayan interference. The road, still somber as it was, turned from mud to a drier, packed earth. A thin ray of hope dared to peek into the adventurer's spirits.

Dead trees still crept in around them, crowding the morass with brittle wood and shades of gray, but they seemed to have crossed the worst of it. But no one felt confident enough to voice that thought and risk cursing them all by tempting the fates.

Furtaevell paced the length of the hall as he waited for the king.

Leidergelth arrived a few moments later and returned the enchanter's journal. The king's face had set to a grim mask; he didn't bother with pleasantries. "You are certain that this vision will come to pass?"

"With magic, nothing is ever certain," Furtaevell insisted, "and we have no indication of a timeline."

"So, you believe that fate is not predetermined."

Furtaevell stared at the ground, refusing to meet his king's gaze. "I can't be certain. But I recognized my daughter

Elorall in the dream. I refuse to believe that there is nothing I can do."

Leidergelth frowned. "We are bound up in this together, Furtaevell; we cannot allow your child and mine to suffer, so. We must do everything within our power to intervene." He chuffed with a disappointing raspberry. "We cannot let the vagha rush to our children's' aide while we stand idly by. Are we not coral elves? We'd never forgive ourselves, especially if Mantieth and Elorall *did* survive the encounter in your vision, but only by the hand of Hy'Mandr."

Furtaevell tightened his lips, afraid to argue. Truthfully, he didn't care *where* any assistance came from if it rescued his daughter—Elorall was the only part of his wife that remained on Esfah. "How can we possibly reach them in time? The vagha have a head start." He glanced at his journal. "If they failed to arrive in time and my dream was a warning of that outcome, then we must arrive even faster."

"Eagles? Where would we get enough?"

"The only ones left in the eyrie right now are too damaged to fly. The dwarven delegate's aide broke their wings during his escape."

"Coral Airships? We have three. That could carry up to…"

"Too slow."

Leidergelth furrowed his brow. "Magic. It's the only way to transport enough of us to the ivory wastes with enough speed… but even then, we cannot send too many. It is a taxing magic."

Furtaevell gulped and nodded. "Beyond sending one or two with the magic artifacts we possess, that might prove impossible. It's not a magic that any in our arcane alignments possesses. Such a spell does not come from Ailuril or Aguarehl," he lamented. The selumari could not channel magics aligned with the other two gods, Eldurim and Firiel, not without outside intervention.

An unspoken thought hung pregnant between them.

"There is a way," Leidergelth insisted. "I have heard the rumors."

"That would mean a visit to… her." Furtaevell bit his lip.

"You have been keeping an eye on her, right?"

The enchanter nodded measuredly. "Yes, as instructed. But to make such a request puts you at her mercy. Do you trust *anyone* with your life, my king, let alone a non-selumari?"

King Leidergelth tightened his face. "We might not have a choice if we hope to save Mantieth and Elorall. And I am not willing that my son should perish because I could not request aid from the vagha."

CHAPTER TWENTY-ONE

Days passed. Their voices seemed like echoes of the previous day as Hy'Targ and his crew languished through the winding paths. Only hisses and splashes of an occasional, solitary sarslayan interrupted the constant monotony of the cursed wood which Mantieth only knew as the Black Glades.

The washed-out light that bled through the fungal, mossy canopy faded all the colors to dusky hues and the traveling crew gathered in a circle. They pooled whatever foodstuffs remained between them. It proved a paltry accounting.

"Might as well enjoy it all together... a last meal, if it were," Hy'Targ said. His mind drifted back to his father. *Did the Adventurer King ever starve in the bleak, gray wastes? He must not have, or why would he love quests so much.*

Varanthl sat next to the dwarf and beckoned the others to follow suit. Rhyll crouched as low as possible. The homunculus gave his friends an exasperated smile. "What an eclectic family we are. Three dwarves, two elves, a treefolk, and whatever it is that I am."

Chuckles rippled around the circle. "Do this with me." He bowed his head and closed his eyes. Waiting a few moments for the others to follow his lead, he prayed the only prayer he knew, the one Jordyll had spoken at the farm. "Father Tarvanehl and Mother Ghaeial, we thank you for continued protection and for our food... gods watch over us." He began humming a note, as he'd been taught.

One by one, the others each intoned their own note to match, building a unique chord that none on Esfah had ever heard before.

Varanthl ended it, and they shared the meager meal together. With a somehow optimistic sigh, they crawled to their feet and resumed their trek, tightening their belts as they journeyed.

Barely fifteen minutes into their walk, Elorall sniffed the air and arched her brows with suspicion. She tapped Mantieth. He noticed it too.

"I smell salt," he said.

The others tried to detect it, but couldn't ascertain any detectable difference. Minutes later, however, they saw a point of light on the bleak horizon. Hope energized their steps, and the trail turned gradually more healthy. Greener trees and rushes struggled through the foul, swampy soil. They did not appear well, stymied by scrubby weeds and hardy spots of discoloration and black knot—but they lived. The black pools of Necralluvium had been in short supply for the last day and were almost nonexistent as they neared the edge where the blighted forest emptied into a barren hillside.

A wasted patch of land spread like a bowl before them, desolate and cursed from the wars waged upon the soil in the previous age. Below, the broken remnants of the Ivory Citadel stood above a cliff face. Its far side fell down to the shores of the Far Sea.

The tower was partially reborn. Black stone had been recently grafted onto the age-stained ivory of the original. Below the tower, a grid of broken foundations and footprints from the ancient site surrounded the tower in lace-like patterns.

They could all smell the salt, now.

The wilded moors seemed eerily still, and a sense of trepidation lodged deep in their hearts. Few things moved in the distance, and Hy'Targ took out a spyglass from his pack. He extended his telescopic lens and spotted the subtle activity, mostly around the top of the tower. "It looks like... they're building something? Repairing the tower, most likely."

Hy'Targ swallowed the lump in his throat. After all the trials and dangers of the road, they'd finally arrived in the deadlands of Lurneville. He wasn't certain any longer that he had the heart to continue. Conviction rang a note deep in his core; the quest, until now, had been mostly bluster... he'd merely been doing whatever it was he figured his father would do.

With thoughts returning to his father, he glanced to his new friend, Varanthl. His eyes glanced down at the homunculus's chest.

The dwarf chewed his lip and looked anxiously at his party. The reality of the place suddenly robbed him of his confidence.

A faint shimmer flashed behind them on the edge of the trees as a carboniferous gnarltree cracked and shifted. Opening from root to branch, a seam in the trunk's xyloid flesh split like hands opening after prayer.

Stepping out from the portal came a figure. She stood tall once she stepped back onto the soil from her treewalk spell. The dryad could've passed for a selumari or morehl except for her earthy green skin. Shades of cinnamon streaked her otherwise smooth and slender form.

The dryad searched each of their faces and then looked up at Rhyll'ee-vrng-nrnnnvv who bent down to commune with her. They held a brief conversation in treespeak and she glanced at Rhyll's damaged hands.

She took his huge hands into her own and said something in their shared tongue.

Rhyll hunched with sorrow. His low, long wail wafted ethereally on the wind as if he'd somehow tapped into the very nature of sorrow.

His friends understood what the dryad had told him without needing to know the language. His beloved Lavrildr was dead.

Varanthl laid a hand gently on him. "She is gone?"

Rhyll sobbed, "Y-yes. But not just her... my whole family. Gray Blight took them all."

The dryad leaned in and hugged Rhyll, saying a few words to comfort him in the unknown language.

Identifying with his pain, the homunculus turned his bracelets and looked at his wrists. "You talked about family before. 'Whenever we are together in heart and mind, we are family,'" he quoted. Varanthl removed one of his bracelets and slid it over one of Rhyll's massive fingers like a ring. "*We are family*, Rhyll."

With a thankful shudder, Rhyll smeared the sticky sap-tears leaking near his eyes.

The dryad spoke again to the efflorah, and he shot back something in seeming disagreement. She wanted him to follow her back to their home.

Hanging her head mournfully, she walked slowly back towards her portal.

"She goes to burn the grove and prevent the spread of any more disease. I am the last of us, there" Rhyll explained. "But I must see our quest through to the end. If Melkior is responsible for the blight, then he must be defeated and held accountable. None else should suffer Lavrildr's fate."

Turning to address Rhyll's companions, the dryad said in common, "Take care of him." Her voice carried a hint of threat. She looked at her treefolk. "When you are finished, please come home to me." With that, the sylvan returned to her portal and disappeared. The others turned and stared at the overwhelming, impossible task before them: to kill the lich before he regained full strength and conquered the planet.

Mantieth dropped into a washout ravine. The others crept behind him, and they used the crevasse as cover while they foraged ahead. They had yet to see any absolute evidence of Melkior, but they needed to get closer to the tower in order to look for him. Their entire trip would be for naught if they tipped their hand too soon.

Shrill winds blasted through the micro canyon. They peppered the invaders with silica and chilled their fingers. Mantieth stepped on something that cracked. He backed up and then jumped. *A skeleton!*

It did not move. The group caught and then held their collective breath. This fallen warrior had been dead for hundreds of years and laid half-buried in the ravine. Scanning further down the slope, they noticed hundreds more of them laying in similar repose.

Mantieth composed himself, and then moved forward again with the others stalking close behind. He put a finger to his lips and then hunched against the wall of the ravine. Footsteps crunched on the gravel above them.

Slow and methodical steps approached, and it sounded like something scraped. *A scout.* It either had a limp, or it dragged something, perhaps a weapon. The elf made himself as small as he could, not daring to look up and satisfy his curiosity. The shambling footsteps continued unabated, and the sentry walked past them without noticing the intruders in their midst.

Mantieth waited a few long moments after the scout had passed, so it couldn't hear him anymore. He wondered if the undead heard the same way the living did, shook away the stray thought, and then poked his head over the lip of the cracked earth and looked for any sign of the enemy.

All he saw were copses of thorny bracken and busted rubble from a world gone by. The wind howled behind them, and then it shattered as a skeleton shrieked, leaping onto them from above. It latched onto Varanthl, who shouted with surprise. He shrugged it off and then crushed it with his hammer.

They held their breath for a tense few seconds, hoping nobody else had heard the commotion. As the wind in their half-tunnel faded, they heard the chatter of the shrieking undead; their bones clacked, and footsteps stomped the dirt.

Rhyll stood to his full height, easily enough to see out from the rift. "We are discovered," he reported, "Ten of them."

Everyone readied their weapons for battle. Mantieth drew his blade and gripped it tight. His heart pounded in his ears. He promised himself that it was time to be the hero his father had always bragged he was.

From his perch in the tree, Nohdan watched his former companions, unwilling though he had been, separate from the green elf. The lava elf usually spent most of his time in urban areas and had never actually seen a dryad before. With the sylvan finally gone, the others scanned the land and looked for the best possible route to sneak closer towards Melkior's keep.

He'd been following them ever since they'd fled Undrakull. Despite the murder of the drider, Undrakull's soldiers had no intention of chasing their enemies through the Black Glades—and their trail had not been difficult to follow.

The morehl knew Hy'Targ's plan. As foolish as he thought it was, he had to admire the adventurers at least a little—even if they were his enemies. After all, the selumari *had* imprisoned him and then left him in chains with the burned skeletons on their tail.

Mantieth, the cocksure coral elf prince, pointed to the winding ravine and led the way. The others followed his path.

Nohdan lost sight of them in the crack, and so he climbed up further and balanced upon the uppermost branches. This time, he'd checked the tree thoroughly before ascending. He wouldn't be caught a second time by a stray efflorah.

His keen, elven eyes picked the others out in the distance and he saw the skeletal scout leap onto them from above. Varanthl crushed it easily, but he spotted a small scouting party rushing to their fallen comrade's aide. A small skirmish was imminent.

He didn't feel any particular attachment to the party that had recently held him prisoner, but he had earlier set a brilliant plan in motion—a joke that would set him back financially, but which would bring him endless enjoyment. He rubbed the spot where the vorpal sword, turned into a needle, had been inserted under the top layer of his skin in place of the dragonstaff.

If he'd gone to this length so far, he intended to see it through to completion and insisted that his investment into his personal satisfaction pay a dividend. He grinned deviously and watched as Mantieth yanked the magical sword from its sheath.

Nohdan whispered with rapt interest and chuckled, "The fool still has no idea."

CHAPTER TWENTY-TWO

"A dozen of them," corrected Rhyll as the skeleton chargers poured over the lip of the washout with blades drawn. Their empty eye sockets burned with the fury of the void as they shrieked.

As the dwarves flanked their enemy, Rhyll obliterated the nearest scout, dashing him to pieces with explosive fury.

Hurling itself over the edge, the largest of the fiends tackled Mantieth. They tumbled through the broken shale and scree. The bloodless clutched for his throat and the two locked into a grapple, kicking each other's weapons beyond reach.

Two wights crept behind Rhyll and chopped hunks of wood from his legs before Varanthl could shatter their chitinous skulls with his hammer. The second creature snarled, rocking back on its heels and with its jaw hanging on by only one hinge.

The homunculus charged and kicked it further back, turning to help Rhyll. The bony warrior tripped over Mantieth and the larger skeleton he was locked together with, freeing them both from their entanglement. Each lunged for their weapons.

Mantieth whirled around and crossed blades with the skeletal champion. The bloodless swung and hacked, causing the elf to block and dodge. It was not fast—but neither was it slow—and its blows came with the strength and ferocity of the undead and all the fury of the Abyss.

With a grin, the blue elf flung himself at the enemy. Stakes were never higher for him. He bet his life that actual combat was much like the training he'd received daily since he was a child—only losing would be more permanent. Mantieth swung repeatedly, pushing the enemy back as he tried to find an opening in its defenses.

Lunging at it with a whirling spin attack, Mantieth finally powered through his defensive posture and shoved the fiend backwards while knocking its sword wide. The enemy's blade skittered to the dirt five cubits away.

With a snarl, the skeleton recognized its imminent defeat. It snatched a pair of glass bulbs from the pouch on its hip and smashed them together against a rock. Their contents reacted with an alchemical spark, and a plume of vibrant, roiling color spat skyward.

Mantieth seized the opening and slashed through his enemy. The keen edge of his magic blade bit into the ossein material and chopped the fiend apart. Though it was not blood and meat, the magic weapon sank through the rigid material of the undead, severing periosteum and marrow.

The elven blade rang like a hammer against a gong and a concussive shockwave staggered everyone in the vicinity while shooting a brilliant, arcane beacon into the stratosphere like a strobing ball lightning.

Both friend and enemy traded momentary glances before resuming their fight.

Elorall grabbed Mantieth by the arm. "I felt it... a powerful magic. Some kind of summoning. What *was* that?"

He turned the blade in his hands. She examined it as well. The pommel seemed different from how he remembered it—truthfully, he'd been so busy trying to stay alive that he hadn't thought much about it. Mantieth peeled back a flap of the sash wrapping around the handle and revealed the hard grip made of a pearl-like, ossified material... dragon bone.

"Nohdan switched the sword," the spell-caster hissed.

"Guys? I-I don't think this is my vorpal blade."

Melkior paced back and forth through the third floor of his citadel. Age-stained ivory block gave way to the dark stone that his minions milled as they had rebuilt the busted tower. Scaffold and rope pulls hung against the edges of his keep as the building crew worked slowly but methodically to restore the place to some semblance of its former glory. The tower would be the capital of the new world that Melkior build: a home for his bride.

He bent over the table in the studio space. Nearby workbenches housed the items he'd gathered: phylacteries, alchemy tools, and tomes of forbidden magic. His dark necromancy could begin as soon as he had the final ingredients… Ailushurai's bones. He'd already prepared the tefillin to receive her soul; once he bound the leather box and its contents to her skeleton, Ailushurai would live again.

A silk pillow rested on the table, laid out in preparation for the spell. Melkior demanded comfort for his would-be bride as he returned her to the realm of Esfah.

His beloved could be no mere shambling corpse. Melkior touched the tattoo embedded upon his chest. The mark gave him the authority to reclaim this one soul from the Abyss—to make Ailushurai the selumari whole again—alive and yet undying, forever exempt from death and decay. Selurehl could never again touch her.

The undead sorcerer only needed her bones, he could recreate the rest of her with flesh stolen from the living. He intended to reupholster the small phylactery box with the inked skin from his chest and then insert it in the body, making her live again while freeing her from the torments of the eternal void.

He'd already sensed that his minions succeeded in finding her and directed the mighty Rahkawmn to acquire them. He possessed her remains and already drew near with them.

A horn bellowed a warning nearby; it split the air with an urgent message and pulled him from his reverie. Melkior had stationed several zombified sentries on the highest level of the tower to provide watch.

The lich walked to the window and stared out across the wasteland. A cloud of furious color marked the location of an incident. He focused his eyes and spotted movement in the ravine. A party of adventurers furiously beat back one of his teams of patrolling minions.

Melkior sneered when he recognized the dwarf and the four-armed creature he'd encountered at his earlier awakening in the crypt.

Licking his lips, the death lord tasted more familiarity through his communion with his Burned One, the black skeletal seeker… this was also the dwarf responsible for stealing the bones from the morehl stronghold.

Melkior grinned. "So, you've been trying to stop this day ever since releasing me from that crypt?" He closed his eyes and stretched out his senses. He felt Rahkawmn in the distance; it would not be long before the dracholich's arrival. "This should prove an amusing distraction until my beloved returns."

He turned away briefly as a bright light strobed from the battlefield and a pulse shot up and into the sky.

Melkior narrowed his eyes to slits, recognizing the familiar magic. "This will be amusing indeed."

Hy'Targ's beard wagged as he lifted his head and looked to the tower. Some vile creature atop the partially finished citadel blew a siren.

The dwarf rushed to the signal smoke and tried to stamp it out, but the chemicals refused to be extinguished. He settled for digging a shallow hole with his boot and kicked it in before covering it over; without air the smoke lessened, but it still seeped upwards through the soil.

Rhyll and Varanthl finished off the last of the skeletons and joined the rag-tag group as they scrambled through the ravine. It emptied into a steppe at the bottom of the bowl. This blackened plain had once been Lurneville.

"Behind the wall!" Hy'Targ said.

He and his crew darted behind a section of old wreckage tall enough to hide even Rhyll, so long as he crouched. They held their breaths as a cadre of undead trotted past, heading towards the wisps of colored smoke in the ravine.

Varanthl pointed to the tower. Getting there would require an uphill run, and they would have to navigate the crumbled remains of old foundations that made a sort of hurdle-high maze walls. Time had disintegrated most segments of them, beating them down to dust and pebble, but they'd still have to crawl or leap over some impassable sections. Storming Melkior's keep would prove harder now that they'd lost the element of surprise.

Hy'Targ glowered at the distance. The sky boiled black and a dark cloud blocked out much of the sun. He gripped his axe and felt the vagha blood heat up in his veins. "I think Melkior knows we're here."

A second group of scouts spotted them and wailed like ghosts. They charged ahead with rusty blades held high and poised to strike; crossing the broken ground with ravenous, predatory speed, they moved like macabre, quickened marionettes.

Varanthl and Hy'Targ slipped around to the other side of the wall. Mantieth protected Elorall as she hit them with a blast of magic. Her icy gale slowed their steps and locked joints in place.

Rhyll swept his mighty arm sidelong, smashing the chilled bones against the lower foundation. Varanthl and Hy'Targ dashed out from around the other side and fell upon the others, blindsiding and demolishing them.

They looked around for any more bloodless, but did not spot more troops. At least, none were visible.

Moving back around the corner of the foundation to a better protected location, they regrouped. "If that's the hardest this is gonna be, I think we stand a serious shot at this," Mantieth grinned, "element of surprise or not. Maybe he hasn't regained as much power as we feared."

"Don't get cocky, kid," Vy'Danis cautioned. "There're bound to be much worse things on this hillside than tiny pockets of skeletons." He snuffled, "these ain't even been the stronger kind—the ones that reassemble."

Mantieth's hubris welled up, and he challenged the old adventurer. "Worse things? Like what?"

Thunder tore the sky, and then the noise took definition. It did not sound like weather, despite the burnt and roiling sky. Another peal echoed overhead, shaking pebbles where they lay upon the ground as it hit crescendo and shaped into the guttural, reptilian screech of a dragon.

The party held their breath and stiffened as if they had ice in their veins. Hiding behind their protective wall they could not see it, but intuition buzzed in their ears; a dragon approached from over the cursed woods to their back, pinning them between the beast and the wall.

Mantieth suddenly recognized the blade in his grip. It was most definitely the same dragon staff that Nodhan had stolen months ago.

Vy'Danis cocked a bushy eyebrow at Mantieth. "You just had to go and jinx us, didn't ye kid?"

The elf bit his lip and frowned, rubbing his palm over the pommel of his sword with the inlaid, pearloid dragon. He hung his head, knowing that things were suddenly about to get much worse.

CHAPTER TWENTY-THREE

Birds scattered in flocks and screamed farewells to their swampy perches. They abandoned both nest and home as they fled for the horizon over the Far Sea, drowning out all other sounds in their cacophony of throaty calls.

Nohdan clutched his belly. He laughed so hard that he nearly fell out of his treetop vantage point as his former captors panicked and scrambled to find cover.

The lava elf ducked down tight and clung to the main trunk of the tree as a red and white drake floated over the treetops. The dragonstaff had called a hybrid without its wielder attempting to control the summoning, and what answered the call was unpredictable and random. Its roar shook the branches as it answered the call of the dragon staff.

After cresting the edge of the deadlands, it turned a wide arc and belched fire, immolating wide swaths of land. Deep pockets of flammable oils and peat deposits ignited, sparking rivers of fire like magma flows.

As it flew over, the dragon snorted a fiery breath towards the wall where Mantieth and the others hunkered down for shelter. Flames splashed against the water like a water jet.

Nohdan's gut twisted. He hadn't intended for them to die… not that it mattered to him personally, but he'd hoped the show might have lasted longer. The lava elf acknowledged that, as calculating as he was, he didn't always think his pranks through to completion.

His eyes brightened as the singed heads of his former companions popped back up and into sight. All of them had survived the initial scorching, but the bloodless began pouring in towards their flanks as waves of fire zigzagged across the land. Pandemonium broke out everywhere; dragon fire slagged a capstone covering a buried ether tunnel. The buried gas chamber lit it up, shooting a geyser of yellow and blue flames eighty cubits high.

With a grin, the lava elf sat back to watch. This wasn't over yet. He only wished that he'd brought something to snack on during the show.

At the lich's bidding, a cloud of black mist exploded and shrouded the area with wispy, onyx tentacles. It sucked in and imploded as quickly as it formed, transporting the necromancer and his minions.

Melkior dropped the wayfare orb, depleting the last of its power with the short jump. With a host of his ghoulish warriors, he stood barely sixty-five cubits away from the intruders. The lich snarled and hurled a writhing, black ball of death magic at the interlopers while a handful of his undead soldiers charged at their prey.

Elorall threw her hands up barely in time to erect a wall of protective magic. She extended a hand and eradicated the chargers with a string of lightning that laced between the skeletons, burning them beyond recognition.

Sneering, the lich pointed his finger at her as if it were a morehl flintlock and fired a killing bolt from his finger.

She screamed with surprise, but managed to catch the deadly black magic with her arcane shield. It crackled and dispelled under the force of his necromancy, but the thing exploded into a shrapnel-like ether. It would have killed her in an instant had she been any slower.

Melkior howled and pulled out his massive, eldarim blade, which he'd rescued from the fort. The shrieking warriors of old who remained standing behind him screeched battle-cries in response and surged past him.

Hy'Targ and his party stood their ground, howling defiantly and with weapons prepared and ready. Elorall blasted them with a flash flood, drawing upon the mystic seas in the reserves of the Aguarehl's domain. The tidal forces spewed out from the party's caster.

As the blast of water smashed apart the front line of the bloodless, Melkior howled an incantation of his own. The ground rumbled and split, breaking open a new chasm.

Elorall's eyes widened. She'd never seen a spell so raw and powerful before. Her water spilled into the breach, dumping into the magma at the bottom and shooting geysers of vapor upwards like a curtain which the drake circled overhead in angry arcs.

Skeletons suddenly appeared within the vapor, answering their master's call. They leapt through the veil of steam with reckless abandon. Mantieth, Rhyll, and Varanthl rushed to protect the selumari caster.

Hy'Targ, Vy'Danis, and Jr'Orhr jumped into the fray with axes swinging wildly. The dull sound of axe-head on bone nearly drowned out the hiss of steam and the cackles of undead screechers. The roar of the oncoming dragon overwhelmed even that.

Through the waning drapes of cascading mist, Hy'Targ locked eyes with his fiendish enemy. Ice seemed to grip his heart, but the dwarf refused to acknowledge his fear or wilt beneath the undead demon's glare.

Melkior roared at the dwarf's simple act of defiance and pointed his blade at the vagha and his friends, hissing an order to press the attack.

Suddenly, a brilliant orange illumination lit everything with intense light and powerful heat.

A sheet of flames exploded in the ground between the warring parties as the dragon made another pass. Both sides recoiled from the fiery wall.

Most of Melkior's forces that had pressed ahead fell apart under the infernal blast. Several of the thicker skeletons managed to survive the leap beyond the dragon's fire. Flames darkened their bones and any scraps of leather or fabrics that still hung to them smoldered and fell off as they screeched and hissed, splitting their party.

Hy'Targ and his friends glared at the lich whose forces, still formidable, had just been decimated by the drake's breath. Melkior whirled and began the trek back towards his keep, no doubt to draw upon reinforcements or eliminate the draconic threat which harried his forces as well as the intruders; only a small contingent of bloodless minions flanked him for protection.

The dwarves ran ahead with raging fervor, hoping to cut Melkior off before he could get to the tower; they expected the others would follow and didn't see the plight of their friends.

Those of Melkior's minions that survived the flames cut off the escape path from the non-vagha adventurers.

Mantieth cut through a swath of them before the undead clustered thick enough to overwhelm him. He grabbed Elorall and retreated, taking a longer path around as the elves tried to regroup with the others.

The skeletons managed to topple an ancient support pillar. It landed with meteoric force, and a patch of the fire exploded in a whirlwind of scattered embers that sizzled like angry bees. The felled colonnade created a bridge over the river of fire and the team of undead sprinted across it, flanking the elves, squeezing them like a vice, cutting them off from Varanthl and Rhyll as they smashed any threats that grew near enough.

The big treefolk recoiled from the flames with obvious fear. The heat dried his bark and limbs. He and Varanthl retreated around the far side, looking for another way around, backtracking to where the fires hadn't yet set everything ablaze. They smashed the dwindling population of skeletons behind them. The largest cluster of incoming enemies came from over the bridge.

Varanthl and Rhyll leapt the fence-like rows of ancient foundations and disappeared.

Mantieth and Elorall clawed for space; their enemies had successfully isolated them from their peers. The selumari prince valiantly held off the most aggressive of them, but they had no retreat from the semicircle of enemies which pressed against them. Undead forces backed them against an old stone wall.

The hybrid red dragon with ivory fins and crests swooped down and beat his wings with gale force, scattering swarms of glowing embers into the winds where they lodged on dry leaf and bracken. He hovered for three beats, and then locked the female elf in his devious gaze. The drake unloaded a hot blast of magmic fury upon the elves.

Elorall screamed so urgently that even the skeletons turned their heads.

She flashed her magic bubble up to shield them. Elorall screamed again, holding off the blast with a furious surge of protective blue magic. The impact of the blazing crimson against the fierce blue crackled with violent, arcane dissonance. The violent noise was enough to catch the ears of the dwarves.

Hy'Targ and his two companions stopped their mad charge and turned to watch as if there was something they could do from such a distance.

Mantieth waived them off and screamed, "Leave us! You've got to stop Melkior!"

The dragon's eyes narrowed to slits when the elf repelled the attack, and it stepped up its intensity, tightening its throat and pouring on even more flame. The heat incinerated the bones of all those enemies that had cornered the elves only moments ago.

The selumari shrieked under the stress of her ward, unable to hold out much longer when Rhyll suddenly stood to his full height. He summoned a copse of wild growth from the callery scrub. The thorny brush dotted the broken lands, immune to even the salted and barren soil. Rhyll stretched his hand tall and bid it to grow high. He poured the strength of the wild growth into one sharp thorn at the tip, made of darkwood, and as hard as any steel ever made.

Rhyll plucked the spear from the soil and hurled it with monstrous strength. The javelin streaked through the sky with ballista force and bounced off the drake's hide, knocking a patch of scales free from the beast with such incredible force; they scattered through the sky like a cascade of stone rain.

The dragon shrieked and relented. He snapped the air with wounded confusion and then flew off and circled high around the corrupted citadel. It scanned the dirt, searching for an easy victim and burned with a new hate for whatever thing it was that had wounded it.

Spent, Elorall collapsed with exhaustion, falling into Mantieth's arms; tears streamed down her cheeks. The prince scooped her up and ran in search of some new, safe location, looking for some place more defensible than the flame streaked patch of wastelands where they'd been caught.

CHAPTER TWENTY-FOUR

"What do you mean, 'she said no?'" King Leidergelth snapped as he angrily tromped through the streets amid his group of four generals. They all wore hoods pulled over their head and had dressed in whatever plain-clothes they could find

on short notice. Leidergelth had, in fact, stopped a commoner on the streets and demanded his clothes.

Syldan and Genmenor walked in front of Leidergelth and Furtaevell. Elalamin and Waesro walked behind. They kept their distance, trying to remain inconspicuous, but failing in that task.

The party received nothing more than passing glances on their trek through the city. They drew slightly longer looks as they moved into the outskirts where wealth was less common; but the elves' strong, eager eyes below their hoods warned off any who thought to approach them.

"Why didn't we take a carriage?" Leidergelth muttered to Furtaevell. With time as a premium, donning disguises and walking to the witch's hovel seemed a waste of it. "I am the king; surely she would open her doors to us."

Furtaevell kept his face neutral. "She already denied your request to meet at the castle. She has proven standoffish in the past. We don't understand why—this seemed the safest bet to getting an audience."

"What is the spell-caster's name and family?"

"Sh'Zzar. Hers is the Shree family."

Leidergelth's mouth crooked. That explained a lot. The Shree family was the last of them released from slavery, and by none other than King Hy'Mandr, long before he had assumed the throne. Very few Shree remained of the continent of Charnock.

The king looked at Furtaevell cross-eyed. "One old dwarf couldn't stop us from entering her house if I demanded it. I am the king and Niamarlee is my home."

Furtaevell gave him a skeptical glance. "Trust me. If she wanted to deny that meeting, she certainly could." The enchanter cocked an eyebrow at him and spoke honestly, "Don't underestimate the power of magic, my king."

Leidergelth grimaced, but quietly followed the party until the buildings began to thin and diminish in quality. Overgrown yards and ill-kept properties dotted the fringes of Niamarlee. Finally, they arrived at a peculiar house. The small bungalow stood in poor repair, but the yard had been meticulously groomed. Ornamental plants sprouted in brilliant blooms, boasting colors and arrangements like fireworks. They hung from planters and trellises and leapt from raised beds arranged along a walking path that circled the dilapidated house.

Waesro and Elalamin caught up with the others and rapped on the door. The planks rattled tenuously beneath the knock. The wood sounded soft and decayed.

The barrier opened slightly to reveal a dwarf woman with silver hair and the most brilliant eyes Leidergelth had ever seen. She somehow radiated beauty, despite her advanced age and foreign race. The fairness of the Shree had made them the most sought after vaghan slaves by selumari nobility.

She scanned the elves and immediately saw through their disguises. "What brings King Leidergelth and his council of war generals to my door?"

Furtaevell pulled back his hood. The king followed suit and asked, "You are the sorceress named Sh'Zzar?"

"I am."

"May we enter?"

Sh'Zzar paused, seeming to ponder it for a moment. Finally, she responded with a curt nod. "You may."

The old dwarf took a seat at her modest table and stared at her guests, waiting for them to voice whatever request they had brought. She offered them no hospitality, only her inquisitive look.

"Do you receive many guests?" Leidergelth asked.

"Enough to afford me what I need," she stated. "But that is not the question that brings you to my door. The crown is not normally concerned with foreigners who live peacefully within its borders… no matter what their family name is."

"You are both right and wrong," Leidergelth said. "My real question is coming, but I am certainly interested in any individuals of significant ability who live under my domain… especially when I hear such colorful stories about them, however dubious."

Sh'Zzar raised an eyebrow. She ignored the king's assertions about her character or past. "Then ask your question."

Furtaevell stepped forward. "We have need of dwarven magic… of a spell that only one who serves the god Eldurim can effect."

The king interjected again, "Your name is really Sh'Zzar? That is not a false one?"

"I really am Sh'Zzar."

"Then you must be of the same family as Sh'Ttil? I know that hers was a small family… they live now beyond the Talvatic Coast, near Gundakhor? I hear they are wealthy."

"So I've been told. I'm not sure I can help you," she stated flatly.

Furtaevell glowered at the king, afraid that Leidergelth's badgering was harming any chances of securing her help. Without her, they had no way to accomplish their end goal.

"As you can see, I have no great love nor need for money," Sh'Zzar insisted.

"Please," Furtaevell's eyes welled up, and he interrupted the king's negotiations, jettisoning protocol. "I cannot cast a Path spell on my own. Both of our children are in danger."

Leidergelth nodded. He frowned, but let Furtaevell steer the conversation. "It is true. We must move many of our forces to the Ivory wastes, and we must do it as soon as possible. We fear that a threat is amassing there; Mantieth and Elorall are in grave danger."

"I will not send an invasion force up the coast for you," Sh'Zzar insisted, afraid of setting a dangerous precedent and unmoved by their appeal. Her face was like flint. "You have my answer. It will not change for any reason."

The King took the seat adjacent to Furtaevell across the table, equally resilient.

Sh'Zzar raised her eyebrow.

"I have certain skills," the king professed. "One of them is deciphering truth from lies. It's not magic, mind you... the clues are in the facial expressions, the little ticks and shifts. This comes in handy when I hear rumors or when others try to feed me falsehoods—though it comes in most handy when interviewing someone with firsthand knowledge of the truth. It is not foolproof, mind you, but it is a skill I have learned. Do you know what rumors they spread about you?"

Sh'Zzar stiffened, but said nothing.

Leidergelth met and held her gaze. "If we send no aide, Mantieth and Elorall—our children—will certainly die, along with their companions. Furtaevell has seen this in a vision." He maintained steady eye contact. "One of those companions is Prince Hy'Targ, son of Hy'Mandr and Sh'Ttil." He let his eyelids flutter when he said the name of the long missing queen. He knew who she was... or he thought he did.

Sh'Zzar stood and turned her back. "You may indeed know some secrets, King Leidergelth." She sighed and turned back to the king and his entourage while she looked off and away through her window. "I will help my nephew. If it is truly as you say, we must hurry. There will be some necessary preparations to make, and they will take some time—haste without error is the most difficult kind. The sort of mobilization you need will require the use of several artifacts."

"I will take you to my study while the army assembles," Furtaevell promised.

Sh'Zzar turned to Leidergelth as he stood to face her. "Can I assume you are leading the army?" she asked the king.

Leidergelth nodded. "I cannot abandon my son on the hopes that Hy'Mandr's efforts alone will safeguard him."

Sh'Zzar gave him a stern gaze, wondering exactly how much of her history the capricious elf knew. It was apparent by their faces that he had not divulged any extra information about her to his peers. She nodded her tenuous agreement and followed the selumari out the door and departed for the castle.

Varanthl jumped from the crumbled steps and over the next chunk of wall. He caught sight of his friends as he leaped. Mantieth had almost caught up with the dwarves.

"Come on," Varanthl urged Rhyll. "We've got to meet them at the tower."

They dashed through what might once have been an old courtyard. A marvelous tunnel cut through at an angle, leading from the upper level of the old city and down to the beach under the section of old Lurneville which hung over the sea on a massive, shelf-like overhang of stone.

Varanthl balked. The steep highway hid more troops. Within, the tunnel was filled with skeletons lying in wait— thousands of them crowding inside the underpass. Below them, more bloodless dotted the seashore so thickly that they blotted out whatever shoreline he could see.

They snapped their heads to attention, locking four thousand empty eye-sockets on the homunculus as if they were of one mind. The crowd surged forward, quickly swarming into the old city square.

Rhyll swept back as many as he could and yanked his arms back quickly. Against so many enemies, chips and bites had been taken out of his arms by ancient steel blades.

Varanthl yelled, "Run!" as he sprinted up another busted stair and leapt over a rift and onto the next section of the ruins. More skeletons filled in the gaps and he smashed them with his hammer while Rhyll stomped them to pieces like tiny bundles of crunchy kindling.

Their zone had been suddenly overrun with a new wave of bloodless fiends. The two heroes pressed forwards, anyway. Their friends might have need of them and they dared not abandon them to fight Melkior alone,

Rhyll stepped ahead of his new family member and kicked the cluster of enemies, scattering bones through the sky like a child kicking leaves in autumn. The treefolk snapped his head around as Varanthl whirled his weapon and leveled the next team of champions that dared test them.

He scooped up the homunculus and clutched him to his chest, rashing Varanthl's skin with his rugged bark and branches. "Hey!" Varanthl howled, suddenly ripped out of the action.

"Family protects its own..." Rhyll whispered, and then Varanthl heard the whoosh of flame as the drake streaked down from the sky and spat a stream of caustic energy like a beam. It wiped out a huge swath of the undead and obliterated the efflorah that had nearly knocked it from the sky.

Rhyll collapsed as he shielded his screaming friend from the heat. The treefolk's bark dried instantly and cracked, splitting leaf and branch.

"Nooooo!" Varanthl howled from within the protection of Rhyll's unyielding arms; he hadn't even seen the monster approaching. Moments later, Varanthl pried himself free and tried to rouse his friend, searching in vain for something to extinguish the inferno with. "It's okay! You're okay. Rhyll? Rhyll wake up—you're on fire."

His body crumbled to ash and ember when Varanthl touched it. Rhyll was gone, only the sterner parts of his husk remained. One blackened stump rose above the others in the smoldering heap; curled and gnarled from the fire, a gold bracelet encircled the twisted branch like a ring upon a broken finger.

Shaking with rage, Varanthl clutched his weapon and shook it at the sky. He screamed at the futility of it all. Varanthl turned his eyes to the citadel and spotted the vagha as they chased Melkior through the gates. The dragon may have killed his companion—his family—but it had also burned a clear path all the way to the tower's front door.

CHAPTER TWENTY-FIVE

Hy'Targ took one glance back at Mantieth and Varanthl. Mantieth held Elorall in his arms. He paused near a busted segment of ancient wall where he tended to her and tried to get her back on her feet. Hy'Targ watched Varanthl and Rhyll run from the dragon as it swooped upon them. It blasted them with volcanic breath, and a moment later, only Varanthl remained. The dwarf's nose flared, and he bit his lip. *All this needless death needs to stop!*

He rushed through the open citadel entrance with his father's axe in hand. Vy'Danis and Jr'Orhr followed him.

"It's always up to us dwarves," the older one said gleefully gripping the haft of his own weapon. "And I wouldn't have it any other way."

They burst into the main chamber, barely sixty cubits wide on both sides, and scanned the room. "It's smaller than it looks from outside," Hy'Targ observed. "Some kind of old living quarters."

Remnants of a moldered rug lay in scraps. Collapsed furnishings lined the walls. Cautiously, the vagha climbed the footings as they led upwards.

The upper level was more of the same as below, plus a heap of old weapons and mostly disintegrated pelts and mounts that may have once been a collection of hunting trophies and an armory. Decay's rot of the building was worse here, and the next flight of steps lay partially crumbled; missing treads had been replaced by graduated heaps of rubble.

So far, there had been no resistance. Worry seated firmly in Hy'Targ's gut.

Floor three was in the worst repair, but looked the most frequently used. Here, glass jars on decrepit shelves were cleared of dust. Books laid open and arranged neatly, as were the necromancer's implements laid on benches near a table at the room's center. A fine silk pillow and a surgical knife rested upon it.

Hoping to find Melkior here, the dwarves checked behind every post of the rugged scaffolding and pilasters erected to support the renovations. Once ivory bricks of the deteriorated walls and ceiling gave way to ebon stones where Hy'Targ had seen the black and white transition from afar, before they'd been forced to make their reckless charge.

They all turned and looked at the final stair. A chill wind blew through the open windows.

A decrepit stair nestled between the scaffolding racks accessed the next level. Vy'Danis grabbed his prince before he could make the first step. They locked eyes. "Your father would be proud of you," Vy'Danis said and then nodded.

Hy'Targ tightened his lips and then charged up to meet their enemy.

Melkior stood atop the freshly completed floor of the fourth level. The walls hadn't yet been completed except on two sides where the bloodless masons had only just begun building; block pieces sat at uneven heights like merlons of a battlement.

Melkior, wearing barely more than the tattered rags of the grave, sneered at them and maintained his calm repose. The fiend stood with his back to the steep, far side of the platform where the edge fell away and over the cliff, stretching all the way down to the beach below.

"So, you have come to my home thinking to defeat me?" Melkior held his bastard sword at the ready. "I am the servant of Malgrimm. I am the terror in the dark. I am the destroyer of Esfah and..."

"Ye talk too much," Vy'Danis interrupted with a surly grunt. He charged the lich with his axe held ready; Jr'Orhr followed on his heels, with Hy'Targ following close behind.

Melkior stepped between them and split their attacks with a deft maneuver. He batted away their axes and kicked Hy'Targ in the face, sprawling the dwarf prince backwards before turning to attack the others.

Hy'Targ scrambled to his feet as Melkior chopped and whirled at the others.

Vy'Danis ducked the wicked, eldari blade, but it caught Jr'Orhr and cut a slash across his ribcage, spilling red down his side. The two vagha teetered precariously near the edge as the lich pressed them towards it.

"No!" Hy'Targ yelled as he rushed towards the enemy.

Melkior sidestepped a cleaving blow, and the vagha suddenly found an advantage. The dwarves swung heavy blades in sequence, driving Melkior back. He stepped again and slid aside, putting several lengths between them. The lich curled a lip, reached out with his hands, and flung a wave of debilitating plague at them.

Hy'Targ raised Glorybringer. Both sides of the double-edged battle-axe ignited, ripping the air with arcane fire; it blocked the wave of death magic.

Jr'Orhr and Vy'Danis rocked on their heels, suddenly wiped out from the crippling sickness. They had no such protection from Magestorm artifacts. Vy'Danis fell to one knee and vomited. His aged constitution succumbed while Jr'Orhr proved better at resisting it.

Melkior didn't seem to notice that Hy'Targ hadn't faltered. The dwarf leapt towards the enemy who'd stepped near the lip of the sheer drop and swung Glorybringer with a wild swing.

The lich grinned and his eyes flashed; he *had* noticed, and he'd baited the prince into such a reckless move. He ducked under the blow that could have taken his head off and planted a foot upon the dwarf's toes.

Hy'Targ couldn't pivot like he needed, and he tumbled to his back. The lich raised his sword high, about to plunge its pointy tip into his chest.

Jr'Orhr screamed and charged at Melkior before he could kill the prince. Melkior snarled and released Hy'Targ, stepping back. He batted Jr'Orhr across his rump with a fierce shove and sent the dwarf sailing over the edge, plummeting to the depths below.

Vy'Danis staggered to his feet and lumbered awkwardly towards the lich, drawing him away from Hy'Targ long enough that the prince could get to his feet.

Melkior snatched Vy'Danis by the throat and lifted the sickly vagha off his feet. He stood at the very edge of the tower and dangled Vy'Danis over the lip. Hy'Targ hesitated, and the lich locked eyes on him. The evil one smiled at the prince and then squeezed, crushing Vy'Danis's windpipe and snapping his neck.

"Nooooo!" Hy'Targ screamed as Melkior cackled deviously and released the body, letting it, too, tumble into the cliffs and surf below.

Mantieth pulled Elorall to her feet, trying to shake her back to her senses. "Come on. This is what we came for—to stop this great evil! We can't stop now"

She wobbled on her feet, but stabilized herself against a scrubby tree. "You're bleeding," she noticed, touching Mantieth's scalp.

He ignored her words, just like he ignored the pain from the jagged wound that crisscrossed his hairline. "I don't have time to entertain pain. I can bleed later—once Melkior is dead... er... dead again."

They spotted Varanthl rushing like madness had taken him. He fled a bonfire heap and leapt over collapsed structures and then flung himself down a charred corridor that led towards the citadel.

The elves saw axes flash high above and could barely make out the vagha figures battling against the lich at the top of the tower as their homunculus friend rushed to their aid.

Mantieth urged Elorall forward. "He's got a path over there. We've got to follow him." They hurried towards the burning heap that marked the beginning of Varanthl's trail and spotted a growing horde of skeletons in the courtyard, gathering near the fiery heap.

Tired as she was, Elorall blasted them with a frosty incantation. Mantieth rushed past her and sliced a broad, wild stroke, hacking them down like corn sheaves. They burst into crystalline shards as the selumari swordsman mowed them down.

The last one broke apart and Mantieth stood back on his heels, aghast at the charwood pile. A hand-like branch stuck up prominently. Its finger wore a distinct gold bracelet on its woody digit.

"Rhyll—no! Gods, why?" Mantieth ignored the cinders and flames that lapped from the treefolk's burning body. He climbed the mound high enough to retrieve the ring. From his vantage, he saw over the top of the smoking mound and spotted the broad tunnel leading to the shore and ducked back into hiding.

Mantieth goose-stepped and crawled back down. He scooped together a tiny pile of frozen shards and laid the hot circlet upon it to cool it down. He bent to one knee. "Bad news," the prince said. "There's a whole army on the other side of Rhyll's body."

Elorall cocked an eyebrow and leaned to the side. "I don't see anything."

He shook his head. "Not enough angle right here. There's an old street, it cuts through the cliff and empties down onto the beach. I couldn't see its size, but the tunnel is filled, and so is the shoreline behind it. We've got to assume there are thousands."

Mantieth glanced back to Melkior's tower, but couldn't see any more of the action atop it. The partially built walls blocked any view from this side. "We've got to hold off his army and make sure it can't give any support to Melkior." He winked at her and tested the metal ring. It had cooled to his touch. "What do you say, Elorall? *You and me?* We can beat all the odds. We'll fight against them—just us against the thousands?" He held up Rhyll's ring and gingerly placed it over her wrist.

Elorall blushed. "Yes," she said breathily. The pool of arcane energy welling within her seemed to spark anew. "I've just been waiting for you to ask... You know I'd follow you anywhere."

With a nod and a smile, they darted around the corpse pyre in tandem, cutting down the undead and blasting them with magic as they took the mouth of the tunnel. "We've got to hold this road," he yelled over the ringing of his blade and the sizzling noise of her spells.

"What about the vagha and Varanthl?"

Mantieth didn't bother looking; he knew they wouldn't be able to see anything from where they stood, anyway. "We've got to trust that they'll be able to deal with Melkior. After all, it's four versus one... surely the odds are in their favor." He turned and lifted his sword, staring down dozens of the undead, and with even more that kept coming.

CHAPTER TWENTY-SIX

Varanthl howled as he emerged from the stairs at the top level of the tower. He watched Melkior break Vy'Danis's neck with a sickly, wet cracking sound and then defiantly dropped the wizened old vagha over the edge.

Hy'Targ's axe burned with the furious blessing of Firiel, and he charged at the lich. Pain wracked his heart, and he verged on tears.

Varanthl leapt forward to join him. As Melkior sidestepped the dwarf's wild, powerful strokes, the homunculus tried to smash him with his hammer.

Melkior leapt aside as the mallet crushed the newer stone with thunderous impact, grinding tile to dust. He swung his keen blade, trying to disrupt or divide the two warriors, but neither relented.

They worked in unison. One defended against the lich's attacks, and the other pressed their advantage. Melkior lost a step at a time. He growled, releasing hundreds of years-worth of pent up rage as he stepped back, throwing minor cantrips at them to introduce a dose of chaos.

Hy'Targ staved off its effects as he'd done before by bringing Glorybringer to bear. The device on Varanthl's chest glowed and dispelled the effect.

Melkior snarled when his magic had no impact on them. He glared at Varanthl curiously, and then his eyes locked on the artifact. He twisted his upper lip in a menacing sneer.

The adventurers brought weapons to bear again. Melkior ducked and slipped through them like a wraith, retaking the center of the citadel as he drew them back in again.

They hacked and chopped as he whirled and evaded their weapons. The lich studied them, searching for any exploitable weakness.

Melkior stepped in closer towards Hy'Targ, concentrating all of his attacks on the dwarf and positioning the prince to put Hy'Targ between him and the homunculus, keeping the four-armed creature in his shadow so he could not bring his hammer to bear.

The two fighters pushed their assault and steered Melkior towards the edge of the tower, shrinking the ground he owned.

Finally, Melkior saw the opening he searched for. As Varanthl moved, Melkior swung his blade high and then kicked the vagha in the face, knocking him backwards and cracking his skull upon the stone. The lich launched a furious assault on the homunculus, attacking him with an overwhelming flurry of blows. Several of them glanced off Varanthl's weapon and cut into his flesh as Hy'Targ struggled to right himself.

"You're like every dwarf I've ever known," Melkior taunted the prince without looking at him. "You fall for the same move every time. You all do." He whirled his bastard blade in an impressive arc, cutting away a space cushion between the lich and Varanthl. "How shall I punish you for your foolish invasion, I wonder?"

Hy'Targ was on his feet as Melkior began his spell, staring daggers at the Kreethaln attached to Varanthal's sternum; he might not have known its origins, but he could guess at its purpose. The first words of his sorcery shot a jolt of energy from Melkior's hand where it hit the exo-skeleton-like casing of the artifact. The Kreethaln went suddenly dark and Varanthl looked down at his chest, confused at the sudden sensation.

Melkior's vile words dripped with the black speech of the abyss. As Hy'Targ tackled the lich, the spell caster's hands wreathed with black fire and he shot them like a blast at the homunculus. He cackled even as the force of Hy'Targ's blow knocked him onto uneven footing.

The black fire poured into Varanthl. Without the Kreethaln to dispel the effects, he took the full brunt of the spell and he staggered on his feet, skin smoldering.

Melkior tried to right himself from Hy'Targ's maneuvers, but stumbled, finding no more ground to stand on. His toes caught the lip of the tower and curled, trying to find a purchase. Melkior howled with surprise and then tumbled over the sheer, vertical edge, disappearing into the misty gray that swelled between the ground and the heights above the cliff face.

Panting heavily, Hy'Targ said, "I-I did it. I did it, Varanthl!" he turned to look at his friend even as Varanthl crumpled into a heap, lying all too still and precariously close to the edge where they'd pushed Melkior over.

"No, no, no…" on his knees, he slid to the homunculus's side and cradled his lifeless body in his lap. "Come on, Varanthl," he slapped his face. "Come on—you can't die on me, not after all this!"

The four-armed body didn't move.

Hy'Targ checked for breath. Found none. Looked for a pulse, but couldn't find it. He shook the body and roared angrily at the gods, not even sure that Varanthl had ever needed to breathe or had a heart to beat. Though Hy'Targ was no healer, he some basic knowledge; he scanned the body. Cuts from Melkior's blade had drawn blood, although it no longer flowed from the wounds—that seemed to indicate a circulatory system.

A long moment of silent finality draped over the citadel roof.

Grieving, he bit his lip hard enough to split it open. Hy'Targ folded both sets of his friend's arms reverently. With a gentle sob, he took one of Varanthl's bracelets and slid it onto his own wrist in remembrance of the dead. The dwarven prince skootched closer to the dangerous edge of the fortification and stared down, hoping to spot his enemy's busted body. He had to see it… to know for sure that Melkior was dead.

The billowing mists cleared enough for a view, and Hy'Targ's breath caught in his chest at the sight. Crowded upon the beach milled a massive skeleton army. They mustered on the beach, loitering and awaiting attack orders. The bloodless legion had gathered for Melkior, thousands strong, ready to begin a new war on life… all this, and the lich had still not regained his full strength!

He searched frantically through the endless waves of gathered undead, looking for one particular corpse among the many.

Finally, Hy'Targ spotted Melkior, who stood and gathered himself from the grainy sands, some distance away from the bone-white multitude. Melkior stood between the broken bodies of his two vagha companions who laid like broken driftwood upon the sandy beach. The lich pointed his sword upwards at Hy'Targ. His eyes glowed with menacing light.

The dwarf's heart plunged into his belly. "He-he's unbeatable," Hy'Targ despaired. Melkior remained alive, but Hy'Targ had also just returned him to his army's side.

Hy'Targ's vision swam, and he turned away from the ledge, scrambling on his knees. Every instinct in his body told him to flee—to run back to Irontooth and hope stronger heroes would rise and throw down this villain. He looked down at Varanthl's body and his eyes locked on the Kreethaln. The device had been right there—with him the whole time—the original object of his quest.

He'd sought the Kreethaln but found something else… and now Varanthl, too, was dead.

The dwarf plucked it from the homunculus's chest and held it gingerly. Its crab-like, metallic arms relaxed as he looked it over. Whatever material it had been made of, it did not appear to be from any metal Hy'Targ was familiar with. It didn't look like anything else he'd *read* about, either. He guessed that it could have originated somewhere other than Esfah. Religious sects had often whispered about such things as elemental relics and inter-planar objects sent by both merciful and vengeful gods beyond those of Esfah's pantheon.

Hy'Targ shook the device as he examined it. Its gentle glow relit, sparking a dim light within the jewel and startling the dwarf with its imitation of the spark of life, and it began to glow more strongly as he held it. He snorted a heavy, pained breath through his nose, torn between possible decisions. Hy'Targ spoke aloud to the dead, as if only he could provide enough insight to battle against such a powerful lich.

"What do I do, now, Varanthl? How did the Champions of the First Age defeat him?" He searched his memories for the story.

An idea formed in his mind. A terrible, dangerous idea. A plan filled with wild assumptions about the Kreethaln's capabilities and of Melkior's goals. A potentially disastrous plan. The Adventurer King would have loved it.

"I could return home and use the Kreethaln to restore my father," he wondered aloud. "It is what I set out to do in the first place, and he would know what to do next..." But he already knew what he had to do. He stared at Varanthl's still body. "I know, I know," he argued with it.

"I have one chance. This crazy strategy of ours had better work," he chastised the corpse. "It's risky, and one of us is going to have to get in real close to him in order to pull it off."

Hy'Targ smiled with a half-grin. "Well, don't look at *me*," he argued with the cadaver and began pulling it across the tower's flat rooftop. "I don't want to do it. And besides, *you're already dead…* Fine. Maybe we draw straws?"

CHAPTER TWENTY-SEVEN

"You're asking the impossible," Sh'Zzar stated with a worried look upon her face. She stood within the High Enchanter's tower among Furtaevell and his corps of spell crafters. Arcane texts and items lay sprawled out upon a table at their center. "It takes an incredible amount of magic to open a Path spell and send even *one* soldier through to his or her destination. What you are asking is beyond the ability of the selumari; even where you all vagha, this would be a difficult task."

Syldan, one of the selumari generals, stood in the corner, waiting to relay official orders to the assembled soldiers who had gathered below.

King Leidergelth stood next to the vagha sorceress and bit his lip. She'd met with the king and his generals in the headquarters within the Ministry of Magic, a university dedicated to developing a strong corps of selumari magic users at the disposal of the crown. It lay within the shadow of the king's keep and had never admitted any race but coral elves. Sh'Zzar's presence indicated how dire their need had become.

Leidergelth stroked his chin. "How many... how many can you send?"

The small army waiting outside in the courtyard was nowhere near an adequate number for an invasion force. That fact alleviated the vagha's conscience in case this had all been a ruse on behalf of the selumari.

Standing at attention along the walls of Furtaevell's office, a dozen spell casters awaited orders. Sh'Zzar scanned them, gaging their aptitude, and then assessed the artifacts at her disposal: several sightstones and a few Rings of the Stars. Each could concentrate their magics and amplify the casters' innate abilities. Furtaevell had set his Magi's Crown out as well, a prized artifact that would allow him to mimic whatever arcane forces Sh'Zzar drew upon.

She turned the artifacts over in her hands and read the inscriptions upon the rings. Magic rings could prove dangerous things. One such artifact, disguised as a Ring of Stars, had long ago been used to drag chunks of the Daybringer comets from the sky in year 532 of the First Age, not that the rare lost ring could cause a mishap; the comet chain had not passed for twenty years.

Sh'Zzar set the items down and sighed with a shrug. "At our best, we can mobilize perhaps half of your troops?"

Leidergelth puffed a disappointed blast through his nose. He'd already culled his numbers down to the smallest contingent he felt comfortable taking. The selumari king pulled his confidant close. They spoke in hushed tones, having an animated conversation. Finally, the king approached. We have something to show you. He eyed the sorceress for a lingering moment. "Your discretion is assumed."

She nodded and followed him as Syldan gave an order for his troops to move out.

Several minutes later, they'd hurried past the outskirts of Niamarlee and up a hill towards a military garrison that seemingly had been placed in the middle of nowhere.

Syldan nodded to the local commander, who allowed them all to pass unmolested, though he eyed the vagha suspiciously. The army paused near the peak of the mound and left the magicians and their king to climb to the apex alone. Atop the secret hill, several large, ancient stones stood stacked upon each other in reverence. Engravings upon the old markers dedicated them to the dwarven deities, Firiel and Eldurim, the specific pair of gods worshiped by the vagha.

The site was old, far predating the community of Niamarlee which had stood nearly since the dawn of the First Age.

Sh'Zzar frowned at the implication of the selumari's secret. Her people had suffered for untold ages under what now looked to be a foreign occupation. Her mood soured and she wanted to glare daggers at the capricious selumari—but this was such secret information that it would be a secret worth killing to keep.

"We must save our children," Leidergelth whispered. "This place must remain a secret."

"Your secret will remain so," Sh'Zzar slowly nodded. She looked Leidergelth in the eyes, "so long as *my secrets* remain a mystery, as well as any involvement on my part, then so shall yours. I was never here, and I did not cast this spell."

Leidergelth nodded.

Sh'Zzar looked from the esoteric site and then over the ridge and at the gathered forces. "Yes. This should work."

Furtaevell nodded to his corps of trusted arcanists when Sh'Zzar put a hand on his arm.

"One final condition," she insisted. "Nobody carries with them any enchanted items that could allow for an instant wayfare."

Furtaevell glanced nervously to Leidergelth.

"This is a one-way trip," Sh'Zzar insisted. "If your words have been true, there should be no problem. But if you go this way, then you must honor your pledge to prevent harm to Hy'Targ; you must fight to the bitter end. I'll not give you a chance to cast a wayfare spell and immediately return if the battle looks too pitched, or if you secure your son and daughter and then decide to abandon any rescue of my… nephew."

King Leidergelth reached around his neck and removed the gold medallion he wore at his neck. The sigil upon it marked it as capable of doing exactly that.

"No, you can't," Furtaevell insisted, glaring at the vagha caster. "If you cannot bring this, then you should not go at all. You are the king, and far too valuable to risk losing. We can manage without you. I know I vouched for this dwarf, but after all, there must be a limit to our trust. We're already putting the fate of your kingdom—of Niamarlee—in the hands of the vagha. Don't..."

Leidergelth warned him back with a stern glance. "No. I will not let Furtaevell and Hy'Mandr both rush into danger on behalf of their children while I remain home in the safety of my walls." He tossed the wayfare artifact to Sh'Zzar. "Do what must be done. Send us to the busted Ivory Citadel."

Hy'Targ tore his eyes away from the massive bloodless army as it began moving down the coast. He rushed to the other side of the citadel, wondering how he could lure Melkior back up to face him. His lips twisted as if sour; Melkior would come—he knew the lich had too much pride to leave the dwarf alive. Hy'Targ had thrown him from the tower—hubris demanded he kill the dwarf.

The vagha prince glanced down to the courtyard. Mantieth and Elorall held their ground and blocked the primary passage up from the Far Sea's shore, but they could not see how large this army actually was. Skeletons swarmed around them and threatened to overwhelm the couple. The dwarf could tell, even from this distance, that fatigue had worn them down, despite the benefit of holding the high ground.

He rushed back to Varanthl's body. Surely Melkior would come up that passage; Hy'Targ and Varanthl would need to be here when the lich did if his desperate plan was going to work. He gritted his teeth and refused to think of the repercussions. It likely meant that Mantieth and Elorall would fall to the army before Melkior made his way back to the tower.

The dwarf whirled around when he spotted movement in his peripheral.

With a whoosh of air, Melkior landed behind him with cat's grace. He had leapt the entirety of the cliff face.

Hy'Targ whistled through his teeth, reminded of all the times his father had lamented the pains of fighting against spell casters.

Melkior snarled, his eyes ringed with red. Gone was the relative calm that he'd operated with until now. The black rage that filled him manifested as animalistic grunts while he chopped and slashed with his sword.

Hy'Targ lost a step at a time as the lich channeled his furor into jagged pain. He recoiled, nearly tripping over the body of Varanthl who wore the Kreethaln upon his breast. The force of Melkior's blows rattled Glorybringer in his hands.

The dwarf maneuvered slowly, slightly, keeping an eye on the beast.

Melkior swung his blade high while the lich grinned deviously.

Everything in the vagha's instincts screamed at him not to fall for the same dirty trick a third time in a row. He refused to yield and let Melkior deliver a cheap shot again.

The monster pulled his sword back as quickly as he began, feinting the move and outmaneuvering Hy'Targ. With a roar of victorious finality, he plunged the wicked blade deep into Hy'Targ's midsection, angling the sword so that it would reach under the ribcage and cleave the chambers of his vaghan heart.

Hy'Targ gasped, not expecting the ferocity or speed of the enemy's attack.

"It is finished," Melkior hissed into his ear and then released the bastard sword's fine handle. He screamed at the sky, "I will have Ailushurai!"

Hy'Targ hunched over the weapon and toppled to the stone floor. He laid near Varanthl's body with the blade protruding from his midsection.

Faintly—barely discernible to him through the blood rushing panickedly between his ears, he heard a noise: a far-off noise like that of a signal horn. He grimaced as pain wracked his body. The sword had lodged firmly in his abdomen, and the dwarf was afraid he'd heard the signal horns of Tarvanehl welcoming him to the Eternal Lands. His vision swam, and he laid his head back upon the cracked tile below.

CHAPTER TWENTY-EIGHT

Hy'Targ laid on the ground, curled in the fetal position and hunched with the blade in his belly. The pain was unbearable. Far below, between the balustrade-like stacks of stone, he caught sight of Mantieth and Elorall. They faltered as the waves of evil crashed around them; they barely managed to keep from the weapons of the enemies. Bones pile around them like mountains, hemming them in.

His gaze shifted to Varanthl whose body lay at his side. Hy'Targ closed his eyes and prayed silently. *Father Tarvanehl, if you are real, give me the strength of a champion—give me the power to defeat Melkior! Grant me the power of Eldurim and Firiel.*

The dwarf squeezed his eyelids tight and felt the hot tears leak from their corners. He concentrated, listening for the voice of the gods. After several long seconds, the pain in his gut lessened, and he heard a small note carried by the wind—a familiar tone he'd heard a moment ago. His mind suddenly recalled Mi'Lazlee's final moments before dying in the lair of the drider... *he'd heard the horns of Tarvanehl as he died! Am I dying?*

Hy'Targ rolled over and coughed, mindful of the blade. He opened his eyes and sat up straight, remembering what else had happened in the lair of Sshkkryyahr and what he'd taken from it.

Melkior stiffened as the dwarf stood to his feet. The dwarf clutched the sword and pulled it from his shirt and cloak where it had caught.

That ain't the sound of the Undying Lands' horns... he suddenly realized what it was.

The dwarf grinned and rubbed the growing bruise he knew laid under the magic armor woven by Sshkkryyahr during her captivity. He felt suddenly grateful that his father had insisted he wear it.

Melkior's eyes narrowed as they met the vagha's.

"Do not think that we are done here," Hy'Targ spat. He chucked the Eldari sword over the edge and picked up his axe. He snorted a hot blast of air through his nostrils and held Glorybringer at the ready; it burst into flames.

The combatants stared each other down for a long moment. Hy'Targ roared and leapt forward, propelled by the righteous fury he felt over his friends' deaths.

Swinging wildly with broad, lethal strokes, the lich jumped out of the way and leapt to a safe distance where he could summon black orbs of churning black magic. He hurled them at the dwarf, but Hy'Targ caught each of them.

Hy'Targ spun Glorybringer with the deft skill of a seasoned warrior. He hit his stride and pressed the attack again when Melkior summoned a weapon using his dark magic; jagged and lethal, he dragged the shard of blackened bone from the Abyss itself, stitched it together from the power of the void.

Melkior blocked and reengaged the dwarf, snarling as they locked weapons.

Hy'Targ rocketed to his tiptoes and head-butted the lich, drawing black blood from his enemy's lips and nose. Without a pumping heart, it only trickled.

Melkior reeled and clutched his face—undead did not mean he could not feel pain.

"*I am the Hammer of Tarvanehl*," Hy'Targ screamed at him, chasing him across the tower. The lich barely managed to fend off his attacks. "This is my destiny—here and now—*your destruction!*"

Melkior scrambled to the far corner and shook off the discomfort of the broken nose, regaining his bearings. He raised the obsidian blade at the ready and hissed. "I think not."

Melkior and Hy'Targ rushed at each other and collided in a whirlwind of edged weapons, dancing with delicate and deadly grace. They shoved and scuffled, trying to knock each other over the edge.

Hy'Targ rocked his weapon back and forth over the fulcrum edge of blade pressed against haft, trying to score Melkior's face with the edge of his weapon.

Grimacing as flames on the dwarf's weapon scalded his skin, Melkior groaned and then stepped back. He feinted and then whirled his blade high and swung it like a furious whirlwind.

Hy'Targ blocked and batted each attack away as he moved backwards. They traded blows back and forth, evenly matched, as they worked their way across the top of the citadel.

Melkior flung a shower of spear-like, deadly fingers from his splayed hands. Hy'Targ raised Glorybringer to catch the magic missiles as they streaked towards him like shadowy hornets.

The lich hooked Hy'Targ's foot and swept his legs out from under him. The dwarf scrambled to his feet immediately and caught the deadly blow Melkior had followed it up with.

Hy'Targ grunted as their weapons rattled, locked together.

Melkior reached through the gap above the weapons and punched the dwarf prince, breaking his nose in return.

Hy'Targ fell to the ground a shoulder's width away. He scrambled backwards on his rump in order to stay out of range. His back hit the short wall, trapping him against the brick.

"Hammer of Tarvanehl! *Ha,*" Melkior scoffed. "Your god is the great abandoner and betrayer. He left me to suffer-and I will not bow to his forces, nor to his chosen ones! *I serve a new god, now*! I am the First-Born son Malgrimm." He pointed the tip of his blade at the fallen dwarf.

Hy'Targ locked eyes with him and grinned. Blood dripped from his mouth and pooled in his beard. He merely laughed.

The lich bared his teeth, but halted his attack. "What is so funny?"

Hy'Targ remained silent. He ignored the blood as it pooled between his whiskers and soaked his chin. The dwarf saw it in his peripheral vision, but he refused to look directly at the red and ivory dragon as it circled high overhead.

"Tell me!" Melkior roared.

Hy'Targ wiped his chin with his wrist. "I know something you don't."

A dwarven battle horn pealed in the distance, echoing across the wasteland.

Melkior whirled and stepped to the edge in order to look over the battlefield. The dragon screamed overhead and descended towards the horizon.

An army of vagha crested the hill of old Lurneville where the Great Coastal Road emptied into the weathered steppe. General Mi'Darrio rode at the front of the army upon a large war mammoth. The ribcages and skulls of the black skeleton bone-seekers hung dismantled from its tusks.

The air flashed as a ball of light pulsed like a shooting star. It sizzled across the sky, hitting the crimson drake.

Hy'Targ began to chortle again as he pushed off his legs and slid to his feet with his back against the block masonry. "I see my father's army brought a dragon lord. You're not the only eldarim in these parts."

The drake screeched again and whirled above the army that had enthralled it, bent it to its desires. vagha poured over the breach nearest the road. They surged forward, shouting battle cries as they rumbled towards the tower, shaking the ground with the sounds of mammoth steps and the massive feet of lizard mounts.

"Hammer of Tarvanehl," Hy'Targ spat insistently, jabbing a thumb into his chest. He turned his head and watched them approach. The dragon swooped over the courtyard as dwarves rushed onto the field.

Mantieth and Elorall abandoned their last stand when they saw the dragon's approach.

The drake belched a line of fire down the corridor where the elves had posted, clearing it out and immolating the undead army all the way down to the sea's edge.

"It's over, Melkior." Hy'Targ shouted. "You can't beat the vagha… we have a dragon!"

The lich sneered, regaining his haughty composure. "You underestimate my power, little hero, if you think I was ill prepared to deal with dragons. Even dragons are subject to the power of death—even dragons are ruled by the Void—neither drake nor wyrm can hear the name of Malgrimm and fail to shudder!"

Melkior's eyes burned, and a raspy roar echoed all around them. A steady *whumph, whumph* sound blew on the wind.

The red and ivory drake screeched and craned its neck. The dreaded white dragon, Rahkawmn, soared over the battlefield, attuned to his undead master's call. "What my loyal pet lacks in speed, he makes up for with raw power!"

Rahkawmn glided towards the citadel and dropped the charred and mangled carcass of the wooly mammoth it carried in one claw. The cadaver tumbled across the ground near the tower's entrance before skidding to a stop with a grisly sound.

Hy'Targ's face blanched.

With another beat of its mighty wings, Rahkawmn flew over the tower and dropped the object it carried in the other claw: the mangled corpse of a vagha. It slapped against the tower floor with a wet smack and rolled over, exposing the velveteen sack tied to the deceased's belt. Melkior snatched the bag up and clutched it tight. The lich held aloft the sack containing Ailushurai's bones and cackled.

"I have them! The bones have returned to me!" he screamed with glee as Rahkawmn touched down for a landing and half-coiled around the ivory keep. Melkior turned to the remnants of the skeletal army gathered along the shore. No matter the distance, the bloodless could hear the voice of their master who had created them. "Kill the vagha intruders! Blot out their names from the face Esfah and then ravage the land! This is your act of worship to our lord, Malgrimm."

The bones on the beach below chattered and wailed as they launched forward up the ramp and the steep stairs built into the cliff-side. They climbed the vertical walls with fearless grips and scaled their way towards the newly arrived army.

"No…" Hy'Targ's heart plummeted. The dwarf turned to look at the Irontooth army. He did not know if his crippled father was among them, but he hoped not. He tried to scan it— to make eye contact and warn away any of the generals, but the massive body of the undead, white dragon blocked his view.

CHAPTER TWENTY-NINE

Rahkawmn beat his wings and leapt from the citadel, scattering a blast of air that blew bone and dust across the wasteland. The white dragon propelled itself into the sky and roared a challenge.

Across the battlefield, the red and ivory drake hovered above the vagha army. It screeched in response before propelling itself towards the white monstrosity on its powerful wings.

They collided mid-air over the wasteland. Flapping shadows darkened the courtyard where Elorall and Mantieth hid. The drake clawed and scratched at its much larger kin. Rahkawmn kicked his scaly, speedier opponent away.

Spinning and flaring his wings, the red one turned and whirled. It dove towards the enemy and blasted Rahkawmn in the face at point blank range. Ducking, it dove downward and away from the white behemoth more quickly than it could react.

Rahkawmn howled with pain and rage. He turned his blackened face and spotted the smaller dragon and then raced towards it.

They whirled around each other, twisting and streaking through the air like a braid of violent energy, each strand snapping and clawing at the next. They crested and peaked their climb high above the ancient citadel.

Rahkawmn beat his mighty wings, trying to get a bead on the drake. The red hybrid flew a ring of circles around the larger white, slashing it with tail barbs and burning Rahkawmn with micro-blasts of its caustic breath.

Holding patiently, Rahkawmn waited until the exact right moment, watching it with cold, calculating eyes. He lunged with open jaws and snapped his scaly maw around the drake. Jagged teeth mangled the red dragon's scales as it shrieked and flapped its wings in panic.

Finally, the trapped dragon pulled itself free and burned the larger monsters face again while trying to speed away. Its wounds slowed the crimson drake enough that the two creatures were now evenly paced. The hybrid turned its face to blast Rahkawmn again.

Gleefully, the huge, white dragon roared. Every time its opponent looked back, it lost more of its lead. The second time it turned back, the drake's eyes widened fearfully. The white enemy bore down on him.

Rahkawmn cut below his prey and yanked his head up, driving his nose-horn into the dragon's flesh where Rhyll's missile had knocked away the patch of armor. Hot dragon blood rained from above and Rahkawmn snatched his prey, crushing the other dragon's head between his mighty jaws before finally smiting the creature down upon the ground.

Whirling around to face the vagha army below, Rahkawmn momentarily glanced aside to meet Melkior's gaze, seeking his master's approval to unleash hell.

He had it.

Rahkawmn swooped overhead of the duelists atop the tower.

"Now you will see my true might," Melkior screamed as he held the bone sack high above his head. The ground began to crack and rumble. He clutched his prize with one hand and stretched the other out in front of him. Earth shook and split as holes opened in the deadlands of old Lurneville.

Melkior cackled as more bloodless crawled from the fissures which continued to grow across the land. Converted selumari and Teldrim skeletons clawed their way back from the grave and formed ranks against Hy'Mandr's army.

"You will die here today." The lich hissed with pleasure as he locked hungry eyes on Hy'Targ. "Fitting. You were the one who released me from my tomb, and it was you who led the Burned Ones to my beloved." He tucked the bones beneath his arm. "Do you hear the sounds of the battle below? It is the noise of a new beginning—the birth of a great new age of Esfah."

Hy'Targ grimaced. The clanging of metal on metal and sword cleaving flesh and bone rose from the field below. Dwarven screams pulled at the edges of his heart. With an angry cry, Hy'Targ raised Glorybringer which flamed like a firebrand and charged at Melkior.

Mantieth grabbed Elorall and held her close during the dragon attacks. Her humid breath tickled his neck as they leaned into a crevice.

Finally, they crept from their hiding place and staggered into the courtyard tunnel. Bones still smoldered; metal weapons had slagged and melted upon the trail towards the beachhead. Residual heat from the dragon's fire felt like it might bake them alive if they stayed in the tunnel.

The ground shook around them; skeletons crawled from newly opened cracks in the soil. A small cadre of dwarves from Hy'Mandr's company rushed in behind them, smashing through the newly arrived bloodless that began to hem them in; the dwarves were children of Firiel and undeterred by the heat—at least within a certain tolerance.

Ahead, more undead began to crowd into the tunnel from the beach, filling the underpass with their otherworldly shrieking.

Elorall hung upon Mantieth's arm and tried to shake off the effects of their undead gibbering. Despair welled up within her and she tried to resist the black thoughts—fighting these ones would only further deplete her ability to craft spells.

"We've got to seal this tunnel," Mantieth insisted.

The vagha chargers reached the selumari. "Whatever fer?"

"There's a whole second army on the shore!"

Looking at the skeletal scouts near the bottom, the burly dwarves looked back and saw the whelming swarm begin to crowd into the courtyard above them. Beyond them, the red and ivory drake fell from the sky, smashing into the ground with a sickening thud.

The dwarf gave him a curt nod, understanding the swing of battle tides.

Mantieth and Elorall led the dwarves down the path, hoping they could somehow find a way to collapse it. The temperature had begun to cool as they descended, drawing nearer to the sea, closer to the next wave of bony enemies.

Before the vagha could charge into the fray near the exit, Elorall cast a web of electricity that crawled across the floor; it leapt from skeleton to skeleton with destructive power. They chased the spell to the edge of the tunnel, smashing whatever survivors remained, beating them back to the shore.

Their small company paused when their feet hit the shifting sands. They scanned back and forth along coast to assess the situation.

bloodless forces kept their distance, mustered on the northwest side of the beach. Down the southeast bank they spotted the dwarven army fighting against the white dragon further up the cliff. They made their stand upon a giant piece of stone that jutted out on an overhang that protected the old Lurneville ports. Huge pillars supported the stone plate.

Beneath it, skeletal forces had piled casks of morehl black powder around the massive plinths. Others hammered away at them with mauls and stone-cutting implements.

"They're going to bring the whole slab down!" one of the dwarves yelled.

Mantieth looked back up the tunnel which had begun to fill from the top with the second wave of bloodless; they could not return the way they'd come. He turned back to stare upwards at the harried vagha army. If the dwarves fell, all would be lost. "We've got to stop them," he said, abandoning the tunnel completely, knowing deep in his heart that this was a one-way trip.

Elorall looked up where Hy'Targ and the others fought Melkior. The citadel towered into the sky high above them. "I hope that those dwarves and Varanthl are having better luck than we are."

"They'll have to find a way." Mantieth suddenly recognized a familiar form on the sands nearby. Next to them a vagha laid broken open and smashed upon a rock outcropping, Vy'Danis's body laid twisted in gruesome repose.

Not far beyond the jagged stones, another dwarf laid face down in the sand. Elorall prayed it was not Hy'Targ as she rushed over to him and rolled Jr'Orhr onto his back.

The dwarf coughed and spluttered, but opened his eyes. They sparkled with pain and he wheezed with ragged gasps as he tried to sit up. Mantieth offered a hand and pulled him to his tenuous feet.

At the fringes of the undead army, soldiers down the beach had just begun to take notice of intruders on the beach.

Jr'Orhr bobbed his head and wagged his beard at the other dwarves, glad for *some* reinforcements, even if only a few. "Thank ye... but what do we do now?"

CHAPTER THIRTY

Melkior raised his blade and lunged at Hy'Targ. He whirled his bastard sword incredibly fast in his right hand while still clutching the bone sack with his other. The dwarf barely kept up, blocking stroke after stroke as Melkior swung the extra-long weapon impossibly fast.

Behind them, Rahkawmn thrashed the opposing drake whose face was trapped within his powerful mandibles. The sounds of a dragon fight crashed like thunder and earthquake. Melkior's snarls roared above that cacophony, and flecks of his spittle landed in Hy'Targ's beard.

A horrific boom echoed across the battlefield as Hy'Targ jumped over the lich's vicious attack. He tumbled into a somersault and spared a glance across the wasteland. The crimson dragon slammed into the dirt and washed everything nearest the impact zone with a scatter blast of loose gravel and dust.

Crumpled in the ground, the broken dragon croaked weakly, trying to crawl from the impact crater that become its makeshift grave. The vagha army stood near the edge of the debris field and stood stiffly, holding its collective breath.

Hy'Targ surged forward, growling with pent up determination—he refused to let the undead have their way with the Irontooth clan—Hy'Targ included!

Glorybringer ignited again, fueled by the dwarf's inner fire. He chopped and slashed, spinning with momentum and skill he never knew he possessed, as if he channeled the light of some bygone hero or combat talents he'd only seen before in competitions or books.

His flurry of edged attacks moved the enemy systematically back one step at a time. With a shout, he whirled Glorybringer around for one final blow.

The lich raised his jagged blade to block it. The fiery axe split it into a million shards when they collided and Melkior reeled backwards.

Melkior threw the busted weapon over the edge of the tower and tossed his sack of bones to the middle of the floor where the two dueled. They slid to a stop near Varanthl's body. Placing his second hand atop his other, Melkior merely summoned another of the foul bone spikes and held it at the ready. His eyes blazed more intensely than ever, and he bared his teeth at Hy'Targ.

Below them, Rahkawmn hovered low above the struggling beast. He angled his head and belched a line of molten, black fury. It boiled and clung to the shrieking drake as the liquid putrescence burned at a molecular level, eating through even dragon scale and hide as it thrashed in the pit. It dissolved as the putrefying disease rampaged through the drake's collapsing body.

"I will blot out your family's name, heir of Klagend. Never again will champions emerge—never again will life prevail in the face of the lord Malgrimm." Melkior shouted orders to his companion. "Rahkawmn, find the vagha king and destroy him!"

The white dragon, fresh from his victory over the drake, turned and soared towards the dwarven forces. Rahkawmn scanned the army. Ignoring their shouts, he shrugged off the missiles they launched as they ricocheted off his thick hide.

Mantieth and Jr'Orhr finished crushing the last of the skeletons below the pillars. However, Melkior had animated them, he had not granted them much intellect, and the scullions barely reacted as the living soldiers attacked them.

Fissures split the noble stone in massive webs that stretched dozens of vertical lengths. Chunks of rock already began busting free, and the supports weakened. Perhaps twenty or more casks of explosive powder had been stacked three tall against each of the structures.

Elorall had already begun trying to dismantle the bombs, dragging the heavy barrels away from the effective range—a task that would take the lot of them hours, even without another army of bloodless bearing down on them.

Down the beach, the group of vagha scouts battled back any undead that dared draw closer to their defensive line.

Zah-pwang-roooo!

Mantieth and Jr'Orhr snapped their heads around as the bullet skipped off the stone nearest their heads.

In the distance, a mostly decomposed and zombified morehl sharpshooter reloaded his carbine. The dwarf and elf looked at each other and then behind them… the explosive casks were right behind them.

"Get out!" Mantieth howled to Elorall as they sprinted away from the dangerous alcove. "Sniper fire…"

Another shot cracked the air and busted open one wooden drum. One of the dwarves furthest down the beach turned his head and recognized the danger. His eyes widened as he understood the gravity of the circumstances.

An undead lava elf rammed the pusher rod down the barrel to load another of the ancient pieces of ballshot. He carried the older kind that had long ago faded from use—the kind of firearm powered by dark magics and bloody alchemy. They demanded a toll on their owners' soul, but could be fired without powder and paper, making their speed and efficacy far superior—for only the heavy cost of damning its wielder's service to Malgrimm's desires. Few remained in Esfah.

One nameless Irontooth dwarf charged down the sandy beach on an intercept course.

Jr'Orhr and the elves ran as fast as they could, eyes fixed on the vagha who closed in on the sniper. He raised his axe even as the dead-shot lifted his flintlock. The assassin's skeletal bodyguards leapt in front of the dwarf as he swung his melee weapon. Too little, too late.

The muzzle flashed with fire and blue smoke as the dwarf tackled the animated remains of the lava elf. Ball shot hit the targeted cask, exploding the pillars each in turn as the flames from each one ignited the next, shattering stone footings. The concussive force flung Jr'Orhr, Mantieth, and Elorall to the sand.

Skeletal troops furiously stabbed the vagha intruder to death, and their defensive line faltered without him. Other skeletons began a new push, suddenly interested in deploying to the battle now that the explosive dangers had passed. They overwhelmed and consumed the dwarven line, swallowing them whole in the undead flood.

Jr'Orhr crawled to his feet slowly, holding his wounded arm at a crooked angle. An odd bulge formed that was likely a broken bone trying to burst its way free of the skin. Mantieth and Elorall immediately scrambled to their feet and turned to watch the entire layer of strata begin to crack and shift where it hung over the bay.

Lurneville's foundation buckled near the cliff face and splintered. The stone plate teetered with a god-like groan and began to slide towards the depths of the Far Sea, threatening to take the entire vagha army above them with it.

Rahkawmn swooped over the dwarven army again even as a huge seam split the soil near their edge—this fissure was different from the others that had released the bloodless, more terrifying in many ways. The ground the dwarves had mustered over began to rumble and slide, grating along the edge as gravity pulled it towards the frothing sea.

Dwarven missilers huddled in knots while their infantry battled the undead hordes. They continued to pelt Rahkawmn's thick scales even as the army slid towards their doom. Their pitiful missiles bounced off him like pebbles from a wall.

His keen, draconic eyes shifted back and forth as he searched for the leader of the nuisance below. The chaos of the lurching ground made it easy: one group moved more quickly than the others as they tried to usher their leader to safety at all costs.

Vagha knights and banner-bearers flanked and guided a burly vagha who wore a crown. Purple vestments draped off him, overlaid by gilded armor. The army cleared a path as each tried to save his own life, but they prioritized even this figure. *It must be the dwarven king?*

Before they could clear the edge of the collapsing land and get him to safety, Rahkawmn plunged into their path. He flared his broad wings and bellowed, halting them in their tracks.

The corptic beast glowered at the king. He sucked in the scorched air of the deadlands and blasted both king and crew with a pestilent breath meant to incinerate them with scorching boils, black flame, and contagion filth.

Rahkawmn paused to admire his handiwork, but the king remained. A glowing sphere of energy protected him as three nearby magi worked their protective spells. One of the knights nearest the leader launched a barbed arrow, which hit Rahkawmn in the face.

The undead dragon roared, feeling real pain for the first time since Melkior had brought him back from the Abyss.

The dragon opened his jaws and belched a stream of energy at the protective bubble. The fierce, caustic squall nearly crushed the magi beneath the force of its impact, and the waves of plague breath that rolled off devoured any dwarves nearby the king who were not under the mystic dome.

Rahkawmn intensified the fire, channeling all his master's hatred and the very power he'd drawn from the Void. The Necralluvium boiled in his body, burning within his age-hollowed bones and redoubling the breath's potency.

His eyes narrowed to slits as the rage consumed him. Nothing would stop him until the king's bones smoldered in the bottom of an ashen pit. His master willed it—and so, then, did he.

Hy'Targ spared another furtive glance back to the Irontooth army. Crunching with a horrific noise, he saw the ground lurch and teeter as the whole upper layer of the cliffs threatened to pitch itself into the seas below. More importantly, the decaying white dragon blasted the army with its fearsome breath.

Black magic spewed from the white dragon as if it were somehow caught between the spectrums of magic. It hammered against an arcane shield like a comet against an anvil.

Hy'Targ's heart plunged as he recognized those dwarves in the bubble. Hunched together, between a trio of terrified vagha spell casters, one of who was Ne'Vistar, were familiar faces. Taryl, the eldarim dragon lord that his father kept on retainer, stood head and shoulders above Mi'Darrio. Between them stood the familiar, regal king, Hy'Mandr.

"What is he doing here?" Hy'Targ groaned, worried for his father. "Things must be dire if he came to lead the army in his state!"

King Irontooth shielded his face from the intensity of the blast. Rahkawmn poured more deadly breath upon them like a wellspring of black magic; even if he did relent, Hy'Mandr and his friends would all fall into the sea in a matter of moments.

Hy'Targ exploded into action, enraged by his enemy's devious plan.

Melkior deflected the prince's wild shots, letting him tire himself out. Glorybringer flashed with a burst of intense magic and shattered Melkior's second blade.

The bloodless eldarim hooked Hy'Targ's arm and hip checked him as the second weapon sundered. Melkior knocked Glorybringer from the vagha's hands and it skittered towards the edge of the tower before slipping over the edge and falling out of sight.

Hy'Targ screamed as it disappeared and scrambled to his feet.

Melkior pummeled him with blows, hand to hand. The dwarf recoiled, backing away as he took punch after punch from the lich.

Staggering like a winded brawler, Hy'Targ lurched on his feet and took a roundhouse kick to the teeth. The dwarf collapsed, hitting his head against the tile. He dripped blood and saliva and could feel a smooth, puffy space where he'd lost a tooth.

"Fool!" Melkior crowed. "You never had any chance of defeating me!" He walked nonchalantly to the middle of their dueling grounds and retrieved the bag containing the bones of his beloved Ailushurai.

Hy'Targ huffed and puffed, barely able to turn his body over. Every inch of him hurt. Defeated, he seated himself on his rump, rolling his head as his vision swum with a punch-drunk stupor.

Melkior never took his eyes from the canny vagha; he'd learned not to underestimate the seemingly mundane dwarf. Melkior walked a slow, predatory circle around Varanthl's body as he gloated. "Perhaps I should make an example of you to any others who dare stand in the way of Lord Malgrimm and his glorious vision?" He grinned and stared deviously at the body near his feet.

"Perhaps I will make this one, your four-armed friend, into my new general? I could force him to murder you slow… and then he will lead my armies against any who dare stand against the bloodless. He will be my new Leisterbane while I spend my time restoring my lover to her former glory." He traced the lines of ink embedded in his flesh, the contract he'd struck with Selurehl—Void, and god of the Abyss—gave him the right to do exactly that.

Far below, undead minions dashed madly up the tunnel road to attack the vagha and keep them hemmed in upon the buckling ground. Those fiends still on the beachhead scaled the vertical walls, swarming up the side like warring ants, ready to destroy any of the dwarves that might manage to make it off of the sinking layer of strata before it fell into the depths.

Melkior stood victorious on the roof of the ivory citadel and cackled. "Death will reign supreme and all of Esfah will bow before Melkior and his corpse bride, Ailushurai!" He narrowed his gaze and skewered the bruised and bleeding dwarf with an evil eye, "And there is nothing that anyone can do to stop this."

CHAPTER THIRTY-ONE

Mantieth grabbed Elorall by the shoulders and shook her. "You've got to do something!"

A blank look of despair sucked the light from her eyes as she stared at the cataclysmic shift of stone that hung nearby. "I-I can't! I'm totally spent…"

"You *have* to," Mantieth howled as he chopped through a cadaver that ran towards her in a jerky fashion. He rushed to rescue Jr'Orhr from the skeletons piling in on his weak side where he nursed a wounded limb.

Further down the beach, the last of the Irontooth scouts disappeared beneath the crushing tide of undead.

As they crept closer and closer, they drove the remaining three survivors towards the shadow of the teetering, grinding tectonic plate. Jr'Orhr and Mantieth bumped each other and stood back to back, close to Elorall.

"If you can't stop it, this thing will crush us both," Mantieth shouted. "Don't let me die here, Elorall!"

The blue-skinned elf looked at her prince and reached deep down, drawing on the inner spark placed deep inside her by Ailuril and Aguarehl. She laid a hold of those innate gifts and cried out as the power coursed through her—threatened to break her. Upon her hand, she wore one of her father's rings: a gift that she'd received on her own Name Day just as Mantieth had received a sword. It crackled blue as she stretched her hands towards the busted pillars, which still crumbled even now.

Elorall looked at Mantieth, who valiantly beat back the enemies that continued to press in towards them. She screamed as that inner spark threatened to ignite and consume her—but she would do whatever it took to save her prince—even if it meant sacrificing herself to save Mantieth.

The sea roared and steamed as water molecules flash boiled with arcane energy and a mist solidified below the stone shelf. It turned deep white and grew, rising to meet the tilting rock. It cracked with the sounds of shifting ice as intense cold rolled off the ice and built a glacier; it hardened and even lifted the plate back to its original height.

She screamed again, unable to release her hold on the powerful magic. The glacial ridge rose further, tipping the great slab in the opposite direction. It expanded and grew towards them, limiting their options for any potential escape, crowding them against the bloodless.

Finally, Elorall's eyes rolled back and her legs gave out. She fell to the sand unconscious.

Mantieth glanced to his limp friend and then to Jr'Orhr. The foamy water was barely fifty cubits away; it was the only avenue left open to them. "I think I can get to her... do you think the undead can swim?"

Jr'Orhr grimaced. "I only know that I cannot." He hacked down a swath of enemies like grass.

Mantieth frowned and saluted him with his sword. "To the end, then."

Jr'Orhr tried to protest, but ultimately nodded, not daring to impinge the prince's desire for a noble sacrifice. "We shall see each other in the Eternal Lands."

In a flash of cerulean light, the shoreline ripped open, and the veil parted as a path spell took hold. King Leidergelth stepped onto the shore and hacked a bewildered skeletal champion apart with his blade.

A wave of selumari from Niamarlee poured onto the shore and crashed against the walking dead. Leidergelth and

Mantieth locked gazes and the selumari army moved down the coastline to protect its own.

The king and his knights cut a swath through the crowd to encircle the prince and his two companions. Mantieth collapsed as soon as he was safe.

Jr'Orhr did likewise. The dwarf ignored the fact that his rescuers scowled at him, seeming almost as likely to attack him as they were any of the bloodless.

Leidergelth finally caught up to his son and embraced him. On the king's heels followed Furtaevell, who scooped his daughter up in his arms.

"She saved us," Mantieth insisted. "She saved the Vagaha above, too." He wiped the grime away from his once fair cheeks and nodded towards the mountain of ice.

Furtaevell's eyebrows raised. "She did this by herself?"

Mantieth nodded.

The enchanter looked down at his daughter. "She's more powerful than I ever imagined," he whispered.

Sword in hand, Leidergelth glanced down at the crippled dwarf. "What of this one? Was he one of the intruders who helped that thief escape my dungeon?"

"He's saved my life many times over," Mantieth insisted.

King Leidergelth's face softened. He nodded. "And Melkior?"

Mantieth and Jr'Orhr both looked to the spire that towered far above them, and then over to the white dragon that flapped above the next tier of the battlefield while he belched black flames.

"The Irontooth dwarves are up there," a scout reported.

Leidergelth turned back to the coast. More skeletons poured in from around the bend where they'd been hidden behind the cliffs. They'd arrived in time to save Mantieth, but had nowhere to go in the face of the overwhelming army. "We can't win," he whispered, recognizing that the new wave of bloodless outnumbered them ten to one.

"Out of the frying pan and into the fire," Furtaevell said.

Mantieth growled at the two leaders. "Aren't we Coral Elves? We are the selumari—we cannot simply let these fiends have their way—and especially not on the shores of the Far Sea, of all places! This coast belongs to us!"

Leidergelth perked up. "No. No, we cannot." He turned to his veteran enchanter. "Do something about that dragon." He drew his blade again and nodded to his son. "We are not going to lose this beach without a fight," the king rallied those nearest him.

"Sir?" Furtaevell cautioned. "I can attack it, but that might very well lure it down here."

The King nodded measuredly and repeated his earlier line of proud logic. "We are coral elves, are we not?"

Furtaevell frowned, but accepted his orders. With the Magi's Crown glowing atop his brow, he laid his daughter in the sand and summoned arcane forces to his hands. The elven High Enchanter bent them to his will, praying to Ailuril that the King knew what he was doing.

Taryl and Mi'Darrio hung over Hy'Mandr, attempting to shield him from the mounting heat as the necrotic fire-breath pounded against the magic shield. Ne'Vistar and his wizards groaned under the stress. Their protective dome shrank exponentially with every passing second.

Rahkawmn's eyes darted sideways, and he momentarily lessened the blast.

From the shore, a spear of ice wreathed in lightning flew across the blasted earth. It slammed into the dragon's chest and hammered him backwards. Rahkawmn shrieked as frozen patches of armored hide splintered and fell off his body.

His putrescent breath dissipated and the vagha magicians gasped a momentary respite.

Taryl, the dragon lord, flung a bolt of specialized magic at him to try to usurp his mind. The dazzling blast of magic hit Rahkawmn between the eyes with meteoric impact.

Rahkawmn blinked and chuffed, shaking his head. He beat his wings and put some distance between him and the vagha. The mighty dragon flailed his head, trying to shake free the creeping, crawling feeling between his ears. Taryl's voice echoed through Rahkawmn's mind.

The dragon felt the hold of the Necralluvium weaken and his freewill returned as the dragon lord's eldritch powers wrested the vile power away from a more noble mind; Rahkawmn snuffed the dark seed of evil magic that burned in his throat. Confusion set in. *Why am I attacking these dwarves? Why am I alive again?*

The dragon barked a final note at the dwarven army and then beat his wings, climbing higher into the air, unsure of anything beyond his longstanding loyalties to the lord of the Ivory Citadel. Rahkawmn located Melkior atop the tower. He'd cornered a dwarf, but Rahkawmn did not know why. Plunged into sudden confusion, he'd understood his friend's pain and the necessity of eradicating the Teldrim, even if he disagreed with the logic... but this? He had no idea what they were doing, or what had happened to Melkior since Rahkawmn had fallen to Leisterbane in the First Age.

Like scales had fallen from his eyes, he'd only just now realized any time had passed between the sacking of Lurneville and this present moment.

Reawakened, Rahkawmn could feel the internal changes. The Necralluvium had invaded his soul—tried to turn him into a dracolich, but the white dragon refused to be fully converted—the magic of the dragons was older and more powerful than whatever stuff the black ichor was made of—he would resist it even if that meant he lingered in this world as some sort of anomaly. He refused to wholly throw in with his master's evil... refused to fully give in to the dark temptations *or* abandon his long-time friend to his terrible decisions.

The white fire in his desiccated, leathery heart re-lit and refused to extinguish.

Rahkawmn climbed further into the sky, leaving the vagha and the selumari to squabble amongst themselves or fight the forces of the bloodless as they willed. He had transcended their problems and took to the clouds.

Hy'Targ watched from the floor as Melkior bent low to lay a hold of Varanthl. The lich reeled in surprise when the homunculus's eyes opened and locked onto the undead leader.

Varanthl snatched Ailushurai's bones with one hand and yanked them from Melkior's grasp while he grappled with the lich with another two of his four strong arms. "Sorry to have fooled you. We've been waiting for you to get close enough."

Melkior spluttered and cursed at the treachery. Hy'Targ hopped to his feet, ready to help, however he could. Finally, Varanthl put to use his last remaining free arm.

"Goodbye, my friend," Varanthl said. He grabbed the kreethaln that had been re-affixed to his chest and removed it. He quickly pressed it against Melkior's sternum, and then the homunculus collapsed.

The arcane artifact pulsed and glowed, infusing the lich with the essence of life—something anathema to the creature's design.

Melkior screamed as chunks of his body crumbled and withered; patches of skin flaked like ash and dust. He flailed out of his limp captor's hands and grabbed at the device as if it pumped fire through his veins. He dug it out from his flesh, tearing skin away; the wounds leaked dust. Melkior threw the

Kreethaln to the floor as his body wasted away. Some of it seemed to even fade out of existence, phasing between elements as his form lost structure.

Life-giver clattered as it landed upon the tile. Wisps of smoke curled into the air from it as the device's arms folded in like the legs of some boiled, metallic crustacean. The lich screeched and fled for the edge of the tower, stopping only when he realized he had nowhere to go.

Behind him, Hy'Targ had hefted Varanthl's warhammer.

A shadow momentarily darkened the floor as Rahkawmn's body blotted out the light. The darkness intensified and then quickly passed as the dragon swooped down like a raptor and then disappeared, hurrying towards the horizon.

Hy'Targ stood on uneasy legs as he surveyed the scene; the dwarf dropped the weapon, glad the enemy had fled—he hadn't any strength left to wield it. Melkior was gone, and the rotting, white dragon flew out of sight, disappearing among the silver-sheened clouds that hung above the Far Sea.

After the dwarf watched the dragon shrink to nothing on the horizon, he turned towards his friend. He took one step towards Varanthl and then the hitch in his leg bent of its own accord and Hy'Targ collapsed.

CHAPTER THIRTY-TWO

Hy'Targ crawled across the ground and heard the tromps of footsteps coming up the stairs. He retrieved the Kreethaln and clutched the contraption as he moved towards his fallen friend, crawling on his arms and knees.

The jewel on the front of the machine dimmed slowly as Hy'Targ held it out before him. The artifact had lost its functionality.

His heart sank. Then Varanthl was truly dead, and so was the Kreethaln. With it went his hopes of completing his original quest. The dwarf turned aside to find Mi'Darrio clearing the entryway. Following him up came his father, King Hy'Mandr Irontooth, who carried Glorybringer with him.

Hy'Mandr looked directly at him with new, albeit milky, eyes. "I think you dropped this," he gruffed.

"Father!" Hy'Targ limped as he scrambled off his knees and embraced the old dwarf. "Your eyes?"

Hy'Mandr winked at his son as he took in what he could of the sight. "Ye did all this just to try to get my sight back?" he asked.

Hy'Targ looked at his cloudy oculars. "But… how?"

"It just started coming back, a few days ago, all on its own." He smiled at his son approvingly. "Where is Brentésion?"

The prince's lips tightened. "I'm sorry, father. I lost her in the moors… the trogs have her."

The Adventurer King squeezed his son into an embrace again. "Dunna worry, son. We'll get her back—by Firiel, we will. I'm just glad ye escaped whatever was strong enough to claim her."

Hy'Targ nodded. He licked his split lips and checked himself for further damage and then told his father everything. They placed the timeline of his father's slowly returning vision at about the same time as Sshkkryyahr's death.

"You did good back there—an adventure worth a fine song... even if that durned dragon ate your bard," his father laughed and slapped Hy'Targ on the back. He said with a wink, "His journal was hard to read though... mostly filled with bawdy limericks... not that I disapprove."

The prince looked suddenly worried and whirled on his heel, realizing there were more enemies to deal with along the coast. "The skeletons. There's a whole army on the beach!"

Mi'Darrio leaned over the edge of the citadel and whistled. "Not anymore, there's not."

Hy'Targ and Hy'Mandr joined him.

Far below, Leidergelth's army camped with their backs against a glacial wall. A massive army of the undead stretched along the coast. The bloodless had fallen apart piece by piece; some even crumbled to dust as Melkior's dark and sustaining will withered away in his absence.

The vagha prince locked eyes with Leidergelth. The coral elf king stood next to Mantieth and gave Hy'Targ a respectful nod before leading his army on a slow voyage towards the tunnel that would allow them passage to the next level.

"Is that it... the thing you came all this way for?" King Hy'Mandr pointed to the Kreethaln.

"Yes, but it's broken... or maybe just depleted."

Hy'Mandr glanced at Varanthl. "And this the one who had it?"

"It is. I would use it on him if it still worked." Hy'Targ bent over Varanthl and laid a hand on his neck. "He was my friend... my family."

Varanthl suddenly groaned and tried to sit up.

"Varanthl! You're alive?"

The homunculus sat up with a pained grunt. He grimaced and sucked air sharply through his teeth. "I think so. But the way I'm feeling makes me wish otherwise."

Hy'Mandr helped haul the four-armed warrior to his feet. He handed Glorybringer back to Hy'Targ.

"It-it's yours," Hy'Targ said.

"Nonsense," the king said. "You've more claim to it now than I've got." Hy'Mandr thrust it back at him. "You are an adventurer, Hy'Targ. You'll need the best tools fer the job that ye can get."

Footsteps rushed up from the stairwell, and Mantieth joined Hy'Targ's company. He bowed before the vagha king. "Hy'Targ… you're alive," he exclaimed, almost surprised at the findings.

The dwarf grinned through his busted smile and purpled, puffy face. "Elorall?"

Mantieth nodded. "She's alive… but unconscious. Jr'Orhr lives, too. He's with my father and the healers."

"Rhyll?"

Mantieth shook his head mournfully. "I found his remains in the courtyard. I'm sure it was him… I found Varanthl's ring and gave it to Elorall."

Varanthl rotated the jewelry on his wrist and turned his thoughts inward. Finally, he removed the remaining bracelets and gave the final one to Mantieth and smiled at the complete the set. "Family?"

Mantieth and Hy'Targ nodded, responding, "Family."

CHAPTER THIRTY-THREE

A mixed army passed the gates of Niamarlee with runners going on ahead of the main assembly to report of their king's glorious return. Confetti rained from windows and second floor terraces as the armies paraded triumphantly through the streets of the elven city. Hy'Targ and Mantieth grinned. Their previous flight from the city had gone quite differently than their return.

The Irontooth dwarves looped around to meet the coral elves from the opposite side, coming to a meeting in front of the gates to the inner curtain wall. They merged in the bailey; the portcullis opened and the selumari and vagha armies entered the royal grounds together as comrades.

With the population of Niamarlee gathered to watch, the vaghan and selumari kings walked across a platform to greet each other. Leidergelth and Hy'Mandr stood upon the dais and simultaneously bowed, acknowledging the alliance accords their kingdoms had drawn up under the shadow of Melkior's keep.

Elves and the other odd assortment of races living within Niamarlee cheered the proclamation. A strong coalition promised more than just physical safety. Increased trade and economic prosperity seemed likely outcomes that could further bolster Niamarlee. Merchants in the audience buzzed about how demands for dwarven steel had increased in demand over recent years and how the roots of the Irontooth Mountain ran deep with ore deposits.

One lone figure in the crowd made sure to keep her distance as she watched the ceremony. Sh'Zzar stood on her toes in order to get a proper look at Hy'Mandr. A ball knotted in her stomach when she finally got a chance to see Prince Hy'Targ. Bruised and bedraggled, he and Mantieth, the two sons of kings, took a bow as the crier announced them as the heroes of the battle. The dwarf grinned; despite a missing tooth and matted beard, that smile proved contagious.

Sh'Zzar's heart trembled, and a solitary tear spilled down her cheek. The vaghan enchantress wiped her face and then slinked away, weaving through the crowd so that none would notice her. She returned to her hut in the outskirts before any persons could spot her—before the prince could see that kindred spark in her eyes and realize that he had family closer than he realized.

Leidergelth held his arms wide for the proclamation. "And now we feast!"

The audience cheered, even though they weren't each invited to the king's dining hall where the dwarves and elven royalty would share meat and mead.

Feasting went late into the night. Br'Derluch, released from the prison, sat at the king's table with the other royals and dignitaries. He wore a vindicated grin.

Elorall walked with a staff to help keep her steady on her feet. Furtaevell hovered around her, cautious and doting all at once.

"I'm fine," she insisted, finally shooing him away as she linked up with Mantieth and Hy'Targ. They'd stood a few paces back from their fathers, who sat at the head table and tried to remain vertical following the feast. They had survived the dragons and the undead, but it was the wine that threatened to defeat them.

Their father's celebrated, and by the end of it spoke in slurred words and as if they had been long-time friends. "S'funny to think," Hy'Mandr admitted. "I was nearly on your doorstep, ready to siege yer city when my wizards sent word that the dragon had attacked."

Leidergelth laughed. "That would have been unfortunate… for both of us," he chuckled into his fresh goblet of strong drink.

"That explains how I was close nuff to get to the citadel in time… but how did *you* get there?"

The selumari king waved his hands in the air. "Magic."

Hy'Mandr smirked, several flagons deep already, and began belting out an old vagha hymn from the *Song of the Land*. He sang,

> Earth and air, fire and water,
> Intermingled in the land.
> Vagha earth and fire master.
> Selumar air, water tend.
> Intermixed, as Nature planned…

He was a warrior, not a bard. Nearby revelers did their best not to cringe, but hearing the old song made Hy'Targ smile, anyway.

The dwarven prince noticed the way Elorall leaned on her staff and scanned Mantieth admiringly. "Let's step out for some air," the dwarf suggested. He rubbed his face as the salt air hit him, helping wake him up. The stars speckled the night sky and Rhaudian lit the city below as brightly as any oil lamp could. Leguin burned near the horizon, only slightly brighter than the neighboring stars.

They found Varanthl already standing on the balcony that overlooked the courtyard. He stared out at the evening's horizon.

"What are you thinking about?" Elorall asked.

Varanthl's face remained expressionless. "Rhyll. Family. My father. Nohdan. Melkior."

"Do you think Melkior's still out there?" Mantieth asked.

Hy'Targ and Varanthl, the last ones to have seen the lich, grimaced at the thought. "I hope not," Varanthl said.

"I don't know if he's gone, but the Kreethaln certainly crippled him," Hy'Targ sighed.

"If he's still out there, we'll be ready," Mantieth insisted. "Our kingdoms are stronger together."

Hy'Targ nodded. He could agree with at least the second part of that.

"But as for the lava elf, Nohdan," Mantieth's face twisted as if it had soured, "he can rot for all I care. Rhyll and the others might have lived if he hadn't swapped my vorpal blade for the dragon staff."

Mantieth pulled the sword from his hip and held the sword out. "This is one of the fabled dragon staffs," he insisted. "That red-skinned sewer rat swapped them out on me..." His voice trailed off when he noticed the pommel had changed yet again. It was most definitely the vorpal sword his father had given him. This was *not* the dragon staff.

The selumari prince growled and looked around from rooftop to terrace, suddenly convinced that Nohdan could be anywhere nearby. At some point the thief had made yet another switch.

"What is it?" Elorall asked.

Mantieth muttered something below his breath. "Nothing. I was wrong... I'm sure it's all a strange coincidence."

The vaghan caravan headed home to the Irontooth domain. It slowed in the plains as mammoths carrying Hy'Targ and Jr'Orhr split off. Varanthl went with them as well and the trio sped off towards the village where the trouble had all began.

Varanthl paid little attention to how the villagers looked at him. He no longer cared what they thought. He had found his true family among others.

Their mounts brought them to Murthak's tent and the tribal chief, Geru, met them at the skald's tent. He followed them in, and they told the two humans their tale.

After the telling, Varanthl laid the Kreethaln on the table before Murthak.

"We figured we ought to return it to its guardians," Hy'Targ said. "It does not appear to function any longer, but regardless, we have no right to keep it. I figured it may be what Trandlurthan wanted."

"I'm not certain what he wanted," Murthak said. "But my brother always wanted good to triumph over evil."

Varanthl cocked his head at the admission of his skald's relationship. Murthak stared into his eyes, and his face softened with sudden understanding. "You have your father's eyes. The eyes of his son," he said, scanning the homunculus. He recognized the patchwork of bronze skin that the minority of local amazons had, a mark of the mixed, Teldrim bloodline. "You will always have a home here in my tent. We are family."

Varanthl nodded slightly and absentmindedly turned the bracelet that encircled his wrist. "Thank you. Perhaps someday, but I already have a family."

Hy'Targ's cheeks warmed.

Murthak put Life-bringer into his nephew's hands. "Keep it. Perhaps there is some greater purpose for it yet that remains a mystery to us, but for now, whatever powered Lifebringer seems to have bonded with *you*, nephew." He locked eyes with Varanthl, "Will you search for the other pieces of the kreethaln, now?"

Varanthl glanced aside at Hy'Targ. They had already talked about this at length. "No. We fear that, whatever the devices' main purposes may be, and whatever good they might represent, they could also bring great evil and destruction. It may be best to leave them hidden, wherever they may lie." He turned the device over in his hands. "I think we shall keep this one secret and safe in the Irontooth Mountain."

"What will you do now?" Jr'Orhr asked the old human. "I mean, without the Kreethaln to protect… what is your mission?"

Chief Geru bit his lip. "Few ever knew that we were its watchers. Secrecy helped us keep it hidden this long," he admitted.

"I have a new task for you, if you would accept it," Hy'Targ said.

The amazons leaned forward to hear more.

Hy'Targ set a velvet sack containing the bones of Ailushurai before them. "You had also kept these safe for all these generations. I can't think of any place better to leave them for safekeeping. I think that this may be the last place anybody looks for them—back where it all started. Perhaps you can seal them back inside the tomb?"

Murthak accepted the sack and reverentially pledged to return them to their resting place. The task would prove easier since Varanthl had eliminated the monster living within the belly of the crypt.

The travelers rose to leave when the old shaman took Hy'Targ by the hand. He looked into his eyes and spoke an omen. "Prepare yourself for battle, Prince Irontooth. Dark days are coming."

Hy'Targ raised his eyebrows at the elderly man. "I think they've been plenty dark already."

Murthak's expression remained severe as he escorted the dwarf from his home. "No. This is only the beginning. A new time of champions is at hand—and it will come barely in time. Strengthen your sword hand, son of Klagend. You may very well need it by the end."

Hy'Targ looked over his shoulder as he and his two companions left the village. He mulled over the cryptic warning, hoping that above all else, the old guardian would prove senile in the end. He knew Klagend was the name of the dwarven Champion of old, but his family had no ties to him. Something deep in his gut, however, seemed to whisper that this old seer knew more than he'd let on.

Nobody saw the disguised intruder hiding upon the plains. Wrapped in layers of tattered clothing that camouflaged its wearer in fabrics that looked like scrubby brush, the watcher peered through the spyglass he'd stolen when he'd swapped the elven swords for the final time.

Nohdan lowered the lens and collapsed it before dropping it in a pocket. He rubbed away the dust and silt gathered at the corners of his eyes. From his perch in the rugged elm, he grinned as he watched his former comrades deliver the highly coveted sack of remains to the same place he'd stolen them from more than a decade ago.

The morehl tucked the info away in the back of his mind. He didn't anticipate needing that knowledge anytime soon, but knowledge was at least as valuable as gold… usually even more so.

He dropped from the tree and rubbed an itch on the callous where he'd hidden the stolen dragon staff he'd reclaimed from the cocky coral elf prince. He angled away from the caravan of vagha as it journeyed and headed in a different direction. The morehl had more lucrative places to be at the moment, but he'd wanted to see the final result of the bone's journey—and his peace of mind needed some closure and the assurance that he wouldn't have to face down a black-burned skeleton anytime soon.

Within a few days' time, Nohdan would be able to sell the stolen dragon staff to his original buyers. He wouldn't get the extra coin for assassinating a selumari prince, but Nohdan was fine with that. He was a thief, not an assassin. He cared more for gold and comfort than for the love of pure chaos. His race had mostly moved beyond such base instincts after the Magestorm Wars. They may have once been motivated by impulses instilled into them by Death at their creation, but self-interest proved a stronger force in the most recent era of Esfah's history.

Nodhan expected to collect additional bonuses to compensate him for all the additional complications he'd endured during this job. He took out the tome he'd stolen from the drider's lair. The *Book of the Void* was priceless, and possibly one of a kind. He also retrieved another item and grinned as he turned it over in his hand. Nodhan had taken the golden nut from the feral folk after finally catching up to his former traveling companions in the Black Glades—during the night they'd slept and not kept a watch.

The golden nut resembled a large peach pit, although smoother. He'd taken it from the badly unkempt ghwereste while he'd slept amongst his former peers. That had been days before the battle at the Ivory Citadel, and he'd swapped it for a stone the same size and shape in the middle of the night. As Nohdan stared at it, the thing seemed to momentarily consume his attention, altering his thoughts... he even felt a twinge of guilt in his morehl heart.

The elf turned his head, sure he'd heard whispering behind him... *all around him*. He glared back at the seed, more convinced than ever that this item was the real deal.

Nohdan ignored the still small voice and shoved the object back into his pocket, afraid to even acknowledge the arcane whisperings it had implanted in his mind. Nohdan would find a way to cash in and be rid of it soon enough.

Between the sword and the book, he could retire comfortably if he wanted. The golden seed could buy him an entire country if he could somehow fence it without being murdered in the process.

Nohdan smiled as he wrapped up the ancient codex in a protective shawl. He spat a raspberry and flicked away a locust that clung to a nearby dry stalk of heather. "Retire? Me? Not likely."

His job was too much fun. He looked back over his shoulder one final time at the vaghan troop and their homunculus. Nohdan could only guess at the likelihood of their paths crossing again.

EPILOGUE

The smell of salt and dead things hung heavy and cloy in the air. A steady thrum of crashing waves drowned the cave in white noise.

Tucked away within the deep crevasse of salt and broken coral, Rahkawmn curled up like a giant, beaten dog. He kept one wary eye open, but appeared otherwise asleep as Melkior wrapped his damaged limbs with torn cloth strips to bind his skin together—he had to find a way to keep himself from crumbling further.

Splatters decorated the walls with dark stains. Here, Malgrimm's crazed cultists had conducted countless sacrifices in his honor over the years. A pile of bones at the rear of the tunnel indicated the sorrow and misery of their victims. It was that flavor that drew Melkior to the hiding place: a haven for him… it had become a festration.

He wrapped another strip and tied it off to keep his arm from disintegrating. The Kreethaln had damaged him far worse than he cared to admit. It would take a considerable amount of time for him to recover from such an egregious wound… if that were even possible.

Melkior's ever-present rage filled the cavern like warm humidity, and he looked up when he saw a man walking in. The stranger raked his fingers along the wall, leaving deep, claw-like furrows in his wake. He meandered along as if he knew this place well.

"Lord Malgrimm… Father," Melkior bowed.

Malgrimm refused to look at his servant. Instead, he walked through the cave looking, as if searching for something—someone worthy of addressing. He pursed his lips and scanned the darkness, but refused to acknowledge Melkior.

Melkior bled hot tears and pleaded for his attention. "Master? Lord Malgrimm… Death? I've failed… and now I've lost Ailushurai all over again."

Malgrimm turned casually, almost capriciously. He took two steps to leave.

"Father! I cannot accomplish this thing. I've tried my hardest… but I am wounded."

Malgrimm turned his head and fixed his dark eyes upon him. They burned with the intensity and depth of the Abyss. "Try harder!" he snapped, and then disappeared, leaving the cave somehow darker than when he'd entered.

THE END

Appendices

GLOSSARY OF TERMS

Abyss - the home of the Void, a realm where silence reigns aside from pockets of terror and chaos where unknown gods reign. This is a similar concept to Greek myths of an underworld.

Ailuril - the secondborn of the Esfahan gods. She is represented by the color blue and has power over the air elements.

Aguarehl - the fourthborn of the Esfahan gods. He is represented by the color green and has power over the water elements.

Amazon - the race of mankind said to have been deposited whole upon Esfah as one of the few races created by Tarvanehl himself. Amazons are the warrior caste of human race.

Areosa - commonly known as the frostwings, a frigid felinoid, winged race with magic resistance.

Bloodless - another common name for the undead.

Deadzone – synonym for the Abyss, except from the point of view of the trogs or morehl. Within their respective religions, versions of the afterlife differ wildly and as often as they align in geopolitical goals, neither could imagine spending an eternal afterlife in the company of the other.

Death - the half-brother god who is the child of Nature and Void.

Dragons – these beasts come in two forms: Drake and Wyrm. Drakes have wings, and wyrms do not. Though the dragonkin are a kind of subspecies, they are not the same thing, no matter how similar they are. They used to live hidden across Esfah, but were nearly eradicated in the Dragoncrusades. Dragons have eternal spirits and when they die, they return to to the plane where they now dwell. Dragonmagic came in two forms and it summons them from this realm or from nearby (the older form of this magic which has now been forgotten since these mythic beasts have largely gone out from Esfah.)

Drakufreet - the dragonkin come from the same realm as dragons and appear as a type of draconic hybrid race.

Eldarim – a human-like race that emerged over eons from Esfah's primordial soup and predated the gods-made races. The eldarim are versatile and have proven the capacity to breed with many of Esfah's races. They are called eldarim, meaning "from the earth."

Eldurim - the firstborn of the Esfahan gods. He is represented by the color gold and has power over the earth elements.

Efflorah - the race of treefolk.

Esfah - the world and one of two planets revolving around Soll.

Empyrea - known commonly as the firewalkers, a war-loving mercenary race.

Faeli - commonly known as scalders or steam dancers. These creatures are fickle and capricious and were once captured and tormented by Death.

Festration - a kind of location so tainted by evil activity that the very land itself has become corrupt and avails itself to wickedness.

Firiel - the thirdborn of the Esfahan gods. She is represented by the color red and has power over the fire elements.

First Age - everything from the beginning of creation to the year 863.

Frehlasuhl - also called the Forsaken or Mudbloods. They are the offspring of selumari and morehl unions. They cannot breed with each other to have children, only with one or the other race, but they are rejected wholesale by both.

Ghaeial - the mother goddess known more commonly as Nature.

Ghwereste - called the "feral folk." These are a hybrid of animal and man created at the dawn of the Second Age.

Kreethaln - there are three of these mystical artifacts made of an unknown metal. Little is known about them except that they each possess some kind of arcane power. Their names are Life-bringer, Wisdom-giver, and Spell-crafter.

Leguin - a sister planet to Esfah that also orbits Sol; it can often be seen in the night sky appearing above the horizon like a bright star.

Lich - a powerful undead spellcaster. Lichs often possess necromantic capabilities, though their created undead are maintained by force of will, rather than by other means, such as the Necralluvium.

Morehl - commonly called lava elves. They have red skin in addition to their elf-like features and their blood is said to smoke when exposed to air.

Necralluvium - a kind of magical potion with a seeming life of its own. This black filth can kill the living. The dead that are exposed to it become animated.

Rhaudian - the name of the moon. It circulates Esfah twice in a daily cycle.

Sarslayan - commonly known as swamp stalkers. These snake-men emerged in the Second Age as a result of Death using magic to twist the creations of his half-brother Aguarehl. They create more of their kind through magic conversion rather than by reproduction.

Second Age - everything after year 863 of the First Age. This began when Ghaeial walked the face of Esfah and surveyed the damages of the myriad of wars. The 864th year is year 1 of the Second Age.

Selurehl - the name of the second god to emerge after Tarvanehl, usually known as Void.

Selumari - commonly called coral elves. They have blue skin in addition to their elf-like features.

Shara – what the eldarim people refer to themselves as when they communicate with each other. It means "little god-in-the-making."

Soll – the sun.

Tarvanehl - the creator god who came first, according to all mythology and story; he is often known as Father Time, or simply The Father.

Teldrim - a race of extinct horselords that bore many similarities to the Amazons. A creation of Tarvanehl, these were remarkable because the race could intermix with any other. They were eradicated by Melkior shortly after their emergence.

Trog - a synonym for goblin. trogs much prefer to live in boggy areas and tend to pollute the land.

Vagha - commonly known as dwarves.

Void - sometimes used interchangeably with the Abyss or, the power or person of Selurehl who is frequently referred to as Void just as his son Malgrimm is more widely regarded as Death. Context determines the meaning.

Warchief - a title of rank among the vagha. Below the king is a Warchief who leads Warlords and Warcommanders under them. It might commonly be understood as a sort of general.

TIMELINE

Included is the general timeline of major world events in Esfah. Please note that, during the time before the Mother, Ghaeial, became a goddess and the First Age began, prehistory spanned a scope of time measuring eons, and in that time, verily, only *Time* existed. Despite the sage's attempts to capture much data and ancient knowledge, they did not begin tracking time and dates until the first passing of the Daybringer. The first three years of history might very well have been hundreds or even a thousand years as the gods (and the earliest race of eldarim) kept time differently.

Prehistory N.D.

Tarvanehl exists and creates within the realm of Void/Abyss and Esfah and Leguin are born; Ghaeial realizes she is a goddess and falls in love with Tarvanehl.

Turambar courts Leguin.

Selurehl, third of the brother gods grows angry.

Eldurim the firstborn (earth) god-son of Ghaeial and Tarvanehl is born.

Ailuril the secondborn (wind) god-daughter of Ghaeial and Tarvanehl is born.

Firiel thirdborn (fire) god-daughter of Ghaeial and Tarvanehl is born

Aguarehl fourth born god-son (water) of Ghaeial and Tarvanehl is born

Malgrimm cursed bastard son (Death) conceived and birthed after Selurehl's violence upon Ghaeial

Eldarim are birthed by Esfah and slowly emerge from the mire of her lands and water, evolving over long periods of time. They call themselves the Shara in their own tongue.

The First Age

03FA the Daybringer Comet passes Esfah for the First Time, the Sisters of Fate are birthed of Turambar and Leguin, Dragons and the Drakufreet are created during the schism of the god-children.

04FA Earliest creations of the gods: "monsters" are formed

15FA selumari are created

16FA vagha are created, trogs are created

17FA morehl are created

19FA The Dawn of War. morehl invaders overthrow the first selumari

22FA Humans arrive on Esfah via Tarvanehl's intervention

28FA Davian Whisperwynd leaves Maris-ta-Sehlim

32FA The proto-empyreans are birthed in the whirlwind

42FA Gundraokh Shatterfist finds the Bands of Turambar and renames the city of Orelod to Gundakhor

96FA Sshkkryyahr the Dread rises to power

103FA Malgrimm attempts to create a new powerful, destructive force within the Shadowlands, but the Areosan's magic resistance helps them maintain mild independence from the Death god and he abandons them to the frost plains.

143FA Undead created, Melkior is defeated upon the Raithlan Plains by the gods' chosen Champions

167FA Dilution of the eldarim race and the reduction of the Dragon population via the Dragoncrusades that eliminated nearly all the natural dragons of Esfah; the spells that compelled natural dragons that still remained in the realm became forgotten after this date in favor of those drawing eternal dragons through the interplanar rifts

341FA Existence of the empyreans is discovered when they aid the elder races in the first major Undead uprising.

447FA *Book of the Land, 1st Ed.* is published and immediately begins revisions

520FA morehl city of Karakto falls to the selumari

532FA morehl discover cursed bullets and retake Karakto

544FA Large load of Eldrymetallum discovered on the Karakto slopes

562FA Final version of *The Book of the Land* completed after 23 quintennial installments

836FA The Magestorm Wars erupt with the tectonic cataclysm that opens the Netherwold and nearly splits Dereh'Liandor in two; the Arcana Veil stiffens

842FA Disappearance of the gremmlobahnd and the genocide of the drakufreet

863FA Final battle of the Magestorm Wars ends the first age, the faeli are birthed in the Firequags and captured by the forces of Death and subjected to torments in the pits of the World Wound.

The Second Age

01SA Ghaeial walks the earth and surveys the damage of the elder races.

03SA Ghaeial creates the ghwereste

79SA The plagues of the World Wound at its evils continue and the first of the sarslayan emerge from the nearby Snekdenn Bayou

153SA The areosa race emerges from the Shadowlands. They are known mostly as rumors, but their existence is verified to the outside world.

209SA Whether the faeli escaped the torments of the World Wound or were released, none know, but they were so twisted by the centuries of abuse that they have become more children of Malgrimm than Ghaeial

233SA Under Ghaeial's wishes, the sylvan efflorah, existing as trees since even before the humans came to Esfah, picked up their roots and first emerged from forest and grove

829SA Zephras "Thunderfist" dies defending in Cyrea defending Balgavarr from a dragon

967SA Geril sa'Guhren "Dragonsbane" born

1021SA Geril sa'Guhren rules in Balgavarr

1082SA Coryn Sa'Geril is born

1119SA Daybringer Comet makes its pass by Esfah

1122SA Kholkoro Wicebrow writes her commentary *Kholkoro's commentary on Book of the Land*

1127SA The famed "Adventurer King" Hy'Mandr sa'Meril is blinded

1139SA Melkior is revived

1142SA Daybringer Comet makes its circuit

Debnlee
amara Bay
Hadden Bay
Regs Island
Kendall River
Trellan
Stonehome
Garnock Range
Oxforge
Th
Lurneville
Ruins
Ember's Gulf
Undrakull
Niamarlee
Raithlan Plains
People of
the Sun
Lyandrica
The Stonejaw Mountains
Irontooth Mtn
Charnock
Bralanthyr
Great Coastal Road
Gods' Vault
Tenebrakth
Gnome Home
Jagra Flats
The
0   200   400
Leagues

Books
in the Dragon Dice Universe
of Esfah

Rise and Fall of the Obsidian Grotto
Cast of Fate
Tome of Tarvanehl*
Heart of Stone and Flame*
Ashes of Ailushurai
Rise of the Champions
Drakuwar
Chill Wind
Eye of the Storm
Secrets of the Shadowlands
Army of the Dead**

*These two short books were the first produced by TSR and are included inside the re-released (2020) version of Cast of Fate, which was originally produced in 1996.

**This book was scheduled for release by TSR in the late 1990s but never published. A version of this book was released in 2003 but should not necessarily be considered Esfah canon and unless it is rereleased should not be considered part of *the Esfah Sagas*.

About the author:

Christopher D. Schmitz is author of both Sci-Fi/Fantasy Fiction and Nonfiction books and has been published in both traditional and independent outlets. If you've investigated indie writers of the upper Midwest, you may have heard his name whispered in dark alleys with an equal mix of respect and disdain. He has been featured on television broadcasts, podcasts, and runs a blog for indie authors... but you've still probably never heard of him.

As an avid consumer of comic books, movies, cartoons, and books (especially sci-fi and fantasy) this child of the 80s basically lived out Stranger Things, but shadowy government agencies won't let him say more than that. He lives in rural Minnesota with his family where he drinks unsafe amounts of coffee; the caffeine shakes keep the cold from killing him. In his off-time he plays haunted bagpipes in places of low repute, but that's a story for another time.

He has a special offer for readers on the following page.

You can connect with him via the following links:
http://www.authorchristopherdschmitz.com

Follow me on Twitter:
https://twitter.com/cylonbagpiper
Follow me on Goodreads:
www.goodreads.com/author/show/129258.Christopher_Schmitz
Like/Follow me on Facebook:
https://www.facebook.com/authorchristopherdschmitz
Subscribe to my blog:
https://authorchristopherdschmitz.wordpress.com
Favorite me at Smashwords:
www.smashwords.com/profile/view/authorchristopherdschmitz
My Amazon Author Profile:
amazon.com/author/christopherdschmitz
Follow me at Bookbub:
www.bookbub.com/authors/christopher-d-schmitz

SPECIAL OFFER:

As a special bonus for you, I'd like to invite you download FIVE ebooks for free as a part of my Starter Library.

To get your free Starter Library, simply visit this link:
https://www.subscribepage.com/p1o9c9
Enter your email address and then collect your books as they are sent to you. It's that simple!

FREE STARTER BOOK LIBRARY

If you like Sci-Fi and Fantasy, you'll love these books, subscribe now to have them delivered right away.

Dragon Dice™ is SFR Inc.'s core product. We are constantly working to create a quality game that everyone can enjoy. Dragon Dice™ was originally created by Lester Smith and produced by TSR© in 1995. After several years, TSR, now owned by Wizards of the Coast, had put Dragon Dice™ on hold to work on other projects. In October of 2000, SFR Inc. purchased the rights to Dragon Dice™ and now will continue to support and create NEW! products for the game.

Dragon Dice™ is strategy game where players create mythical armies using dice to represent each troop. The game combines strategy and skill as well as a little luck. Each person tries to win the game by outmaneuvering the opponent and capture 2 terrains. Of course, eliminating your opponent completely is another acceptable way of winning.

Get online today and "Roll your way to victory!"

http://www.sfr-inc.com

www.ingramcontent.com/pod-product-compliance
Lightning Source LLC
Chambersburg PA
CBHW032209180726
48284CB00001B/260